City of Saints and Madmen
THE BOOK OF AMBERGRIS

Books by Jeff VanderMeer

The Book of Frog
The Lyric of the Highway Mariner
Dradin, In Love
The Book of Lost Places
Dradin, In Love & Other Stories (Greece)
The Book of Winter
The Hoegbotton Guide to the Early History of Ambergris
The Exchange

City of Saints and Madmen
THE BOOK OF AMBERGRIS

Jeff VanderMeer

"What can be said about Ambergris that has not already been said? Every minute section of the city, no matter how seemingly superfluous, has a complex, even devious, part to play in the communal life. And no matter how often I stroll down Albumuth Boulevard, I never lose my sense of the city's incomparable splendor—its love of ritual, its passion for music, its infinite capacity for the beautiful cruelty." —Voss Bender, *Memoirs of a Composer*, Vol. No. 1, page 558, Ministry of Whimsy Press

Cosmos Books, an imprint of **Wildside Press**
New Jersey . New York . California . Ohio

City of Saints and Madmen:
THE BOOK OF AMBERGRIS

Published by:

Cosmos Books, an imprint of Wildside Press
P.O. Box 45, Gillette, NJ 07933-0045
www.wildsidepress.com

For more information, contact Wildside Press.

ISBN: 1-58715-436-6

SPECIAL THANKS TO:
Ann Kennedy, Erin Kennedy, Eric Schaller, Brian Stableford, Michael Moorcock, Jeffrey Thomas, Garry Nurrish, Wayne Edwards, Stephen Jones, Tom Winstead, Sean Wallace, Richard and Mardelle Kunz, Mark Roberts, Terri Windling and Ellen Datlow.

CREDITS:
"Dradin, In Love" first appeared from Buzzcity Press, 1996.
"The Early History of Ambergris" first appeared from Necropolitan Press, 1999.
"The Transformation of Martin Lake" first appeared in *Palace Corbie 8*, 1999.
"The Strange Case of X" first appeared in *White of the Moon*, 1999.
The versions set out in this collection constitute definitive revisions.

ACKNOWLEDGMENTS:
"The Early History of Ambergris": Some quoted material in the novella has been adapted from material written by such ancient chroniclers and leaders as: the Byzantines Michael Psellus and Theodore of the Studium; Ruskin; the Romans Eusebius and Lactantius; the Papal diplomat Liuprand; and the Venetian Doge Andrea Gritti. My thanks to Eric Schaller for the flotation device illustration and to David Griffin for allowing me to steal an idea from an unpublished short story for Tonsure's final journal entry. I am also indebted to John Julius Norwich, a magnificent historian, for his style, which I perhaps appropriated, lovingly, for this story.

"The Transformation of Martin Lake": Quotes attributed to "Leonard Venturi" adapted from commentary by Lioneli Venturi in his book *Chagall*.

"The Strange Case of X": Thanks to Eric Schaller for providing the mushroom dwellers illustration.

For Ann, who means more to me than words

Contents

THE REAL VANDERMEER
An Introduction by Michael Moorcock

"You'll be familiar, of course, with VanderMeer." Schomberg's fat red fingers fondled the notes he had counted. He placed them in his box and took a sideways look at me before pretending to hide it under the table. "Captain VanderMeer? First mate of *The Shriek* until she hit that reef. Master of *The Frog* when he next came back to the Islands."

"There was a woman involved, I take it?" I sipped my vortex water. It was locally made and suspiciously piquant.

"He knew Shriek himself and did his dirty work." Schomberg grimaced with his habitual distaste for every villainy and moral weakness not his own. The big fans overhead fluttered and rattled and stirred the thick, damp air. "Dradin did it to him. That's the view round here. You can tell what happened. It's all in the final story, if you're not afraid to give it your full attention."

"So X was, after all, his muse, his love?"

Schomberg shrugged. It was clear he wanted me to leave. As I removed myself from his story, I heard him breathe heavily in relief. I would miss his earthy explanations, but my presence made him uneasy. I strolled back to my place and was again absorbed in VanderMeer...

- Josef Conrad, *The Rescued*, 1900

In those earlier years, to which we all look back with longing, there was no captain more respected than VanderMeer. He sailed the Mirage Islands and the Ambergris Peninsula. His memoirs had been eagerly awaited by the cognoscenti of the ports from Jannquork to San Francisco; but when they were published not everyone was satisfied the account was genuine. The methods he chose were often grotesque, baroque and fantastical, as if he strove to mirror in his writing style the visions he had witnessed. To be sure, this density of narrative was a little demanding to the reader used to the single sentimental plot which passes for story in most modern tales, as if there were only one truth, and only one way of uttering it, one character of central interest, one view to which you should be sympathetic,

If our author's response to his own experience was instinctively post-modern, this should be no reason for anyone's surprise. As one of a remarkable group of contemporary captains who follow their own psychic maps, Captain VanderMeer is a master of keel and sail and at the wheel can take his vessel anywhere he chooses, whether skimming over rocky shallows or plunging her prow aggressively into the crowded waters of the Further Depths. For curiophilia, a wild curiosity and a love of exotic treasure, a fascination with complex architecture, a taste for the strangeness in the apparently ordinary, is what drives him on, carrying a peculiar miscellany of equipment into corners of the universe no intelligence has explored before and returning with remarkable rarities, so valuable they have yet to find their true price or, indeed, connoisseurs.

While we are inevitably reminded of Captain Smith's *Mercury* or Ashton Smith's *Zothique*, Jack Vance's *Dying Earth*, 'Crastinator Harrison's *Viriconium* or Lady Brackett's *Old Mars* or of the borderlands explored by the famous Hope Hodgson expedition, while Dunsany and even Lovecraft can be used in respectful comparison, we perhaps find more useful similarities in those recent reporters from the imagination's margins.

We recall Captain Aylett's *Beerlight* and Pilot Etchells' *Endland,* whose mores and customs are at once so familiar and so strange to us. Since the great expansion, Captains DiFilippo, Constantine, Mieville, Gentle and Newman all return with alien currency from new worlds. Others with a taste for exotic geographies continue to seek the Unending Parallel. All have left accounts.

Yet of course few of these have the weighty grandeur of *Ambergris,* which is reminiscent more of Peake's fine, almost-finished *Titus Alone.* Here is the complex surreality of fresh-discovered history, only a shade or two inland from our most familiar harbors. It shares resonances with Sir David Britton's monumental wasteland offered to us in the dark memories of *Lord Horror* and *The Auschwitz of Oz.* We are also reminded of labyrinthine Whittemore of the *Sinai Tapestry* and lands explored by the Welsh captains from Cowper Powys to Rhys Hughes and the strangely named Captain Taffy Sinclair. Robert Irwin, the *Arabiste,* has been another to draw his own maps and follow them. With VanderMeer, all are commanders of their chosen literary destinies, as courageous a company of psychic navigators as any you could hope to find.

Examining VanderMeer one is reminded of the glories of Angkor and Anudhapura combined with the bustle and swagger of Captain Conrad's Indonesia, the adventurous intrigues of Byzantium and Venice, the brutal Spice Wars of the Dutch. But sometimes it is as if Proust intrudes, insensed and reminiscent. VanderMeer describes a world so rich and exaggerated and full of mysterious life that it draws you away from any intended moral or pasquinade deep into the wealth of the world's womb. There is, I know, some suspicion he made over-free, even fictional, use of his material, perhaps to point an irony or two, even to present some kind of personal vision? Has this created a material change in his world? Would the Ambergris we next visit be anything like VanderMeer's romantic version? And what of the rumor that there is a delicious tinge of an obscure heresy in these pages?

I believe I am not the only one to have calibrated the references to Giant Squid and detected emotional involvements more appropriate in a child to a mother than in man to cephalopod. But it isn't our place or intention to analyze Captain VanderMeer's character or predilections, such as he offers us in these pages. Rather we should admire the rare texture of the writing, the engaging vividness of his description and the quirks of his idiosyncratic mind which conducts its network of realities with celebratory panache.

Make the most of the tapestry of tales and visions before you. It is a rare treasure, to be tasted with both relish and respect. It is the work of an original. It's what you've been looking for.

ho can see her eye color from th street?

DRADIN, IN LOVE

I

Dradin, in love, beneath the window of his love, staring up at her while crowds surge and seethe around him, bumping and bruising him all unawares in their rough-clothed, bright-rouged thousands. For Dradin watches *her*, she taking dictation from a *machine*, an inscrutable block of gray from which sprouts the earphones she wears over her delicate egg-shaped head. Dradin is struck dumb and dumber still by the seraphim blue of her eyes and the cascade of long and lustrous black hair over her shoulders, her pale face gloomy against the glass and masked by the reflection of the graying sky above. She is three stories up, ensconced in brick and mortar, almost a monument, her seat near the window just above the sign that reads "Hoegbotton & Sons, Distributors." Hoegbotton & Sons: the largest importer and exporter in all of lawless Ambergris, that oldest of cities named for the most valuable and secret part of the whale. Hoegbotton & Sons: boxes and boxes of depravities shipped for the amusement of the decadent from far, far Surphasia and the nether regions of the Occident, those places that moisten, ripen, and decay in a blink. And yet, Dradin surmises, she looks as if she comes from more contented stock, not a stay-at-home, but uncomfortable abroad, unless traveling on the arm of her lover. Does she have a lover? A husband? Are her parents yet living? Does she like the opera or the bawdy theatre shows put on down by the docks, where the creaking limbs of laborers load the crates of Hoegbotton & Sons onto barges that take the measure of the mighty River Moth as it flows, sludge-filled and torpid, down into the rapid swell of the sea? If she likes the theatre, I can at least afford her, Dradin thinks, gawping up at her. His long hair slides down into his face, but so struck is he that he does not care. The heat withers him this far from the river, but he ignores the noose of sweat round his neck.

look up

Dradin, dressed in black with dusty white collar, dusty black shoes, and the demeanor of an out-of-work missionary (which indeed he is), had not meant to see the woman. Dradin had not meant to look up at all. He had been looking *down* to pick up the coins he had lost through a hole in his threadbare trousers, their seat torn by the lurching carriage ride from the docks into Ambergris, the carriage drawn by a horse bound for the glue factory, perhaps taken to the slaughter yards that very day—the day before the Festival of the Freshwater Squid as the carriage driver took pains to inform him, perhaps hoping Dradin would require his further services. But it was all Dradin could do to stay seated as they made their way to a hostel, deposited his baggage in a room, and returned once more to the merchant districts—to catch a bit of local color, a bite to eat—where he and the carriage driver parted company. The driver's mangy beast had left its stale smell on Dradin, but it was a necessary beast nonetheless, for he could never have afforded a mechanized horse, a vehicle of smoke and oil. Not when he would soon be down to his last coins and in desperate need of a job, the job he had come to Ambergris to find, for his former teacher at the Morrow Religious Academy—a certain Cadimon Signal—preached from Ambergris' religious quarter, and surely, what with the festivities, there would be work?

But when Dradin picked up his coins, he regained his feet rather too jauntily, spun and rattled by a ragtag gang of jackanapes who ran past him, and his gaze had come up on the gray, rain-threatening sky, and swung through to the window he now watched with such intensity.

The woman had long, delicate fingers that typed to their own peculiar rhythms, so that she might as well have been playing Voss Bender's Fifth, diving to the desperate lows and soaring to the magnificent highs that Voss Bender claimed as his territory. When her face became, for the moment, revealed to Dradin through the glare of glass—a slight forward motion to advance the tape, perhaps, or a hand run through her hair—he could see that her features, a match for her hands, were reserved, streamlined, artful. Nothing in her spoke of the rough rude world surrounding Dradin, nor of the great, unmapped southern jungles from which he had just returned; where the black panther and the blacker mamba waited with such malign intent; where he had been so consumed by fever and by doubt and by lack of converts to his religion that he had come back into the charted territory of laws and governments, where, sweet joy, there existed women like the creature in the window above him. Watching her, his blood simmering within him, Dradin wondered if he was dreaming her, she a haloed, burning vision of salvation, soon to disappear mirage-like, so that he might once more be cocooned within his fever, in the jungle, in the darkness.

But it was not a dream and, of a sudden, Dradin broke from his reverie, knowing she might see him, so vulnerable, or that passersby might guess at his intent and reveal it to her before he was ready. For the real world surrounded him, from the stink of vegetables in the drains to the *sweet* of half-gnawed hamhocks in the trash; the clip-clop-stomp of horse and the rattled honk of motored vehicles; the rustle-whisper of mushroom dwellers disturbed from daily slumber and, from somewhere hidden, the sound of a baroque and lilting music, crackly as if played on a phonograph. People knocked into him, allowed him no space to move: merchants and jugglers and knife salesmen and sidewalk barbers and tourists and prostitutes and sailors on leave from their ships; even the odd pale-faced young tough, smiling a gangrenous smile.

Dradin realized he must act, and yet he was too shy to approach her, to fling open the door to Hoegbotton & Sons, dash up the three flights of stairs and, unannounced (and perhaps unwanted) and unwashed, come before her dusty and smitten, a twelve o'clock shadow upon his chin. Obvious that he had come from the Great Beyond, for he still stank of the jungle rot and jungle excess. No, no. He must not thrust himself upon her.

But what, then, to do? Dradin's thoughts tumbled one over the other like distraught clowns and he was close to panic, close to wringing his hands in the way his mother had disapproved of but that indicated nothing unusual in a missionary, when a thought came to him and left him speechless at his own ingenuity.

A bauble, of course. A present. A trifle, at his expense, to show his love for her. Dradin looked up and down the street, behind and below him for a shop that might hold a treasure to touch, intrigue, and, ultimately, keep her. Madame Lowery's Crochets? The Lady's Emporium? Jessible's Jewelry Store? No, no, no. For what if she were a Modern, a woman who would not be kept or kept pregnant, but moved in the same circles as the artisans and writers, the actors and singers? What an insult such a gift would be to her then. What an insensitive man she would think him to be, and what an insensitive man he *would* be. Had all his months in the jungle peeled away his common sense, layer by layer, until he was as naked as an orangutan? No, it would not do. He could not buy clothing, chocolates, nor even flowers, for these gifts were too forward, unsubtle, uncouth, and lacking in imagination. Besides, they—

—and his roving gaze, touching on the ruined aqueduct that divided the two sides of the street like the giant fossilized spine of a long, lean shark, locked in on the distant opposite shore and the modern sign with the double curlicues and the bold lines of type that proclaimed *Borges Bookstore*, and right there, on Albumuth Boulevard, the filthiest, most sublime, and richest thoroughfare in all of Ambergris, Dradin realized he had found the perfect gift. Nothing could be better than a book, or more mysterious, and nothing could draw her more perfectly to him.

The most beautiful woman he'd ever seen.

Still dusty and alone in the swirl of the city—a voyeur amongst her skirts—Dradin set out toward the opposite side, threading himself between street players and pimps, card sharks and candy sellers, through the aqueduct, and, braving the snarl of twin stone lions atop a final archway, came at last to *Borges Bookstore*. It had splendid antique windows, gilt embroidered, with letters that read:

GIFTS FOR ANY OCCASION:

* THE HISTORY OF THE RIVER MOTH *
* GAMBLING PRACTICES OF THE OUTLANDS *
* THE RELIGIOUS QUARTER ON 15 Ls. A DAY *
* SQUID POACHING ON THE HIGH SEAS *
* CORRUPTION IN THE MERCHANT DISTRICT *
* ARCHITECTURE OF ALBUMUTH BOULEVARD *
ALSO, The Hoegbotton Series of Guidebooks & Maps
to the Festival, Safe Places, Hazards, and Blindfolds.

Book upon piled book mentioned in the silvery scrawl, and beyond the glass the quiet, slow movements of bibliophiles, feasting upon the genuine articles. It made Dradin forget to breathe, and not simply because this place would have a gift for his dearest, his most beloved, the woman in the window, but because he had been away from the world for a year and, now back, he found the accoutrements of civilization comforted him. His father, that tortured soul, was still a great reader, between the bouts of drinking, despite the erosion of encroaching years, and Dradin could remember many a time that the man had, honking his red, red nose—a monstrosity of a nose, out of proportion to anything in the family line—read and wept at the sangfroid exploits of two poor debutantes named Juliette and Justine as they progressed from poverty to prostitution, to the jungles and back again, weepy with joy as they rediscovered wealth and went on to have wonderful adventures up and down the length and breadth of the River Moth, until finally pristine Justine expired from the pressure of tragedies wreaked upon her.

It made Dradin swell with pride to think that the woman at the window was more beautiful than either Juliette or Justine, far more beautiful, and likely more stalwart besides. (And yet, Dradin admitted, in the delicacy of her features, the pale gloss of her lips, he espied an innately breakable quality as well.)

Thus thinking, Dradin pushed open the glass door, the lacquered oak frame a-creak, and a bell chimed once, twice, thrice. On the thrice chime, a clerk dressed all in dark greens, sleeves spiked with gold cuff links, came forward, shoes soundless on the thick carpet, bowed, and asked, "How may I help you?"

To which Dradin explained that he sought a gift for a woman. "Not a woman I know," he said, "but a woman I should like to know."

The clerk, a rake of a lad with dirty brown hair and a face as subtle as mutton pie, winked wryly, smiled, and said, "I understand, sir, and I have *precisely* the book for you. It arrived a fortnight ago from the Ministry of Whimsy imprint—an Occidental publisher, sir. Please follow me."

The clerk led Dradin past mountainous shelves of history texts perused by shriveled prunes of men dressed in orange pantaloons—buffoons from university, no doubt, practicing for some baroque Voss Bender revival—and voluminous mantels of fictions and pastorals, neglected except by a widow in black and a child of twelve with thick, thick glasses, then exhaustive columns of philosophy on which the dust had settled thicker still, until finally they reached a corner hidden by "Funerals" entitled "Objects of Desire."

The clerk pulled out an elegant eight-by-eleven book lined with soft velvet and gold leaf. "It is called *The Refraction of Light in a Prison* and in it can be found the collected wisdom of the last remaining Truffidian monks, who have long been imprisoned in the dark towers of the Kalif. It was snuck out of those dark towers by an intrepid adventurer who—"

"Who was not a son of Hoegbotton, I hope," Dradin said, because it was well known that Hoegbotton & Sons dealt in all sorts of gimmickry and mimicry, and he did not like to think that he was giving his love an item she might have unpacked and catalogued herself.

"Hoegbotton & Sons? No, sir. Not a son of Hoegbotton. We do not deal with Hoegbotton & Sons (except inasmuch as we are contracted to carry their guidebooks), as their practices are . . . how shall I put it? . . . *questionable*. With neither Hoegbotton nor his sons do we deal. But where was I? The Truffidians.

"They are experts at the art of cataloguing passion, with this grave distinction: that when I say to you, sir, 'passion,' I mean the word in its most general sense, a sense that does not allow for intimacies of the kind that might strike the lady you *wish to know better* as too vulgar. It merely speaks to the general—the *incorporeal*, as one more highly witted than I might say. It shall not offend; rather, it shall lend to the gift-giver an aura of mystery that may prove permanently alluring."

The clerk proffered the book for inspection, but Dradin merely touched the svelte cover with his hand and said no, for he had had the most delightful thought: that he could explore those pages at the same time as his love. The thought made his hands tremble as they had not trembled since the fever ruled his body and he feared he might die. He imagined his hand atop hers as they turned the pages, her eyes caressing the same chapter and paragraph, the same line and word; thus could they learn of passion together but separate.

"Excellent, excellent," Dradin said, and, after a tic of hesitation—for he was much closer to penniless than penniful—he added, "but I shall need two," and then as the clerk's eyebrows rose like the startled silhouettes of twin sea gulls upon finding that a fish within their grasp is actually a snark, he stuttered, "A-a-and a map. A map of the city. For the festival."

"Of course," said the clerk, as if to say, *Converts all around, eh?*

Dradin, dour-faced, said only, "Wrap this one and I will take the other unwrapped, along with the map," and stood stiff, brimming over with urgency, as the clerk dawdled and digressed. He knew well the clerk's thoughts: *a rogue priest, ungodly and unbound by any covenant made with God.* And perhaps the clerk was right, but did not canonical law provide for the unforeseen and the estranged, for the combination of beauty and the bizarre of which the jungle was itself composed? How else could one encompass and explain the terrible grace of the Hull Peoples, who lived within the caves hewn by a waterfall, and who, when dispossessed by Dradin and sent to the missionary fort, complained of the silence, the silence of God, how God would not talk to them, for what else was the play of water upon the rocks but the voice of God? He had had to send them back to their waterfall, for he could not bear the haunted looks upon their faces, the disorientation blossoming in their eyes like a deadly and deadening flower.

Dradin had first taken a lover in the jungles: a sweaty woman priest whose kisses smothered and suffocated him even as they brought him back to the world of flesh. Had she infected his mission? No, for he had tried so very hard for conversions, despite their scarcity. Even confronted by savage beast, savage plant, and just plain savage he had persevered. Perhaps persevered for too long, in the face of too many obstacles, his hair proof of his tenacity—the stark black streaked with white or, in certain light, stark white shot through with black, each strand of white attributable to the jungle fever (so cold it burned, his skin glacial), each strand of black a testament to being alive afterwards.

Finally, the clerk tied a lime green bow around a bright red package: gaudy but serviceable. Dradin dropped the necessary coin on the marble counter, stuck the map in the unwrapped copy, and with a frown to the clerk, walked to the door.

Out in the gray glare of the street, the heat and the bustling confusion struck Dradin and he thought he was lost, lost in the jungles that he had only just fled, lost so he would never again find his lady. His breaths came ragged and he put a hand to his temple, for he felt faint yet giddy.

Gathering his strength, he plunged into the muddle of sweating flesh, sweating clothes, sweating cobblestones. He rushed past the twin lions, their asses waggling at him as if they knew very well what he was up to, the arches, and then a vanguard of mango sellers, followed by an army of elderly dowager women with brimming stomachs and deep-pouched aprons, determined to buy up every last fruit or legume; young pups in play nipped at his heels, and, lord help him, he was delivered pell-mell in a pile, delivered with a stumble and a bruise to the opposite sidewalk, there to stare up once again at his lady love. Could any passage be more perilous than that daylight passage across Albumuth Boulevard, unless it was to cross the Moth at flood time?

Undaunted, Dradin sprang to his feet, his two books secure, one under each arm, and smiled to himself.

The woman. She had not moved from her station on the third floor; Dradin could tell, for he stood exactly as he had previous, upon the same crack in the pavement, and she was exactly as before, down to the pattern of shadows across the glass. Her rigid bearing brought questions half-stumbling to his lips. Did they did not give her time for lunch? Did they make a virtue out of vice and virtually imprison her, enslave her to a cruel schedule? What had the clerk said? That Hoegbotton & Sons practices were *questionable*? He wanted to march into the building and talk to her superior, be her hero, but his dilemma was of a more practical kind: he did not wish to reveal himself as yet and thus needed a messenger for his gift.

Dradin searched the babble of people and his vision blurred, the world simplified to a sea of walking clothes: cufflinks and ragged trousers, blouses dancing with skirts, tall cotton hats and shoes with loose laces. How to distinguish? How to know whom to approach?

Fingers tugged at his shoulder and someone said, "Do you want to buy her?"

Buy her? Glancing down, Dradin found himself confronted by a singular man. This singular soul looked to be, it must be said, almost one muscle, a squat man with a low center of gravity, and yet perhaps the source of levity despite this: in short, a dwarf. How could one miss him? He wore a jacket and vest red as a freshly slaughtered carcass and claribel pleated trousers dark as crusted blood and shoes tipped with steel. A permanent grin molded the sides of his mouth so rigidly that, on second glance, Dradin wondered if it might not be a grimace. Melon bald, the dwarf was tattooed from head to foot.

The tattoo—which first appeared to be a birthmark or fungal growth—rendered Dradin speechless so that the dwarf said to him not once, but twice, "Are you all right, sir?"

While Dradin just stared, gap-jawed like a young jackdaw with naive fluff for wing feathers. For the dwarf had, tattooed from a point on the top of his head, and extending downward, a precise and detailed map of the River Moth, complete with the names of cities etched in black against the red dots that represented them. The river flowed a dark blue-green, thickening and thinning in places, dribbling up over the

dwarf's left eyelid, skirting the midnight black of the eye itself, and
down past taut lines of nose and mouth, curving over the generous chin
and, like an exotic snake act, disappearing into the dwarf's vest and chest
hair. A map of the lands beyond spread out from the River Moth. The
northern cities of Dradin's youth—Belezar, Stockton, and Morrow (the
last where his father still lived)—were clustered upon the dwarf's brow
and there, upon the lower neck, almost the back, if one were to niggle,
lay the jungles of Dradin's last year: a solid wall of green drawn with a
jeweler's precision, the only hint of civilization a few smudges of red
that denoted church enclaves. Dradin could have traced the line that
marked his own dismal travels. He grinned, and he had to stop himself
from putting out a hand to touch the dwarf's head for it had occurred to
him that the dwarf's body served as a time line. Did it not show Dradin's
birthplace and early years in the north as well as his slow descent into the
south, the jungles, and now, more southern still, Ambergris? Could he
not, if he were to see the entire tattoo, trace his descent further south, to
the seas into which flowed the River Moth? Could he not chart his future, as it were? He would have laughed if not aware of the impropriety
of doing so.

"Incredible," Dradin said.

"Incredible," echoed the dwarf, and smiled, revealing large yellowed
teeth scattered between the gaping black of absent incisors and molars.
"My father Alberich did it for me when I stopped growing. I was to be
part of his show—he was a riverboat pilot for tourists—and thus he traced
upon my skin the course he plotted for them. It hurt like a thousand
devils curling hooks into my flesh, but now I am, indeed, incredible. Do
you wish to buy her? My name is Dvorak Nibelung." From within this
storm of information, the dwarf extended a blunt, whorled hand that,
when Dradin took it, was cool to the touch, and very rough.

"My name is Dradin."

"Dradin," Dvorak said. "Dradin. I say again, do you wish to buy her?"

"Buy who?"

"The woman in the window."

Dradin frowned. "No, of course I don't wish to buy her."

Dvorak looked up at him with black, watery eyes. Dradin could smell
the strong musk of river water and silt on the dwarf, mixed with the
sharp tang of an addictive, *ghittlnut.*

Dvorak said, "Must I tell you that she is only an image in a window?
She is no more real to you. Seeing her, you fall in love. But: if you desire,
I can I find you a woman who looks like her. She will do anything for
money. Would you like such a woman?"

"No," Dradin said, and would have turned away if there had been
room in the swirl of people to do so without appearing rude. Dvorak's
hand found his arm again.

"If you do not wish to buy her, what do you wish to do with her?" Dvorak's voice was flat with miscomprehension.

"I wish to . . . I wish to woo her. I need to give her this book." And, then, if only to be rid of him, Dradin said, "Would you take this book to her and say that it comes from an admirer who wishes her to read it?"

To Dradin's surprise, Dvorak began to make huffing sounds, soft but then louder, until the River Moth changed course across the whorls of his face and something fastened to the inside of his jacket clicked together with a hundred deadly shivers.

Dradin's face turned scarlet.

"I suppose I will have to find someone else."

He took from his pocket two burnished gold coins engraved with the face of Trillian, the Great Banker, dead these forty years, and prepared to turn sharply on his heel.

Dvorak sobered and tugged yet a third time on his arm. "No, no, sir. Forgive me. Forgive me if I've offended, if I've made you angry," and the hand pulled at the gift-wrapped book in the crook of Dradin's shoulder. "I will take the book to the woman in the window. It is no great chore, for I already trade with Hoegbotton & Sons, see," and he pulled open the left side of his jacket to reveal five rows of cutlery: serrated and double-edged, made of whale bone and of steel, hilted in engraved wood and thick leather. "See," he said again. "I peddle knives for them outside their offices. I know this building," and he pointed at the solid brick. "Please?"

Dradin, painfully aware of the dwarf's claustrophobic closeness, the reek of him, would have said no, would have turned and said not only no, but *How dare you touch a man of God?*, but then what? He must make acquaintance with one or another of these people, pull some ruffian off the dusty sidewalk, for he could not do the deed himself. He knew this in the way his knees shook the closer he came to Hoegbotton & Sons, the way his words rattled around his mouth, came out mumbled and masticated into disconnected syllables.

Dradin shook Dvorak's hand off the book. "Yes, yes, you may give her the book." He placed the book in Dvorak's arms. "But hurry about it." A sense of relief lifted the weight of heat from his shoulders. He dropped the coins into a pocket of Dvorak's jacket. "Go on," and he waved a hand.

"Thank you, sir," Dvorak said. "But, should you not meet with me again, tomorrow, at the same hour, so you may know her thoughts? So you may gift her a second time, should you desire?"

"Shouldn't I wait to see her now?"

Dvorak shook his head. "No. Where is the mystery, the romance? Trust me: better that you disappear into the crowds. Better indeed. Then she will wonder at your appearance, your bearing, and have only the riddle of the gift to guide her. You see?"

"No, I don't. I don't see at all. I must be confident. I must allow her to—"

"You are right—you do not see at all. Sir, are you or are you not a priest?"

"Yes, but—"

"You do not think it best to delay her knowing of this until the right moment? You do not think she will find it odd a priest should woo her? Sir, you wear the clothes of a missionary, but she is no ordinary convert."

And now Dradin did see. And wondered why he had not seen before. He must lead her gently into the particulars of his occupation. He must not boldly announce it for fear of scaring her off.

"You are right," Dradin said. "You are right, of course."

Dvorak patted his arm. "Trust me, sir."

"Tomorrow then."

"Tomorrow, and bring more coin, for I cannot live on good will alone."

"Of course," Dradin said.

Dvorak bowed, turned, walked up to the door of Hoegbotton & Sons, and—quick and smooth and graceful—disappeared inside.

Dradin looked up at his love, wondering if he had made a mistake. Her lips still called to him and the entire sky seemed concentrated in her eyes, but he followed the dwarf's advice and, lighthearted, disappeared into the crowds.

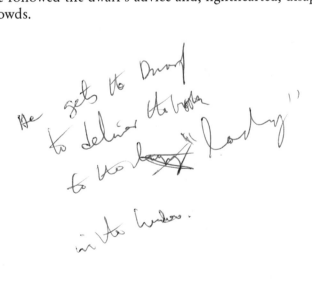

II

Dradin, happier than he had been since dropping the fever at the Sisters of Mercy Hospital, some five hundred miles away and three months in the past, sauntered down Albumuth, breathing in the smell of catfish simmering on open skillets, the tangy broth of codger soup, the sweet regret of overripe melons, pomegranates, and leechee fruit offered for sale. Stomach grumbling, he stopped long enough to buy a skewer of beef and onions and eat it noisily, afterwards wiping his hands on the back of his pants. He leaned against a lamppost next to a sidewalk barber and—aware of the sour effluvium from the shampoos, standing clear of the trickle of water that crept into the gutter—pulled out the map he had bought at Borges Bookstore. It was cheaply printed on butcher paper, many of the street names drawn by hand. Colorless, it compared unfavorably with Dvorak's tattoo, but it was accurate and he easily found the intersection of streets that marked his hostel. Beyond the hostel lay the valley of the city proper; north of it stood the religious district and his old teacher, Cadimon Signal. He could make his way to the hostel via one of two routes. The first would take him through an old factory district, no doubt littered with the corpses of rusted out motored vehicles and railroad cars, railroad tracks cut up and curving into the air with a profound sense of futility. In his childhood in the city of Morrow, Dradin, along with his long-lost friend Anthony Toliver (Tolive the Olive, he had been called, because of his fondness for the olive fruit or its oil), had played in just such a district, and it did not fit his temperament. He remembered how their play had been made somber by the sight of the trains, their great, dull heads upended, some staring glassily skyward while others drank in the cool, dark earth beneath. He was in no mood for such a death of metal, not with his heartbeat slowing and rushing, his manner at once calm and hyperactive.

No, he would take the second route—through the oldest part of the city, over one thousand years old, so old as to have lost any recollection of itself, its stones worn smooth and memory-less by the years. Perhaps such a route would settle him, allow him this bursting joy in his heart and yet not make his head spin quite so much.

Dradin moved on—ignoring an old man defecating on the sidewalk (trousers down around his ankles) and neatly sidestepping an Occidental woman around whom flopped live carp as she, armed with a club, methodically beat at their heads until a spackle of yellow brains glistened on the cobblestones.

After a few minutes of walking, the wall-to-wall buildings fell away, taking the smoke and dust and babble of voices with them. The world became a silent place except for the scuff of Dradin's shoes on the cobblestones and the occasional muttering chug-chuff of a motored vehicle, patched up and trundling along, like as not burning more oil than fuel. Dradin ignored the smell of fumes, the angry retort of tailpipes. He saw only the face of the woman from the window—in the pattern of lichen on a gray-stained wall, in the swirl of leaves gathered in a gutter.

The oldest avenues, thoroughfares grandfatherly when the Court of the Mourning Dog had been young and the Days of the Burning Sun had yet to scorch the land, lay a-drowning in a thick soup of honeysuckle, passion fruit, and bougainvillea, scorned by bee and hornet. Such streets had the lightest of traffic: old men on an after-lunch constitutional; a private tutor leading two children dressed in Sunday clothes, all polished shoes and handkerchief-and-spit cleaned faces.

The buildings Dradin passed were made of a stern, impervious gray stone, and separated by fountains and courtyards. Weeds and ivy smothered the sides of these stodgy, baroque halls, their windows broken as if the press of vines inward had smashed the glass. Morning glories, four o'clocks, and yet more ivy choked moldering stone street markers, trailed from rusted balconies, sprouted from pavement cracks, and stitched themselves into fences or gates scoured with old fire burns. Whom such buildings had housed, or what business had been conducted within, Dradin could only guess. They had, in their height and solidity, an atmosphere of states-craft about them, bureaucratic in their flourishes and busts, gargoyles and stout columns. But a bureaucracy lost to time: sword-wielding statues on horseback overgrown with lichen, the features of faces eaten away by rot deep in the stone; a fountain split down the center by the muscular roots of an oak. There was such a staggering sense of lawlessness in the silence amid the creepers.

Certainly the jungle had never concealed such a cornucopia of assorted fungus, for between patches of stone burned black Dradin now espied rich clusters of mushrooms in as many colors as there were beggars on Albumuth Boulevard: emerald, magenta, ruby, sapphire, plain brown, royal purple, corpse white. They ranged in size from a thimble to an obese eunuch's belly.

Such a playful and random dotting delighted Dradin so much that he began to follow the spray of mushrooms as much as he could without abandoning his general direction.

Their trail led him to a narrow avenue blocked in by ten-foot high gray stone walls, and he was soon struck by the notion that he traveled down the throat of a serpent. The mushrooms proliferated, until they not only grew in the cobblestone cracks, but also from the walls, speckling the gray with their bright hoods and stems.

The sun dimmed between clouds. A wind came up, brisk on Dradin's face. Trees loured ever closer, darkening the sky ever more. The street continued to narrow until it was wide enough for two men, then one

man, and finally so narrow—narrow as any narthex Dradin had ever encountered—that he moved sideways crablike, and still tore a button.

Eventually, the street widened again. He stumbled out into the open
space—only to be met by a *crack!* loud as the severing of a spine, a sound
that shot up, over, and past him. He cried out and flinched, one arm
held up to ward off a blow, as a sea of wings thrashed toward the sky.

He slowly brought his arm down. Pigeons. A flock of pigeons. Only
pigeons.

Ahead, when the flock had cleared the trees, Dradin saw, along the
street's right hand side, the rotting columbary from which the birds had
flown. Its many covey holes had the bottomless gaze of the blind. The
stink of pigeon droppings made his stomach queasy. Beside the
columbary, separated by an alleyway, stood a columbarium, also rotting
and deserted, so that urns of ashes teetered on the edge of a windowsill,
while below the smashed window two urns lay cracked on the cobblestones, their black ash spilling out.

A columbary and a columbarium! Side by side, no less, like old and
familiar friends, joined in decay.

Much as the sight intrigued him, the alley between the columbary
and columbarium fascinated Dradin more, for the mushrooms that had
crowded the crevices of the street and dotted the walls like the pox now
proliferated beyond all imagining, the cobblestones thick with them in a
hundred shades and hues. Down the right hand side of the alley, ten alcoves had been carved, complete with iron gates, a hundred hardened
cherubim and devils alike caught in the metalwork. The gate of the nearest alcove stood open and from within spilled lichen, creepers, and
mushroom dwellers, their red flags droopy. Surrounded by the vines, the
mushroom dwellers resembled human headstones or dreamy, drowning
swimmers in a green sea.

Beside Dradin—and he jumped back as he realized his mistake—lay a
mushroom dweller that he had thought was a mushroom the size of a
small child. It mewled and writhed in half-awakened slumber as Dradin
looked at it with a mixture of fascination and distaste. Stranger to Ambergris that he was, still Dradin knew of the mushroom dwellers, for, as
Cadimon Signal had taught him in Morrow, "they form the most out-
landish of all known cults," although little else had been forthcoming
from Cadimon's dried and withered lips.

Mushroom dwellers smelled of old, rotted barns and spoiled milk,
and vegetables mixed with the moistness of dark crevices and the dryness
of day-dead dung beetles. Some folk said they whispered and plotted
among themselves in a secret language so old that no one else, even in
the far, far Occident, spoke it. Others said they came from the subterra-
nean caves and tunnels below Ambergris, that they were escaped con-
victs who had gathered in the darkness and made their own singular reli-

gion and purpose, that they shunned the light because they were blind from their many years underground. And yet others, the poor and the under-educated, said that newts, golliwogs, slugs, and salamanders followed in their wake by land, while above bats, nighthawks, and whip-poorwills flew, feasting on the insects that crawled around mushroom and mushroom dweller alike.

Mushroom dwellers slept on the streets by day, but came out at night to harvest the fungus that had grown in the cracks and shadows of grave-yards during sunlit hours. Wherever they slept, they planted the red flags of warning, and woe to the man who, as Dradin had, disturbed their wet and lugubrious slumber. Sailors on the docks had told Dradin that the mushroom dwellers were known to rob graves for compost, or even mur-der tourists and use the flesh for their midnight crop. If no one ques-tioned or policed them, it was because during the night they tended to the garbage and carcasses that littered Ambergris. By dawn the streets had been picked clean and lay shining and innocent under the sun.

Fifty mushroom dwellers now spilled out from the alcove gateway, macabre in their very peacefulness and the even hum-thrum of their breath: stunted in growth, wrapped in robes the pale gray-green of a frog's underbelly, their heads hidden by wide-brimmed gray felt hats that, like the hooded tops of their namesakes, covered them to the neck. Their necks were the only exposed part of them—incredibly long, pale necks; at rest, they did indeed resemble mushrooms.

And yet, to Dradin's eye, they were disturbingly human rather than inhuman—a separate race, developing side by side, silent, invisible, chained to ritual—and the sight of them, on the same day that he had fallen so irrevocably in love, unnerved Dradin. He had already felt death upon him in the jungles and had known no fear, only pain, but here fear burrowed deep into his bones. Fear of death. Fear of the unknown. Fear of knowing death before he drank deeply of love. Morbidity and sullen curiosity mixed with dreams of isolation and desolation. All those ob-sessions of which the religious institute had supposedly cured him.

Positioned as he was, at the mouth of the alley, Dradin felt as though he were spying on a secret, forbidden world. Did they dream of giant mushrooms, gray caps agleam with the dark light of a midnight sun? Did they dream of a world lit only by the phosphorescent splendor of their charges?

Dradin watched them for a moment longer and then, his pace consid-erably faster, made his way past the alley mouth.

Eventually, under the cloud-darkened eye of the sun, the maze of al-leys gave way to wide, open-ended streets traversed by carpenters, clerks, blacksmiths, and broadsheet vendors, and he soon came upon the depressing but cheap Holander-Barth Hostel. (In another, richer, time he never would have considered staying there.) He had seen all too many such establishments in the jungles: great mansions rotted down to their foundations, occupied by the last inbred descendants of men and women who had thought the jungle could be conquered with machete and fire, only to find that the jungle had conquered them; where yesterday they had hacked down a hundred vines a thousand now writhed and interlocked in a fecundity of life. Dradin could not even be sure that the Sisters of Mercy Hospital still stood, untouched by such natural forces.

The Holander-Barth Hostel, once white, now dull gray, was a salute to pretentiousness, the dolorous inlaid marble columns crumbling from the inside out and laundry spread across ornately filigreed balconies black with decay. Perhaps once, a long time ago, jaded aristocrats had owned it, but now tubercular men walked its halls, hacking their lungs out while fishing in torn pockets for cigars or cigarettes. The majority were soldiers from long-forgotten campaigns who had used their pensions to secure lodging, blissfully ignorant (or ignoring) the cracked fixtures, curled wallpaper, communal showers and toilets. But, as the hansom driver had remarked on the way in, "It is the cheapest" and had added, "It is also far away from the festival." Luckily, the proprietors respected a man of the cloth, no matter how weathered, and Dradin had managed to rent one of two second story rooms with a private bath.

Heart pounding now not from fear, but rather from desire, Dradin dashed up the warped veranda—past the elderly pensioners, who bowed their heads or made confused signs of the cross—up the spiral staircase, came to his door, fumbled with the key, and once inside, fell on the bed with a thump that made the springs groan, the book thrown down beside him. The cover felt velvety and smooth to his touch. It felt like her skin must feel, he thought, and promptly fell asleep, a smile on his lips, for it was still near midday and the heat had drained his strength.

III

Mouth dry, hair tousled, and chin scratchy with stubble, Dradin woke to a pinched nerve in his back that made him moan and turn over and over on the bed, his perspective notably skewed, though not this time by the woman. Still, he could tell that the sun had plummeted beneath the horizon, and where the sky had been gray with clouds, it now ranged from black to a bruised purple, the moon mottled, the light measured out in rough dollops. Dradin yawned and scrunched his shoulders together to cure the pinchedness, then rose and walked to the tall but slender windows. He unhooked the latch and pulled the twin panes open to let in the smell of approaching rain, mixed with the sweet stink of garbage and honeysuckle.

The window looked down on the city proper, which lay inside the cupped hands of a valley veined with tributaries of the Moth. It was there that ordinary people slept and dreamt not of jungles and humidity and the lust that fed and starved men's hearts, but of quiet walks under the stars and milk-fat kittens and the gentle hum of wind on wooden porches. They raised families and doubtless missionaries never moved amongst their ranks, but only full-fledged priests, for they were already converted to a faith. Indeed, they—and people like them in other cities—paid their tithes and, in return, had emissaries sent out into the wilderness to spread the word, such emissaries nothing more than the physical form of their own hopes, wishes, fears; their desires made flesh. Dradin found the idea a sad one, sadder still, in a way he hesitated to define, that were it not for his chosen vocation, he could have had such a life: settling down into a daily rhythm that did not include the throbbing of the jungles, twinned to the beating of his heart. Anthony Toliver had chosen such a life, abandoning the clergy soon after graduation from the religious institute.

Around the valley lay the fringe, like a roughly circular smudge of wine and vulgar lipstick. The Holander-Barth Hostel marked the dividing line between the valley and fringe, just as the beginning of Albumuth Boulevard marked the end of the docks and the beginning of the fringe. It was here, not truly at a city's core, that Dradin had always been most comfortable, even back in his religious institute days, when he had been more severe on himself than the most pious monks who taught him.

On the fringe, jesters pricked and pranced, jugglers plied their trade with babies and knives (mixing the two as casually as one might mix apples and oranges). The life's blood swelled at a more exhilarating pace, a pace that quickened beyond the fringe, where the doughty sailors of the River Moth sailed on barges, dhows, frigates, and the rare steamer: anything that could float and hold a man without sinking into the silt.

Beyond the river lay the jungles, where the pace quickened into madness. The jungles hid creatures that died after a single day, their lives condensed beyond comprehension, so that Dradin, in observation of their own swift mortality, had sensed his body dying, hour by hour, minute by minute, a feeling that had not left him even when he lay down with the sweaty woman priest.

Dradin let the breeze from the window brush against him, cooling him, then returned to the bed, circling around it to the bed lamp, turned the switch, and lo!, a brassy light to read by. He plopped down on the bed, legs akimbo, and opened the book to the first page. Thus began the fantasy: that in some other room, some other house—perhaps even in the valley below—the woman from the window lay in her own bed by some dim light and turned these same pages, read these same words. The touch of the pages to his fingers was erotic; they felt damp and charged his limbs with the short, sharp shock of a ceremonial cup of liqueur. He became hard, but resisted the urge to touch himself. Ah, sweet agony! Nothing in his life had ever felt half so good, half so tortuous. Nothing in the bravely savage world beyond the Moth could compare: not the entwining snake dances of the Magpie Women of the Frangipani Veldt, nor the single, aching cry of a Zinfendel maid as she jumped headfirst into the roar of a waterfall. Not even the sweaty woman priest before the fever struck, her panting moans during their awkward love play more a testimonial to the humidity and ever-present mosquitoes than any skill on his part.

Dradin looked around his room. How bare it was for all that he had lived some thirty years. There was his red-handled machete, balanced against the edge of the dresser drawers, and his knapsack, which contained powders and liquids to cure a hundred jungle diseases, and his orange-scuffed boots beside that, and his coins on the table, the gold almost crimson in the light, but what else? Just his suitcase with two changes of clothes, his yellowing, torn diploma from the Morrow Institute of Religiosity, and daguerreotypes of his mother and father, them in their short-lived youth, Dad not yet a red-faced, broken-veined lout of an academic, Mom's eyes not yet squinty with surrounding wrinkles and sharp as bloodied shards of glass.

What did the woman's room look like? No doubt it too was briskly clean, but not bare, oh no. It would have a bed with white mosquito netting and a place for a glass of water, and her favorite books in a row beside the bed, and beyond that a white and silver mantel and mirror, and below that, her dresser drawers, filled to bursting with frilly night things and frilly day things, and filthily frilly twilight things as well. Powders and lotions for her skin, to keep it beyond the pale. Knitting needles and wool, or other less feminine tools for hobbies. Perhaps she kept a vanilla kitten close by, to play with the balls of wool. If she lived at home, this might be the extent of her world, but if she lived alone, then Dradin had three, four, other rooms to fill with her loves and hates. Did she enjoy small talk and other chatter? Did she dance? Did she go to social events? What might she be thinking as she read the book, on the first page of which was written:

THE REFRACTION OF LIGHT IN A PRISON
(Being an Account of the Truffidian Monks
Held in the Dungeons of the Kalif,
For They Have Not Given Up Sanity, or Hope)

BY:
Brother Peek
Brother Prowcosh
Brother Witamoor
Brother Sirin
Brother Grae

(and, held unfortunately in separate quarters,
communicating to us purely
by the force of her will, Sister Stalker)

And, on the next page:

BEING CHAPTER ONE:
THE MYSTICAL PASSIONS

The most mystical of all passions are those practiced by the water people of the Lower Moth, for though they remain celibate and spend most of their lives in the water, they attain a oneness with their mates that bedevils those lesser of us who equate love with intercourse. Surely their women would never become the objects of their desire, for then these women would lose an intrinsic eroticism.

Dradin read on impatiently, his hands sweaty, his throat dry, but, no, no, he would not rise to drink water from the sink, nor release his tension, but must burn, as his love must burn, reading the self-same words. For now he was in truth a missionary, converting himself to the cause of love, and he could not stop.

Outside, along the lip of the valley, lights began to blink and waver in phosphorescent reds, greens, blues, and yellows, and Dradin realized that preparations for the Festival of the Fresh Water Squid must be underway. On the morrow night, Albumuth Boulevard would be cleared for a parade that would overflow onto the adjacent streets and then the entire city. Along the avenues, candles wrapped in boxes of crepe paper would appear, so that the light would be like the dancing of the squid, great and small, upon the midnight salt water where it met the mouth of the Moth. A celebration of the spawning season, when males battled mightily for females of the species and the fisher folk of the docks would set out for a month's trawling of the lusting grounds, hoping to bring back enough meat to last until winter.

If only he could be with her on the morrow night. Among the sights the hansom driver had pointed out on the way into Ambergris was a tavern, *The Drunken Boat*, decked out with the finest in cutlery and clientele, and featuring, for the festival only, the caterwauling of a band called The Ravens. To dance with her, her hands interwoven with his, the scent of her body on his, would make up for all that had happened in the jungle and the humiliations since: the hunt for ever more miserable jobs, accompanied by a general lightening of coin in his pockets.

The clocks struck the insomniac hours after midnight and, below the window, Dradin heard the moist scuttle of mushroom dwellers as they gathered offal and refuse. Rain followed the striking of the clocks, falling softly, as light in touch as Dradin's hand upon *The Refraction of Light in a Prison*. The smell of rain, fresh and sharp, came from the window.

Drawn by that smell, Dradin put the book aside and rose to the window, watched the rain as it caught the faint light, the drops like a school of tiny silver-scaled fish, here and gone, back a moment later. A vein of lightning, a boom of thunder, and the rain came faster and harder.

Many times Dradin had stared through the rain-splashed windows of the old gray house on the hill from his childhood in Morrow (the house with the closed shutters like eyes stitched shut) while relatives came up the gray, coiled road: the headlights of expensive motored vehicles bright in the sheen of rain. They resembled a small army of hunched black, white, and red beetles, like the ones in his father's insect books, creeping up the hill. Below them, where it was not fogged over, the rest of Morrow: industrious, built of stone and wood, feeding off of the River Moth.

From one particular window in the study, Dradin could enjoy a double image: inside, at the end of a row of three open doors—library, living room, dining room—his enormous opera singer of a mother (tall and big-boned) stuffed into the kitchen. No maid helped her, for they lived, the three of them, alone on the hill, and so she would be delicately placing mincemeats on plates, cookies on trays, splashing lemonade and punch into glasses, trying very hard to keep her hands clean and her red dress of frills and lace unstained. She would sing to herself as she worked, in an unrestrained and husky voice (it seemed she never spoke to Dradin, but only sang) so that he could hear, conducted through the various pipes, air ducts, and passageways, the words of Voss Bender's greatest opera:

Come to me in the Spring
When the rains fall hard
For you are sweet as pollen,
Sweet as fresh honeycomb.

When the hard brown branches
Of the oak sprout green leaves,
In the season of love, come to me.

Into the oven would go the annual pheasant, while outside the window Dradin could see his father, thin and meticulous in tuxedo and tails, picking his way through the puddles in the front drive, carrying a big, ragged black umbrella. Dad would walk *precisely*, as if by stepping first *here* and then *there*, he might escape the rain drops, slip between them because he knew the umbrella would do no good, riddled as it was with rips and moth holes. But, oh, what a pantomime for the guests!, while Dradin laughed and his mother sang. Apologies for the rain, the puddles, the tattered appearance of the umbrella. In later years, Dad's greetings became loutish, slurred by drink and age until they were no longer generous. But back then he would unfold his limbs like a good-natured mantis and with quick movements of his hands switch the umbrella from left to right as he gestured his apologies. All the while, the guests would be half-in, half-out of the car—Aunt Sophie and Uncle Ken, perhaps—trying hard to be polite, but meanwhile drenched to the skin. Inside, Mom would have time to steel herself, ready a greeting smile by the front door, and—one doomful eye on the soon-to-be-burnt pheasant—call for Dradin.

In a much more raging rain, Dradin had first been touched by a force akin to the spiritual. It occurred on a similarly dreary day of visiting relatives, Dradin only nine and trapped: trapped by dry pecks on the cheek; trapped by the smell of damp, sweaty bodies brought close together; trapped by the dry burn of cigars and by the alarming stares of the elderly men, eyebrows inert white slugs, moustaches wriggly, eyes enormous and watery through glasses or monocles. Trapped, too, by the ladies, even worse at that advanced age, their cavernous grouper mouths intent on devouring him whole into their bellies.

Dradin had begged his mother to invite Anthony Toliver and, against his father's wishes, she had said yes. Anthony, a fearless follower, was a wiry boy with sallow skin and dark eyes. They had met in public school, odd fellows bonded together by the simple fact that both had been beaten up by the school bully, Roger Gimmell.

As soon as Tony arrived, Dradin convinced him to escape the party. Off they snuck, through a parlor door into a backyard bounded only at the horizon by a tangled wilderness of trees. Water pelted them, splattered on shirts, and pummeled flesh, so that Dradin's ears rang with the force of it and dull aches woke him the morning after. Grass was swept away, dirt dissolving into mud.

Tony fell almost immediately and, scrabbling at Dradin, made him fall too, into the wet, grasping at weeds for support. Tony laughed at the surprised look on Dradin's face. Dradin laughed at the mud clogging Tony's left ear. Splash! Slosh! Mud in the boots, mud in the trousers, mud flecking their hair, mud coating their faces.

They grappled and giggled. The rain fell so hard it stung. It bit into their clothes, cut into the tops of their heads, attacked their eyes so they could barely open them. In the middle of the mud fight they stopped battling each other and started battling the rain. They scrambled to their feet, no longer playing, then lost touch with each other, Tony's hand slipping from Dradin's, so that Tony said only, "Come on!" and ran toward the house, never looking back at Dradin, who stood still as a frightened rabbit, utterly alone in the universe.

As Dradin stands alone in the sheets of rain, staring at the heavens that have opened up and sent the rains down, he begins to shake. The rain, like a hand on his shoulders, presses him down; the electric sensation of water on his skin rinses away mud and bits of grass, leaves him cold and sodden. He shudders convulsively, sensing the prickle of an immensity up in the sky, staring down at him. He knows from the rush and rage of blood, the magnified beat of his heart, that nothing this *alive*, this out of control, can be random.

Dradin closes his eyes and a thousand colors, a thousand images, explode inside his mind, one for each drop of rain. A rain of shooting stars, and from this conflagration the universe opening up before him. For an instant, Dradin can sense every throbbing artery and arrhythmic heart in the city below him—every darting quicksilver thought of hope, of pain, of hatred, of love. A hundred thousand sorrows and a hundred thousand joys ascending to him.

The babble of sensation so overwhelms him that he can hardly breathe, cannot feel his body except as a hollow receptacle. Then the sensations fade until, closer at hand, he feels the pinprick lives of mice in the nearby glades, the deer like graceful shadows, the foxes clever in their burrows, the ladybugs hidden on the undersides of leaves, and then nothing, and when it is gone, he says, shoulders slumped, but still on his feet, *Is this God?*

When Dradin—a husk now, his hearing deafened by the rain, his bones cleansed by it—turned back toward the house; when he finally faced the house with its shuttered windows, as common sense dictated he should, the light from within fairly burst to be let out. And Dradin saw (as he stood by the window in the hostel) not Tony, who was safely inside, but his mother. His mother. The later memory fused to the earlier seamlessly, as if they had happened together, one, of a piece. That he had turned and she was there, already leveling a blank stare toward him; that, simple as breath, the rain brought redemption and madness crashing down on both their heads, the time span no obstacle and of no importance.

... he turned and there was his mother, on her knees in the mud, in her red dress spattered brown. She scooped the mud up with her hands, regarded it, and began to eat, so ravenously that she bit into her little finger. The eyes on the face of stone—the face as blank as the rain—looked up at him with the most curious expression, as if trapped as Dradin had felt trapped inside the house, trapped and asking Dradin ... to do something. And him, even then, already fourteen, not knowing what to do, calling for Dad, calling for a doctor, while the mud smudged the edges of her mouth and, unconcerned, she ate more and stared at him after each bite, until he cried and came to her and hugged her and tried to make her stop, though nothing in the world could make her stop, or make him stop trying. What unnerved him more than anything, more than the mud in her mouth, was the complete silence that surrounded her, for he had come to define her by her voice, and this she did not use, even to ask for help.

Dradin again heard the mushroom dwellers below and closed the window abruptly. He sat back on the bed. He wanted to read more of the book, except that now his thoughts floated, rose and fell like waves and, before he realized it, before he could stop it, he was, as it were, not quite dead, but merely asleep.

***

In the morning, Dradin rose rested and spry, his body almost certainly recovered from the jungle fever. For months he had risen to the ache of sore muscles and bruised internal organs; now he had only a fever of a different sort. Every time Dradin glanced at *The Refraction of Light in a Prison*—as he washed his face in the green-tinged basin, as he dressed, not looking at his pant legs so it took him several tries to put them on—he thought of her. What piece of glitter might catch her eye for him? For now, surely, if she had read the book, was the time to appraise her worth to him, to let her know that serious is as serious does. In just

such a manner had his dad wooed his mom, Dad a rake-thin but
puff-bellied proud graduate of Morrow's University of Arts & Facts
(which certainly defined Dad). She, known by the maiden name of
Barsombly, the famous singer with a voice like a pit bull—almost bari-
tone, but husky enough, Dradin admitted, to conceal a sultry sexuality.
He could not remember when he had not either felt the *thrulling* vibra-
tions of his mother's voice or heard the voice itself. Or a time when he
had not watched as she applied raucous perfumes and powders to herself, after putting on the low-bodiced, gold-satin costumes that rounded
her taut bulk like an impenetrable wall. He could remember her taking
him into theatres and music halls through the back entrance, bepuddled
and muddened, and as some helpful squire would escort him sodden to
his seat, so too would she be escorted atop the stage, so that as Dradin
sat, the curtain rose, simultaneous with the applause from the audience—an ovation like the crashing of waves against rock.

Then she would sing, and he would imagine the thrull of her against
him, and marvel at the power of her voice, the depths and hollows of it,
the way it matched the flow and melody of the orchestra only to diverge,
coursing like a secret and perilous undertow, the vibration growing and
growing until there was no longer any music at all, but only the voice devouring the music.

Dad did not go to any of her performances and sometimes Dradin
thought she sang so loud, so full of rage, that Dad might still hear her
faintly, him up late reading in the study of the old house on the hill with
the shutters like eyes stitched shut.

His mother would have been proud of his attempts to woo, but, alas,
she had been gagged and trussed for her own good and traveled now
with the Bedlam Rovers, a cruising troupe of petty psychiatrists—sailing
down the Moth on a glorified houseboat under the subtitle of "Boat
Bound Psychiatrists: Miracle Workers of the Mind"—to whom, finally,
Dad had given over his dearest, the spiced fig of his heart, Dradin's
mother—for a fee, of course; and didn't it, Dad had raged and blustered,
come to the same thing? In a rest home or asylum; either situated in one
place, or on the move. It was not so bad, he would say, slumping down in
a damp green chair, waving his amber bottle of Smashing Ted's Finest;
after all, the sights she would see, the places she would experience, and
all under the wise and benevolent care of trained psychiatrists who *paid*
to take that care. Surely, his father would finish with a belch or burp,
there is no better arrangement.

Youngish Dradin, still smarting from the ghost of the strap of a half
an hour past dared not argue, but thought often: yes, but all such locu-
tions of thought are reliable and reliant upon one simple supposi-
tion—to whit, that she be insane. What if not insane but sane "south by
southwest" as the great Voss Bender said? What if, inside the graying but

leopardesque head, the burgeoning frame, lay a wide realm of sanity, with only the outer shell susceptible to hallucinations, incantations, and inappropriate metaphors? What then? To be yanked about thus, like an animal on a chain, could this be stood by a sane individual? Might such parading and humiliation lead a person to the very insanity hitherto avoided?

And, worse thought still, that his father had driven her to it with his cruel, carefully-planned indifference.

But Dradin—remembering the awful silence of that day in the rain when Mom had stuffed her mouth full of mud—refused to dwell on it. He must find a present for his darling, this accomplished by rummaging through his pack and coming up with a necklace, the centerpiece an un-cut emerald. It had been given to him by a tribal chieftain as a bribe to go away ("There is only One God," Dradin had said. "What's his name?" the chieftain asked. "God," replied Dradin. "How bloody boring," the chieftain said. "Please go away.") and he had taken it initially as a dona-tion to the Church, although he had meant to give it to the spiced fig of his heart, the sweaty woman priest, only to have the fever overtake him first. As he held the necklace in his hand, he recognized the exceptional workmanship of the blue-and-green beads. If he were to sell it, he might pay the rent at the hostel for another week. But, more attractive, if he gave it to his love, she would understand the seriousness of his heart's de-sire.

With uncharacteristic grace and a touch of inspired lunacy, Dradin tore the first page from *The Refraction of Light in a Prison* and wrote his name below the name of the last monk, like so:

Brother Dradin Kashmir -
Not truly a brother, but devout
in his love for you alone

Dradin looked over his penmanship with satisfaction. There. It was done. It could not be undone.

IV

Over breakfast, his sparse needs tended to by a gaunt waiter who looked like a malaria victim, Dradin examined his dull gray map. Toast without jam for him, nothing richer like sausages frying in their own fat, or bacon with white strips of lard. The jungle climate had, from the start, made his bowels and bladder loosen up and pour forth their bile like the sludge of rain in the most deadly of monsoon seasons. Dradin had avoided rich foods ever since, saying no to such jungle delicacies as fried grasshopper, boiled peccary, and a local favorite that baked huge black slugs into their shells.

From dirty gray table-clothed tables on either side, war veterans coughed and harrumphed, their bloodshot eyes perked into semi-awareness by the sight of Dradin's map. Treasure? War on two fronts? Mad, drunken charges into the eyeteeth of the enemy? No doubt. Dradin knew their type, for his father was the same, if with an academic bent. The map would be a mystery of the mind to his father.

Nonetheless, ignoring their stares, Dradin found the religious quarter on the map, traced over it with his index finger. It resembled a bird's eye view of a wheel with interconnecting spokes. No more a "quarter" than drawn. Cadimon Signal's mission stood near the center of the spokes, snuggled into a corner between the Church of the Fisherman and the Cult of the Seven-Edged Star. Even looking at it on the map made Dradin nervous. To meet his religious instructor after such a time. How would Cadimon have aged after seven years? Perversely, as far afield as Dradin had gone, Cadimon Signal had, in that time, come closer to the center, his home, for he had been born in Ambergris. At the religious institute Cadimon had extolled the city's virtues and, to be fair, its vices many times after lectures, in the common hall. His voice, hollow and echoing against the black marble archways, gave a raspy voice to the gossamer-thin cherubim carved into the swirl of white marble ceilings. Dradin had spent many nights along with Anthony Toliver listening to that voice, surrounded by thousands of religious texts on shelves gilded with gold leaf.

The question that most intrigued Dradin, that guided his thoughts and bedeviled his nights, was this: Would Cadimon Signal take pity on a former student and find a job for him? He hoped, of course, for a missionary position, but failing that a position which would not break his back or tie him in knots of bureaucratic red tape. Dad was an unlikely ally in this, for Dad had recommended Dradin to Cadimon and also recommended Cadimon to Dradin.

Before the fuzzy beginnings of Dradin's memory, Dad had, when still young and thin and mischievous, invited Cadimon over for tea and conversation, surrounded in Dad's study by books, books, and more books.

Books on culture and civilization, religion and philosophy. They would, or so Dad told Dradin later, debate every topic imaginable, and some that were unimaginable, distasteful, or all too real until the hours struck midnight, one o'clock, two o'clock, and the lanterns dimmed to an ironic light, brackish and ill-suited to discussion. Surely this bond would be enough? Surely Cadimon would look at him and see the father in the son?

After breakfast, necklace and map in hand, Dradin wandered into the religious quarter, known by the common moniker of Pejora's Folly after Midan Pejora, the principal early architect, to whose credit or discredit could be placed the slanted walls, the jumble of Occidental and accidental, northern and southern, baroque and pure jungle, styles. Buildings battled for breath and space like centuries-slow soldiers in brick-to-brick combat. To look into the revolving spin of a kaleidoscope while heavily intoxicated, Dradin thought, would not be half so bad.

The rain from the night before took the form of sunlit droplets on plants, windowpanes, and cobblestones that wiped away the dull and dusty veneer of the city. Cats preened and tiny hop toads hopped while dead sparrows lay in furrows of water, beaten down by the storm's ferocity. Dradin felt fresh and clean, and breathed deeply of the breezy, damp air.

He snorted in disbelief as he observed followers of gentle Saint Solon the Decrepit placing the corpses of rain victims such as the sparrows into tiny wooden coffins for burial. In the jungle deaths occurred in such thick numbers that one might walk a mile on the decayed carcasses, the white clean bones of deceased animals, and after a time even the most fastidious missionary gave the crunching sound not a second thought.

As he neared the mission, Dradin tried to calm himself by breathing in the acrid scent of votive candles burning from alcoves and crevices and balconies. He tried to imagine the richness of his father's conversations with Cadimon—the plethora of topics discussed, the righteous and pious denials and arguments. When his father mentioned those conversations, the man would shake off the weight of years, his voice light and his eyes moist with nostalgia. If only Cadimon remembered such encounters with similar enthusiasm.

The slap-slap of punished pilgrim feet against the stones of the street pulled him from his reverie, and he stood to one side as twenty or thirty mendicants slapped on past, cleansing their sins through their calluses, on their way to one of a thousand shrines. In their calm but blank gaze, their slack mouths, Dradin saw the shadow of his mother's face, and he wondered what she had done while his father and Cadimon talked.

Gone to sleep? Finished up the dishes? Sat in bed and listened through the wall?

At last, Dradin found the Mission of Cadimon Signal. Set back from the street, the mission remained almost invisible among the sky-ward-straining cathedrals surrounding it—remarkable only for the emp-tiness, the silence, and the swirl of swallows skimming through the air like weightless trapeze artists. The building that housed the mission was an old tin-roofed warehouse reinforced with mortar and brick, opened up from the inside with ragged holes for skylights, which made Dradin wonder what they did when it rained. Let it rain on them, he supposed.

Christened with fragmented mosaics that depicted saints, monks, and martyrs, the enormous doorway lay open to him. All around, aco-lytes frantically lifted sandbags and long pieces of timber, intent on bar-ricading the entrance, but none challenged him as he walked up the steps and through the gateway; no one, in fact, spared him a second glance, so focused were they on their efforts.

Inside, Dradin went from sunlight to shadows, his footfalls hollow in the silence. A maze of paths wound through lush green Occidental-style gardens. The gardens centered around rock-lined pools cut through by the curving fins of corpulent carp. Next to the pools lay the eroded ruins of ancient, pagan temples, which had been reclaimed with gaily-colored paper and splashes of red, green, blue, and white paint. Among the tem-ples and gardens and pools, unobtrusive as lampposts, acolytes in gray habits toiled, removing dirt, planting herbs, and watering flowers. The air had a metallic color and flavor to it and Dradin heard the buzzing of bees at the many poppies, the soft *scull-skithing* as acolytes wielded their scythes against encroaching weeds.

The ragged, blue grass-fringed trail led Dradin to a raised mound of dirt on which stood a catafalque, decorated with gold leaf and the legend "Saint Philip the Philanderer" printed along its side. In the shadow of the catafalque, amid the blue grass, a gardener dressed in dark green robes planted lilies he had set on a nearby bench. Atop the catafalque, halting Dradin in mid-step, stood Signal. He had changed since Dradin had last seen him, for he was bald and gaunt, with white tufts of hair sprouting from his ears. A studded dog collar circled his withered neck. But most disturbing, unless one wished to count a cask of Solomon's Wine that dangled from his left hand—no doubt shipped in by those reli-able if questionable purveyors of spirits Hoegbotton & Sons, perhaps even held, caressed, by his love—*the man was stark staring naked!* The ob-ject of no one's desire bobbed like a length of flaccid purpling sausage, held in some semblance of erectitude by the man's right hand, the hand currently engaged in an up-and-down motion that brought great plea-sure to its owner.

"Ccc-Cadimon Ssss-sigggnal?"

"Yes, who is it now?" said the gardener.

"I beg your pardon."

"I said," repeated the gardener with infinite patience, as if he really would not mind saying it a third, a fourth, or a fifth time, "I said 'Yes, who is it now?' "

"It's Dradin. Dradin Kashmir. Who are you?" Dradin kept one eye on the naked man atop the catafalque.

"I'm Cadimon Signal, of course," the gardener said, patiently pulling weeds, plotting lilies. *Pull, plot, pull.* "Welcome to my mission, Dradin. It's been a long time." The small, green-robed man in front of Dradin had mannerisms and features indistinguishable from any wizened beggar on Ambergris Boulevard, but looking closer, Dradin thought he could see a certain resemblance to the man he had known in Morrow. Perhaps.

"Who is he, then?" Dradin pointed to the naked man, who was now ejaculating into a rose bush.

"He's a Living Saint. A professional holy man. You should remember that from your theology classes. I know I must have taught you about Living Saints. Unless, of course, I switched that with a unit on Dead Martyrs. No other kind, really. That's a joke, Dradin. Have the decency to laugh."

The Living Saint, no longer aroused, but quite tired, lay down on the smooth cool stone of the catafalque and began to snore.

"But what's a Living Saint doing here? And naked?"

"I keep him here to discomfort my creditors who come calling. Lots of upkeep to this place. My, you have changed, haven't you?"

"What?"

"I thought *I* had gone deaf. I said you've changed. Please, ignore my Living Saint. As I said, he's for the creditors. Just trundle him out, have him spill his seed, and they don't come back."

"I've changed?"

"Yes, I've said that already." Cadimon stopped plotting lilies and stood up, examined Dradin from crown to stirrups. "You've been to the jungle. A pity, really. You were a good student."

"I have come back from the jungle, if that's what you mean. I took fever."

"No doubt. You've changed most definitely. Here, hold a lily bulb for me." Cadimon crouched down once more. *Pull, plot, pull.*

"You seem . . . you seem somehow less imposing. But healthier."

"No, no. You've grown taller, that's all. What are you now that you are no longer a missionary?"

"No longer a missionary?" Dradin said, and felt as if he were drowning, and here they had only just started to talk.

"Yes. Or no. Lily please. Thank you. Blessed things require so much dirt. Good for the lungs exercise is. Good for the soul. How is your father these days? Such a shame about your mother. But how is he?"

"I haven't seen him in over three years. He wrote me while I was in the jungle and he seemed to be doing well."

"Mmmm. I'm glad to hear it. Your father and I had the most wonderful conversations a long time ago. A very long time ago. Why, I can remember sitting up at his house—you just in a crib then, of course—and debating the aesthetic value of the Golden Spheres until—"

"I've come here looking for a job."

Silence. Then Cadimon said, "Don't you still work for—"

"I quit." Emphasis on *quit*, like the pressure on an egg to make it crack just so.

"Did you now? I told you you were no longer a missionary. I haven't changed a whit from those days at the academy, Dradin. You didn't recognize me because you've changed, not I. I'm the same. I do not change. Which is more than you can say for the weather around here."

It was time, Dradin decided, to take control of the conversation. It was not enough to counter-punch Cadimon's drifting dialogue. He bent to his knees and gently placed the rest of the lilies in Cadimon's lap.

"Sir," he said. "I need a position. I have been out of my mind with the fever for three months and now, only just recovered, I long to return to the life of a missionary."

"Determined to stick to a point, aren't you?" Cadimon said. "A point stickler. A stickler for rules. I remember you. Always the sort to be shocked by a Living Saint rather than amused. Rehearsed rather than spontaneous. Oh well."

"Cadimon . . ."

"Can you cook?"

"Cook? I can boil cabbage. I can heat water."

Cadimon patted Dradin on the side of his stomach. "So can a hedgehog, my dear. So can a hedgehog, if pressed. No, I mean cook as in the Cooks of Kalay, who can take nothing more than a cauldron of bilge water and a side of beef three days old and tough as calluses and make a dish so succulent and sweet it shames the taste buds to eat so much as a carrot for days afterwards. You can't cook, can you?"

"What does cooking have to do with missionary work?"

"Oh, ho. I would have thought a jungle veteran would know the answer to that! Ever heard of cannibals? Eh? No, that's a joke. It has nothing to do with missionary work. There." He patted the last of the lilies and rose to sit on the bench, indicating with a wave of the hand that Dradin should join him.

Dradin sat down on the bench next to Cadimon. "Surely, you need experienced missionaries?"

Cadimon shook his head. "We don't have a job for you. I'm sorry. You've changed, Dradin."

"But you and my father . . . " Blood rose to Dradin's face. For he could woo until he turned purple, but without a job, how to fund such adventures in pocketbook as his new love would entail?

"Your father is a good man, Dradin. But this mission is not made of money. I see tough times ahead."

Pride surfaced in Dradin's mind like a particularly ugly crocodile. "I am a good missionary, sir. A very good missionary. I have been a missionary for over five years, as you know. And, as I have said, I am just now out of the jungle, having nearly died of fever. Several of my colleagues did not recover. The woman. The woman . . . "

But he trailed off, his skin goose-pimpled from a sudden chill. Layeville, Flay, Stern, Thaw, and Krug had all gone mad or died under the onslaught of green, the rain and the dysentery, and the savages with their poison arrows. Only he had crawled to safety, the mush of the jungle floor beneath his chest a-murmur with leeches and dung bugs and "molly twelve-step" centipedes. A trek into and out of hell, and he could not even now remember it all, or wanted to remember it all.

"Paugh! Dying of fever is easy. The jungle is easy, Dradin. I could survive, frail as I am. It's the city that's hard. If you'd only bother to observe, you'd see the air is overripe with missionaries. You can't defecate out a window without fouling a brace of them. The city bursts with them. They think that the festival signals opportunity, but the opportunity is not for them! No, we need a cook, and you cannot cook."

Dradin's palms slickened with sweat, his hands shaking as he examined them. What now? What to do? His thoughts circled and circled around the same unanswerable question: How could he survive on the coins he had yet on his person and still woo the woman in the window? And he must woo her; he did not feel his heart could withstand the blow of *not* pursuing her.

"I am a good missionary," Dradin repeated, looking at the ground. "What happened in the jungle was not my fault. We went out looking for converts, and when I came back the compound was overrun."

Dradin's breaths came quick and shallow and his head felt light. Suffocating, that was it, he was suffocating under the weight of jungle leaves closing over his nose and mouth.

Cadimon sighed and shook his head. In a soft voice he said, "I am not unsympathetic," and held out his hands to Dradin. "How can I explain myself? Maybe I cannot, but let me try. Perhaps this way: Have you converted the Flying Squirrel People of the western hydras? Have you braved the frozen wastes of Lascia to convert the ice cube-like Skamoo?"

"No."

"What did you say?"

"No!"

"Then we can't use you. At least not now."

Dradin's throat ached and his jaw tightened. Would he have to beg, then? Would he have to become a mendicant himself? On the catafalque, the Living Saint had begun to stir, mumbling in his half-sleep.

Cadimon rose and put his hand on Dradin's shoulder. "If it is any consolation, you were never really a missionary, not even at the religious academy. And you are definitely not a missionary now. You are . . . something else. Extraordinary, really, that I can't put my finger on it."

"You insult me," Dradin said, as if he were the gaudy figurehead on some pompous yacht sailing languid on the Moth.

"That is not my intent, my dear. Not at all."

"Perhaps you could give me money. I could repay you."

"Now *you* insult *me*. Dradin, I cannot lend you money. We have no money. All the money we collect goes to our creditors or into the houses and shelters of the poor. We have no money, nor do we covet it."

"Cadimon," Dradin said. "Cadimon, I'm desperate. I need money."

"If you are desperate, take my advice—leave Ambergris. And before the festival. It's not safe for priests to be on the streets after dark on festival night. There have been so many years of calm. Ha! I tell you, it can't last."

"It wouldn't have to be much money. Just enough to—"

Cadimon gestured toward the entrance. "Beg from your father, not from me. Leave. Leave now."

Dradin, taut muscles and clenched fists, would have obeyed Cadimon out of respect for the memory of authority, but now a vision rose into his mind like the moon rising over the valley the night before. A vision of the jungle, the dark green leaves with their veins like spines, like long, delicate bones. The jungle and the woman and all of the dead . . .

"I will not."

Cadimon frowned. "I'm sorry to hear you say that. I ask you again, leave."

Lush green, smothering, the taste of dirt in his mouth; the smell of burning, smoke curling up into a question mark.

"Cadimon, I was your student. You owe me the—"

"Living Saint!" Cadimon shouted. "Wake up, Living Saint."

The Living Saint uncurled himself from his repose atop the catafalque.

"Living Saint," Cadimon said, "dispense with him. No need to be gentle." And, turning to Dradin, "Goodbye, Dradin. I am very sorry."

The Living Saint, spouting insults, jumped from the catafalque and—his penis, purpling and flaccid as a sea anemone, brandished menacingly—ran toward Dradin, who promptly took to his heels, stumbling

through the ranks of the gathered acolytes and hearing directly behind
him as he navigated the blue grass trail not only the Living Saint's
screams of "Piss off! Piss off, you great big baboon!" but also Cadimon's
distant shouts of: "I'll pray for you, Dradin. I'll pray for you." And,
then, too close, much too close, the unmistakable hot and steamy sound
of a man relieving himself, followed by the hands of the Living Saint
clamped down on his shoulder blades, and a much swifter exit than he
had hoped for upon his arrival, scuffing his fundament, his pride, his
dignity.

   "And stay out!"

   When Dradin stopped running he found himself on the fringe of the
religious quarter, next to an emaciated macadamia salesman who
cracked jokes like nuts. Out of breath, Dradin put his hands on his hips.
His lungs strained for air. Blood rushed furiously through his chest. He
could almost persuade himself that these symptoms were only the aftershock of exertion, not the aftershock of anger and desperation. Actions
unbecoming a missionary. Actions unbecoming a gentleman. What
might love next drive him to?

   Determined to regain his composure, Dradin straightened his shirt
and collar, then continued on his way in a manner he hoped mimicked
the stately gait of a mid-level clergy member, to whom all such earthly
things were beneath and below. But the bulge of red, red veins at his
neck, the stiffness of fingers in claws at his sides, these clues gave him
away, and knowing this made him angrier still. How dare Cadimon treat
him as though he were practically a stranger! How dare the man betray
the bond between his father and the church!

   More disturbing, where were the agents of order when you needed
them? No doubt the city had ordinances against public urination. Although that presupposed the existence of a civil authority, and of this
mythic beast Dradin had yet to convince himself. He had not seen a single blue, black, or brown uniform, and certainly not filled out with a
body lodged within its fabric, a man who might symbolize law and order
and thus give the word flesh. What did the people of Ambergris do when
thieves and molesters and murderers traversed the thoroughfares and alleyways, the underpasses and the bridges? But the thought brought him
back to the mushroom dwellers and their alcove shrines, and he abandoned it, a convulsion traveling from his chin to the tips of his toes. Perhaps the jungle had not yet relinquished its grip.

   Finally, shoulders bowed, eyes on the ground, in abject defeat, he admitted to himself that his methods had been grotesque. He had made a
fool of himself in front of Cadimon. Cadimon was not beholden to
him. Cadimon had only acted as he must when confronted with the ungodly.

Necklace still wrapped in the page from *The Refraction of Light in a Prison*, Dradin came again to Hoegbotton & Sons, only to find that his love no longer stared from the third floor window. A shock traveled up his spine, a shock that might have sent him gibbering to his mother's side aboard the psychiatrists' houseboat, if not that he was a rational and rationalizing man. How his heart drowned in a sea of fears as he tried to conjure up a thousand excuses: she was out to lunch; she had taken ill; she had moved to another part of the building. Never that she was gone for good, lost as he was lost; that he might never, ever see her face again. Now Dradin understood his father's addiction to sweet-milled mead, beer, wine and champagne, for the woman was his addiction, and he knew that if he had only seen her porcelain-perfect visage as he suffered from the jungle fevers, he would have lived for her sake alone.

The city might be savage, stray dogs might share the streets with grimy urchins whose blank eyes reflected the knowledge that they might soon be covered over, blinded forever, by the same two pennies just begged from some gentleman, and no one in all the fuming, fulminous boulevards of trade might know who actually ran Ambergris—or, if anyone ran it at all, but, like a renegade clock, it ran on and wound itself heedless, empowered by the insane weight of its own inertia, the weight of its own citizenry, stamping one, two, three hundred thousand strong; no matter this savagery in the midst of apparent civilization—still the woman in the window seemed to him more ruly, more disciplined and in control and thus, perversely, malleable to his desire, than anyone Dradin had yet met in Ambergris: this priceless part of the whale, this over brimming stew of the sublime and the superlative.

It was then that his rescuer came: Dvorak, popping up from betwixt a yardstick of a butcher awaiting a hansom and a jowly furrier draped over with furs of auburn, gray, and white. Dvorak, indeed, dressed all in black, against which the red dots of his tattoo throbbed and, in his jacket pocket, a dove-white handkerchief stained red at the edges. A mysterious, feminine smile decorated his mutilated face.

"She's not at the window," Dradin said.

Dvorak's laugh forced his mouth open wide and wider still, carnivorous in its red depths. "No. She is not at the window. But have no doubt: she is inside. She is a most devout employee."

"You gave her the book?"

"I did, sir." The laugh receded into a shallow smile. "She took it from me like a lady, with hesitation, and when I told her it came from a secret admirer, she blushed."

"Blushed?" Dradin felt lighter, his blood yammering and his head a puff of smoke, a cloud, a spray of cotton candy.

"Blushed. Indeed, sir, a good sign."

Dradin took the package from his pocket and, hands trembling, gave it to the dwarf. "Now you must go back in and find her, and when you find her, give her this. You must ask her to join me at *The Drunken Boat* at twilight. You know the place?"

Dvorak nodded, his hands clasped protectively around the package.

"Good. I will have a table next to the festival parade route. Beg her if you must. Intrigue her and entreat her."

"I will do so."

"U-u-unless you think I should take this gift to her myself?"

Dvorak sneered. He shook his head so that the green of the jungles blurred before Dradin's eyes. "Think, sir. Think hard. Would you have her see you first out of breath, unkempt, and, if I may be so bold, there is a slight smell of *urine*. No, sir. Meet her first at the tavern, and there you shall appear a man of means, at your ease, inviting her to the unraveling of further mysteries."

Dradin looked away. How his inexperience must show. How foolish his suggestions. And yet, also, relief that Dvorak had thwarted his brashness.

"Sir?" Dvorak said. "Sir?"

Dradin forced himself to look at Dvorak. "You are correct, of course. I will see her at the tavern."

"Coins, sir."

"Coins?"

"I cannot live on kindness."

"Yes. Of course. Of course." Damn Dvorak! No compassion there. He stuck a hand into his pants pocket and pulled out a gold coin, which he handed to Dvorak. "Another when you return."

"As you wish. Wait here." Dvorak gave Dradin one last long look and then scurried up the steps, and disappeared into the darkness of the doorway.

Dradin discovered he was bad at waiting. He sat on the curb, got up, crouched to his knees, leaned on a lamp post, scratched at a flea biting his ankle. All the while, he looked up at the blank window and thought: If I had come into the city today, I would have looked up at the third floor and seen nothing and this frustration, this impatience, this *ardor*, would not be practically bursting from me now.

Finally, Dvorak scuttled down the steps with his jacket tails floating out behind him, his grin larger, if that were possible, positively a leer.

"What did she say?" Dradin pressed. "Did she say anything? Something? Yes? No?"

"Success, sir. Success. Busy as she is, devout as she is, she said little, but only that she will meet you at *The Drunken Boat*, though perhaps not until after dusk has fallen. She looked quite favorably on the emerald and the message. She calls you, sir, a gentleman."

A gentleman. Dradin stood straighter. "Thank you," he said. "You have been a great help to me. Here." And he passed another coin to Dvorak, who snatched it from his hand with all the swiftness of a snake.

As Dvorak murmured goodbye, Dradin heard him with but one ear, cocooned as he was in a world where the sun always shone bright and uncovered all hidden corners, allowing no shadows or dark and glimmering truths.

V

Dradin hurried back to the hostel. He hardly saw the flashes of red, green, and blue around him, nor sensed the expectant quality in the air, the huddled groups of people talking in animated voices, for night would bring the Festival of Freshwater Squid and the streets would hum and thrum with celebration. Already, the clean smell of fresh-baked bread, mixed with the treacly promise of sweets, began to tease noses and turn frowns into smiles. Boys let out early from school played games with hoops and marbles and bits of brick. The more adventurous imitated the grand old Kraken sinking ships with a single lash of tentacle, puddle-bound toy boats smashed against drainpipes. Still others watched the erection of scaffolding on tributary streets leading into Albumuth Boulevard. Stilt men with purpling painted faces hung candy and papier-mâché heads in equal quantities from their stilts.

At last, Dradin came to his room, flung open the door, and shut it abruptly behind him. As the citizens of Ambergris prepared for the festival, so now he must prepare for his love, putting aside the distractions of joblessness and decreasing coin. He stripped and took a shower, turning the water on so hot that needles of heat tattooed his skin red, but he felt clean, and more than clean, cleansed and calm, when he came out after thirty minutes and wiped himself dry with a large green towel. Standing in front of the bathroom mirror in the nude, Dradin noted that although he had filled out since the cessation of his fever, he had not filled out into fat. Not even the shadow of a belly, and his legs thick with muscle. Hardly a family characteristic, that, for his randy father had, since the onset of Mom's river adventures, grown as pudgy as raw bread dough. Nothing for Dad to do but continue to teach ethics at the university and hope that the lithe young things populating his classes would pity him. But for his son a different fate, Dradin was sure.

Dradin shaved, running the blade across his chin and down his neck, so that he thrilled to the self-control it took to keep the blade steady; and yet, when he was done, his hand shook. There. Now various oils worked into the scalp so that his hair became a uniform black, untainted by white except at the outer provinces, where it grazed his ears, and it did not fall back into his face. Then a spot of rouge to bring out the muddy green of his eyes—a scandalous habit, perhaps, learned from his mother of course, but Dradin knew many pale priests who used it.

For clothing, Dradin started with clean underwear and followed with fancy socks done up in muted purple and gold serpent designs. Then the trousers of gray—gray as the slits of his father's eyes in the grip of spirits, gray as his mother's listless moods after performances at the music halls. Yes, a smart gray, a deep gray, not truly conservative, and then the shirt: large on him but not voluminous, white with purple and gold buttons, to match the socks, and a jacket over top that mixed gray and purple thread so that, from heel to head, he looked as distinguished as a debutante at some political gala. It pleased him—as much a uniform as his missionary clothes, but the goal a conversion of a more personal nature. Yes, he would do well.

Thus equipped, his pockets jingly with his last coins, his stomach wrapped in coils of nerves (an at-sea sensation of *notenoughmoney*, *notenoughmoney* beating inside his organs like a pulse), Dradin made his way out onto the streets.

The haze of twilight had smothered Ambergris, muffling sounds and limiting vision, but everywhere also: lights. Lights from balconies and bedrooms, signposts and horse carriages, candles held by hand and lanterns swinging on the arms of gristled caretakers who sang out, from deep in their throats, "The dying of the light! The dying of the light! Let the Festival begin."

Wraiths riding metal bars, men on bicycles swished past, bells all a-tinkle, and children in formal attire, entow to the vast and long-suffering barges of nannies, who tottered forward on unsteady if stocky legs. Child mimes in white face approached Dradin, prancing and pirouetting, and Dradin clapped in approval and patted their heads. They reminded him of the naked boys and girls of the Nimblytod Tribe, who swung through trees and ate birds that became lost in the forest and could not find their way again into the light.

Women in the red and black of hunter's uniforms crossed his path. They rode hollow wooden horses that fit around their waists, fake wooden legs clacking to either side as their own legs cantered or galloped or pranced, but so controlled, so tight and rigid, that they never broke formation despite the random nature of their movements. The horses had each been individually painted in grotesque shades of green, red, and white: eyes wept blood, teeth snarled into black fangs. The women's lips were drawn back against the red leer of lipstick to neigh and nicker. Around them, the gathering crowd shrieked in laughter, the riders so entranced that only the whites of their eyes showed, shockingly pale against the gloom.

Dradin passed giant spits on which spun and roasted whole cows, whole pigs, and a host of smaller beasts, the spits rotated by grunting, muscular, ruddy-faced men. Everywhere, the mushroom dwellers uncurled from slumber with a yawn, picked up their red flags, and trundled off to their secret and arcane rites. Armed men mock-fought with saber and with knife while youths wrestled half-naked in the gutters—their bodies burnished with sweat, their eyes focused not on each other but on the young women who watched their battles. Impromptu dances devoid of form or unified steps spread amongst the spectators until Dradin had to struggle through their spider's webs of gyrations, inured to the laughter and chatter of conversations, the tap and stomp of feet on the rough stones. For this was the most magical night of the year in Ambergris, the Festival of the Freshwater Squid, and the city lay in trance, spellbound and difficult, and everywhere, into the apparent lull, glance met glance, eyes sliding from eyes, as if to say, "What next? What will happen next?"

At last, after passing through an archway strung with nooses, Dradin came out onto a main boulevard, *The Drunken Boat* before him. How could he miss it? It had been lit up like an ornament so that all three stories of slanted dark oak decks sparkled and glowed with good cheer.

A crowd had lined up in front of the tavern, waiting to gain entrance, but Dradin fought through the press, bribed the doorman with a gold coin, and ducked inside, climbing stairs to the second level, high enough to see far down the boulevard, although not so high that the sights would be uninvolving and distant. A tip to the waiter secured Dradin a prime table next to the railing of the deck. The table, complete with lace and embroidered tablecloth, engraved cutlery, and a quavery candle encircled by glass, lay equidistant from the parade and the musical meanderings of The Ravens, four scruffy-looking musicians who played, respectively, the mandolin, twelve-string guitar, the flute, and the drums:

In the city of lies
I spoke in nothing
but the language of spies.

In the city of my demise
I spoke in nothing
but the language of flies.

Their music reminded Dradin of high tide crashing against cliffs and, then, on the down-tempo, of the back-and-forth swell of giant waves rippling across a smooth surface of water. It soothed him and made him seasick both, and when he sat down at the table, the wood beneath him lurched, though he knew it was only the surging of his own pulse, echoed in the floorboards.

Dradin surveyed the parade route, which was lined with glittery lights rimmed with crepe paper that made a crinkly sound as the breeze hit it. A thousand lights done up in blue and green, and the crowd gathered to both sides behind them, so that the street became an iridescent replica of the Moth, not nearly as wide, but surely as deep and magical.

Around him came the sounds of laughter and polite conversation, each table its own island of charm and anticipation: ladies in white and red dresses that sparkled with sequins when the light caught them, gentlemen in dark blue suits or tuxedos, looking just as ridiculous as Dad had once looked, caught out in the rain.

Dradin ordered a mildly alcoholic drink called a Red Orchid and sipped it as he snuck glances at the couple to his immediate right: a tall, thin man with aquiline features, eyes narrow as paper cuts, and rich, gray sideburns, and his consort, a blonde woman in an emerald dress that covered her completely and yet also revealed her completely in the tightness of its fabric. Flushed in the candlelight, she laughed too loudly, smiled too quickly, and it made Dradin cringe to watch her make a fool of herself, the man a bigger fool for not putting her at her ease. The man only watched her with a thin smile splayed across his face. Surely when the woman in the window, his love, came to his table, there would be only traces of this awkwardness, this ugliness in the guise of grace?

His love? Glass at his lips, Dradin realized he didn't know her name. It could be Angeline or Melanctha or Galendrace, or even—and his expression darkened as he concentrated *hard,* felt an odd tingling in his temples, finally expelled the name—"Nepenthe," the name of the sweaty woman priest in the jungles. He put down his glass. All this preparation, his nerves on edge, and he didn't even know the name of the woman in the window. A chill went through him, for did he not know her as well as he knew himself?

Soon, the procession made its way down the parade route: the vast, engulfing cloth kites with wire ribs that formed the shapes of giant squid, paper streamers for tentacles running out behind as, lit by their own inner flames, they bumped and spun against the darkened sky. Ships followed them—floats mounted on the rusted hulks of mechanized vehicles, their purpose to re-enact the same scene as the boys with their toy boats: the hunt for the mighty Kraken, the fresh water squid, which made its home in the deepest parts of the Moth, in the place where the river was wide as the sea and twice as mad with silt.

Dradin clapped and said, "Beautiful, beautiful," and, with elegant desperation, ordered another drink, for if he was to be starving and penniless anyway, what was one more expense?

On the parade route, performing wolfhounds followed the floats, then jugglers, mimes, fire-eaters, contortionists, and belly dancers. The gangrenous moon began to seep across the sky in dark green hues. The drone of conversations grew more urgent and the cries of the people on the street below, befouled by food, drink, and revelry, became discordant: a fragmented roar of fragmenting desires.

Where was his love? Would she not come? Dradin's head felt light and hollow, yet heavy as the earth spinning up to greet him, at the possibility. No, it was not a possibility. Dradin ordered yet another Red Orchid.

She would come. Dressed in white and red she would come, around her throat a necklace of intricate blue and green beads, a rough emerald

dangling from the center. He would stand to greet her and she would offer her hand to him and he would bow to kiss it. Her skin would be
warm to the touch of his lips and his lips would feel warm and electric to
her. He would say to her, "Please, take a seat," and pull out her chair. She
would acknowledge his chivalry with a slight leftward tip of her head.
He would wait for her to sit and then he would sit, wave to a waiter, order her a glass of wine, and then they would talk. Circling in toward how
he had first seen her, he would ask her how she liked the book, the necklace. Perhaps both would laugh at the crudity of Dvorak, and at his own
shyness, for surely now she could see that he was not truly shy. The hours
would pass and with each minute and each witty comment, she would
look more deeply into his eyes and he into hers. Their hands would
creep forward across the table until, clumsily, she jostled her wine glass
and he reached out to keep it from falling—and found her hand instead.

From there, her hand in his, their gaze so intimate across the table, everything would be easy, because it would all be unspoken, but no less elo-
quent for that. Perhaps they would leave the table, the tavern, traverse
the streets in the aftermath of festival. But, no matter what they did,
there would be this bond between them: that they had drunk deep of the
desire in each other's eyes.

Dradin wiped the sweat from his forehead, took another sip of his
drink, looked into the crowd, which merged with the parade, crashing
and pushing toward the lights and the performers.

War veterans were marching past: a grotesque assembly of ghost
limbs, memories disassembled from the flesh, for not a one had two
arms and two legs both. They clattered and shambled forward in their
odd company with crutches and wheelchairs and comrades supporting
them. They wore the uniforms of a hundred wars and ranged in age from
seventeen to seventy; Dradin recognized a few from his hostel. Those
who carried sabers waved and twirled their weapons, inciting the crowd,
which now pushed and pulled and divided amongst itself like a replicat-
ing beast, to shriek and line the parade route ever more closely.

Then, with solemn precision, four men came carrying a coffin, so
small as to be for a child, each lending but a single hand to the effort. On
occasion, the leader would fling open the top to reveal the empty interior and the crowd would moan and stamp its feet.

Behind the coffin came a caged jungle cat that spat and snarled and
worked one enormous pitch paw through bamboo bars. Looking into
the dulled but defiant eyes of the cat, Dradin gulped his Red Orchid and
thought of the jungle. *The moist heat, the ferns curling into their fetid green-
ness, the flowers running red, the thick smell of rich black soil on the shovel, the
pale gray of the woman's hand, the suddenness of coming upon a savage village,
soon to be a ghost place, the savages fled or struck down by disease, the dark eyes
and questioning looks on the faces of those he disturbed, bringing his missionary*

word, the way the forest could be too green, so fraught with scents and tastes and
sounds that one could become intoxicated by it, even become feverish within it,
drowning in black water, plagued by the curse of no converts.

Dradin shuddered again from the cold of the drink, and thought he
felt the deck beneath him roll and plunge in time to the music of The Ravens. Was it possible that he had never fully recovered from the fever?
Was he even now stone-cold mad in the head, or was he simply woozy
from Red Orchids? Or could he be, in his final distress, drunk on love?
He had precious little else left, a realization accompanied by a not unwelcome thrill of fear. With no job and little money, the only element of
his being he found constant and unyielding, undoubting, was the
strength of his love for the woman in the window.

He smiled at the couple at the next table, though no doubt it came
out as the sort of drunken leer peculiar to his father. Past relationships
had been of an unfortunate nature; he could admit that to himself now.
Too platonic, too strange, and always too brief. The jungle did not cotton to long relationships. The jungle ate up long relationships, ground
them between its teeth and spat them out. Like the relationship between
himself and Nepenthe. Nepenthe. Might the woman in the window also
be called Nepenthe? Would she mind if he called her that? Now the deck
beneath him really did roll and list like a ship at sea, and he held himself
to his chair, pushed the Red Orchid away when he had come once more
to rest.

Looking out at the parade, Dradin saw Cadimon Signal and he had to
laugh. Cadimon. Good old Cadimon. Was this parade to become like
Dvorak's wonderfully ugly tattoo? A trip from past to present? For there
indeed was Cadimon, waving to the crowds from a float of gold and
white satin, the Living Saint beside him, diplomatically clothed for the
occasion in messianic white robes.

"Hah!" Dradin said. "Hah!"

The parade ended with an elderly man leading a live lobster on a
leash, a sight that made Dradin laugh until he cried. The lights along the
boulevard began to be snuffed out, at first one by one, and then, as the
mob descended, ripped out in swathes, so that whole sections were
plunged into darkness at once. Beyond them, the great spits no longer
turned, abandoned, the meat upon them blackened to ash, and beyond
the spits bonfires roared and blazed all the more brightly, as if to make
up for the death of the other lights. Now it was impossible to tell parade
members from crowd members, so clotted together and at-sea were they,
mixed in merriment under the green light of the moon.

Around Dradin, busboys hastily cleaned up tables, helped by bar-
keepers, and he heard one mutter to another, "It will be bad this year.
Very bad. I can feel it." The waiter presented Dradin with the check, tap-
ping his feet while Dradin searched his pockets for the necessary coin,

and when it was finally offered, snatching it from his hand and leaving in a flurry of tails and shiny shoes.

Dradin, hollow and tired and sad, looked up at the black-and-green-tinged sky. His love had not come and would not now come, and perhaps had never planned to come, for he only had the word of Dvorak. He did not know how he should feel, for he had never considered this possibility, that he might not meet her. He looked around him—at the table fixtures, the emptying tables, the sudden lull. Now what could he do? He could take a menial job and survive on scraps until he could get a message to his father in Morrow—who then might or might not take pity on him. But for salvation? For redemption?

Fireworks wormholed into the sky and exploded in an umbrella of sparks so that the crowds screamed louder to drown out the noise. Someone jostled him from behind. Wetness dripped down his left shoulder, followed by a curse, and he turned in time to see one of the waiters scurry off with a half-spilled drink.

The smoke from the fireworks descended, mixed with the growing fog come traipsing off the River Moth. It spread more quickly than Dradin would have thought possible, the night smudged with smoke, thick and dark. And who should come out of this haze and into Dradin's gloom but Dvorak, dressed now in green so that the dilute light of the moon passed invisibly over him. His head cocked curiously, like a monkey's, he approached sideways toward Dradin, an appraising look on his face. Was he poisonous like the snake, Dradin thought, or edible, like the insect? Or was he merely a bit of bark to be ignored? For so did Dvorak appraise him. A spark of anger began to smolder in Dradin, for after all Dvorak had made the arrangements and the woman was not here.

"You," Dradin said, raising his voice over the general roar. "You. What're you doing here? You're late . . . I mean, she's late. She's not coming. Where is she? *Did you lie to me, Dvorak?*"

Dvorak moved to Dradin's side and, with his muscular hands under Dradin's arms, pulled Dradin halfway to his feet with such suddenness that he would have fallen over if he hadn't caught himself.

Dradin whirled around, intending to reprimand Dvorak, but found himself speechless as he stared into the dwarf's eyes—dark eyes, so impenetrable, the entire face set like sculpted clay, that he could only stand there and say, weakly, "You said she'd be here."

"Shut up," Dvorak said, and the stiff, coiled menace in the voice caught Dradin between anger and obedience. Dvorak filled the moment with words: "She is here. Nearby. It is Festival night. There is danger everywhere. If she had come earlier, perhaps. But now, now you must meet her elsewhere, in safety. For her safety." Dvorak put a clammy hand on Dradin's arm, but Dradin shook him off.

"Don't touch me. Where's safer than here?"

"Nearby, I tell you. The crowd, the festival. Night is upon us. She will not wait for you."

On the street below, fist fights had broken out. Through the haze, Dradin could hear the slap of flesh on flesh, the snap of bone, the moans of victims. People ran hither and thither, shadows flitting through green darkness.

"Come, sir. *Now*." Dvorak tugged on Dradin's arm, pulled him close, whispered in Dradin's ear like an echo from another place, another time, the map of his face so inscrutable Dradin could not read it: "You must come *now*. Or not at all. If not at all, you will never see her. She will only see you now. Now! Are you so foolish that you will pass?"

Dradin hesitated, weighing the risks. Where might the dwarf lead him?

Dvorak cursed. "Then do not come. Do not. And take your chances with the Festival."

He turned to leave but Dradin reached down and grabbed his arm.

"Wait," Dradin said. "I will come," and taking a few steps found to his relief that he did not stagger.

"Your love awaits," Dvorak said, unsmiling. "Follow close, sir. You would not wish to become lost from me. It would go hard on you."

"How far—"

"No questions. No talking. Follow."

VI

Dvorak led Dradin around the back of *The Drunken Boat* and into an alley, the stones slick with vomit, littered with sharp glass from broken beer and wine bottles, and guarded by a bum muttering an old song from the equinox. Rats waddled on fat legs to eat from half-gnawed drumsticks and soggy buns.

The rats reminded Dradin of the religious quarter and of Cadimon, and then of Cadimon's warning: *"It's not safe for priests to be on the streets after dark during Festival."* He stopped following Dvorak, his head clearer.

"I've changed my mind. I can see her tomorrow at Hoegbotton & Sons."

Dvorak's face clouded like a storm come up from the bottom of the sea as he turned and came back to Dradin. He said, "You have no choice. Follow me."

"No."

"You will never see her then."

"Are you threatening me?"

Dvorak sighed and his overcoat shivered with the blades of a hundred knives. "You will come with me."

"You've already said that."

"Then you will not come?"

"No."

Dvorak punched Dradin in the stomach. The blow felt like an iron ball. All the breath went out of Dradin. The sky spun above him. He doubled over. The side of Dvorak's shoe caught him in the temple, a deep searing pain. Dradin fell heavily on the slick slime and glass of the cobblestones. Glass cut into his palms, his legs, as he twisted and groaned. He tried, groggily, to get to his feet. Dvorak's shoe exploded against his ribs. He screamed, fell onto his side where he lay unmoving, unable to breath except in gasps. Clammy hands put a noose of hemp around his neck, pulled it taut, brought his head up off the ground.

Dvorak held a long, slender blade to Dradin's neck and pulled at the hemp until Dradin was on his knees, looking up into the mottled face. Dradin gasped despite his pain, for it was a different face than only moments before.

Dvorak's features were a sea of conflicting emotions, his mouth twisted to express fear, jealousy, sadness, joy, hatred, as if by encompassing a map of the world he had somehow encompassed all of worldly experience, and that it had driven him mad. In Dvorak's eyes, Dradin saw the dwarf's true detachment from the world and on Dvorak's face he saw the beatific smile of the truly damned, for the face, the flesh, still held the memory of emotion, even if the mind behind the flesh had forgotten.

"In the name of God, Dvorak," Dradin said.

Dvorak's mouth opened and the tongue clacked down and the voice came, distant and thin as memory, "You are coming with me, sir. On your feet."

Dvorak pulled savagely on the rope. Dradin gurgled and forced his fingers between the rope and his neck.

"On your feet, I said."

Dradin groaned and rolled over. "I can't."

The knife jabbed into the back of his neck. "Soft! Get up, or I'll kill you here."

Dradin forced himself up, though his head was woozy and his stomach felt punctured beyond repair. He avoided looking down into Dvorak's eyes. To look would only confirm that he was dealing with a monster.

"I am a priest."

"I know you are a priest," Dvorak said.

"Your soul will burn in Hell," Dradin said.

A burst of laughter. "I was born there, sir. My face reflects its flames. Now, you will walk ahead of me. You will not run. You will not raise your voice. If you do, I shall choke you and gut you where you stand."

"I have money," Dradin said heavily, still trying to let air into his lungs. "I have gold."

"And we will take it. Walk! There is not much time."

"Where are we going?"

"You will know when we get there."

When Dradin still did not move, Dvorak shoved him forward. Dradin began to walk, Dvorak so close behind he imagined he could feel the point of the blade against the small of his back.

The green light of the moon stained everything except the bonfires the color of toads and dead grass. The bonfires called with their siren song of flame until crowds gathered at each one to dance, shout, and fight. Dradin soon saw that Dvorak's route—through alley after alley, over barricades—was intended to avoid the bonfires. There was now no cool wind in all the city, for around every corner they turned, the harsh rasp of the bonfires met them. To all sides, buildings sprang up out of the fog—dark, silent, menacing.

As they crossed a bridge, over murky water thick with sewage and the flotsam of the festivities, a man hobbled toward them. His left ear had been severed from his head. He cradled part of someone's leg in his arms. He moaned and when he saw Dradin, Dvorak masked by shadow, he shouted, "Stop them! Stop them!" only to continue on into the darkness, and Dradin helpless anyway. Soon after, following the trail of blood, a hooting mob of ten or twelve youths came a-hunting, tawny-limbed and fresh for the kill. They yelled catcalls and taunted Dradin, but when they saw that he was a prisoner they turned their attentions back to their own prey.

The buildings became black shadows tinged green, the street underfoot rough and ill hewn. A wall stood to either side.

A deep sliver of fear pulled Dradin's nerves taut. "How much further?" he asked.

"Not far. Not far at all."

The mist deepened until Dradin could not tell the difference between the world with his eyes shut and the world with his eyes open. Dradin sensed the scuffle of feet on the pavement behind and in front, and the darkness became claustrophobic, close with the scent of rot and decay.

"We are being followed," Dradin said.

"You are mistaken."

"I hear them!"

"Shut up! It's not far. Trust me."

"*Trust me?*" Did Dvorak realize the irony of those words? How foolish that they should converse at all, the knife at his back and the hushed breathing from behind and ahead, stalking them. Fear raised the hairs along his arms and heightened his senses, distorting and magnifying every sound.

Their journey ended where the trees were less thick and the fog had been swept aside. Walls did indeed cordon them in, gray walls that ended abruptly ten feet ahead in a welter of shadows that rustled and quivered like dead leaves lifted by the wind, but there was no wind.

Dradin's temples pounded and his breath caught in his throat. On another street, parallel but out of sight, a clock doled out the hours, one through eleven, and revelers tooted on horns or screamed out names or called to the moon in weeping, distant, fading voices.

Dvorak shoved Dradin forward until they came to an open gate, ornately filigreed, and beyond the gate, through the bars, the brooding headstones of a vast graveyard. Mausoleums and memorials, single tombs and groups, families dead together under the thick humus, the young and the old alike feeding the worms, feeding the earth.

The graveyard was overgrown with grass and weeds so that the headstones swam in a sea of green. Beyond these fading statements of life after death writ upon the fissured stones, riven and made secretive by the moonlight, lay the broken husks of trains, haphazard and strewn across the landscape. The twisted metal of engines, freight cars, and cabooses gleamed darkly green and the patina of broken glass windows, held together by moss, shone especially bright, like vast, reflective eyes. Eyes that still held a glimmer of the past when coal had coursed through their engines like blood and brimstone, and their compartments had been busy with the footsteps of those same people who now lay beneath the earth.

The industrial district. Dradin was in the industrial district and now he knew that due south was his hostel and southwest was Hoegbotton & Sons, and the River Moth beyond it.

"I do not see her," Dradin said, to avoid looking ahead to the squirming shadows.

Dvorak's face as the dwarf turned to him was a sickly green and his mouth a cruel slit of darkness. "Should you see her, do you think? I am leading you to a graveyard, missionary. Pray, if you wish."

At those words, Dradin would have run, would have taken off into the mist, not caring if Dvorak found him and gutted him, such was his terror. But then the creeping tread of the creatures resolved itself. The sound grew louder, coming up behind and ahead of him. As he watched, the shadows became shapes and then figures, until he could see the glinty eyes and glinty knives of a legion of silent, waiting mushroom dwellers. Behind them, hopping and rustling, came toads and rats, their eyes bright with darkness. The sky thickened with the swooping shapes of bats.

"Surely," Dradin said, "surely there has been a mistake."

In a sad voice, his face strangely mournful and moonlike, Dvorak said, "There have indeed been mistakes, but they are yours. Take off your clothes."

Dradin backed away, into the arms of the leathery, stretched, musty folk behind. Cringing from their touch, he leapt forward.

"I have money," Dradin said to Dvorak. "I will give you money. My father has money."

Dvorak's smile turned sadly sweeter and sweetly sadder. "How you waste words when you have so few words left to waste. Remove your clothes or they will do it for you," and he motioned to the mushroom dwellers. A hiss of menace rose from their assembled ranks as they pressed closer, closer still, until he could not escape the dry, piercing rot of them, nor the sound of their shambling gait.

He took off his shoes, his socks, his trousers, his shirt, his underwear, folding each item carefully, until his pale body gleamed and he saw himself in his mind's eye as switching positions with the Living Saint. How he would have loved to see the hoary ejaculator now, coming to his rescue, but there was no hope of that. Despite the chill, Dradin held his hands over his penis rather than his chest. What did modesty matter, and yet still he did it.

Dvorak hunched nearer, hand taut on the rope, and used his knife to pull the clothes over to him. He went through the pockets, took the remaining coins, and then put the clothes over his shoulder.

"Please, let me go," Dradin said. "I beg you." There was a tremor in his voice but, he marveled, only a tremor, only a hint of fear.

Who would have guessed that so close to his own murder he could be so calm?

"I cannot let you go. You no longer belong to me. You are a priest, are you not? They pay well for the blood of priests."

"My friends will come for me."

"You have no friends in this city."

"Where is the woman from the window?"

Dvorak smiled with a smugness that turned Dradin's stomach. A spark of anger spread all up and down his back and made his teeth grind together. The graveyard gate was open. He had run through graveyards once, with Anthony—graveyards redolent with the stink of old metal and ancient technologies—but was that not where they wished him to go?

In the name of God, what have you done with her?

"You are too clever by half," Dvorak said. "She is still in Hoegbotton & Sons."

"At this hour?"

"Yes."

"W-w-why is she there?" His fear for her, deeper into him than his own anger, made his voice quiver.

Dvorak's mask cracked. He giggled and cackled and stomped his foot. "Because, because, sir, sir, I have taken her to pieces, I have dismembered her!" And from behind and in front and all around, the horrible, galumphing, harrumphing laughter of the mushroom dwellers.

Dismembered her.

The laughter, mocking and cruel, set him free from his inertia. Clear and cold he was now, made of ice, always keeping the face of his beloved before him. He could not die until he had seen her body.

Dradin yanked on the rope and, as Dvorak fell forward, wrenched free the noose. He kicked the dwarf in the head and heard a satisfying howl of pain, but did not wait, did not watch—he was already running through the gate before the mushroom dwellers could stop him. His legs felt like cold metal, like the churning pistons of the old coal-chewing trains. He ran as he had never run in all his life, even with Tony. He ran like a man possessed, recklessly dodging tombstones and high grass, while behind came the angry screams of Dvorak, the slithery swiftness of the mushroom dwellers. And still Dradin laughed as he went—bellowing as he jumped atop a catacomb of mausoleums and leapt between monuments, trapped for an instant by abutting tombstones, and then up and running again, across the top of yet another broad sepulcher. He found his voice and shouted to his pursuers, "Catch me! Catch me!", and cackled his own mad cackle, for he was as naked as the day he had entered the world and his beloved was dead and he had nothing left in the world to lose. Lost as he might be, lost as he might always be, yet the feeling of freedom was heady. It made him giddy and drunk with his own power. He crowed to his pursuers, he needled them, only to pop up elsewhere, thrilling to the hardness of his muscles, the toughness gained in the jungle where all else had been lost.

Finally, he came to the line of old trains, byzantine and convoluted and dark, surrounded by the smell of dank, rusting metal. One backward glance before entering the maze revealed that the mushroom dwellers, led by Dvorak, had reached the last line of tombstones, fifty feet away—

—but a glance only before he swung himself into the side door of an engine, walked on the balls of his feet into the cool darkness. Hushed quiet. This was what he needed now. Quiet and stealth in equal measures so that he could reach the relative safety of the street beyond the trains. His senses heightened, he could hear *them* coming, the whispers between them as they spread out to search the compartments.

Spider-like, Dradin moved as he heard them move, shadowing them but out of sight—into their clutches and out again with a finesse he had not known he possessed—always working his way farther into the jungle of metal. Train tracks. Dining cars. Engines split open by the years, so that he hid among their most secret parts and came out again when danger had passed him by, a pale figure flecked with rust.

Ahead, when he dared to take his gaze from his pursuers, Dradin could see the uniform darkness of the wall and, from beyond, the red flashes of a bonfire. Two rows of cars lay between him and the wall. He crept forward through the gaping doorway of a dining car—

—just as, cloaked by shadow, Dvorak entered the car from the opposite end. Dradin considered backing out of the car, but no: Dvorak would hear him. Instead, he crouched down, hidden from view by an overturned table, a salt-and-pepper shaker still nailed to it.

Dvorak's footsteps came closer, accompanied by raspy breathing and the shivery threat of the knives beneath his coat. A single shout from Dvorak and the mushroom dwellers would find him.

Dvorak stopped in front of the overturned table. Dradin could smell him now, the *must* of mushroom dweller, the *tang* of Moth silt. The breathing.

Dradin sprang up and slapped his left hand across Dvorak's mouth, spun him around as he grunted, and grappled for Dvorak's knife. Dvorak opened his mouth to bite Dradin. Dradin stuck his fist in Dvorak's mouth, muffling his own scream as the teeth bit down. Now Dvorak could make no sound and the dwarf frantically tried to expel Dradin's fist. Dradin did not let him. The knife seesawed from Dvorak's side up to Dradin's clavicle and back again. Dvorak thrashed about, trying to dislodge Dradin's hold on him, trying to face his enemy. Dradin, muscles straining, entangled Dvorak's legs in his and managed to keep him in the center of the compartment. If they banged up against the sides, it would be as loud as a word from Dvorak's mouth. But the knife was coming too close to Dradin's throat. He smashed Dvorak's hand against a railing, a sound that sent up an echo Dradin thought the mushroom dwellers must surely hear. No one came as the knife fell from Dvorak's hand. Dvorak tried to grasp inside his jacket for another. Dradin pulled a knife from within the jacket first. As Dvorak withdrew his own weapon, Dradin's blade was already buried deep in his throat.

Dradin felt the dwarf's body go taut and then lose its rigidity, while the mouth came loose of his fist and a thick, viscous liquid dribbled down his knife arm.

Dradin turned to catch the body as it fell, so that as he held it and lowered it to the ground, his hand throbbing and bloody, he could see Dvorak's eyes as the life left them. The tattoo, in that light, became all undone, the red dots of cities like wounds, sliding off to become merely a crisscross of lines. Dark blood coated the front of his shirt.

Dradin mumbled a prayer under his breath from reflex alone, for some part of him—the part of him that had laughed to watch the followers of St. Solon placing sparrows in coffins—insisted that death was unremarkable, undistinguished, and, ultimately, unimportant, for it happened every day, everywhere. Unlike the jungle, Nepenthe's severed hand, here there was no amnesia, no fugue. There was only the body beneath him and an echo in his ears, the memory of his mother's voice as she *thrulled* from deep in her throat a death march, a funeral veil stitched of words and music. How could he feel hatred? He could not. He felt only emptiness.

He heard, with newly preternatural senses, the movement of mushroom dwellers nearby, and resting Dvorak's head against the cold metal floor, left the compartment, a shadow against the deeper shadow of the wrecked and rotted wheels.

Now it was easy for Dradin, slipping between tracks, huddling in dining compartments, the mushroom dwellers blind to his actions. The two rows of cars between him and the wall became one row and then he was at the wall. He climbed it tortuously, the rough stone cutting into his hands and feet. When he reached the top, he swung up and over to the other side.

Ah, the boulevard beyond, for now Dradin wondered if he should return to the graveyard and hide there. Strewn across the boulevard were scaffolds and from the scaffolds men and women had been hung so that they lolled and, limp, had the semblance of rag dolls. Rag dolls in tatters, the flesh pulled from hindquarters, groins, chests, the red meeting the green of the moon and turning black. Eyes stared sightless. The harsh wind carried the smell of offal. Dogs bit at the feet, the legs, the bodies so thick that as Dradin walked forward, keen for the sound of mushroom dwellers behind him, he had to push aside and duck under the limbs of the dead. Blood splashed his shoulders and he breathed in gasps and held his side, as if something pained him, though it was only the sight of the bodies that pained him. When he realized that he still wore a noose of his own, he pulled it over his head with such speed that it cut him and left a burn.

Past the hanging bodies and burning buildings and flamed out motored vehicles, only to see . . . stilt men carrying severed heads, which they threw to the waiting crowds, who kicked and tossed them . . . a man disemboweled, his intestines streaming out into the gutter as his attackers continued to hack him apart and he clutched at their legs . . . a woman assaulted against a brick wall by ten men who held her down as they cut and raped her . . . fountains full of floating, bloated bodies, the waters turned red-black with blood . . . glimpses of the bonfires, bodies stacked for burning in the dozens . . . a man and woman decapitated, still caught in an embrace, on their knees in the murk of rising mist . . . the unearthly screams, the taste of blood rising in the air, the smell of fire and burning flesh . . . and the female riders on their wooden horses, riding over the bodies of the dead, splashing in the blood, their eyes still turned inward, that they might not know the horrors of the night.

Oh, that he could rip his own eyes from his sockets! He did not wish to see and yet could not help but see if he wished to live. In the face of such carnage, his killing of Dvorak became the gentlest of mercies. Bile rose in his throat and, sick with grief and horror, he vomited beside an abandoned horse buggy. When the sickness had passed, he gathered his wits, found a landmark he recognized, and by passing through lesser alleys and climbing over the rooftops of one-story houses set close together, came once again to his hostel.

The hostel was empty and silent, and Dradin crept, limping from glass in his foot and the ache in his muscles, up to the second floor and his room. Once inside, he did not even try to wash off the blood, the dirt, the filth, did not put on clothes, but stumbled to his belongings and stuffed his pictures, *The Refraction of Light in a Prison*, and his certificate from the religious college into the knapsack. He stood in the center of the room, knapsack over his left shoulder, the machete held in his right hand, breathing heavily, trying to remember who he might be and where he might be and what he should do now. He shuffled over to the window and looked down on the valley. What he saw made him laugh, a high-pitched sound so repugnant to him that he closed his mouth immediately.

The valley lay under a darkness pricked by soft, warm lights. No bonfires raged in the valley below. No one hung from scaffolding, tongues blue and purpling. No one bathed in the blood of the dead.

Seeing the valley so calm, Dradin remembered when he had wondered if, perhaps, his beloved lived there, amid the peace where there were no missionaries. No Living Saints. No Cadimons. No Dvoraks. He looked toward the door. It was a perilous door, a deceitful door, for the world lay beyond it in all its brutality. He stood there for several beats of his heart, thinking of how beautiful the woman had looked in the third story window, how he had thrilled to see her there. What a beautiful place the world had been then, so long ago.

Machete held ready, Dradin walked to the door and out into the night.

VII

When Dradin had at last fought his way back to Hoegbotton & Sons, Albumuth Boulevard was deserted except for a girl in a ragged flower print dress. She listened to a tattered phonograph that played Voss Bender tunes.

In the deep of winter:
Snatches of song
Through the branches
Brittle as bone.

You'll not see my face
But there I'll be,
Frost in my hair,
My hunger hollowing me.

The sky had cleared and the cold, white pricks of stars shone through the black of night, the green-tinge of moon. The black in which moon and stars floated was absolute; it ate the light of the city, muted every-thing but the shadows, which multiplied and rippled outward. Behind Dradin, sounds of destruction grew nearer, but here the stores were ghostly but whole. And yet here too men, women, and children hung from the lamp posts and looked down with lost, vacant, and wondering stares.

The girl sat on her knees in front of the phonograph. Over her lay the shadow of the great lambent eye, shiny and saucepan blind, of one of the colorful cloth squid, its tentacles rippling in the breeze. Bodies were caught in its *faux* coils, sprawled and sitting upright in the maw and craw of the beast, as if they had drowned amid the tentacles, washed ashore still entangled and stiffening.

Dradin walked up to the girl. She had brown hair and dark, unread-able eyes with long lashes. She was crying, although her face had long ago been wiped clean of sorrow and of joy. She watched the phonograph as if it were the last thing in the world that made sense to her.

He nudged her. "Go. Go on! Get off the street. You're not safe here."

She did not move, and he looked at her with a mixture of sadness and exasperation. There was nothing he could do. Events were flowing away from him, caught in the undertow of a river stronger than the Moth. It was all he could do to preserve his own life, his bloody machete proof of the dangers of the bureaucratic district by which he had come again to Albumuth. The same languid, nostalgic streets of daylight had become killing grounds, a thousand steely-eyed murderers hiding amongst the vetch and honeysuckle. It was there that he had rediscovered the white-faced mimes, entangled in the ivy, features still in death.

Dradin walked past the girl until Hoegbotton & Sons lay before him. The dull red brick seemed brighter in the night, as if it reflected the fires burning throughout the city.

And so it ends where it began, Dradin thought. In front of the very same Hoegbotton & Sons building. Were he not such a coward, he should have ended it there much sooner.

Dradin stole up the stairs to the door. He smashed the glass of the door with his already mangled fist, grunting with pain. The pain pulsed far away, disconnected from him in his splendid nakedness. *Pinpricks on the souls of distant sinners.* Dradin swung the door open and shut it with such a clatter that he was sure someone had heard him and would come loping down the boulevard after him. But no one came and his feet, naked and dirty and cut, continued to slap the steps inside so loudly that surely she would run away if she was still alive, thinking him an intruder. But where to run? He could hear his own labored breathing as he navigated the stairs: the sound filled the landing; it filled the spaces between the steps; and it filled him with determination, for it was the most vital sign that he still lived, despite every misfortune.

Dradin laughed, but it came out ragged around the edges. His mind sagged under the weight of carnage: the cries of looting, begging; the sound of men swinging by their necks or their testicles or their feet. Swinging all across a city grown suddenly wise and quiet in their deaths.

But that was out there, in the city. In here, Dradin promised, he would not lose himself to such images. He would not lose the threads.

Curious, but on reaching the door to the third floor, Dradin paused, halted, did not yet grasp the iron knob. For this door led to the window. He had engraved her position so perfectly on the interstices of his memory that he knew exactly where she must be . . . One moment more of hesitation, and then Dradin entered her.

A room. Darkened. The smell of sawdust packing and boxes. Not the right room. Not her room. The antechamber only, for receiving visitors, perhaps, the walls lined with decadent objects d' arte, and beyond that, an open doorway, leading to . . .

The next room was lined with Occidental shadow puppets that looked like black scars, seared and shaped into human forms: bodies entwined in lust and devout in prayer, bodies engaged in murder and in business. Harlequins and pierrotts with bashful red eyes and sharp teeth lay on their backs, feet up in the air. Jungle plants trellised and cat's cradled the interior, freed from terrariums, while a clutter of other things hidden by the shadows beckoned him with their strange, angular shapes. The smell of moist rot mixed with the stench of mushroom dweller and the sweet bitter of sweat, as if the very walls labored for the creation of such wonderful monstrosities.

She still faced the window, but set back from it, in a wooden chair, so that the curling curious fires ravaging the city beyond could not sear her face. The light from these fires created a zone of blackness and Dradin could see only her black hair draped across the chair back.

It seemed to Dradin as he looked at the woman sitting in the chair that he had not seen her in a hundred, a thousand, years; that he saw her across some great becalmed ocean or desert, she only a shape like the shadow puppets. He moved closer.

His woman, the woman of his dreams, gazed off into the charred red-black air, the opposite street, or even toward the hidden River Moth beyond. He thought he saw a hint of movement as he approached her—a slight uplifting of one arm—she no longer concerned with the short view, but with the long view, the perspective that nothing of the moment mattered or would ever matter. It had been Dvorak's view, with the map that had taken over his body. It was Cadimon's view, not allowing the priest to take pity on a former student.

"My love," Dradin said, and again, "My love," as he walked around so he could see the profile of her face. A white sheet covered her body, but her face, oh, her face . . . her eyebrows were thin and dark, her eyes like twin blue flames, her nose small, unobtrusive, her skin white, white, white, but with a touch of color that drew him down to the sumptuous curve of her mouth, the bead of sweat upon the upper lip, the fine hairs placed to seduce, to trick; the way in which the clothes clung to her body and made it seem to curve, the arms placed upon the arms of the chair, so naturally that there was no artifice in having done so. Might she . . . could she . . . still be . . . alive?

Dradin pulled aside the white sheet—and screamed, for there lay the torso, the legs severed and in pieces beneath, but placed cleverly for the illusion of life, the head balanced atop the torso, dripping neither blood nor precious humors, but as dry and slick and perfect as if it had never known a body. Which it had not. From head to toe, Dradin's beloved was a mannequin, an artifice, a deception. *Hoegbotton & Sons, specialists in all manner of profane and Occidental technologies . . .*

Dradin's mouth opened and closed but no sound came from him. Now he could see the glassy finish of her features, the innate breakability of a creature made of papier-mâché and metal and porcelain and clay, mixed and beaten and blown and sandpapered and engraved and made up like any other woman. A testimony to the clockmaker's craft, for at the hinges and joints of the creature dangled broken filaments and wires and gimshaw circuitry. Fool. He was thrice a fool.

Dradin circled the woman, his body shivering, his hands reaching out to caress the curve of cheekbone, only to pull back before he touched skin. The jungle fever beat within him, fell away in *decrescendo*, then again *crescendo*. Twice more around and his arm darted out against his will and he touched her cheek. Cold. So cold. So monstrously cold against the warmth of his body. Cold and dead in her beauty despite the heat and the bonfires roaring outside. Dead. Not alive. Never alive.

As he touched her, as he saw all of her severed parts and how they fit together, something small and essential broke inside him; broke so he couldn't ever fix it. Now he saw Nepenthe in his mind's eye in all of her darkness and grace. Now he could see her as a person, not an idea. Now he could see her nakedness, remember the way she had felt under him—smooth and moist and warm—never moving as he made love to her. As he took her though she did not want to be taken. If ever he had lost his faith it was then, as he lost himself in the arms of a woman indifferent to him, indifferent to the world. He saw again the flash of small hand, severed and gray, and saw again his own hand, holding the blade. Her severed hand. His hand holding the blade. Coming to in the burning missionary station, severed of his memory, severed from his faith, severed from his senses by the fever. Her severed gray hand in his and in the other the machete.

Dradin dropped the machete and it landed with a clang next to the mannequin's feet.

Feverish, he had crawled back from his jungle expedition, the sole survivor, only to find that the people he had gone out to convert had come to the station and burned it to the ground . . . fallen unconscious, and come to with the hand in his, Nepenthe naked and dead next to him. Betrayal.

The shattered pieces within came loose in an exhalation of breath. He could not contain himself any longer, and he sobbed there, at the mannequin's feet, and as he hugged her to him, the fragile balance came undone and her body scattered into pieces all around him, the head staring up at him from the floor.

"I killed her I did I killed her I didn't kill her I didn't mean to I meant to I didn't mean to she made me I let her I wanted her I couldn't have her I never wanted her I wanted her not the way I wanted I couldn't I meant to I couldn't have meant to but I did it I don't know if I did it—*I can't remember!* "

Dradin slid to the floor and lay there for a long while, exhausted, gasping for breath, his mouth tight, his jaw unfamiliar to him. He welcomed the pain from the splinters that cut into his flesh from the floorboards. He felt hollow inside, indifferent, so fatigued, so despairing that he did not know if he could ever regain his feet.

But, after a time, Dradin looked full into the woman's eyes and a grim smile spread across his face. He thought he could hear his mother's voice mixed with the sound of rain thrumming across a roof. He thought he could hear his father reading the adventures of Juliette and Justine to him. He knelt beside the head and caressed its cheek. He lay beside the head and admired its features.

He heard himself say it.

"I love you."

He still loved her. He could not deny it. Could not. It was a love that might last a minute or a day, an hour or a month, but for the moment, in his need, it seemed as permanent as the moon and the stars, and as cold.

It did not matter that she was in pieces, that she was not real, for he could see now that she was his salvation. Had he not been in love with what he saw in the third story window, and had what he had seen through that window changed in its essential nature? Wasn't she better suited to him than if she had been real, with all the avarices and hungers and needs and awkwardnesses that create disappointment? He had invented an entire history for this woman and now his expectations of her would never change and she would never age, never criticize him, never tell him he was too fat or too sloppy or too neat, and he would never have to raise his voice to her.

It struck Dradin as he basked in the glow of such feelings, as he watched the porcelain lines of the head while shouts grew louder and the gallows jerked and swung merrily all across the city. It struck him that he could not betray this woman. There would be no decaying, severed hand. No flowers sprayed red with blood. No crucial misunderstandings. The thought blossomed bright and blinding in his head. He could not betray her. Even if he set her head upon the mantel and took a lover there, in front of her, as his father might once have done to his mother, those eyes would not register the sin. This seemed to him, in that moment, to be a form of wisdom beyond even Cadimon, a wisdom akin to the vision that had struck him as he stood in the backyard of the old house in Morrow.

Dradin embraced the pieces of his lover, luxuriating in the smooth and shiny feel of her, the precision of her skin. He rose to a knee, cradling his beloved's head in his shaking arms. Was he moaning now? Was he screaming now? Who could tell?

With careful deliberateness, Dradin took his lover's head and walked into the antechamber, and then out the door. The third floor landing was dark and quiet. He began to walk down the stairs, descending slowly at first, taking pains to slap his feet against each step. But when he reached the second floor landing, he became more frantic, as if to escape what lay behind him, until by the time he reached the first floor and burst out from the shattered front door, he was running hard, knapsack bobbing against his back.

Down the boulevard, seen through the folds of the squid float, a mob approached, holding candles and torches and lanterns. Stores flared and burned behind them . . .

Dradin spared them not a glance, but continued to run—past the girl and her phonograph, still playing Voss Bender, and past *Borges Bookstore*, in the shadow of which prowled the black panther from the parade, and then beyond, into the unknown. Sidestepping mushroom dwellers at their dark harvest, their hands full of mushrooms from which spores broke off like dandelion tufts, and the last of the revelers of the Festival of the Freshwater Squid, their trajectories those of pendulums and their tongues blue if not black, arms slack at their sides. Through viscera and the limbs of babies stacked in neat piles. Amongst the heehaws and gimgobs, the drunken dead and the lolly lashers with their dark whips. Weeping now, tears without end. Mumbling and whispering endearments to his beloved, running strong under the mad, mad light of the moon—headed forever and always for the docks and the muscular waters of the River Moth, which would take him and his lover as far as he might wish, though perhaps not far enough.

[like a twilight zone story — depends on a plot twist to inspire wonder]

THE HOEGBOTTON GUIDE TO
THE EARLY HISTORY OF AMBERGRIS
by Duncan Shriek

I

The history of Ambergris, for our purposes, begins with the legendary exploits of the whaler-cum-pirate Cappan John Manzikert,[1][2][3] who, in the Year of Fire—so called for the catastrophic volcanic activity in the Southern Hemisphere that season—led his fleet of 30 whaling ships up the Moth River Delta into the River Moth proper. Although not the first reported incursion of Aan whaling clans into the region, it is the first incursion of any importance.

---

[1]   By Manzikert's time, the rough southern accent of his people had permanently changed the designation "Captain" to "Cappan." "Captain" referred not only to Manzikert's command of a fleet of ships, but also to the old Imperial titles given by the Saphants to the commander of a *see* of islands; thus, the title had both religious and military connotations. Its use, this late in history, reflects how pervasive the Saphant Empire's influence was: 200 years after its fall, its titles were still being used by clans that had only known of the Empire secondhand.

[2]   A footnote on the purpose of these footnotes: This text is rich with footnotes to avoid inflicting upon you, the idle tourist, so much knowledge that, bloated with it, you can no longer proceed to the delights of the city with your customary mindless abandon. In order to hamstring your predictable attempts—once having discovered a topic of interest in this narrative—to skip ahead, I have weeded out all of those cross references to other Hoegbotton publications that litter the rest of this pamphlet series like a plague of fungi.

[3]   I should add to footnote 2 that the most interesting information will be included only in footnote form, and I will endeavor to include as many footnotes as possible. Indeed, information alluded to in footnote form will later be expanded upon in the main text, thus confusing any of you who have decided not to read the footnotes. This is the price to be paid by those who would rouse an elderly historian from his slumber behind a teaching desk in order to coerce him to write for a common travel guide series.

Manzikert's purpose was to escape the wrath of his clansman Michael Brueghel, who had decimated Manzikert's once-proud 100-ship fleet off the coast of the Isle of Aandalay. Brueghel meant to finish off Manzikert for good, and so pursued him some 40 miles upriver, near the current port of Stockton, before finally giving up the chase. The reason for this conflict between potential allies is unclear—our historical sources are few and often inaccurate; indeed, one of the most infuriating aspects of early Ambergrisian history is the regularity with which truth and legend pursue separate courses—but the result is clear: in late summer of the Year of Fire, Manzikert found himself a full 70 miles upriver, at the place where the Moth forms an inverted "L" before straightening out both north and south. Here, for the first time, he found that the fresh water flowing south had completely cleansed the salt water seeping north.[4]

Manzikert anchored his ships at the joint of the "L," which formed a natural harbor, at dusk of the day of their arrival. The banks were covered in a lush undergrowth very familiar to the Aan, as it would have approximated the vegetation of their own native southern islands.[5] They had, encouragingly enough, seen no signs of possibly hostile habitation, but could not muster the energy, as dusk approached, to launch an expedition. However, that night the watchmen on the ships were startled to see the lights of campfires clearly visible through the trees and, as more than one keen-eared whaler noticed, the sound of a high and distant chanting. Manzikert immediately ordered a military force to land under cover of darkness, but the Truffidian monk Samuel Tonsure persuaded him to rescind the order and await the dawn.

Tonsure—who, following his capture from Nicea (near the mouth of the Moth River Delta), had persuaded the Cappan to convert to Truffidism and thus gained influence over him—plays a major role, perhaps the major role, in our understanding of Ambergris' early history.[6] It

---

[4]   Today, the salinity of the river changes to fresh water a mere 25 miles upriver; the reason for this change is unknown, but may be linked to the build-up of silt at the river's mouth, which acts as a natural filter.

[5]   Almost 500 years later, the Petularch Dray Mikal would order the uprooting of native flora around the city in favor of the northern species of his youth, surely among the most strikingly arrogant responses to homesickness on record. The Petularch would be dead for 50 years before the transplantation could be ruled a success.

[6]   And yet, what is our understanding of the monk's early history? Obscure at best. The records at Nicea contain no mention of a Samuel Tonsure, and it is possible he was just passing through the city on his way elsewhere and so did not actively preach there. "Samuel Tonsure" may also be a name that Tonsure created to disguise his true identity. A handful of scholars, in particular the truculent Mary Sabon, argue that Tonsure was none other than the Patriarch of Nicea himself, a man who is known to have disappeared at roughly the same time Tonsure appeared with Manzikert. Sabon offers as circumstantial evidence the oft repeated story that the Patriarch sometimes traversed his city incognito, dressed as a simple monk to spy on his subordinates. He could easily have been captured without knowledge of his rank—which, if revealed, would have given Manzikert such leverage over Nicea that he might well have been able to take the city and settle behind its walls, safe from Brueghel. If so, how-

is from Tonsure that most histories descend—both from the discredited (and incomplete) *Biography of John Manzikert I of Aan and Ambergris*,[7] obviously written to please the Cappan, and from his secret journal, which he kept on his person at all times and which we may assume Manzikert never saw since otherwise he would have had Tonsure put to death.

The journal contains a most intricate account of Manzikert, his exploits, and subsequent events. That this journal appeared (or, rather, reappeared) under somewhat dubious circumstances should not detract from its overall validity, and does not explain the derision directed at it from certain quarters, possibly because the name "Samuel Tonsure" sounds like a joke to a few small-minded scholars. It certainly was not a joke to Samuel Tonsure.[8]

At daybreak, Manzikert ordered the boats lowered and with 100 men, including Tonsure, set off on a reconnaissance mission to the shore. It must have been a somewhat ridiculous sight, for as Tonsure writes of Manzikert, a man possessed of a cruel and mercurial temper, "he must occupy one boat himself, save for the oarsman, such a large man was he and the boat beneath him a child's toy."[9] Here, as Manzikert is rowed toward the site of the city he will found, it is appropriate to quote in full Tonsure's famous appraisal of the Cappan:

> I myself marveled at the man; for nature had combined in his person all the qualities necessary for a military commander. He stood at the height of almost seven feet, so that to look at him men would tilt back their heads as if toward the top of a hill or a high mountain. Possessed of startling blue eyes and furrowed brows, his countenance was neither gentle nor

---

ever, why didn't the Patriarch make any attempt to escape once he had gained Manzikert's trust? The case, despite some of Sabon's other evidence, seems wrong-headed from its inception. My own research, corroborated by the Autarch of Nunk, indicates that the Patriarch's disappearance coincides with that of the priestess Caroline of the Church of the Seven Pointed Star, and that the Patriarch and Caroline eloped together, the ceremony performed by a traveling juggler hastily ordained as a priest.

[7]   For reasons which will become clear, Tonsure could no longer complete it; therefore, 10 years later, Manzikert's son had another Truffidian monk summoned from Nicea for this purpose. Unfortunately, this monk, whose name is lost to us, believed in wearing hair shirts, daily flagellation, and preaching "the abomination of the written word." He did indeed complete the biography, but he might as well have spared himself the effort. Although edited by Manzikert II himself, it contains such prose as "And his highly exhulted majesty set foot on land like a swaggorin conquor from daes of your." Clearly this abominator's abominations against the Written Word far outweigh any crimes It may have perpetrated upon him.

[8]   If the careful historian needs further proof that Sabon is wrong, he need look no further than the inscription on the monk's journal: "Samuel Tonsure." Why would he bother to maintain the pretense since the contents of the journal itself would condemn him to death? And why would he, if indeed the Patriarch (a learned and clever man by all accounts), choose such a clumsy and obvious pseudonym?

[9]   All quotes without attribution are from Tonsure's journal, not the biography.

pleasing, but put one in mind of a tempest; his voice was like thunder and his hands seemed made for tearing down walls or for smashing doors of bronze. He could spring like a lion and his frown was terrible. Those who saw him for the first time discovered that every description that they had heard of him was an understatement.[10]

Alas, the Cappan possessed no corresponding wisdom or quality of mercy. Tonsure obviously feared his master's mood on this occasion, for he tried to persuade Manzikert to remain onboard his flagship and allow the more reasonable of his lieutenants—perhaps even his son John Manzikert II,[11] who would one day govern his people brilliantly—to lead the landing party, but Manzikert, Truffidian though he was, would have none of it. The Cappan also actively encouraged his wife, Sophia, to accompany them. Unfortunately, Tonsure tells us little about Sophia Manzikert in either the biography or the journal (her own biography has not survived), but from the little we do know Tonsure's description of her husband might fit her equally well; the two often waxed romantic on the pleasures of being able to pillage together.

And so, Manzikert, Sophia, Tonsure, and the Cappan's men landed on the site of what would soon be Ambergris. At the moment, however, it was occupied by a people Tonsure christened "gray caps," known today as "mushroom dwellers."

Tonsure reports that they had advanced hardly a hundred paces into the underbrush before they came upon the first inhabitant, standing outside of his "rounded and domed single-story house, built low to the ground and seamless, from which issued a road made of smooth, shiny stones cleverly mortared together." The building had once served as a sentinel post, but was now used as living quarters.

Clearly Tonsure found the building more impressive than the native standing outside of it, for he spends three pages on its every minute detail and gives us only this short paragraph on the building's inhabitant:

> Stout and short, he came only to the Cappan's shoulder: swathed from head to foot in a gray cloak that covered his tunic and trousers, these made from lighter gray swatches of animal skin stitched together. Upon his head lay a hat the color of an Oliphaunt's skin: a tall, wide contrivance that covered his face from the sun. His features, what could be seen of

---

10   Quote taken from the biography. One wonders: if the Cappan was so fierce, how much more fearsome must Michael Brueghel have been to make him flee the south?

11   The Cappan's appending "II" to his son's name gives us an early indication that he meant to settle on land and found a dynasty. The Aan clan would have thought the idea of a dynasty odd, for usually cappans were chosen from among the ablest sailors, with hereditary claims a secondary consideration.

them, were thick, sallow, innocent of knowledge. When the
Cappan inquired as to the nature and name of the place, this
unattractive creature could not answer except in a series of
clicks, grunts, and whistles that appeared to imitate the song
of the cricket and locust. It could not be considered speech or
language. It was, as with insects, a warning or curious sound,
devoid of other meaning.[12]

We can take a farcical delight from imagining the scene: the giant
leaning down to communicate with the dwarf, the dwarf speaking a language so subtle and sophisticated that it has resisted translation to the
present day, while the giant spits out a series of crude consonants and
vowels that must have seemed to the gray cap a sudden bout of apoplexy.

Manzikert found the gray cap repellent, resembling as it did, he is
quoted as saying, "both child and mushroom,"[13] and if not for his fear of
retaliation from a presumed ruling body of unknown strength, the
Cappan would have run the native through with his sword. Instead, he
left the gray cap to its incomprehensible vigil, still clicking and whis-
tling to their backs,[14] and proceeded along the silvery road until they
reached the city.

---

[12] I find it necessary to interject three observations here. First, that the paragraph on the
gray caps written for the Cappan's biography is far worse, describing as it does "small,
piglike eyes, a jowly jagged crease for a mouth, and a nose like an ape." The gray caps actually
looked much like the mushroom dwellers of today—which is to say, like smaller versions of
ourselves—but the Cappan was already attempting to dehumanize them, and thus create a
justification, a rationalization, for depriving them of life and property. Second, and surpris-
ingly, evidence suggests that the gray caps wove their clothing from the cured pelts of field
mice. Third, Tonsure appears to have given away a secret—if, in fact, the gray caps they met
came "only to the Cappan's shoulder" and the gray caps averaged, by Tonsure's own admission, three-and-one-half feet in height (as do the modern mushroom dwellers), then the
Cappan could only have stood four and one-half feet to five feet in height, something of a
midget himself. (Is it of import that in a letter concerning future trade relations written to
the Kalif, Brueghel calls Manzikert "my insignificant enemy," since "insignificant" in the
Kalif's language doubles as a noun meaning "dwarf" and Brueghel, who wrote his own letters
of state, loved word play?) Perhaps Tonsure's description of Manzikert in the biography was
dictated by the Cappan, who wished to conceal his slight stature from History. Unfortunately, the Cappan's height, or lack thereof, remains an ambiguous subject, and thus I will
stay true to the orthodox version of the story as related by Tonsure. Still, it is delicious to
speculate. (If indeed Manzikert was short, we might have hoped he would look upon the gray
caps as long-lost cousins twice removed. Alas, he did not do so.)

[13] We can only speculate as to why Manzikert should find children and mushrooms repul-
sive. He certainly ate mushrooms and had had a child with Sophia. Perhaps, if indeed
undertall, his nickname growing up had been "little mushroom?"

[14] As this is the first and last time the gray caps actively attempted to communicate with
the Aan, one wonders just what the gray cap was saying to Manzikert. A friendly greeting? A
warning? The very loquaciousness of this particular gray cap in relation to the others they
were to encounter has led more than one historian to assume that he (or she—contrary to
popular opinion, there are as many female gray caps as male; the robes tend to make them all
look unisexual) had been assigned to greet the landing party. What opportunities did
Manzikert miss by not trying harder to understand the gray cap's intent? What tragedies
might have been averted?

Although Tonsure has, criminally, neglected to provide us with the re-actions of Manzikert and Sophia upon their first glimpse of the city proper—and, from the monk's description of aqueducts, almost certainly the future site of Albumuth Boulevard—we can imagine that they were as impressed as Tonsure himself, who wrote:

> The buildings visible beyond the increasingly scanty tree cover were decorated throughout by golden stars, like the very vault of heaven, but whereas heaven has its stars only at intervals, here the surfaces were entirely covered with gold, is-suing forth from the center in a never-ending stream. Sur-rounding the main building were other, smaller buildings, themselves surrounded completely or in part by cloisters. Structures of breathtaking complexity stretched as far as the eye could see. Then came a second circle of buildings, larger than the first, with lawns covered in mushrooms of every pos-sible size and color—from gigantic growths as large as the Oliphaunt[15] to delicate, glassy nodules no larger than a child's fingernail. These mushrooms—red capped and blue capped, their undersides dusted with streaks of silver or emer-ald or obsidian—gave off spores of the most varied and re-markable fragrances, while the gray caps themselves tended their charges with, in this one instance, admirable delicacy and loving concern . . .[16] There were also fountains which filled basins of water; gardens, some of them hanging, full of exotic mosses, lichens, and ferns, others sloping down to the level ground; and a bath of pure gold that was beautiful be-yond description.[17]

We can only imagine the slavering delight of Manzikert and his wife upon seeing all that gold; unfortunately, as they would soon find out, much of the "gold" covering the buildings was actually a living organ-

---

[15]   Tonsure was criminally fond of Oliphaunts. References to them, usually preceded by mundanea like "as large as" or "as gray as," occur 30 times in the journal. Possessed of infi-nite mercy, I shall spare you 28 of these comparisons.

[16]   Tonsure's description in the biography also includes a series of mushroom drawings by Manzikert—an attempt to "appear sensitive," Tonsure sneers in his journal—from which I provide three samples for the half dozen of you who are curious as to the Cappan's illustra-tive skills:

 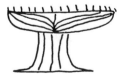 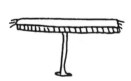

[17]   Apparently, since Tonsure fails to describe it.

ism similar to lichen that the gray caps had trained to create decorative patterns; not only was it *not* gold, it wasn't even edible.

Nonetheless, Manzikert and his men began to explore the city. The most elemental details about the buildings they ignored, instead remarking upon the abundance of tame rats as large as cats,[18] the plethora of exotic birds, and, of course, the large quantities of fungus, which the gray caps appeared to harvest, eat, and store against future famine.[19]

While Manzikert explores, I shall pass the time by relating a few facts about the city. According to the scant gray cap records that have been found and, if not translated, then haltingly understood, they called the city "Cinsorium," although the meaning of the word has been lost, or, more accurately, never been found. It is estimated by those who have studied the ruins lying beneath Ambergris[20] that at one time Cinsorium could have housed 250,000 souls, making it among the largest of all ancient cities. Cinsorium also boasted highly advanced plumbing and water distribution systems that would be the envy of many a city today.[21]

However, at the time Manzikert stumbled upon Cinsorium, Tonsure argued, it was well past its glory years. He based this conclusion on rather shaky evidence: the "undeniable decadence" of its inhabitants. Surely Tonsure is prejudicial beyond reason, for the city appeared fully functional—the high domed buildings in sparkling good repair, the streets swept constantly, the amphitheaters looking as if they might, within minutes, play host to innumerable entertainments.

Tonsure ignored these signs of a healthy culture, perhaps fearing to admit that an almost certainly heretical people might be superior. Instead, he argued, in the biography especially, but also in his journal, that

[18]   The mammologist Xaver Daffed maintains that these were "actually cababari, a stunted relation of the pig that resembles a rat." (Quote taken from *The Hoegbotton Guide to Small, Indigenous Mammals*.) If so, then, as subsequent events will show, the rats of Ambergris have managed something of a public relations coup; the poor cababari are today extinct in the southern climes.

[19]   James Lacond has suggested that the fungus had hallucinogenic qualities. Tonsure, for his part, sampled a "fungus that resembled an artichoke" and found it tasted like unleavened bread; he reports no side effects, although Lacond claims that the rest of Tonsure's account must be considered a drug-induced dream. Lacond further claims that Tonsure's later account of Manzikert's men glutting themselves on the fungi—some of which tasted like honey and some like chicken—explains their sudden mercilessness. But Lacond contradicts himself: if the rest of Tonsure's account is a fever dream, then so is his description of the men eating the fungus. As always when discussing the gray caps, debate tends to describe the same circles as their buildings. (A similar circularity drove Lacond, late in his life, to declare that the world as we know it is actually a product of the dream dreamt by Tonsure. Since our knowledge of our identity as Ambergrisians, where we came from, is so dependent on Tonsure's journal, this is close to the heresy of madness.)

[20]   Admittedly, a perilous and notoriously inaccurate undertaking; the mushroom dwellers tend to look unkindly upon intrusions into their territory.

[21]   The question of where the gray caps came from and why they were concentrated only in Cinsorium remains a mystery. The subject has frustrated many a historian and, to avoid a similar fate, I shall pass over it entirely.

the current inhabitants—numbering no more, he estimates, than 700—had no claim to any greatness once possessed by their ancestors, for they were "clearly the last generations of a dying race," unable to understand the processes of the city, unable to work its machines, unable to farm, "reduced to hunting and gathering."[22] Their watch fires scorched the interiors of great halls, whole clans wetly bickering with one another within a territory marked by the walls of a single building. They did not a one of them, according to Tonsure, comprehend the legacy of their heritage.

Tonsure's greatest argument for the gray caps' degeneracy may also be his weakest. That first day, Manzikert and Sophia entered what the monk described as a library, a structure "more immense than all but the most revered ecclesiastical institutions I have studied within." The shelves of this library had rotted away before the onslaught of a startling profusion of small dark purple mushrooms with white stems. The books, made from palm frond pulp in a process lost to us, had all spilled out upon the main floor—thousands of books, many ornately engraved with strange letters[23] and overlaid by the now familiar golden lichen. The use the current gray caps had made of these books was as firewood, for as Manzikert watched in disbelief, gray caps came and went, collecting the books and condemning them to their cooking fires.

Did Tonsure correctly interpret what he saw in the "library?" I think not, and have published my doubts in a monograph entitled "An Argument for the Gray Caps and Against the Evidence of Tonsure's Eyes."[24] I believe the "library" was actually a place for religious worship, the "books" prayer rolls. Prayer rolls in some cultures, particularly in the far Occident, are consigned to the flames in a holy ritual. The "shelves" were rotted wooden planks *specifically* inserted into the walls to foster the growth of the special purple mushrooms, which grew nowhere else in Cinsorium and may well have had religious significance.[25] Another clue lay in the large, mushroom-shaped stone erected just beyond the library's front steps, since determined to have been an altar.

---

22   But surely they farmed the fungus?

23   Tonsure reports the following symbol showed up repeatedly:

24   Volume XX, Issue 2, of *The Real History Newsletter*, published by the Ambergrisians For The Original Inhabitants Society.

25   In a city otherwise so pristine, such blatant "disorder" should have made Tonsure suspicious. Was he now so completely set, as was his master, on the goal of discrediting and dehumanizing the gray caps, that he could see it no other way?

Sophia chose this moment to remark upon what she termed the "primitivism" of the natives, chiding her husband for his "cowardice." Faced with such a rebuke, Manzikert became more aggressive and free of any moral restraints. Fortunately, it took several days for this new attitude to manifest itself, during which time Manzikert moved more and more of his people off the ships and onto the lip of the bay, where he commenced building docks. He also appropriated several of the round, squat structures on the fringes as living quarters, evicting the native inhabitants who, burbling to themselves, complacently walked into the city proper.

Not only were Manzikert's clan members glad to stretch their legs, but the land that awaited them proved, upon exploration, to be ideal. Abundant springs and natural aquifers fed off of the Moth, while game, from pigs to deer to a flightless bird called a "grout," provided an ample food source. The curve of the river accentuated the breeze that blew from the west, generally cooling the savage climate, and with the breeze came birds, swallows in particular, to swoop down at dusk and devour the vast clouds of insects that hovered over the water.

Tonsure spent these five or six days wandering the city, which he still found a marvel. He had, he wrote in his journal, "squandered" much of his early life in the realm of the Kalif, where architectural marvels crowded every city, but never had he seen anything like Cinsorium.[26] First of all, the city had no corners, only curves. Its architects had built circles within circles, domes within domes, and circles within domes. Tonsure found the effect soothing to the eye, and more importantly to the spirit: "This lack of edges, of conflicting lines, makes of the mind a plateau both serene and calm." The possible truth of this observation has been confirmed by modern-day architects who, on review of the reconstructed blueprint of Cinsorium, have described it as the structural equivalent of a tuning fork, a vibration in the soul.

Just as delightful were the huge, festive mosaics lining the walls, most of which depicted battles or mushroom harvesting, while a few consisted of abstract shiftings of red and black; these last gave Tonsure as much unease as the lack of corners had given him comfort, although again he could not say why. The mosaics were made from lichen and fungus skillfully placed and trained to achieve the desired effect. Sometimes fruits, vegetables, or seeds were also used to form decorative patterns—cauliflower to depict a sheep-like creature called the "lunger," for example—with the gray caps replacing these weekly. If Tonsure can be believed, one mosaic used the eggs of a native thrush to depict the eyes of a gray cap; when the eggs hatched, the eyes appeared to be opening.

---

[26]   Unfortunately, this claim strengthens Sabon's assertion with regard to the Patriarch of Nicea—see footnote 6.

The library yielded the most magnificent of Tonsure's discoveries: a mechanized golden tree, its branches festooned with intricate jeweled shrikes and parrots, while on the circular dais by which it moved equally intricate deer, stalked by lions, pawed the golden ground. By use of a winding key, the birds would burst simultaneously into song while the lions roared beneath them. The gray caps maintained it in perfect working condition, but had no appreciation for its beauty, as if they "were themselves clockwork parts in some vast machine, fated to retrace the same movements year after year."

Yet, as Tonsure's appreciation for the city grew, so to did his loathing of its inhabitants. Runts, he calls them—cripples. In their ignorance of the beauty of their own city, he wrote (in the biography), they "had become unfit to rule over it, or even to live within its boundaries." Their "pallor, the sickly moistness of their skin, even the rheumy discharge from their eyes," all pointed to the "abomination of their existence, mocking the memory of what they once had been."[27]

Why the normally tolerant Tonsure came to espouse such ideas we may never know; certainly, there is none of the element of pity that marks his journal comments about Manzikert, whom he calls "a seething mass of emotions, a pincushion of feelings who would surely be locked away if he were not already a leader of men." Although Tonsure's disparaging comments in his journal seem overwrought, similar comments in the biography are easily attributed to Manzikert himself, for if the monk reviled the natives, the Cappan hated them with an intensity that can have no rational explanation. Tonsure records that whenever Manzikert had cause to walk through the city, he would casually murder any gray cap in his path. Perhaps even more chilling, other gray caps in the vicinity ignored such unprovoked murder, and the mortally wounded themselves expired without a struggle.[28]

---

27 Poor Tonsure. Just preceding this diatribe, the monk describes a kind of hard mushroom, about seven inches tall, with a stem as thick as its head. When squeezed, this mushroom suddenly throbs to an even greater size. While walking innocently between the "library" and the amphitheater, Tonsure came across a group of gray cap women using these mushrooms in what he calls a "lascivious way." So perhaps we should forgive him his hyperbole. Still, shocked or not—and he was a more worldly monk than many—Tonsure should have noticed that for every such "perversion," the gray caps had developed a dozen more useful wonders. For example, another type of mushroom stood two feet tall and had a long, thin stem with a wide hood that, when plucked, could be used as an umbrella; the hood even collapsed into the stem for easy storage.

28 Here, for once, Lacond proves useful. He puts forth two theories for the gray caps' passivity: first, that Manzikert had landed in the midst of a religious festival during which the gray caps were forbidden to take part in any aggressive acts, even to defend themselves; second, that the gray cap society resembled that of bees or ants, and thus none of the "units" in the city had free will, being extensions of some hive intellect. This second theory by Lacond seems extreme to some historians, but the idea of passivity being bred into particular classes of gray cap society cannot be ruled out. This would support my own theory that the entire city of Cinsorium was a religious artifact, a temple, if you will, in which violence was not permitted to be inflicted by its keepers. Were Manzikert's actions tantamount to desecration?

At the end of the first week, Manzikert and Sophia held a festival not only to celebrate the completion of the docks, but also "this new beginning as dwellers on the land." Due to its timing, this celebration must be considered the forerunner of the Festival of the Freshwater Squid.[29] During the festivities, Manzikert christened the new settlement "Ambergris," after the "most secret and valuable part of the whale"[30]—over Sophia's objections, who, predictably enough, wanted to call the settlement "Sophia."

The next morning, Manzikert, groggy from grog the night before, got up to relieve himself and, about to do so beside one of the gray caps' round dwellings, noticed on the wall a small, flesh-colored lichen that bore a striking resemblance to the Lepress Saint Kristina of Malfour, a major icon in the Truffidian religion. Menacing the Saint was a lichen that looked uncannily like a gray cap. Manzikert fell into a religious rage and, presumably after relieving himself, gathered his people and told them of his vision. In the biography Tonsure dutifully reports the jubilant reaction of Manzikert's men upon learning they were going to war because of a maliciously-shaped fungus,[31] but neglects to mention this reaction in his journal, presumably out of shame.[32]

Late in the afternoon, Sophia and Tonsure at his side, Cappan Manzikert I of Aan and Ambergris led a force of 200 men into the city. The sun, Tonsure writes, shone blood red, and the streets of Cinsorium soon reflected red independent of the sun, for at Manzikert's order, his men began to slaughter the gray caps. It was a horribly mute affair. The gray caps offered no resistance, but only stared up at their attackers as

---

[29]   Typically, Sabon cannot bite her tongue and disagrees, citing the Calabrian Calendar used by the Aan as schismatic—most definitely *not* synchronized with the modern calendar. However, Sabon fails to take into account that *Tonsure*, as the non-Aan author of the biography and the journal, would have used the Kalif's calendar, which is identical to our own.

[30]   Cynically, Tonsure reports, "Better to name a city after the anus of a whale than to actually go whaling, for Manzikert, lazy as he is, finds piracy much easier than whaling: when you harpoon an honest sailor, he is less likely to drag you 300 miles across open water and then, turning, casually devour you and drown your companions." Other names Manzikert considered include "Aanville," "Aanapolis," and "Aanburg," so we may be fairly certain that Tonsure suggested "Ambergris," despite his ridicule of the name.

[31]   Or, as Sabon put it, "how cunning a fungus."

[32]   Tonsure does, in his journal, write that the lichen in question "more closely resembled one blob rutting with another blob, but who is to doubt the vision of cappans?" Are we to believe that the carnage to come was all the result of two unfortunately-shaped lichen? Sabon points to the Holy Visitation of Stockton (alternately known by historians as the Sham Involving Jam), where a stain of blueberry jam resembling the heretic Ibonof Ibonof sparked seven days of riots. Lacond, in agreement with Sabon, relates the story that the Kalif's order to attack the Menite town of Richter was the direct result of a Richter lemon squirting him in the eye when he cut it open. Unfortunately, Sabon and Lacond have joined forces to support an idea that lacks merit given the context. It is my opinion that, lichen or no lichen, Manzikert would have attacked the gray caps.

they were cut down.[33] Perhaps if they had resisted, Manzikert might have
shown them mercy, but their silence, their utter willingness to die rather
than fight back, infuriated the Cappan, and the massacre continued un-
abated until dusk. By this time "the newly-christened city had become
indistinguishable from a charnel house, so much blood had been spilled
upon the streets; the smell of the slaughter gathered in the humid air,
and the blood itself clung to us like sweat." The bodies were so numerous that they had to be stacked in piles so that Manzikert and his men
could navigate the streets back to the docks.

Except that Manzikert, as the sunset finally bled into night and his
men lit their torches, did *not* return to the docks.

For, as they passed the great "library" and the inert shapes sprawled
on its front steps, Manzikert espied a gray cap dressed in purple robes
standing by the red-stained altar. This gray cap not only clicked and
whistled at the Cappan, but, after making an unmistakably rude gesture
(in any language), fled up the steps. At first shocked, Manzikert quickly
pursued with a select group of men,[34] shouting out to Sophia to lead the
rest back to the ships; he would follow shortly. Then he and his men—including, for some reason, Tonsure, journal in his pocket—disappeared
into the "library." Sophia, always a good soldier, followed orders and returned to the docks.

The night passed without event—except that Manzikert did not return. At first light, Sophia immediately re-entered the city with a force of
300 men, larger by a third than the small army that had slaughtered the
gray caps the evening before.

It must have been an odd sight for Sophia and the young Manzikert
II.[35] The morning sun shone down upon an empty city. The birds called
out from the trees, the bees buzzed around their flowers, but nowhere
could be found a dead gray cap, a living man—not even a trace of blood,
as if the massacre had never happened and Manzikert himself had never
walked the earth. As they walked through the silent streets, fear so over-
came them that by the time they had reached the library, which lay near
the city's center, more than half the men had broken ranks and headed

---

33   Tonsure never indicates what he did during the massacre—whether to participate or intervene; later circumstantial evidence indicates he may have tried to intervene. Nonetheless,
Tonsure's description of the massacre has a disturbingly cold, disinterested edge to it. Predictably, the biography account speaks of Manzikert's bravery as, surrounded by "dangerous
gray caps armed to the teeth," (read: "wide-eyed, weaponless midgets") he managed to cut his
way through them to safety.

34   The bersar, an honorary title peculiar to the Aan and awarded only to men who had
shown great bravery in combat.

35   All the information we have about the events that follow comes from Manzikert II, who
is not nearly as entertaining as Tonsure, lacking both his wit and powers of description.
Manzikert II was serious and 17—a disastrous combination for historical writing, as I can at-
test—and I have resisted direct quotation for the most part.

back to the docks. Although Sophia and Manzikert II did not lose their nerve, it was a close thing. Manzikert II writes that:

> Not only had I not seen my Mother so afrightened before, I had never thought to see the day; and yet it was undeniable: she shook with fear as we went up the library steps. Her hands whitest white, her eyes nervous in her head, that something might any moment leap out of bluest sky, the gentle air, the unshadowed dwellings, and set upon her. Seeing my Mother so afeared, I thought myself no coward for my own fear.

Within the library, which had been emptied of its books, its mushrooms, its "shelves," they found only a single chair,[36] and sitting in that chair, Manzikert,[37] who wept and covered his face with his hands. Behind him, in the far wall: a gaping hole with stairs that led down into Cinsorium's extensive network of underground tunnels. Into this hole the night before, Manzikert I would later divulge, he, Tonsure, and his bersar had entered in pursuit of the fleeing gray cap.

But at the moment, all Manzikert I could do was weep, and when Sophia finally managed to pry his hands from his face, she could see that there were no tears, for his "eyes had been plucked from their sockets so cleanly, so expertly, that to look at him, this pitiable man, one might think he had been born that way." Of Tonsure, of the cappan's men, there was no sign, and no sign of any except for the monk would ever turn up. They had effectively vanished for all time.

Manzikert I remained incoherent for several days, screaming out in the night, vomiting, and subject to fits that appear to have been epileptic in nature. He also had lost his bearings, for he claimed to have been underground for more than a month, when clearly he had only just gone underground the night before.

During this difficult time—her husband incapacitated, her son stricken with immobility by the double trauma of his father's condition and Tonsure's disappearance—Sophia's grief and fear turned into rage. On the third day after discovering her husband in the library, she reached a decision that has divided historians throughout the ages: she put Cinsorium to the torch.[38]

---

[36]   The gray caps must also have taken the fabulous golden tree, for there is no mention of it in Manzikert II's account, or in any future chronicle. It defies the laws of probability that such a remarkable invention would *not* be mentioned somewhere, in some account, had it not already been taken back by the gray caps.

[37]   I will call him Manzikert I from this point on, so as to avoid confusing him with his son.

[38]   Lacond: "An act of utter barbarism, destroying the finest artifacts of a culture that has never been found anywhere else in the known world and destroying a people both peaceful and advanced. Genocide is too kind a word." Sabon: "Without Sophia's bravery, the new-born city of Ambergris would soon have perished, undone by the treachery of the gray

The conflagration began in the library, and she is said to have expressed great regret that no "books" remained to feed to the fire. The city burned for three days, during which time, due to a miscalculation, the Aan were forced to work long hours protecting the docks which, when the winds shifted, were in serious danger of going up in flame as well. Finally, though, the city burned to the ground, leaving behind only the fleeting descriptions in Tonsure's journal, a few other scattered accounts from Manzikert I's clan, and a handful of buildings that proved resistant to the blaze.[39] Chief among these were the walls of the library itself, which proved to have been made of a fire-repellent stone, the aqueducts, and the altar outside of the library (these last two still stand today). Sophia realized the futility, not to mention the economic consequences, of dismantling the aqueducts, and so took out her frustrations on the altar and the library. The altar was made of a stone so strong they could not crack it with their hammers and other tools. When they tried to dig it out, they discovered it was a pillar that descended at least 100 feet, if not farther, and thus impregnable. The library, however, she had taken apart until "not one stone stood upon another stone." As for the entrances to the underground sections of the ancient city, Sophia had these blocked up with several layers of burned stones from the demolished buildings, and then topped this off with a crude cement fashioned from mortar, pebbles, and dirt. This layer was reinforced with wooden planks stripped from the ships. Finally, Sophia posted sentries, in groups of ten, at each site, and five years later we find a description of these sentries in Manzikert II's journal, still manning their posts.

By this time, Sophia's husband had regained his senses—or, rather, had regained as much of them as he ever would . . .

Manzikert I refused to discuss what had occurred underground, so we will never know whether he even remembered the events that led up to his blinding. He would talk of nothing but the sleek, fat rats that, hiding from the carnage and the fires, had re-emerged to wander the cindered city, no doubt puzzled by the changes. Manzikert I claimed the rats were the reincarnated spirits of saints and martyrs, and as such must be worshipped, groomed, fed, and housed to the extent that they had known such comforts in their former lives.[40] These claims drove Sophia to distraction, and many were the screaming matches aboard the flagship over

---

caps. By destroying these degenerates, and with them their heretical artifacts, she saw to it that they would never recover. As night dwellers exclusively, although a danger and a nuisance, they at least cannot parade their failings under the sun."

[39]   Sophia, in the biography, would have us believe that she destroyed all of the buildings, but since we find Manzikert II, 10 years later, using several of them for defensive and storage purposes, this seems unlikely.

[40]   We begin to wonder if Manzikert did believe in his heart of hearts that he should massacre the gray caps because of two oddly-shaped lichens.

the next few weeks. However, when she realized that her husband had not recovered, but had, in a sense, died underground, she installed him near the docks, in the very building beside which he had met his first gray cap. There she allowed him to indulge his mania to his heart's content.

Although no longer a fearsome sight, short or tall, Manzikert I lived out his remaining years in a state of perpetual happiness, his gap-toothed grin as prominent as his frown had been in previous years. It was common to see him, with the help of a walking stick, blindly leading his huge charges—sleek, well-fed, and increasingly tame—around the city he had named. At night, the rats all crowded into his new house, and to his son's embarrassment, slept by his side, or even on his bed. Such reverence as he showed the rats, whether the result of insanity or genuine religious epiphany, greatly impressed many of the Aan, especially those who still worshipped the old icons and those who had participated in the slaughter of the gray caps. Soon, he had many helpers.[41] One morning, eight years after the fires, these helpers found Manzikert in his bed, gnawed to death by his "saints and martyrs," and yet, if Manzikert II is to be believed, "with a smile upon his eyeless face."

Thus ended the oddly poignant life of Ambergris' first ruler—a man who thoroughly deserved to be gnawed to death by rats, as a year had not gone by before his blinding when he had not personally murdered at least a dozen people. Brave but cruel, a tactical genius at war but a failure at peace, and an enigma in terms of his height, Manzikert I is today remembered less as the founder of Ambergris, than as the founder of a religion which still has its adherents today in the city's Religious Quarter and which is still known as "Manziism."[42]

---

[41]   So many that Manzikert II had to ban the feeding of rats during a time of famine.

[42]   Much to the disgust of Truffidians everywhere, Manziists often claim to be the Brothers and Sisters of Truff, a claim that has led to riots—and dozens of rats cooked on spits—in the Religious Quarter.

II[43]

To Manzikert I's son, Cappan Manzikert II, would fall the monumental task of converting a pirate/whaling fleet into a viable land-based culture that could supplement fishing with extensive farming and trade
with other communities.[44] Luckily, Manzikert II possessed virtues his father lacked, and although never the military leader his father had been,
neither did he have the impulsive nature that had led to their exile in the
first place.[45] He also had the ghost of Samuel Tonsure at his disposal, for
he had taken the monk's teachings to heart.

Above all else, Manzikert II proved to be a builder—whether it was establishing a permanent town within the old city of Cinsorium or creating friendships with nearby tribes.[46] When peace proved impossible—with, for example, the western tribe known as the Dogghe—
Manzikert II showed no reluctance to use force. Twice in the first ten
years, he abandoned his rebuilding efforts to battle the Dogghe, until, in
a decisive encounter on the outskirts of Ambergris itself, he put to flight
and decimated a large tribal army and, using his naval strength to its best
effect, annihilated the rest as they took to their canoes. The chieftain of
the Dogghe died of extreme gout during the fighting and with his death
the Dogghe had no choice but to come to terms.

Thus, in Manzikert II's eleventh year of rule, he was finally able to focus exclusively on building roads, promoting trade, and, most importantly, designing the layers of efficient bureaucracy necessary to govern a
large area. He himself never conquered much territory, but he laid the
groundwork for the system that would reach its apogee 300 years later

---

[43]   The impatient, feckless reader, posessed of no glimmer of intellectual or historical curiosity, should do an old historian a favor and skip the next few pages, proceeding directly to the
Silence itself (Part III). I would assume that, in these horrid modern times, that will include
most of you. Of course, those readers least likely to read these footnotes, and thus least likely
to appreciate the next few pages, will skip this note and bore themselves upon the ennui of
history . . .

[44]   Sophia was never the same after Manzikert I returned to her blinded and deranged—she
died soon after him and while alive expressed little or no interest in governing, although she
did on at least two occasions, at her son's insistence and with great success, lead punitive expeditions against the southern tribes. Sophia had truly loved her brute of a man, although
not in the maudlin terms described by Voss Bender in his first and least successful opera, *The
Tragedy of John and Sophia*; it is difficult not to laugh while John dances with a man in a rat
suit, which he has mistaken in his madness for Sophia, toward the end of Act III.

[45]   He was, by all accounts, a handsome man, if not possessed of the swarthy, thick, hairy
handsomeness of his father; he had a slender frame, and a head topped with a tangle of black
hair, beneath which his green eyes shone with a cunning fierceness.

[46]   For a long time, these tribes avoided the city and accorded the new settlement an undue
measure of respect—until they began to realize the gray caps had left, apparently for good, after which a vigorous contempt for the Aan became the norm.

during the reign of Trillian the Great Banker.[47]

Manzikert II also laid the groundwork for Ambergris' unique religious flavor by building churches in what would become the Religious Quarter—and, less to his credit, by active plundering of other cities. Obsessed with relics, Manzikert II was forever sending agents to the south and west to buy or steal the body parts of saints, until by the end of his reign he had amassed a huge collection of some 70 mummified noses, eyelids, feet, kneecaps, fingers, hearts, and livers.[48] Housed in the various churches, these relics attracted thousands of pilgrims (along with their money), some of whom stayed in the city, thus helping to spark the rapid growth that made Ambergris a thriving metropolis only 20 years after its foundation. Remarkably, Manzikert II's astute diplomacy averted catastrophe in at least four instances where his thievery of relics so infuriated the plundered cities that they were ready to invade Ambergris.

On the architectural front, Manzikert II built many remarkable structures with the help of his chief architect Midan Pejora, but none so well-known as the Cappan's Palace, which would exist intact until, 350 years later, the Kalif's Grand Vizir, upon his temporary occupation of Ambergris, dismantled much of it.[49] The palace was, by all accounts, a rather peculiar building. The exterior inspired the noted traveler Alan Busker to write:

> The walls, the columns rise until, at last, as if in ecstasy, the
> crests of the arches break into a marble foam, and toss them-
> selves far into the blue sky in flashes and wreaths of sculp-

---

[47]   For a thorough overview of the early political and economic systems, as well as particulars on crops, etc., see Richard Mandible's excellent "Early Ambergrisian Finance and Society," recently published in Vol. XXXII, Issue 3, of *Historian's Quarterly*. Such detailed information lies beyond the brief of this particular essay, not to mention the patience of the reader and the endurance of an old historian with creaky joints.

[48]   A catalog kept during Manzikert II's reign indicates that at least two of these relics were taken from saintly men while still living, and that although the Cappan's agents bargained long and hard for the purchase from the Kalif of the "penis and left testicle of Saint George of Assuf," they managed only to procure the testicle. (We can only imagine the bizarre sight of the testicle's triumphant entrance to the city, borne upon a perfumed, gold-embroidered pillow held high by a senior Truffidian priest while the crowds cheered wildly.) At the height of the religious frenzy, the Church of the Seven Pointed Star even put together an array of different saints' body parts—a head here, an ear there—to make a creature they called the "The Saint of Saints," a sort of super saint. This was put on display for 20 years until several other churches, on the verge of bankruptcy due to their own lack of relics, launched a joint raid and "dismembered" this early golem.

[49]   The rebuilt palace elicited neither condemnation nor praise; indeed, its most interesting features were its many interior murals and portraits, several of which commemorate victories against the Kalif created out of thin air by Ambergrisian historians. Worse, the first two portraits in the Great Hall depict cappans who never existed, to gloss over the Occupation, a period when the city was under the Kalif's control. To this day, Ambergrisian school children are taught the exploits of Cappan Skinder and Cappan Bartine. Braver if less substantial leaders have rarely trod upon the earth . . .

tured spray, as if the breakers on the shore had been frost
bound before they fell, and the river nymphs had inlaid them
with diamonds and amethyst.

However, the interior prompted him to write: "We shall find that the
work is at least pure in its insipidity, and subtle in its vice; but this monument is remarkable as showing the refuse of one style encumbering the
embryo of another, and all principles of life entangled either in diapers
or the shroud." The actual bust of Manzikert II pleased Busker even less:
"A huge, gross, bony clown's face, with the peculiar sodden and sensual
cunning in it which is seen so often in the countenances of the worst
Truffidian priests; a face part of iron and part of clay. I blame the sculptor, not the subject."

Manzikert II ruled for 43 years and sired a son on his sickly wife
Isobel when he was already a gray beard of 45 years. During his reign, he
had managed the impossible task of both consolidating his position and
preparing for future growth. If his religious fervor led him to bad decisions, then at least his gift for diplomacy saved him from the consequences of those decisions.

Following the death of Manzikert II,[50] Manzikert III duly took his
place as ruler of lands that now stretched some 40 miles south of Ambergris and 50 miles north.[51] Manzikert III suffered from mild
oliphauntitus[52] that apparently affected his internal organs, yet oddly
enough he died, after six tumultuous years, of jungle rot[53] received while
on a southern expedition to procure lemur eyelids and kidneys for an ex-

---

[50]   Evidence suggests he may have been poisoned by his ambitious son, whom he was always
careful to bring on campaign with him, so as to keep the boy under a watchful eye.
Manzikert II died suddenly, with no apparent symptoms, his body quickly cremated on his
son's order. If there was little protest, this may have been because he had never been a popular
leader, despite his excellent record. He lacked the necessary charisma for men to follow him
unthinkingly.

[51]   In the north, the Cappandom of Ambergris, as it was now officially known, encountered
implacable resistance from the Menites, adherents to a religion that saw Truffid as heresy.
The Menites would subsequently establish a vast northern commercial empire, based in the
city of Morrow, some 85 miles upriver from Ambergris.

[52]   Sabon insists it was leprosy, while others believe it was epilepsy. Regardless, we can
choose from three spectacular diseases with very different symptoms.

[53]   Jungle rot can have various manifestations, but, according to an anonymous observer,
Manzikert III's jungle rot was among the nastiest ever recorded: "Suddenly an abscess appeared in his privy parts then a deep-seated fistular ulcer; these could not be cured and ate
their way into the very midst of his entrails. Hence there sprang an innumerable multitude
of worms, and a deadly stench was given off, since the entire bulk of his members had,
through gluttony, even before the disease, been changed into an excessive quantity of soft
fat, which then became putrid and presented an intolerable and most fearful sight to those
who came near it. As for the physicians, some of them were wholly unable to endure the ex-
ceeding and unearthly stench, while those who still attended his side could not be of any as-
sistance, since the whole mass had swollen and reached a point where there was no hope of
recovery."

otic meat pie. The Cappan's condition was not immediately diagnosed, perhaps due to his oliphauntitus, and by the time doctors had discovered the nature of his condition, it was too late. Displaying a fine disregard for mercy, Manzikert III's last order before he died was for every last member of the Institute of Medicine to be boiled alive in an eel broth; evidently, he had thought up a new recipe.[54]

Manzikert III had not been a good cappan.[55] During his reign, he had launched numerous futile assaults on the Menites, and although no one ever doubted his personal bravery, he had all of his grandfather's impatience and impulsiveness, but none of that man's charisma or shrewdness. A grotesque gastronome, he put on decadent banquets even during the famine that struck in the third year of his reign.[56] About all that can be said for Manzikert III is that he provided monies for research that resulted in refinements of the mariner's compass and the invention of the double-ruddered ship (useful for maneuvering in narrow tributaries), but Manzikert III is best remembered for his poor treatment of the poet Maximillian Sharp. Sharp came to Ambergris as an emissary of the Menites, and when it came time for him to leave, Manzikert III would not allow him safe passage by the most convenient route. He was consequently obliged to make his way back through malarial swampland as a result of which this greatest of all ancient masters caught a fever and

---

[54]   Although Manzikert III's order (rescinded after his death) was extreme, his charge that the city's doctors knew little of their craft is, unfortunately, true. In an attempt to upgrade its service, the Institute sent representatives to the Kalif's court, as well as to the witchdoctors of native tribes. The Kalif's physicians refused to reveal their methodology, but the witchdoctors proved very helpful. The Institute incorporated such native procedures as applying the freshwater electric flounder as a local anesthetic during surgery. Another procedure, perhaps even more ingenious, solved the problem of infection during the stitching up of intestines. Large senegrosa ants, placed along the opening, clamped the wounds shut with their jaws; the witchdoctor then cut away the bodies, leaving only the heads. After replacing the intestines in the stomach, the witchdoctor would sew up the abdomen. As the wound healed, the ant heads would gradually dissolve.

[55]   Although I have certainly devoted enough footnotes to him.

[56]   One menu for such a banquet included calf's brain custard, roast hedgehog, and a dish rather cruelly known as Oliphaunt's Delight, the incomplete recipe for which was uncovered by the Ambergrisian Gastronomic Association just last year:

> 1 scooped out oliphaunt's skull
> 1 pureed oliphaunt's brain
> 1 gallon of brandy
> 6 oysters
> 2 very clean pigs' bladders
> 24 eggs
> salt, pepper, and a sprig of parsley

I am unhappy to report that the search is on for the missing ingredients.

died.[57] Manzikert III, when brought news of Sharp's death, is said to have joked, "Consider this my contribution to the Arts."[58] Another year and Manzikert III might have exhausted both the treasury and his people's patience. As it was, he managed little permanent damage and all of this was put right by his successor: Manzikert II's illegitimate son by a distant third cousin, the handsome and intelligent Michael Aquelus, arguably the greatest of the Manzikert cappans.[59] If not for Aquelus' firm hand, Ambergris, cappandom and city, might well have crumbled to dust within a generation.

***

We now stand on the threshold of the event known as the Silence. Almost 58 years have passed since the massacre of the gray caps and the destruction of the ancient city of Cinsorium. The new Cappandom of Ambergris has begun to thrive over its ruins and no gray caps have been seen since the day of the massacre. An initial population that may well have flinched in anticipation of some terrible reprisal for genocide has given way to people who have never seen a gray cap, many of them Aan clans folk from the south who also wish to resettle on land. Manzikert II has already, during an exceedingly long reign, overseen the painful transition to a permanent settlement—already, too, a prosperous middle class of merchants, shopkeepers, and bankers has sprung up, supplemented

---

[57]   In all fairness to Manzikert III, Sharp had an insufferable ego. His autobiography, published from the unedited manuscript found on his body, contains such gems as, "From East and West alike my reputation brings them flocking to Morrow. The Moth may water the lands of the Kalif, but it is my golden words that nourish their spirit. Ask the Brueghelites or the followers of Stretcher Jones: they will tell you that they know me, that they admire me and seek me out. Only recently there arrived an Ambergrisian, impelled by an insurmountable desire to drink at the fountain of my eloquence."

[58]   The Scathadian novelist George Leopran—prevented by Manzikert III from sailing home—had an experience almost as bad, returning to Scatha only after much tribulation: "I boarded my vessel and left the city that I had thought to be so rich and prosperous but is actually a starveling, a city full of lies, tricks, perjury and greed, a city rapacious, avaricious and vainglorious. My guide was with me, and after 49 days of ass-riding, walking, horse-riding, fasting, thirsting, sighing, weeping, and groaning, I arrived at the Kalif's court. Even this was not the end of my sufferings, for upon setting out for the final stretch of my journey, I was delayed by contrary winds at Paust, deserted by my ship's crew at Latras, unkindly received by a eunuch bishop and half-starved on Lukas and subjected to three consecutive earthquakes on Dominon, where I subsequently fell in among thieves. Only after another 60 days did I finally return to my home, never again to leave it." If he had known that an arthritic Ambergrisian historian would some day find his account hilarious, he might have cheered up. Or perhaps not. In any event, we can certainly understand historical novelists' tendency to vilify Manzikert III beyond even his due.

[59]   We will never know why Aquelus was accepted so readily, unless Manzikert III had proclaimed him ruler on his deathbed or Manzikert II, knowing his son's sickly nature, had already decreed that if Manzikert III died, Aquelus should take his place. The story that, in his childhood, a golden eagle alighted at Aquelus' bedroom window and told him he would one day be cappan is almost certainly apocryphal.

by farmers who have settled in Ambergris and the outlying minor towns.[60] River trade is booming, and has made the city rich in a short period of time. Compulsory two-year military service has proven a success—the army is strong but civic-minded while Ambergris' enemies appear few and impotent. Units of barter based on a gold standard have been introduced and these coins form the principal form of currency, followed closely by the southern Aan sel, which will gradually be phased out. All of Ambergris' rulers—including Manzikert III—have successfully foiled attempts by the upper classes (mostly descendants of Manzikert I's lieutenants) to form a ruling aristocracy by parceling out most of the land to small farmers. Thus, there are no serious internal threats to the succession. Finally, we are on the cusp of a period of inspired building and invention known as the Aquelus Age.

Everywhere, new ideas take root. The refurbished whaling fleet has focused its efforts on the giant freshwater squid, with great success. Aquelus will not just make freshwater squid products a national industry, but part of the national identity, inadvertently introducing the Festival of the Freshwater Squid, which will remain a peaceful event throughout the rule of the Manzikerts.[61] The old aqueducts have been made functional again and extensive settlement has occurred in the valley beyond the city proper, creating a separate town of craftspeople. Every day a new house goes up and a new street is dedicated, and by the time of Aquelus there are over 30,000 permanent residents in Ambergris: approximately 13,000 men and 17,000 women and children.[62]

And yet, as Aquelus enters his sixth year in power, there is something *dreadfully wrong*, and although no one knows the source of this wrongness, perhaps a few suspect, at least a little. First, there is the sinister way in which the gray caps have entered the collective consciousness of the city: parents tell tales of the old inhabitants of Cinsorium to children at bedtime—that the gray caps will creep up out of the ground on their

[60]   Three centuries later, city mayors all along the Moth would caste off the yoke of cappans and kings and create a league of city-states based on trade alliances—eventually plunging Ambergris into its current state of "functional anarchy."

[61]   The first festival, held by Manzikert I, had been a simple affair: a two-course feast attended by an elderly swordswallower who managed to impale himself. More elaborate entertainments would mark the reign of Aquelus in particular. Such celebrations included a representation of the Gardens of Nicea, 300 yards across, built on rafts between the two banks of the Moth, complete with flowers, trees of brightly-colored crystal, and an artificial lake stocked with fish, from which guests were to choose their dinner before retiring to a banquet. In the year after the Silence, at a touch from the Cappaness' hand, an outsized artificial owl sped around the public courtyard, sparking off a hundred torches as it, finally, came to rest on an 80-foot high replica of the Kalif's Arch of Tarbut. But perhaps the most audacious presentation occurred during the reign of Manzikert VII, who resurrected the gray caps' old coliseum, sealed it off, had the arena flooded with water, and recreated famous naval battles using ships built to 2/3 scale. All this pomp and circumstance served as genuine celebration, but also, in later years, to hide the city's growing poverty and military weakness.

[62]   Fourth Census—on file in the old bureaucratic quarter.

clammy pale hands and feet, crawl in through an open window, and *grab you* if you don't go to sleep.

Or, more frequently now, the term "mushroom dweller" is used instead of "gray cap," no doubt become more common because, rather disturbingly, the only major failure of the civil government and private citizens has been the war against the fungus that has overgrown many areas of Ambergris: cascades of dark and bright mushrooms, gaily festooned with red and green, or somber in jackets of gray or brown, sometimes as thick as the very grass. Public complaints proliferate, for certain types exude a slick poison which, when it comes into contact with legs, feet, arms, hands, leaves the victim in extreme pain and covered with purple splotches for up to a week. More alarmingly, a new type of mushroom with a stem as thick as an oak and four or five feet tall, begins to spring up in the middle of certain streets, wrenching free from the cobblestones. These blue-tinged "white whales,"[63] as some wag nicknamed them, have to be chopped down by either fire emergency workers or the civil police department, causing hours of inconvenience and lost work time. They also smell so strongly of rotten eggs that whole neighborhoods have to be evacuated, sometimes for days.

Certainly the afflicted areas had grown more numerous in those last years before the Silence, almost as if the fungi formed a vast, nonsentient advance guard . . . but for what? At least one prominent citizen, the inventor Stephen Bacilus[64]—the great-great-great grandfather of the influential statistician Gort—appears to have known what for, and to have recognized a potential danger. As he put it to the Home Council, a body created to address issues of citywide security:

> The very fact that we cannot stop their proliferation, that every poison only makes them thrive the more, should alarm us. For it indicates the presence of another, superior, force determined that these fungi should live. The further observation, made by many in this room tonight, that some fungi, after we have uprooted them and placed them in the appointed garbage heaps for burning, mysteriously find their way back to their former location—this should also shock us

---

[63]   Lacond's most ridiculous "theory" according to most historians (and therefore well worth relating) postulates that some mushroom dwellers actually gestated within such mushrooms. This explains both why the axe blows to fell them caused the mushrooms to shriek and why their centers often proved to be composed of a dark, watery mass reminiscent of afterbirth or amniotic fluid. I myself now believe they "shrieked" because this is the sound a certain rubbery consistency of fungi flesh makes when an axe cleaves it; as for the "afterbirth," many fungi contain a nutrient sac. We could wish that Lacond had done more research on the subject before venturing an opinion, but then we would be bereft of his marvelous stupidity.

[64]   By now in his late sixties, Bacilus was a fiery old man with a smoking white beard who must have made quite a spectacle in public.

into action . . . and, finally, I need not remind you, except
that so many of us today have short memories, that several of
these mushrooms are purple in hue. Until a few years ago, a
purple mushroom could not be found in all the city. Somehow, I find this fact more sinister than any other. . .

Unfortunately, the Council dismissed his evidence as based on old
wives' tales, and placed an edict on Bacilus that forbid him to speak
about "mushrooms, fungi, lichen, moss, or related plants so as not to
unwittingly and unnecessarily cause a general panic amongst the populace."[65] After all, the Home Council was responsible for security in the
city.

But did Bacilus have cause for alarm? Perhaps so. According to police
reports, three years before the Silence the city experienced 76 unexplained or unsolved break-ins, up from only 30 the previous year. Two
years before the Silence this figure rose to 99 break-ins, and in the year
before the Silence, almost 150 unexplained break-ins occurred within
the city limits. No doubt some of these burglaries can be attributed to
the large number of unassimilated immigrant adventurers flooding into
Ambergris, and no doubt the authorities' failure to show undue concern
means they had reached a similar conclusion. However, the victims in
an astonishing number of these cases claim, when they saw anyone at all,
that the intruder was a *small person*, usually hidden by shadow and almost always *wearing a large felt hat*. These mystery burglars most often
made off with cutlery, jewelry, and food items.[66] It is unfortunate indeed

---

[65]   In the Council's defense, Bacilus had a rather checkered reputation in Ambergris. We
have, today, the luxury of distance, but the Council had had no time to expunge from memory such Bacilus innovations as artificial legs for snakes, mittens for fish, or the infamous
Flying Jacket. Bacilus reasoned that if trapped air will make an object float upon the water,
then trapped air might also allow an object, in this case a man, to float upon the air. Therefore, Bacilus created a special body suit he called the Flying Jacket. Made from hollowed out
pig and cow stomachs, it consisted of three dozen air sacs sewn together. Without prior test-
ing, Bacilus persuaded his cousin Brandon Map to don the Flying Jacket and, in front of
some of Aquelus' foremost ministers, to jump from the top of the new Truffidian Cathedral.
After the poor man had plummeted to his death, it was generally observed within Bacilus'
earshot, if only to make the loss appear not completely pointless, that yes, perhaps his cousin
had flown a little bit before the end. Another minister, less kindly, remarked that if Bacilus
himself, surely a natural windbag if ever he'd seen one, had donned the jacket, the results
might have been different, for it was obvious that Brandon had no air within him anymore,
nor blood, nor bones . . . The Truffidians were, of course, horrified that their new cathedral
had been christened with such a splatter of blood—and even more upset when they discovered Brandon had been an atheist. (I should note, however, that Truffidians have spent the
last seven centuries being horrified by some event or other.)

[66]   This police report filed by Richard Krokus provides a typical example: "I woke in the
middle of the night to a humming sound from the kitchen. It must have been two in the
morning and my wife was by my side, and we have no children, so I knew no one who was
supposed to be in the house was fixing themselves a midnight snack. So I go into the kitchen
real quiet-like, having picked up a plank of wood for a weapon that I was going to use to rein-
force the mantel, but hadn't gotten around to on account of my bad back—I served like everyone in the army and messed up my back when I fell during training exercises and even got

that the urban legend of the mushroom dwellers had spread so widely, because, reduced to stories to scare children, no one took them seriously. The police passed off such accounts as hysterical or as bald-faced lies, while criminals complicated the situation by disguising themselves in gray cap "garb" when committing burglaries.[67]

Worse still, the efficient government and the network of peace treaties Manzikert II and Aquelus had created proved to be built on a fragile foundation.

At the time of the Silence, it would have seemed that Ambergris was not only secure but richer than ever before. Indeed, Aquelus had just formed an even stronger alliance with the Menites[68]—and took the first step toward the continuation of his bloodline by marrying the old Menite King's daughter Irene,[69] who by all accounts was not only beauti-

---

disability payments for awhile, until they found out I'd slipped on a tomato—and my wife had been nagging me to fix the mantel so I picked up the wood—from the store, first, I mean, and then that night I picked it up, but not so as to fix the mantel, you know, but to defend myself. Where was I? Oh, yes. So I go into the kitchen and I'm already thinking about making myself a sandwich with the left-over bread, so maybe I'm not paying as much attention as I should to the situation, and I'll be f— if there isn't this little person, this wee little person in a great big felt hat just sitting on the countertop, stuffing its face with the missus' chocolate cake. I looked at it and it looked at me, and I didn't move and it didn't move. It had great big eyes in its head, and a small nose, and a grin like all get out, only it had teeth, too, real big teeth, so it kind of spoiled the cheerfulness. Of course, it had already spoiled my wife's cake, so I was going to hit it with my plank of wood, only then it threw a mushroom at me and next thing I know it's morning and not only is the cake completely gone, but my wife is slapping my face and telling me to get up have I been drinking again don't I know I'm late for work. And later that day, when I'm setting the plates for dinner, I can't find any of the knives or forks. They're all gone. Oh, yes, and I almost forgot—I couldn't find the mushroom that hit me, either, but I'm telling you, it was heavier than it looked because it left this great big bump on top of me head. See?"

67   A few local souvenir shops, hoping to cash in on the pilgrim business, had begun to sell small statues and dolls of the mushroom dwellers, as well as potpourris made from mushrooms; a singular tavern called "The Spore of the Gray Cap" even sprouted up. (This tavern still exists today and serves some of the best cold beer in the city.)

68   Aquelus, in a brilliant maneuver, sent, along with his ambassador suggesting marriage, a bevy of Truffidian monks to Morrow, to negotiate a religious compromise that would allow the Menite kingdom and the Truffidian cappandom to reconcile their differences. Many of the arguments were extremely obscure. For example, the Menites believed God was to be found in all creatures, while the Truffidians, in their attempts to disassociate themselves from Manziism, believed rats were "of the Devil"; after weeks of ridiculous testimony on the merits ("their fur is pleasant to stroke") and deficiencies ("they spread disease") of rats, the compromise was that "of the Devil" should be struck from the Truffidian literature and replaced with the language "not of God" (originally changed to "made of God, but perhaps strayed from His teachings," but the Truffidians would not accept this). After a tortuous year of negotiation, and possibly more from exhaustion and boredom than because anyone actually *believed* in it, a settlement was reached, much to the relief of both rulers (who, although religious, had a strong streak of pragmatism). This agreement would last for 70 years, until made void by the Great Schism, and even then the dissolution of the contract transpired through the offices of the main Truffidian Church in the lands of the Kalif.

69   Chroniclers of the period call the marriage one of convenience, as evidence suggests Aquelus was a homosexual. But if begun in convenience, it soon deepened into mutual love. Certainly nothing rules out the possibility of Aquelus being bisexual, much as the homosexual scholar cappan of Ambergris, Meriad, writing two centuries later, would have us believe

ful but intelligent and could be expected to rule jointly with Aquelus, much as had, in their fashion, Sophia and Manzikert I.[70]

The same year, Aquelus secured his western borders against possible attacks by the Kalif[71] with the signing of a treaty in which Ambergrisian merchants would receive preferential treatment (especially the waiver of export taxes) and in return Aquelus promised to hold Ambergris in vassalage to the Kalif.[72]

The depth of Aquelus' deviousness is best illustrated by his response when the Kalif asked Aquelus to help suppress the southern rebellion of Stretcher Jones in return for further trade concessions. The Kalif, a devious man himself, also wrote that Aquelus' two half-brothers, closest successors to the cappanship, had been awarded the honor of studying in the Kalif's court, under the tutelage of his most able instructors, "amongst the most learned men in the civilized world." Aquelus, who had remained neutral in the conflict, replied that a Brueghelite armada of 100 sail already threatened Ambergris—a fleet actually some 200 miles away, contentedly plundering the southern islands—and he could not spare any ships to attack a friendly Truffidian power in the west; nonetheless, he gratefully accepted the privileges so generously offered by the Kalif. As for the invitation to his half-brothers, Aquelus returned his "devout and immense thanks," but they never went. Had they gone, the Kalif would almost certainly have kept them as hostages.[73]

However pleased Aquelus may have been at the adroit deflection of these potential threats, he still, as the annual fresh water squid expedition came ever closer, had two other dangerous situations that required

---

Aquelus was as bent as a broken bow.

[70]   Given Sophia and Manzikert I's example, it is not surprising that, until the fall of Trillian the Great Banker and his Banker Warriors, women served in the army, many of them attaining the highest ranks. Irene herself excelled as a hunter, could outrun and outfight the fastest of her five brothers, and had studied strategy with no less a personage than the Kalif's brilliant general, Masouf.

[71]   Please note that in these several references to the Kalif over the past 60 years, I have been referring to more than one ruler. The Kalif was chosen by secret ballot, and his identity never revealed, so as to protect against assassination attempts. Each Kalif was called simply "the Kalif." It is little wonder that the position of Royal Genealogist has so few rewards and so many frustrations.

[72]   If this arrangement seems extreme, we should consider that in effect the vassalage meant nothing—the Kalif was far too busy consolidating his recent eastern conquests (rebellions in these lands secretly funded by Aquelus, who left nothing to chance) to exact tribute or even send his own administrators to oversee the Cappandom. However, the Kalif may have outmaneuvered Aquelus in this regard, since in later centuries his successors would claim that the Cappandom of Ambergris belonged by right to them and would wage war to "liberate" it.

[73]   When Stretcher Jones was finally defeated, in a bloody battle that consolidated the Kalif's western supremacy for 300 years, Aquelus responded with the following words: "Being a friend of both sovereigns, I can only say, with God: I rejoice with them that do rejoice and weep with them that weep."

swift resolution. First, the clear shortfall in the spring crops, combined with the influx of new settlers (which he had no wish to see slacken) meant the possibility of famine. Second, the Haragck, a warlike clan of nomads who rode sturdy mountain ponies into battle, had begun to make inroads on his western borders.[74] Aquelus had no cavalry, but the Haragck had no fleet, and if it came to armed confrontation, Aquelus must have been confident—now that Morrow, in firm control of the northern Moth, was an ally—that he could stop the barbarians from crossing the river in force.

If the Haragck had been Aquelus' only enemy, he would still have had cause to thank his good fortune, but to the south a old adversary chose this moment to re-assert itself: the Aan descendants of the same Brueghel who had chased Manzikert I upriver. Drawn by the Aan exodus to the rich suburbs of Ambergris, these Brueghelites, as they called themselves, had begun to make trouble in the south. Understandably, they resented the loss of so much potential manpower when they found themselves beset by the still more southerly Gray Tribes. Most damaging, in light of the famine, the Brueghelites waged a trade war instead of a military war, which might at least have been resolved quickly. Some of their weapons included transit dues on Ambergrisian goods, heavy tolls on produce bound for the southern islands, and customs houses (backed by large, well-armed garrisons) along the Moth.[75]

Eventually, Aquelus would find a way to set the Haragck against the Brueghelites, eliminating both as a threat to Ambergris,[76] but as the freshwater squid season approached, Aquelus could not know that his bribes and political maneuverings would bear fruit. Thus, he made the fateful decree that three times as many ships would participate in the hunt as usual. His purpose was to offset the shortfall of crops with squid meat and byproducts, and to provide enough extra food to withstand a siege by either the Brueghelites or the Haragck.[77] In the event there was

---

[74]   Even before Stretcher Jones' fall these fierce warriors had been driven east by the slowly-advancing armies of the Kalif, who most certainly wished for them to weaken Ambergris. They have since passed out of history in a manner both shocking and absurd, but tangential to the concerns of this essay; suffice it to say that exploding ponies do not a pretty sight make, and that no one knows who was responsible for the worms.

[75]   With access to the sea blocked in this way, it is hardly surprising that Ambergris did not become the dominant naval power in the region until the days of Manzikert V, who established the Factory: a world-renowned shipbuilding center that could produce a galley in 12 hours, a fully-armed warship in two days.

[76]   And, coincidentally, providing Aquelus with an excellent example of what happens when an army with a strong cavalry fights a primarily naval force: nothing.

[77]   To this end, Aquelus built land walls to protect against an assault from the north, south, or east. He also set out defensive fortifications on the river side that included provisions for converting ships into floating barricades. Very little remains of any of these structures, as the contractor who won the bid, purportedly a former Brueghelite, used inferior materials; the extreme eastern side of the Religious Quarter still abuts the last nub of the land walls.

no siege, these provisions could accommodate the continuing flow of immigrants. The maneuvers to catch the squid, coincidentally, required a prowess and skill level far greater than necessary during an actual war, and so Aquelus also looked to toughen up his navy.

At the appointed time, Aquelus, at the head of nearly 5,000 men and women, took to the river in his 100 ships.[78] They would be gone for two weeks, the longest period of time Aquelus thought he could safely remain away from the capital. His new wife stayed behind. No two turns of fate—Irene's choice to stay at home and the enormity of the fleet that set off for the southern hunting grounds—would have a more profound effect on Ambergris during its early history.

---

[78] Even if there had been no famine, Aquelus would have been obliged to take nearly as many ships with him, for they would have to pass through the outer edge of Brueghelite waters in order to hunt the squid.

III

Any historian must take extreme care when discussing the Silence, for the enormity of the event demands respect. But when the historian in question, myself, explains the Silence for even a paltry pamphlet series, he must display a degree of solemnity in direct inverse proportion to the frivolity of the surrounding information. I find it unacceptable that you, the reader, should flip—a most disagreeably shallow word—from this pamphlet to the next, which may concern Best Masquerade Festivals or Where to Procure a Prostitute, without being made to grasp the awful ramifications of the Event. This requires no melodramatic folderol on my part, for the facts themselves should suffice: *upon Aquelus' return, the city of Ambergris lay empty, not a single living soul to be found upon any of its boulevards, alleyways, and avenues, nor within its many homes, public buildings, and courtyards.*

Aquelus' ships landed at docks where the only sound was the lapping of water against wood. Arrived in the early morning, having raced home to meet the self-imposed two-week deadline, the cappan found the city cast in a weak light, wreathed in mist come off the river. It must have been an ethereal scene—perhaps even a terrifying one.

At first, no one noticed the severity of the silence, but as the fleet weighed anchor and the crews walked out onto the docks, many thought it odd no one had come out to greet them. Soon, they noticed that the river defenses lay unmanned, and that the boats in the harbor around them, as they came clear of the mist, drifted, under no one's control.

When Aquelus noticed these anomalies, he feared the worst—an invasion by the Brueghelites during his absence—and ordered the crews back onto the ships. All ships but his own sailed back out into the middle of the River Moth, where they remained, laden with squid, at battle readiness.

Then Aquelus, anxious to find his new bride, personally led an expedition of 50 men into the city.[79] His fears of invasion seemed unfounded, for everywhere they went, Ambergris was as empty of enemies as it was of friends.

We are lucky indeed that among the leaders of the expedition was one Simon Jersak, a common soldier who would one day serve as the chief tax collector for the western provinces. Jersak left us with a full account

---

[79]   Aquelus' one weakness was a penchant for taking personal command of military expeditions. Such bravery often helped him win the day, but it would also be the cause of his death a few days shy of his 67th birthday, when, although incapacitated as we shall see, he insisted in riding a specially-trained horse into battle against the Skamoo, who had come down from the frozen tundra to attack Morrow. Aquelus never saw the northern giant who felled him with a battle axe.

of the expedition's journey into Ambergris, and I quote liberally from it
here:

> As the mist, which had hidden the true extent of the city's
> emptiness from us, dissipated, and as every street, every
> building, every shop on every corner, proved to have been
> abandoned, the Cappan himself trembled and drew his cloak
> about him. Men from among our ranks were sent randomly
> through the neighborhoods, only to return with the news
> that more silence lay ahead: meals lay on tables ready to eat,
> and carts with horses stood placidly by the sides of avenues
> that, even at the early hour, would normally have been
> abustle. But nowhere could we find a soul: the banks were un-
> locked and empty, while in the Religious Quarter, the flags
> still weakly fluttered, and the giant rats meandered about the
> courtyards, but, again, no people, even the fungi that had
> been our scourge had gone away. We quickly searched
> through the public baths, the granaries, the porticos, the
> schools—nothing. When we reached the Cappan's palace and
> found no one there—not his bride, not the least retainer—the
> Cappan openly wept, and yet underneath the tears his face
> was set as if for war. He was not the only man reduced to
> tears, for it soon became clear that our wives, our children,
> had all disappeared, and yet left behind all the signs of their
> presence, so we knew we had not been dreaming our lives
> away—they had existed, they had lived, but they were no lon-
> ger in the city . . . And so, disconsolate, robbed of all power to
> act against an enemy whose identity he did not know, my
> Cappan sat upon the steps of the palace and stared out across
> the city . . . until such time as one of the men who had been
> sent out discovered certain items on the old altar of the gray
> caps. At this news, the Cappan donned his cloak once more,
> wiped the tears from his face, drew his sword and sped to the
> site with all haste. As we followed behind our Cappan,
> through that city once so full of lives and now as empty as a
> tomb, there were none among us who did not, in our heart of
> hearts, fear what we would find upon the old altar. . .

What did they find upon the altar? An old weathered journal and two
human eyeballs preserved by some unknown process in a solid square
made of an unknown clear metal. Between journal and squared eyeballs
blood had been used to draw a symbol:[80]

---

[80]   Note the difference between this symbol and the one accompanying footnote 23. No
one has yet deciphered the original symbol, nor the meaning of its "dismemberment."

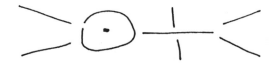

More ominous still, the legendary entrance, once blocked up, boarded over, lay wide open, the same stairs that had enticed Manzikert I beckoning now to Aquelus.

The journal was, of course, the one that had disappeared with Samuel Tonsure 60 years before. The eyes, a fierce blue, could belong to no one but Manzikert I. Who the blood had come from, no one cared to guess, but Aquelus, finally confronted with an enemy—for who could now doubt the return of the gray caps and their implication in the disappearance of the city's citizens?[81]—acted decisively.

Those commanders who argued that a military force should attack the underground found themselves overruled by Aquelus, who, in the face of almost overwhelming opposition, ordered all of his military commanders back to the ships, there to speed up the disembarkation so as to simultaneously process the squid, which otherwise would have rotted, and take up defensive positions throughout the city. Aquelus knew that the Haragck, upon hearing of the developments in Ambergris, might well attack, followed by the Brueghelites. Worse still, if the Cappaness could not be found, the political consequences—regardless of his love for her—would be disastrous. Might not the King of the Menites blame Aquelus for the death of his daughter?

Once the commanders had taken their leave, Aquelus transferred power to his minister of finance, one Thomas Nadal,[82] and announced that he intended to go down below himself.[83] The Cappan's decision

[81] Who but Sabon, of course. Sabon claims the Menites herded up the city's residents, massacred them some fifty miles from the city, and then left behind evidence to implicate the gray caps. She supports this ridiculous theory by pointing out the Cappaness' fate (soon to be revealed).

[82] Aquelus' lover for many years. What Irene thought of this arrangement we do not know, but we do know that she treated Nadal with much more kindness and respect than he treated her. Later, he would lose his position for it.

[83] The reason for this decision appears to have been both political and personal. Although Aquelus never commented on the decision either in public or private, Nadal wrote after the Cappan's death that (much to Nadal's distress) the Cappan truly loved Irene and, in the madness of his grief, was convinced she still lived underground. However, Nadal's account must be considered somewhat disingenuous, for if Aquelus believed his wife was alive, surely he would have allowed the military to send a large force after her? No, his sacrifice served several other purposes: if *he* did not go, then in the current state of anger and anguish, these men would surely take their own actions, possibly overthrowing him if he tried to stop them again. (Further, if his descent was seen as taken on behalf of Irene, perhaps the Menite king would look more kindly upon the Cappan.) Most importantly, Aquelus was an ardent stu-

horrified his ministers.[84] In addition to their personal affection for Aquelus, they feared losing their Cappan after all else that had been taken from them. Many, Nadal included, also feared the Haragck and the Brueghelites, but Aquelus countered these arguments by pointing out, truthfully enough, that his military commanders could easily lead any defense of the city—after all, they had drawn up a plan for just such a situation months ago. However, when Nadal then asked, "Yes, but who other than you can lead us to rebuild the morale of this shattered city?" Aquelus ignored him. Clearly, only he or his disappeared wife could make Ambergris a viable, living metropolis again. Still, down below he went, and down below he stayed for three days.[85]

Above ground, Aquelus' military commanders might well have staged a coup if not for the arrival that first night of Irene, only 12 hours after Aquelus' descent into the domains of the mushroom dwellers. By a quirk of chance both cruel and kind, she had left the capital for a two-day hunting trip in the surrounding countryside.[86]

Faced with the double-edged horror of the Silence and her husband's underground sojourn, Cappaness Irene never faltered, taking quick, decisive action. The rebellious commanders—Seymour, Nialson, and Rayne—she had thrown in prison. Simultaneously, she sent a fast boat to Morrow with a message for her father, asking for his immediate military support.[87] The Cappaness might have thought this ended her immediate

---

dent of history and must have known the details of the gray cap massacre and the subsequent burning of Cinsorium. No doubt he interpreted the gray caps' actions as revenge, and what must be avoided at all costs were reprisals against them, which would only lead to further retaliation on both sides, permanently destabilizing the city and making it impossible to rule. For, if the gray caps could make 25,000 people disappear without a trace, then Aquelus had only two choices: to leave the city forever, or reach some sort of accommodation. Perhaps perceiving that, having taken their revenge, the gray caps might be persuaded to negotiate, knowing also that *some* action must be taken, and even now hoping against hope to rescue his wife, he must have felt he had no choice. If Aquelus saw the situation in this light, then he was among the most selfless leaders Ambergris would ever have; such selflessness would carry a heavy price.

[84]   In the unlikely event that you are wondering how so many ministers survived the Silence, let me draw aside the veils of ignorance: Ministers were in no way exempted from periodic military service—in fact, their positions demanded it, since Aquelus was determined to keep the army as "civilian" as possible. Therefore, at least seven major ministers or their designees had sailed with the fleet.

[85]   Peter Copper, in his biography *Aquelus*, provides a poignant account of the Cappan's departure for the nether regions. Copper writes: "And so down he went, down into the dark, not as Manzikert I had done, for blood sport, but after much thought and in the belief that no other action could deliver his city from annihilation physical and spiritual. As the darkness swallowed him up and his footsteps became an ever fainter echo, his ministers truly believed they would never see him again."

[86]   Near Baudux, where the old ruins of Alfar still stand; grouse and wild pigs are plentiful in the region.

[87]   At the time she meant for such help to strengthen her internal position, not to defend the city from external threats.

problems, but she had severely under-estimated the mood of the men and women who had returned to the city. The soldiers guarding the rebel commanders freed their prisoners[88] and led a drunken mob of naval cadets to the front steps of the palace.

Inside, the Cappan's ministers had succumbed to panic—burning documents, stripping murals for their gold thread, and preparing to abandon the city under cover of darkness. When they came to the Cappaness with news of the insurrection and told her she must flee too, she refused and, as reported by Nadal, said to them:

> Every man who is born into the light of day must sooner or later die; and how could I allow myself the luxury of such cowardice when my husband took all our sins upon himself and went underground? May I never willingly shed the colors of Ambergris, nor see the day when I am no longer addressed by my title. If you, my noble ministers, wish to save your skins, you will have little difficulty in doing so. You have plundered the palace's riches and with luck you can reach the river and your boats moored there. But consider first whether when you reach safety you will not regret that you did not choose death. For those who remain, I shall ask only that you contain your blubbering and your shaking, for we must present a brave face if we are to survive this night.

Shamed by these words, Nadal and his colleagues had no choice but to follow the Cappaness out to the front steps of the palace. What followed must be considered the crowning achievement of early Ambergrisian nationalism—a moment that even today sends "chills down the spine" of the least patriotic city dweller. This daughter of Menites, this Cappaness without a Cappan, made her famous speech in which she called upon the mob to lay down its arms "in the service of a greater good, for the greater glory of a city unique in the history of the world. For if we can overcome this strife now, we shall never fear our-

---

[88]   That the Cappaness even managed to have the commanders imprisoned is testimony not only to Irene's strength of character, but to the civil service system put into place by Manzikert II. Most survivors of the Silence, when the Cappan's decision and the rumor of the mushroom dwellers' involvement became common knowledge, were for an all-out assault on the underground areas of the city. Indeed, despite the Cappaness' reiteration of Aquelus' orders, Red Martigan, a lieutenant on the Cappan's flagship, *did* lead a clandestine operation against the mushroom dwellers while the Cappan was still below ground. He took some 50 men to the city's extreme southeastern corner and entered the sewer system through an open culvert. Some days later, a friend who had not joined Martigan's expedition went down to the culvert to check on them. He found, neatly set out across the top of the culvert, the heads of Red Martigan and his 50 men, their eyes scooped out, their mouths to a one set in a kind of "grimacy" smile that was more frightening than the sight of the heads themselves. As to whether this action on Martigan's part hurt Aquelus' efforts underground, I can only offer the by now familiar, and irritating, refrain of "alas, we shall never know."

selves ever again."[89] She then detailed in cold-blooded fashion exactly who the rebels would have to kill to gain power and the full extent of the repercussions for a severely divided Ambergris: instant assimilation by the Brueghelites.[90] Further, she promised to strengthen the elected position of city mayor[91] and not to pursue reprisals against the mob itself, only its leaders.

Such was the magnetism of her personality and the passion of her speech that the mob turned on its leaders and brought them to the Cappaness in chains. Thus was the most severe internal crisis in the cappandom's short history diffused by Irene—the daughter of a foreign state with a heretical (to the Truffidians) religion. The people would not soon forget her.

But the Cappaness and her people had no time to draw breath, for on the second day of Aquelus' disappearance, 7,000 Haragck crossed the Moth and attacked Ambergris.[92] The Cappaness' forces, although taken by surprise, managed to keep the Haragck pinned down in the region of the docks, except for a contingent of 2,000, whom Irene allowed to break through to the city proper; she rightly sought to split the Haragck army

[89] While we can trust Nadal on the contents of the speech, he is a less trustworthy reporter of the actual verbiage: in his mouth, even the word "nausea" becomes both vainglorious and tediously melodramatic. He is, however, our only source.

[90] In reality, the Haragck were the greater threat.

[91] With the result that in later years, under weak cappans, the mayor actually had equal status.

[92] How did the Haragck cross over in such numbers? Atrocious swimmers, they somehow managed to make 7,000 inflatable animal skins—not, as rumor has it, made from their ponies, which they loved—and, fully armed, floated/dog paddled across the Moth. The reliefs that depict this event are among the only surviving examples of Haragck artwork:

The more perplexing question is: How did the Haragck know to attack so soon? Until recent times, it remained a mystery. Even a good rider could not have reached Ambergris' western borders in less than three days, and it would take three days to return after receiving the news—to say nothing of crossing the Moth itself. Five years ago, a carpenter in the western city of Nysimia accidentally unearthed a series of stone tablets carved with Haragck folk legends, and among these is one, dating from the right time period, that tells of a mushroom that sprang suddenly from the ground, and from which emerged an old man who told them to attack their "eastern enemies." Could it be that the mushroon dwellers managed to coordinate the Haragck attack with their Silence? And could the old man have been Tonsure himself?

in two, and in the labyrinthine streets of Ambergris, her own troops had a distinct advantage.[93]

Outflanked by the Ambergrisian ships behind them, which they had neglected to secure before establishing their beach head, the rest of the Haragck floundered; bereft of their ponies, they fought hand-to-hand on the shore while the Ambergrisian sailors assaulted them from behind with arrows and burning faggots. If the Haragck had managed to fire the ships, they might still have won the day, but instead they tried to capture them (rightly perceiving that without a navy they would never be able to conquer the region). Even so, the defenders barely managed to hold their positions through the night. But at dawn of the third day an advance guard of light horsemen arrived from Morrow and turned the fortunes of the defenders, who, tired and disheartened by all they had lost, would soon have given way to Haragck pressure.

By nightfall, the surviving Haragck had either tried to bob back over the Moth on their inflated animal skins or run north or south. Those who swam were slaughtered by the navy (the inflated animals skins were neither maneuverable nor inflammable);[94] those who fled south ended up as slaves to the Arch Duke of Malid[95] (who, in his turn, would be enslaved by the encroaching Brueghelites); those who fled north managed to evade the Menite army marching south, but then ran into the ferocious Skamoo with their spears made of ice.[96]

---

[93]   Seeking to redeem themselves, some rebel Ambergrisian commanders asked to be put in charge of the dangerous street-to-street fighting, and accounted themselves well enough that although they were deprived of their rank and returned to civilian life after the emergency, their lands were not confiscated, and neither were their lives.

[94]   Worse still, whatever animal they had made their floats from had wide pores and the skins, hastily prepared, suffered slow leakage; although the vast majority had survived the initial crossing, many sank upon the return trip.

[95]   A notorious cannibal with a taste for the western tribes; that Aquelus kept him on retainer as a buffer against the Brueghelites may have been a political necessity, but it was still morally reprehensible.

[96]   The only reason the Haragck regrouped so quickly—they would pose a threat to Ambergris again a mere three years later—is that their great general Heckira Blgkkydks escaped the Skamoo with seven of his men and, his anger fearsome to behold (more fearsome than that of Manzikert I), eventually reached the fortress of Gelis, where the Haragck Khan Grnnck (who had ordered the amphibious attack on Ambergris) had taken refuge. Starving, shoeless, his clothes in tatters, Blgkkydks burst into the Khan's court, reportedly roared out, "*Inflatable animal skins?!*", cut off his ruler's head with a single blow of his sword, and promptly proclaimed himself Khan; he would remain Khan for 20 years before the destruction of the Haragck as a political/cultural entity. Luckily, he spent the next three years annihilating the Skamoo, for he had suffered terribly at their hands, and by the time he refocused on Ambergris, the city had sufficiently recovered to defend itself. (One long-term effect on the Haragck as a consequence of their failed attack on Ambergris was a crucial lack of good translators, almost all of whom had been killed by the burning faggots of Ambergris. Thus, when Blgkkydks issued a formal demand for Ambergrisian surrender as a pretense for declaring war, the threat which accompanied the demand read, "I will put fried eggs up your armpits," when the old Haragck saying *should* have read, "I will tear you armpit to armpit like a chicken.")

That night, Cappan Aquelus made his way back to the surface on his hands and knees, his hair a shocking white and his eyes plucked from him;[97] they would never, even posthumously, be returned to him.[98] Weak with hunger and delirium, Aquelus soon recovered under the personal ministrations of his wife, who was also a noted surgeon. Like Manzikert I, he would never discuss what had happened to him. Unlike Manzikert I, he would rule again, but in the three days of his absence, the dynamics of power had undergone a radical shift. His Cappaness had proven herself quite capable of governing and had demonstrated remarkable toughness in the face of catastrophe. The Cappandom was also indebted to the Menite King for his help.

Finally, not only had Aquelus been blinded, but even many of his own ministers concluded that his underground adventure had been an act of rashness and/or cowardice. Never again would Aquelus be the sole ruling authority; from now on it would be his wife who, backed by her father, ruled in matters of defense and foreign diplomacy. More and more, Aquelus would oversee building projects and provide valuable advice to his wife. That she ever intended to usurp the cappanship is unlikely,[99] but once she had it, the people would not let her abdicate it.[100]

The problem went deeper than this, however. Although Aquelus had sacrificed his sight for them—indeed, many have speculated that Aquelus reached a pact with the mushroom dwellers that saved the

---

[97]   Some horticulturists—none of the ones consulted for this travel guide—have pointed out that the tissue in eyeballs provides excellent nutrient value for fungi.

[98]   We cannot forget the late Voss Bender's opera about the Silence, *The King Underground*, which—although it contains a patently idiotic wish fulfillment sequence in which the Cappan single-handedly slays two dozen midgets dressed as mushroom dwellers, after which "all quaver before him"—has a rather profound and singular beauty to it, especially in the scene where the Cappan crawls back up the steps to the surface, hears the voice of his Irene, and, his hand upon her cheek (aft, not nether), sings:

> *My fingers are not blind,*
> *and they hunger still*
> *for the sight of you;*
> *and you, not seen but seeing,*
> *can you bear the sight of me?*

As Bender's opera is more popular than any history book, his vision has become the popular conception of the event, conveniently ignoring the unfortunate Nadal's passion for the Cappan. Luckily, many subjects—including the Haragck's use of floating animal skins—Bender thought to be unsuitable for opera, and it is in such low domains, far below the public eye, that creatures such as myself are still allowed to crawl about while muttering our "expert" opinions.

[99]   Although the Menite king did pressure her to annex Ambergris for Morrow; already firmly committed to her adopted people, she put him off by invoking the specter of intervention by the Kalif should the Cappandom fall into Menite hands.

[100]   That Aquelus still loved her is undeniable, and he himself made no complaint, although many of his ministers, who effectively lost power as a result, did complain—vociferously.

city—the people no longer trusted him, and would never regain their former love for him. That he had gone below and survived when so many
had not was proof enough for the common naval cadet that their
Cappan had conspired with the enemy. Tales circulated that he snuck
out at midnight to seek council with the mushroom dwellers. It was said
that a tunnel had been dug from his private chambers to the mushroom
dwellers' underground lair. Most ridiculous of all, some claimed that
Aquelus was actually a doppelganger, made of fungus, under the mushroom dwellers' control; he had, after all, forbidden anyone from attacking them.[101]

The latter part of Aquelus' "reign" was marked by increasingly desperate attempts to regain the respect of his subjects. To this end, he would
have himself led out into the city disguised as a blind beggar and listen
to the common laborers and merchants as they walked by his huddled
form. He also gave away huge sums of money to the poor, so seriously
draining the treasury that Irene was forced to order a halt to his largesse.
Aquelus' spending, combined with the promises made to entice people
to settle in Ambergris, led to the selling of titles and, in later years, a
landed aristocracy that would prove a constant source of treasonous ambition.

Despite these failings, Aquelus managed partial redemption by having four children with Irene, although surely the irony of the Cappaness
being the instrument of his salvation was not lost on him. These children—Mandrel, Tiphony, Cyril, and Samantha—became Aquelus' delight and main reason for living. While Irene ruled, he doted on them,
and the people doted on them too. In Aquelus' love for his children,
Ambergrisians saw the shadow of their former love for him, and many
forgave him his involvement with the mushroom dwellers—a charge almost certainly false anyway.

Thus, although in many ways tragic, the partnership of Cappaness
and Cappan would define and redefine Ambergris—both internally and
in the world beyond—for another 30 years.[102] They would be haunted
years, however, for the legacy of the Silence would permeate Ambergris
for generations—in the sudden muting of the voices of children, of
women, of those men who had stayed behind. For those inhabitants
who had lost their families, their friends, the city was nothing more than
a giant morgue, and no matter how they might console one another, no

---

[101]   Nadal, who had stuck by Aquelus through all of this, reports to us a conversation in
which the Cappan chastised Nadal for his anger at the many slurs, saying, "They have suffered a terrible loss. If to heal they must remake me in the image of the villain, let them."

[102]   It is outside the scope of this essay to tell of the continuation of the Manzikert line or of
the mushroom dwellers; suffice it to say, the mushroom dwellers are still with us, while the
Manzikerts exist only as a borderline religion and as a rather obnoxious model of black, bee-
tle-like motored vehicle.

matter how they might set to their tasks with almost super-human intensity, the better to block out the memories, they could never really escape the Silence, for the "City of Remembrance and Memorial," as one poet called it, was all around them.[103] It was common in those early, horrible years—still scarred by famine, despite the reduction in the population—for men and women to break down on the street in a sudden flux of tears.

The Truffidian priest Michael Nysman came to the city as part of a humanitarian mission the year after the Silence and was shocked by what he found there. In a letter to his diocese back in Nicea, he wrote:

> The buildings are gray and their windows often like sad, empty eyes. The only sound in the street is that of weeping. Truly, there is a great emptiness to the city, as if its heart had stopped beating, and its people are a grim, suspicious folk. They will hardly open their doors to you, and have as many locks as can be imagined ... Few of them sleep more than two or three hours at a time, and then only when someone else is available to watch over them. They abhor basements, and have blocked up all the dirt floors with rocks. Nor will they suffer the slightest section of wall to harbor fungus of any kind, but will scrape it off immediately, or preferably, burn it. Some neighborhoods have formed Watches during the night that go from home to home with torches, making sure that all within are safe. Most eerie and discomfiting, the citizens of this bleak city leave lanterns burning all through the night, and in such proliferation that the city, in such a hard, all-seeing light, cannot fail to seem already enveloped in the flames of Hell, it only remaining for the Lord of the Nether World to take up his throne and scepter and walk out upon its streets. Just yesterday some unfortunate soul tried to rob a watchmaker and was torn to pieces before it was discovered he was not a gray cap ... Worst of all: no children; the schools have closed down and their radiant, innocent voices are no longer heard in the church choirs. The city is childless, barren—it has only visions of the happy past, and what parent will bring a child into a city that contains the ghosts of so

---

[103] Little wonder that many moved away, to other cities, and that their places were taken by settlers from the southern Aan islands and, north, from Morrow. Additional bodies were drummed up amongst the tribes neighboring the city; Irene offered them jobs and reduced taxation in return for their relocation. The influx of these foreign cultures into the predominantly Aan city forever diversified and rejuvenated the local culture ... We might well ask *why* so many people were willing to reinhabit a place where 25,000 souls had disappeared, but, in fact, the government deliberately spread misinformation, blaming the invading Haragck and the Brueghelites for the loss of life. In the confusion of the times, it appears many outside of the city did not even hear the real story. Others chose not to believe it, for it was not, after all, a very believable story. Thus, for several centuries, historians who should have known better promulgated false stories of plague and civil war.

many children? Some parents—although usually only one
parent has survived—believe that their children will return,
and some tried to unblock the hole by the old altar before the
Cappaness made it a hanging offense. Still others wait by the
door at dinner, certain that a familiar small shape will walk
by. It breaks my heart to see this. Can such a city ever now
lose a certain touch of cruelty, of melancholy, a lingering
hint of the macabre? Is this, then, the grief of the gray caps 60
years later given palpable form? I fear I can do little more
here at this time; I am caught up in their sadness, and thus
cannot give them solace for it, although unscrupulous
priests sell "dispensations" which they say will protect the
user from the mushroom dwellers while simultaneously ab-
solving the disappeared of their sins.

What are we, in this modern era, to make of the assertion that 25,000
people simply disappeared, leaving no trace of any struggle? Can it be believed? If the number were 1,000 could we believe it? The answer the honest historian reluctantly comes to is that the tale must be believed, because it happened. Not a single person escaped from the mushroom
dwellers. More hurtful still, it left behind a generation known simply as
the Dispossessed.[104] The city recovered, as all cities do, and yet for at least
100 years,[105] this absence, this silence, insinuated itself into the happiest
of events: the coronations and weddings of cappans, the extraordinarily
high birthrate (and low mortality rate), the victories over both Haragck
and Brueghelite. The survivors retook their homes uneasily, if at all, and
some areas, some houses, stood abandoned for a generation, never
re-entered, so that dinners set out before the Silence rotted, moldered,
and eventually fossilized.[106] There remained the terrible conviction
among the survivors that they had brought this upon themselves
through Manzikert I's massacre of the gray caps and Sophia's torching
of Cinsorium. It was hard not to feel that it was God's judgment to see
Ambergris destroyed soul by soul.[107]

---

[104]   Given the magnitude of the loss, remarkably few survivors killed themselves. We must
credit the industriousness of Irene and Aquelus—the example they set and the work they provided.

[105]   For, at the 100-year mark, the mushroom dwellers first began to integrate themselves
with Ambergrisian society, albeit as garbage collectors.

[106]   As recently as 50 years ago, a few homes were found in this state: they had been boarded
up and then built over, and were discovered by accident during a survey expedition to install
street lamps. The surveyors found the atmosphere within these rooms (the dust over everything, the plates and kitchen implements corroded, the smell dry as death, the dried flowers
set out as a memorial) so oppressive that after a brief reconnaissance, they not only boarded
them back up, but filled them in, despite a vigorous protest from myself and various other
old farts at the Ambergrisian Historical Society.

[107]   If so, then the Devil has saved it several times over.

Worst of all, there was never any clue as to the fate of the Disappeared, and in the absence of information, imaginations, as always, imagined the worst. Soon, in the popular folklore of the times, the Disappeared had not only been killed, but had been subjected to terrible tortures and defilements. Although some still claimed the Brueghelites had carried off the 25,000, most people truly believed the mushroom dwellers had been responsible. Theories as to *how* cropped up much more frequently than *why* because, short of revenge, no one could fathom *why*. It was said that the ever-present fungus had released spores that, inhaled, put all of the city's inhabitants to sleep, after which the mushroom dwellers had come out and dragged them underground. Others claimed that the spores had not put the Disappeared to sleep, but had actually, in chemical combination, formed a mist that corroded human flesh, so that the inhabitants had slowly melted into nothing. The truth is, we shall never know unless the mushroom dwellers deign to tell us.

IV[108]

But what of Samuel Tonsure's journal? What, after all these years, did
it contain? Aquelus wisely had it placed in the care of the librarians at
the Manzikert Memorial Library.[109] In essence, the book disappeared
again, as—hidden and known by only a few—it was not part of the public
discourse.[110] Aquelus made the librarians swear not to reveal the contents
of the journal, or even hint at its existence to anyone, on pain of death.
The journal was kept in a locked strong box, which was then put inside
another box. We can certainly understand why Aquelus kept it a secret,
for the journal tells a tale both macabre and frightening. If the general
populace had, at the time, known of its contents, they would no longer
have had anything to fear from their imaginations—only to have their
worst nightmares given validation. The burden on Aquelus and Irene of
not releasing this information was terrible—Nadal, who was privy to
most state secrets, reports that the two frequently fought over whether
the journal should be made public, often switching sides in
mid-argument.

To head librarian Michael Abrasis fell the task of examining the journal, and luckily he kept notes. Abrasis describes the journal as:

> . . . leather-bound, 6 x 9, with at least 300 pages, of which al-
> most all have been used. The leather has been contaminated
> by a green fungus that, ironically, has helped to preserve the
> book; indeed, were the lichen to be removed, the covers
> would disintegrate, so ingrained and so uniform are these
> green "shingles." Of the ink, it would appear that the first 75
> pages are of a black ink easily recognizable as distilled from
> whale's oil. However, the sections thereafter are written using
> a purple ink that, after careful study, appears to have been

---

[108] At this point in the narrative I begin to make my formal farewells, for those of you who
ever even noticed my marginal existence. By now the blind mechanism of the story has sur-
passed me, and I shall jump out of it's way in order to let it roll on, unimpeded by my frantic
gesticulations for attention. The time-bound history is done: there is only the matter of
sweeping the floors, taking out the garbage, and turning off the lights. Meanwhile, I shall retire once more to the anonymity of my little apartment overlooking the Voss Bender Memorial Square. This is the fate of hostorians: to fade ever more into the fabric of their history,
untile they no longer exist outside of it. Remember this while you navigate the afternoon
crowd in the Religious Quarter, your guidebook held limply in your pudgy left hand as your
right hand struggles to balance a half-pint of bitter.

[109]   The library already housed a number of unique manuscripts, including the anonymous
Dictionary of Foreplay, Stretcher Jones' *Memories*, a few sheets of palm-pulp paper with mushroom dweller scrawls on them, and 69 texts on preserving flesh, stolen from the Kalif, that
had been of great use to Manzikert II while conducting his body parts shopping spree among
the saints.

[110]   As it is, when copies were made available 50 years later, it forced Cappan Manzikert VI to
abdicate and join a monastery.

distilled from some sort of fungus. These sections exude a distinctly sweet odor.[111]

Abrasis had copies of the journal made and secreted them away—which accounts for the existence of the text in the city to this day—but, unfortunately, the original was pawned to the Kalif during the tragic last days of Trillian.

We have already discussed the early days of Ambergris as recounted in Tonsure's journal, but what of the last portion of the journal? The first entry Tonsure managed to make following his descent[112] reads:

> Dark and darker for three days. We are lost and cannot find our way to the light. The Cappan still pursues the gray caps, but they remain flitting shadows against the pale, dead glow of the fungus, the mushrooms that stink and writhe and even seem to speak a little. We have run out of food and are reduced to eating from the mushrooms that rise so tall in these caverns we must seek sustenance from the stem alone—maddeningly aware of succulent leathery lobes too high to reach. We know we are being watched, and this has unnerved all but the strongest men. We can no longer afford to sleep except in shifts, for too often we have woken to find another of our party missing. Early yesterday I woke to find a stealthy gray cap about to murder the Cappan himself, and when I gave the alarm, this creature smiled most chillingly, made a chirping sound, and ran down the passageway. We gave chase, the Cappan and I and some 20 others. The gray cap escaped, and when we returned our supplies were gone, as were the 15 men who had remained behind. The gray caps' behavior here is as different as night is to day—here they are fast and crafty and we hardly catch sight of them before they strike. I do not believe we will make it to the surface alive.

Tonsure's composure is admirable, although his sense of time is certainly faulty—he writes that three days had passed, when it must still have been but a single night, for Manzikert I was found in the library the very next morning.[113] Another entry, dated just a few "days" later, is more disjointed and, one feels, soaked through with terror:

---

[111]   Alas, Abrasis never commented on the consistency of the handwriting!

[112]   With the exception of his entry describing the massacre and Manzikert I's decision to go underground.

[113]   No less a skeptic than Sabon half-heartedly documents the folktale that the Manzikert I who reappeared in the library was actually a construct, a doppelganger, created out of fungus. Although ridiculous on the face of it, we must remember how often tales of doppelgangers intertwine with the history of the mushroom dwellers.

Three more gone—taken. In the night. Morning now. What
do we find arranged around us like puppet actors? We find arranged around us the heads of those who have been taken
from us. Ramkin, Starkin, Weatherby, and all the rest.
Staring. But they cannot stare. They have no eyes. I wish I had
no eyes. Cappan long ago gave up on all but the idea of escape. And it eludes us. We can taste it—the air sometimes
fresher, so we know we are near the surface, and yet we might
as well be a hundred miles underground! We must escape
these blind staring heads. We eat the fungus, but I feel it eats
us instead. Cappan near despair. Never seen him this way.
Seven of us. Trapped. Cappan just stares at the heads. Talks to
them, calls them by name. He's not mad. He's not mad. He
has it easier in these tunnels than I.[114] And still they watch
us . . .

Tonsure then describes the deaths of the men still with the Cappan
and Tonsure—two by poisoned mushrooms, two by blow dart, and one
by a trap set into the ground that cut the man's legs off and left him to
bleed to death. Now it is just the Cappan and Tonsure, and, somehow,
Tonsure has recovered his nerve:

We wonder now if there ever were such a dream as above
ground, or if this place has always been the reality and we
simply deluding ourselves. We shamble through this darkness, through the foul emanations of the fungus, like lost
souls in the Nether World . . . Today, we beseeched them to
end it, for we could hear their laughter all around us, could
glimpse the shadows of their passage, and we are past fear.
End it, do not toy with us. It is clear enough now that here,
on their territory, they are our Masters. I looked over my
notes last night and giggled at my innocence. "Degenerate
traces of a once-great civilization" indeed. We have passed
through so many queer and ominous chambers, filled with
otherworldly buildings, otherworldly sights—the wonders I
have seen! Luminous purple mushrooms pulsing in the darkness. Creatures of vivid blue with four legs and with six feeding upon their spores. Eyeless, pulsating, blind salamanders
that slowly ponder the dead darkness through other senses.
Winged animals that speak in voices. Headless things that
whisper our names. And ever and always, the gray caps. We
have even spied upon them at play, although only because
they disdain us so, and seen the monuments carved from
solid rock that beggar the buildings above ground. What I
would give for a single breath of fresh air. Manzikert resists

---

[114] Another indication Manzikert was a little man.

even these fancies; he has become sullen, responding to my words with grunts and clicks and whistles . . . More disturbing still, we have yet to retrace our steps; thus, this underground land must be several times larger than the above ground city, much as the submerged portion of an iceberg is larger than the part visible to a sailor.

Clearly, however, Tonsure never regained his time-sense, for on this day, marked by him as the sixth, Manzikert would already have been five days above ground, eyeless but alive. Perhaps Tonsure deluded himself that Manzikert remained by his side to strengthen his own resolve, or perhaps the fringe-historians have for once been too conservative: instead of a golem Manzikert being returned to the surface, perhaps the underground Manzikert was replaced with a golem. Tonsure certainly never tells us what happened to Manzikert; his entries simply do not mention him after approximately the ninth day. By the twelfth day, the entries become somewhat disjointed, and the last coherent entry, before the journal dissolves into fragments, is this pathetic paragraph:

> They're coming for me. They've had their fun—now they'll finish me. To my mother: I have always tried to be your obedient son. To my illegitimate son and his mother: I have always loved you, although I didn't always know it. To the world that may read this: know that I was a decent man, that I meant no harm, that I lived a life far less pious than I should have, but far better than many. May God have mercy on my soul.[115]

And yet, apparently, they did not "finish" him,[116] for another 150 pages of writing follow this entry. Of these 150 pages, the first two are full of weird scribbles punctuated by a few coherent passages,[117] all writ-

---

[115] Then as now, bastards were a sel-a-dozen amongst the clergy; how much more interesting to know *where* this mother and child resided—Nicea, perhaps?

[116] Sabon dryly writes, "Tonsure was already the most finished man in the history of the world. How then could they improve upon perfection?"

[117] Most of the scribbles are erotic in nature and superfluous. Of the writings, the following lines appear in no known religious text and are accompanied by the notation "d.t.," meaning "dictated to." Scholars believe that the lines are an example of mushroom dweller poetry translated by Tonsure.

> *We are old.*
> *We have no teeth.*
> *We swallow what we chew.*
> *We chew up all the swallows.*
> *Then we excrete the swallows.*
> *Poor swallows—they do not fly*
> *once they are out of us.*

ten using the strange purple ink described by Abrasis as having been distilled from fungus. These pages provide damning evidence of a mind
gone rapidly deranged, and yet they are followed by 148 lucid pages of
essays on Truffidian religious rituals, broken infrequently by glimpses
into Tonsure's captivity. The essays have proven invaluable to pres-
ent-day Truffidians who wish to read an "eyewitness" account of the
early church, but baffle those of us who naturally want answers to the
mysteries inherent in the Silence and the journal itself. The most obvious question is, why did the mushroom dwellers suffer Tonsure to live?
On this subject, Tonsure at least provides his own theory, the explanation inserted into the middle of a paragraph on the Truffidian position
on circumcision:[118]

> Gradually, as they come to me time after time and rub my
> bald head, it has struck me why I have been spared. It is such a
> simple thing that it makes me laugh even to contemplate it: I
> look like a mushroom. Quick! Alert the authorities! I must
> send a message aboveground—tell them all to shave their
> heads! I can hardly contain my laughter even now, which
> startles my captors and makes it hard to write legibly.

Later, stuck between a discussion on the divine properties of frogs and
a diatribe against inter-species marriages, Tonsure provides us with another glimpse into the mushroom dwellers' world that entices the reader
like a flash of gold:

> They have led me to a vast chamber unlike any place I have
> ever seen, above or below. There stands before me a palace of
> shimmering silver built entirely of interlocking mushrooms,
> and festooned with lichen and moss of green and blue. A
> sweet, sweet perfume hangs pungent in the air. The columns
> that support this dwelling are, it appears, made of living tis-
> sue, for they recoil at the touch . . . from the doorway steps
> the ruler of the province, who is herself but a foot soldier
> compared to the mightiest ranks that can be found here. All
> glows with an unearthly splendor and supplicant after sup-
> plicant kneels before the ruler and begs for her blessing. I am
> made to understand that I must come forward and allow the
> ruler to rub my head for luck. I must go.

If this is indeed mushroom dweller poetry, then we must conclude that either the transla-
tor—under stress and with insufficient light—did a less than superlative job, or that the mushroom dwellers had a spectacular lack of poetic talent.

[118] They're for it, by the way.

Other entries hint that Tonsure made at least two attempts to escape, each followed by harsh punishment, the second of which may have been partial blinding,[119] and at least one sentence suggests that afterwards he was led secretly to the surface: "Oh, such torture, to be able to hear the river chuckling below me, to feel the night wind upon my face, to smell the briny silt, but to see *nothing*." However, Tonsure may have been blindfolded or been so old and have existed in darkness for so long that his eyes could not adapt to the outside, day or night. Tonsure's sense of time being suspect, we can only guess as to his age when he wrote that entry.

Finally, toward the end of the journal, Tonsure relates a series of what surely must be waking dreams, created by his long diet of fungus and the attendant fumes thereof:

> They wheeled me into a steel chamber and suddenly a window appeared in the side of the wall and I saw before me a vision of the city that frightened me more than anything I have yet seen below ground. As I watched, the city grew from just the docks built by my poor lost Cappan to such immense structures that half the sky was blotted out by them, and the sky itself fluxed light, dark, and light again in rapid succession, clouds moving across it in a flurry. I saw a great palace erected in a few minutes. I saw carts that moved without horses. I saw battles fought in the city and without. And, in the end, I saw the city reduced to ruins, the towers fallen to the ground and, after a time, when the jungles had eaten the remains of the towers and the river had flooded the streets, the gray caps came out once again into the light and rebuilt their old city and everything was as before. The one I call my Keeper wept at this vision, so surely he must have seen it too?[120]

Then follow the last 10 pages of the journal, filled with so concrete and frenzied a description of Truffidian religious practices that we can only conclude that he wrote these passages as a bulwark against insanity and that, ultimately, when he ran out of paper, he ran out of hope—ei-

---

[119] Lacond's pet theory, sneered at by Sabon: the two shall continue to make war, history itself their battlefield, hands caressing each other's necks, legs entwined for all eternity, and yet neither shall ever win in such a subjective area as theoretical history. (Although *my* pet theory is that Lacond and Sabon are the conflicting sides of the same hopelessly divided historian. If only they could reach some understanding?)

[120] Sabon has suggested that the mushroom dwellers had a form of zoetrope or "magic lantern" that could project images on a wall. As for the reference to a "Keeper," it appears nowhere else in the text and thus is frustratingly enigmatic. Many a historian has ended his career dashed to pieces on the rocks of Tonsure's journal; I refuse to follow false beacons, myself.

ther writing on the walls[121] or succumbing to the despair that must have been a tangible part of every one of his days below ground. Indeed, the last line of the journal reads: "An inordinate love of ritual can be harmful to the soul, unless, of course, in times of great crisis, when ritual can protect the soul from fracture."

Thus passes into silence one of the most influential and mysterious characters in the entire history of Ambergris. Because of Tonsure, Truffidianism and the Cappandom cannot, to this day, be separated from each other. His tutorials informed the administrative genius of Manzikert II, while his counsel both inflamed and restrained Manzikert I. Aquelus studied his journal endlessly, perhaps seeking some clue to which only he, with his own experience below ground, was privy. Tonsure's biography of Manzikert I—never out of print—and his journal remain the sources historians turn to for information about early Ambergris and early Truffidianism.

If the journal proves anything it is that another city exists below the city proper, for Cinsorium was not truly destroyed when Sophia razed its above ground manifestation. Unfortunately, all attempts to explore the under ground have met with disaster,[122] and now that the city has no central government, it is unlikely that there will be further attempts—especially since such authority as does exist would prefer the mysteries remain mysteries for the sake of tourism.[123] It would seem that two separate and very different societies shall continue to evolve side by side, separated by a few vertical feet of cement. In our world, we see their red flags and how thoroughly they clean the city, but we are allowed no similar impact on their world except through the refuse that goes down our sewer pipes.

The validity of the journal has been called into question several times over the years—lately by the noted writer Sirin, who claims that the journal is actually a forgery based on Manzikert I's biography. He points to the writer Maxwell Glaring, who lived in Ambergris some 40 years after the Silence. Glaring, Sirin says, carefully studied the biography written

---

121   I have a certain affection for Lacond's theory that Tonsure's journal is merely the introduction to a vast piece of fiction/nonfiction scrawled on the walls of the underground sewer system, and that this work, if revealed to the world above ground, would utterly change our conception of the universe. Myself, I believe such a work might, at best, change our conception of Lacond—for, if it existed, at least one of his theories might be accepted by mainstream historians.

122   The most recent, 30 years ago, resulting in the loss of the entire membership of the Ambergrisian Historical Society, and two of its dog mascots.

123   Until recently you could take an ostensible tour of the mushroom dwellers' tunnels run by a certain Guido Zardoz. After tourists had imbibed refreshments laced with hallucinogens, Zardoz would lead them down into his basement, where several dwarfs in felt hats awaited the signal to leap out from hiding and say "Boo!" Reluctantly, the district councilor shut the establishment down after an old lady from Stockton had a heart attack.

by Tonsure, incorporated elements of it into his fake, invented the underground accounts, used an odd purple ink distilled from the freshwater squid[124] for the last half, and then "produced" the "journal" via a friend in the administrative quarter who spread the rumor that Aquelus had suppressed it for 50 years. Sirin's theory has its attractions—Glaring, after all, forged a number of state documents to help his friends embezzle money from the treasury, and his novels often contain an amount of desperate derring-do in keeping with the fragments of reason found in the latter portion of the journal.[125] Adding to the controversy, Glaring was murdered—his throat cut as he crossed a back alley on his way to the post office—shortly after the release of the journal.

Sabon prefers the alternate theory that, yes, Glaring *did* forge parts of the journal, but only the sections on obscure Truffidian religious practices[126]—these pages then inserted to replace pages removed by the government for national security reasons. Glaring was then killed by the Cappan's operatives to preserve the secret. Unfortunately, a fire gutted part of the palace's administrative core, destroying the records that might have provided a clue as to whether Glaring was on the national payroll. Sabon further speculates that Glaring's embezzlement had been discovered and was used as leverage to make him forge the journal pages, for otherwise, some of his relatives having disappeared in the Silence, he would have been disinclined to suppress evidence as to mushroom dweller involvement.[127] Sabon explains away the few paragraphs dealing with Tonsure's captivity as Glaring's genius in knowing that a good forgery must address issues of its authenticity—the journal must therefore contain some evidence of Tonsure's underground experiences. These paragraphs, meanwhile, *Lacond* claims are genuine, pulled from the real journal.[128]

Another claim, which has taken on the status of popular myth, suggests that the mushroom dwellers skillfully rewrote and replaced many

---

[124]   And since discontinued—too runny.

[125]   A passage from his *Midnight for Munfroe* reads "It was in this cloying darkness, the lights from Krotch's house stabbing at me from beyond the grave, that I could no longer hold onto the idea that I was going to be all right. I would have to kill the bastard. I would have to do it before he did it to me. Because if he did it to me, there would be no way for me to do it to him."

[126]   Certainly possible—Glaring could have interviewed any number of Truffid monks or read any number of books, few now surviving, on the subject.

[127]   Sabon notes that Glaring kept copies of his forgeries. Further, that a letter Glaring wrote to a friend mentions "a rather unusual memoir of sorts I've been told to duplicate." Sabon believes Glaring made a *true* copy of the original pages. If so, no one has found this true copy.

[128]   It is perhaps too cruel to think of Tonsure not only struggling to express himself, to communicate, underground, but also struggling *above ground* to be heard as Glaring tries equally hard to snuff him out.

pages, to keep inviolate their secrets, but this theory is rendered ridiculous by the fact that the journal was left on the altar—a fact confirmed by Nadal, the then minister of finance. This eyewitness account also nixes the first of Sabon's theories: that the entire journal is a forgery.[129]

To further complicate matters, an obscure sect of Truffidians who inhabit the ruined fortress of Zamilon near the eastern approaches to the Kalif's empire claim to possess the last true page of Tonsure's journal. According to legend, Trillian's men once stayed at the fortress on their way to the Kalif, bearing the journal that, the careful reader will remember, was hocked by the cappandom. A monk crept into the room where the journal was kept and stole the last page, apparently as revenge for the left femur of their leader having been spirited away by agents of Cappan Manzikert II 300 years before.

The front of the page consists of more early Truffidian religious ritual, but the back of the page reads as follows:

> We have traveled through a series of rooms. The first rooms were tiny—I had to crawl into them, and even then barely squeezed through, banging my head on the ceiling. These rooms had the delicate yet ornate qualities of an illuminated manuscript, or one of the miniature paintings so beloved by the Kalif. Golden lichen covered the walls in intricate patterns, crossed through with a royal red fungus that formed star shapes. Strangely, in these rooms I felt as if I had unlimited space in which to move and breathe. Each room we entered was larger and more elaborate than its predecessor—although never did I have the sense that anyone had ever lived in the rooms, despite the presence of chairs, tables, and bookshelves—so that I found myself bedazzled by the light, the flourishes, the engraved ceilings. And yet, oddly enough, as the curious rooms expanded, my sense of claustrophobia expanded too, so that it took over all my thoughts . . . This continued for days and days, until I had become numb to the glamour and dulled to the claustrophobia. When hungry, we broke off pieces of the walls and ate of them. When thirsty, we squeezed the chair arms and greedily drank the drops of mossy elixir that came from them. Eventually, we would push open the now immense doors leading to the next room and see only distantly the far wall . . . Then, just when I thought this journey might never end—and yet surely could not continue—I was brought through one final door (as large as many of the rooms we had passed through). Beyond this door, it was night, lit vaguely by the stars, and we had come out upon a hill of massive columns, through which I could

---

[129]   Although Sabon, predictably, claims Nadal's eyewitness account could also have been forged by Glaring.

see, below us, a vast city that looked uncannily like Cinsorium, surrounded by a forest. A sweet, sweet breeze blew through the trees and lifted the grass along the hill. Above, the immense sky—and I thought, I *thought*, that I had been brought above ground, for the entire world seemed to spread out before me. But no, I realized with sinking heart, for far above me I could see, when I squinted, that, luminous blue against the blackness, the lines of strange constellations had been set out there, using some instrument more precise than known of above ground. And yet the stars themselves *moved* in phosphorescent patterns of blue, green, red, yellow, and purple, and after a moment I discovered that these "stars" were actually huge moths gliding across the upper darkness . . . My captors intend to leave me here; I am given to understand that I have reached the end of my journey—they are done with me, and I am free. I have but a few more minutes to write in this journal before they take it from me. What now to do? I shall not follow the light of the moths, for it is a false light and wanders where it will. But, in the lands that spread out before me, a light beckons in the distance. It is a clear light, an even light, and because light still, to me, means the surface, I have decided to walk toward it in hopes, after all this time, of regaining the world I have lost. I may well simply find another door when I find the source of the light, but perhaps not. In any event, God speed say I.

Surely, *surely*, such visions indicate Tonsure's advanced delirium or, more probably, monkish forgery, but one is almost convinced by the holy reverence in which the inhabitants of Zamilon hold their page, for it means more to them than any other of their possessions, and even now, after many a reading, it moves more than one monk to tears.[130]

To attempt to put the controversy to rest[131]—after all, Tonsure has become a saint to the Truffidians by virtue of his faith in the face of adversity—a delegation from the Morrow-based Institute of Religiosity,[132] led by the distinguished Head Instructor Cadimon Signal,[133] journeyed 20 years ago to the lands of the Kalif, under guarantee of safe passage, to examine the journal in its place of honor in Lepo.

---

[130] I myself have journeyed to Zamilon to see the page, and am cagey enough at this stage of my bizarre career to decline comment on its authenticity or fakery.

[131] Admittedly confined to the pages of obscure history journals and religious pamphlets.

[132] Then called the Morrow Religious Institute.

[133] Cadimon Signal was a friend of mine and so, to avoid a conflict of interest, I shall not expound upon his many virtues—his strength of character, his fine sense of humor, the pedigree of the wines hidden in his basement.

The conditions under which the delegation could view the journal—conditions set after their arrival—could not have been more rigid: they could examine the book for an hour, but, due to the book's fragile condition, they themselves could not touch it; they must allow an attendant to do so for them. Further, the attendant would flip through *all* of the pages once, and then the delegation would be able to study up to 10 individual pages, but no more than 10—and they must name the page numbers in question on the basis of the first flip through[134] The delegation had no alternative but to accept the ridiculous conditions,[135] and resolved to make the most of their time. After half an hour, they found it appeared parts of the book *had* been replaced with different paper, and that the penmanship appeared, in places, somewhat different from Tonsure's own (as compared against the biography). Alas, at the half-hour mark, news reached the Kalif by carrier pigeon that the then mayor of Ambergris had tendered a major personal insult to the Kalif, and he immediately expelled the delegation from the reading room and sent them via fast horses to his borders, where they were unceremoniously dumped with their belongings. Their notes had been taken from them, and they could not remember any useful particulars about the page they had seen. No further examination has been allowed as of the date of this writing.

Thus, although we have copies of the journal, we may never know why pages were replaced in this invaluable primary source of history. We are left with the difficult task of either repudiating the entire document or, as I believe, embracing it all. If you do believe in Samuel Tonsure's journal, in its validity, then your pleasure will be enhanced as you pass the equestrian statue of Manzikert I[136] in the Banker's Courtyard and as you survey the ruined aqueducts on Albumuth Boulevard that are, be-

---

134   The Kalif had had golden page numbers added for his convenience.

135   Signal reports that the attendant "flipped through the pages at such incredible speed that we could hardly see them. When it came time for us to present the 10 page numbers, which we simply chose at random, a great ceremony was made of taking them to the attendant, who made an equally great show of finding the right page, during which we were made to wait outside, for fear we might see a forbidden page. By the time the first page was located and presented to us some 20 minutes had elapsed, and it turned out to be blank, except for the words 'see next page.'"

136   Suitably tall, although the statue's torso and legs (and the horse itself—Manzikert never *saw* a horse, let alone rode on one) are *not* of Manzikert I, but the remains of an equestrian statue dating from the period of the Kalif's brief occupation of the city—onto which someone has rather crudely attached Manzikert's head. The original statue of Manzikert I was of an unknown height and showed Manzikert I surrounded by his beloved rats, rendered in bronze. An enterprising but none too bright bureaucrat sold the statue, sans head, for scrap to the Arch Duke of Banfours a century before the Kalif's invasion; the Arch Duke promptly recast the statue as a cannon affectionately christened "Old Manzikert" and bombarded the stuffing out of Ambergris with it. As for the rats, they now decorate a small altar near the aqueduct, and if they look more like cats than rats, this is because the sculptor's models died half way through the commission and he had to use his tabby to complete it.

sides the mushroom dwellers themselves, the only remaining sign of Cinsorium, the city *before* Ambergris.[137]

---

[137] Surely, after all, it is more comforting to believe that the sources on which this account is based are truthful, that this has not all, in fact, been one huge, monstrous lie? And with that pleasant thought, O Tourist, I take my leave for good.

GLOSSARY

Given the nature of Duncan Shriek's style and the length constraints inherent in production of a travel guide/pamphlet, it should surprise no one that descriptions of certain people, places, and landmarks have been truncated for the sake of brevity. Many of Shriek's original footnotes were easily as long as the finished essay. In many cases, I found it difficult—even enlisting the aid of noted writer and editor Sirin—to know where to cut without damaging the intent of the manuscript. Once finished, we wished to preserve some of the deleted material without compromising the narrative flow of the streamlined essay. Therefore, again with Sirin's help, I have compiled a glossary of the terms that might interest the reader but which fell under the category of "peripheral" to the essay's main thrust. Complicating matters further, Duncan had left behind his own incomplete glossary, which I have attempted to integrate into this new glossary.

All numerals in italics refer to footnotes. Wherever possible, I have preserved the pseudo-informal tone Duncan used in the essay proper. Finally, again in the interests of space constraints, I have sacrificed my original afterword to this essay in favor of this abbreviated version. I hope that my afterword can be published separately at a later date, as I believe it would shed further light on the current whereabouts of my brother, whether above or underground.
- *Janice Shriek*

– A –

AANDALAY, ISLE OF. The mythic homeland of the piratical Aan Tribes. According to the tales of the Aan, the Southern Hemisphere once consisted of a single landmass, the Isle of Aandalay, populated solely by the happy, peaceful Children of Aan. Only after a great cataclysm—the nature of which varies more from tale to tale than the weather in that part of the world—that shattered the Isle into a thousand pieces did the Aan become warlike, each faction certain they possessed the mandate for restoration of a united Isle of Aandalay. Thus did piracy become rationalized as a quest for a homeland. Some Aan even attacked the mainland, claiming it was merely a huge splinter exiled from their beloved Isle. See also: *Calabrian Calendar.*

ABRASIS, MICHAEL. The first head librarian of the Manzikert Memorial Library. Abrasis is best known for his collection of erotic literature and lithographs. When he died, in his sleep, his body could not at first be removed from his apartment because the piles of pornography had blocked the only route from bed to door. Oddly enough, by the time Abrasis' relatives came to collect his things, the apartment had been picked clean. Abrasis also bred prize-winning cababari. See also: *Cababari; Manzikert Memorial Library.*

ALBUMUTH BOULEVARD. A rather famous thoroughfare cutting through the heart of Ambergris. The site of both the Borges Bookstore and the headquarters of Hoegbotton & Sons, Albumuth Boulevard has long been privy to the inner workings of the Festival of the Freshwater Squid. During the civil disturbances of the Reds and the Greens, Albumuth Boulevard served as the main battlefield. Certainly the recent armed struggle between Hoegbotton's publishing arm and the inscrutable Frankwrithe & Lewden could not have occurred without the events that first unfolded on the boulevard. No one can agree on the origin of the name "Albumuth", nor on the limits of the boulevard. As Sirin once said, "Like the Moth, Albumuth Boulevard has a thousand tributaries and streams, so that, ultimately, who can determine its boundaries or the limits of its influence?" See also: *Frankwrithe & Lewden; Sirin.*

ALFAR. The ruins of Alfar form, with Zamilon, the only recorded instances of a particular architectural style reminiscent of gray cap buildings. Specifically, structures at both Alfar and Zamilon consist of circles within circles. Neither location bears witness to a single corner or sharp edge. Alfar, like Zamilon, is of unknown origin, but an additional peculiar tale is told by shepherds in both places: that, on certain nights, Alfar and Zamilon glow iridescent green and red, a sheen that spreads and intensifies so slowly an observer does not at first recognize the change, but finally cannot doubt the evidence of his eyes. No one has as yet confirmed this claim independently, nor has anyone thought to time these "eruptions" of color, one to the other. What would it mean if Alfar and Zamilon both became luminous on the same nights?(86) See also: *Nysman, Michael, and Zamilon.*

AMBERGRISIAN GASTRONOMIC ASSOCIATION. Founded during the days of Trillian the Great Banker, the AGA recently achieved a degree of notoriety by uncovering the lost ingredients for Oliphaunt's Delight: ½-pound of cherries, 17 pounds of freshwater squid, 20 gallons of goat's milk, 5 pounds of fish paste (preferably flounder) and 1 ounce of asparagus.(56)

AMBERGRISIAN HISTORICAL SOCIETY. Completely unlike the Ambergrisians for the Original Inhabitants Society. The most adventure this group has seen is undercooked flounder at the annual Ambergrisian Historical Society Ball and the occasional paper cut (sweet red relief from boredom!)

opening mail sent by similar dullards located in Morrow and Stockton.(*106, 122*) See also: *Ambergrisians for the Original Inhabitants Society.*

AMBERGRISIANS FOR THE ORIGINAL INHABITANTS SOCIETY. Completely unlike the Ambergrisian Historical Society. Never has membership in a historical society been so fraught with peril. Every two or three years, another few members succumb to the temptation to pry open a manhole cover and go spelunking amongst the sewer drains. Inevitably, someone gets stuck in a drainpipe and the others go for help, or the gray caps, presumably, catch them and they disappear forever. One imagines the hapless AFTOIS members waving their official membership cards at the approaching, unimpressed gray caps. When not conspiring to commit assisted suicide, the AFTOIS publishes *The Real History Newsletter.*(*24*) See also: *Martigan, Red,* and *Real History Newsletter, The.*

– B –

BANFOURS, ARCH DUKE OF. Best known for being the first to bombard Ambergris with cannon fire. He ruled Ambergris for exactly 21 days. While sitting at a sidewalk cafe, surrounded by his bodyguards, a waiter casually walked up behind him and slit his throat. There appears to have been no particular motivation for the assassination except for the usual engrained Ambergrisian dislike of foreigner interlopers.(*136*) See also: *Occupation, The.*

BANKER WARRIORS. This sect, the most feared of Trillian's followers, grew out of the predations of highway robbery. Due to the rise of the merchant classes, much money had to be physically moved from one city to another. Generally, a banker's representative accompanied this transfer. Early transfers of this kind met with disaster. After years of robberies and pay offs to avoid robberies, the position of banker's representative evolved from paper-pusher to hardened veteran of weapons' training. By the time Trillian came to power through the Ambergrisian banking system, the banker representatives had become a powerful, feared security force. Trillian himself named them the Banker Warriors and used them to consolidate his hold over Ambergris. Also influential in repelling attacks by the Kalif. Eventually assimilated into the Ambergris Defense Force, at which time women were excluded from participation. Several of these women (including the noted strategist Rebecca Gort, munitions expert Kathleen Lynch, and fencing master Susan Dickerson) founded their own chain of banks, bought several other businesses, including Frankwrithe & Lewden, and moved to Morrow, where they became the core of the most feared security force on the continent. The Ambergris Defense Force, on the other hand, perished to the last man during the Kalif's invasion.(*70*) See also: *Frankwrithe & Lewden; Gort; Kalif, The; Trillian, The Great Banker.*

BARTINE, CAPPAN. Smoke and mirrors. Never was and never will be. (*49*) See also: *Skinder, Cappan.*

BENDER, VOSS. A composer of operas, requiems, and minor rhymes, who, for a period of time, transcended his status as a cultural icon to become a politician and the unofficial ruler of Ambergris. His suspicious death spawned a civil war between the Greens, his most fanatical followers, and the Reds, his most fervent enemies. Famous for his defiant speech to the merchant barons during which he exclaimed, "Art always transforms money!" His many operas include: *The Refraction of Light in a Prison, The Tragedy of John & Sophia, The King Underground, Hymns for the Dead, Trillian, Wilted As the Flower Lay*, and his masterpiece, *The Release of Belacqua*. Bender wrote an autobiography, *Memoirs of a Composer*, which contains more information on his early life.(*44, 98, 108*) See also: *Midnight for Munfroe; Nunk, Autarch of.*

BLGKKYDKS, HECKIRA. A Haragck military officer today best known for his oil paintings of remote landscapes. He often painted in the field and thus the paintings also have historical significance. The night before his amphibious assault on Ambergris, he did the preliminary sketches for a piece he intended to call "The Sack of Ambergris." During the ensuing rout, these sketches came into the possession of the Ambergris navy. For 20 years they were displayed at the Ambergris History Museum. But the trader Michael Hoegbotton found them so compelling that, after the Haragck had largely faded as a political/cultural force, he paid Blgkkydks to live in Ambergris for a year to complete the actual painting. Living in poverty at the time, the old general agreed reluctantly, but fell so in love with Ambergris that he lived out his remaining years there. He eventually became a fixture of Albumuth Boulevard, his craggy visage and rickety easel actually noted on tourist maps of the period.(*96*) See also: *Grnnck, Haragck Khan.*

BROTHERS AND SISTERS OF TRUFF. The contemporaries of the monk simply known as "Truff" who saw him as a conduit to God and followed him during his short, brutal life time. To call someone a Brother or Sister of Truff in modern times is a sarcastic way of saying "This person is pious."(*42*) See also: *Ibonof, Ibonof.*

BRUEGHEL, MICHAEL. John Manzikert's nemesis eventually united the islands of the Aan despite several times coming close to total defeat. During his 50 years of rule, Brueghel not only annihilated the Kalif's troops in three historic naval battles, forever relegating the Kalif's ambitions to the continent, but also established an oligarchic form of government that served the Aan well for the next three generations. Perhaps his greatest achievement was to collect the remnants of the Saphant Empire under his aegis, preserving scientific and cultural advances that would otherwise have been lost. In later years, descendents of Brueghel, calling themselves Brueghelites, would seize large portions of the River Moth to the south of Ambergris and threaten Ambergrisian autonomy. See also: *Calabrian Calendar; Kalif, The; Saltwater buzzard; Saphant Empire, The.*

BUSKER, ALAN. Busker, long known as a fanatical (and often quite critical) traveler in both the north and south, may also have been a spy for the Kingdom of Morrow. Certainly, there was a time when Busker's travels among the northern cities resulted in disaster—Stockton, Belezar, Dovetown, and Tratnor all fell to Morrow shortly after Busker's visits to them. Most famous for attempting to enter the Kalif's Holy City by impersonating the Kalif himself. See also: *Kalif, The; Stockton.*

- C -

CABABARI. Long-snouted, foul-smelling, fungus-eating, dirt-seeking pigs instrumental in the ouster of Trillian the Great Banker as ruler of Ambergris.(*18*) See also: *Fungus; Trillian the Great Banker.*

CALABRIAN CALENDAR. A wonder of inefficiency that used an estimated count of the various islands the Isle of Aandalay had fragmented into as the number of days in its year. Months were named after the nearly unpronounceable monikers of old Aan leaders, but the names of months changed as new leaders rose and fell, with the result that many Aan towns employed month-tellers whose sole function was to untangled the knots of names. Making the situation more confusing, each group of Aan on each island began to name their months differently. The charts created by the month-finders began to dwarf those used by mathematicians and map-makers. Several wars were fought over the allocation of days and months, including the famous War of the Three-Day Weekend, which left over 10,000 people forever unable to enjoy even a one-day weekend. Eventually, under the rule of Michael Brueghel, a reunited Aan people scrapped the Calabrian Calendar altogether in favor of the Kalif's calendar, itself based on the old Saphant Empire's calendar. Thousands of month-finders had to find other types of work. Their color-coded charts still reside in many wealthy art collectors' mansions.(*29*) See also: *Aandalay, Isle of; Brueghel, Michael.*

CAROLINE OF THE CHURCH OF THE SEVEN-POINTED STAR. A heretic from Nicea who left the Cult of the Seven-Edged Star to found her own religion. Unlike the Cult of the Seven-Edged Star, the Church of the Seven-Pointed Star believed that God had seven points rather than seven edges. Therefore, rather than worshipping the journey toward self-realization symbolized by the edges, they worshipped the goals of self-realization as symbolized by the points. The specific points Caroline adhered to were: celibacy (during certain times of the year, if absolutely necessary), truth, beauty, self-realization, self-worth, love of others, and good hygiene (in some translations from the sacred text, literally, "negation of body odor through soapy immersions"). Adherents to the Church of the Seven-Pointed Star used swords with sharp points but no edge, while the Cult of the Seven-Edged Star used swords with sharp edges but no point. Alas, edges proved superior to points in most battles fought in the streets of Nicea. Caroline's followers were forced to either commit sacrilege and switch to edges, or become meals for the ever-present Saltwater Buzzard. Proving, one could say, the point of the edges.(*6*) See also: *Mikal, Dray; Saltwater Buzzard.*

CYRIL. The eldest, but no student of power, he soon retired to a life of leisure and sloth. Although living long, he passed out of the history books with his birth. Death by decades of gluttony at age 71. See also: *Mandrel; Samantha; Tiphony.*

- D -

DAFFED, XAVER. An excellent observer of animal behavior whose reputation in recent years has been sullied by accusations he became too intimately involved with his subject matter. Daffed published numerous books on animals of the southern climes, including *Diary of an Aardvark, My Life Among the Sand Turtles of the Moth River Delta, A History of Animals, Vols. I–X,* and *The Hoegbotton Guide to Small, Indigenous Mammals.* He was found dead, of an apparent heart attack, in the tropical mountains near Nicea, wearing only a wooly monkey suit, several perplexed wooly monkeys watching from the nearby bushes.(*18*) See also: *Cababari; Hoegbotton Guide to Small, Indigenous Mammals, The.*

DISPOSSESSED. Some of the Ambergrisians "dispossessed" of their families because of The Silence became strange and fey to their friends. They would dig up animal bones, eat strange fungus, and visit graveyards, claiming to hear their brothers, sisters, sons, daughters, fathers, mothers, calling to them from the ground. In later years, these individuals became the official Dispossessed, wandering from place to place and burying the bones of their dead in the walls of buildings that others had boarded up after The Silence. For more than 70 years, these urban nomads roamed like lost souls, living by ever more desperate means, their numbers dwindling until they finally disappeared from the city.(40) See also: *Fungus.*

- F -

FESTIVAL OF THE FRESHWATER SQUID, THE. A celebration specific to Ambergris that has, on occasion, been a spark for civil unrest.(*61*)

FRANKWRITHE & LEWDEN. A devious and conniving publishing company run by L. Gaudy and his family. Known for their insidious marketing strategies and accused by some of collaborating with the gray caps. Frankwrithe & Lewden was founded during the wane of the Saphant Empire and claims to be the oldest publisher still extant on the Southern Continent. Books published by F&L have been banned by the Truffidian Antechamber of Ambergris 43 times. See also: *Albumuth Boulevard; Banker Warriors; Manzikert Memorial Library; Midnight for Munfroe; Saphant Empire, The.*

FUNGUS. A type of spore-reproducing "plant" that is usually quite harmless. One of Samuel Tonsure's favorite words—the most frequently-appearing word in his journal after the words "the," "a," "and," "that," "blood," and "fear."(*19, 22, 23, 31, 113*) See also: *Cababari; Dispossessed, The.*

– G –

GLARING, MAXWELL. The author of *Midnight for Munfroe, The Problem With Krotch, Munfroe's Return, Krotch Strikes Back, Munfroe Reborn, Krotch Reborn, Krotch's Triumph, Munfroe's Legacy, Krotch's World, Son of Munfroe, Krotch's Last Stand, A Krotchless World, Krotch's Legacy, Son of Munfroe II, Krotch and Munfroe: The Lost Memoirs,* and, posthumously, *The End of the Legacy of Krotch and Munfroe.(126–129)* See also: *Bender, Voss; Krotch; Munfroe; Midnight for Munfroe.*

GORT. Marmey Gort kept minutely detailed records of city inhabitants' sanitary habits, including their storage of refuse. A typical entry reads: "X—outhouse use increase: av. 7x/day (5 min. av. ea.); note: garbage output up 3x for week: connex?" Gort even managed to track gray cap garbage pickup habits and concluded that, if the vast amounts of garbage were used as food or as mulch to grow food, the population of gray caps under the city could exceed 300,000. No one listened to him. No one likes bad news. But Gort didn't care that no one listened to him—he went right on with his research, leaving behind 3,000 journals of observations when he died at the age of 70. Later, the Kalif would use the journals to successfully invade the city.(27) See also: *Banker Warriors.*

GRAY TRIBES. Successors to the Aan in the Southern Islands. Implacable, cultured and barbaric at the same time. Thrilled to the opening of a book as much as the opening of an enemy's throat. Denied a foothold on the continent by the Arch Duke of Malid, who thrilled only to the opening of throats and therefore put more enthusiasm into the endeavor. See also: *Aandalay, Isle of; Malid, Arch Duke of; Saltwater buzzard.*

GRNNCK, HARAGCK KHAN. Responsible for the failed amphibious attack on Ambergris. Grnnck had complicated tastes—utterly ruthless and without peer in the arts of deception, but also enamored of frogs and all things connected to frogs. He may have possessed the largest collection of frog art in the world—from paintings to sculptures and wood carvings. Torn from his youth in the Southern swamps to join the Haragck who invaded his remote homeland, Grnnck quickly rose through the ranks until, by a stroke of luck, he managed to best the old Khan in single combat and replace him. No doubt love of frogs, a vestige of his youth he did not wish to relinquish, proved his downfall. Who can doubt this love made the idea of an amphibious invasion of Ambergris so attractive?(96) See also: *Blgkkydks, Heckira.*

– H –

HOEGBOTTON GUIDE TO SMALL, INDIGENOUS MAMMALS, THE. The perfect present for friends or suitable for tourists who wish to learn more about the fascinating variety of small, indigenous mammals found in the southern climes. Available at the Borges Bookstore.(*18*) See also: *Cababari; Daffed, Xaver; Trillian the Great Banker.*

- I -

IBONOF, IBONOF. A heretic once named simply Ibonof. A former member of the Truffidian Church. Excommunicated after having a vision in which he appeared to himself and proclaimed himself "divine." Spent the rest of his life talking to himself and seeing double.(*32*) See also: *Brothers and Sisters of Truff.*

INSTITUTE OF RELIGIOUSITY. See also: *Morrow Religious Institute.*

- J -

JERSAK, SIMON. An unusually socially-mobile individual who eventually became known for his funny and insightful pamphlets about tax collecting and tax collectors. Although usually attributed to Sirin, Jersak in fact first sarcastically referred to "Those days when taxation has become a thing of beauty." His advice to ordinary citizens is studded with laconic satire: "When a traveler came to some narrow defile, he would be startled by the sudden appearance of a tax-gatherer, sitting aloft like a thing uncanny."

JONES, STRETCHER. A tragic story, too long to summarize here. Suffice it to say that if Stretcher Jones had been victorious he would have led us all to a better place. There are still those in this world who hold fast to his ideals.(*57, 73, 74, 109*) See also: *Masouf; Nadal, Thomas; Oliphaunt; Saltwater buzzard.*

- K -

KALIF, THE. Any one of 80 anonymous, sequential rulers of the great western empire. Known for taking great risks incognito. Often killed in freak accidents of a macabre but humorous nature. One of the more absurd theories put forth by Mary Sabon is that Samuel Tonsure was an incognito Kalif. See also: *Banker Warriors; Brueghel, Michael; Busker, Alan; Royal Genealogist; Saltwater buzzard.*

KRISTINA OF MALFOUR, LEPRESS SAINT. With each little bit of her that fell off, she came a little bit closer to Sainthood. Other than her ability to shed body parts with apparent nonchalance, no historian has ever found any other reason why she should have been sainted. She appears to have sat around a lot and eaten hundreds of servings of rice pudding while watching her family work in the fields of the communal farm.

KROKUS, RICHARD. One of History's bit players—good for a quote or two in a footnote, but not the kind of fellow you would want to invite into a chapter; soon your book would be swarming with Richard Krokuses and suffocating the life out of your narrative.(*66*)

KROTCH. The villain of Maxwell Glaring's Krotch and Munfroe action/detective series. Krotch is described in the first book, *Midnight for Munfroe*, as "a tall man, so slender that sideways he might melt into the shadows that had already taken his soul. His gaze, when he brought it to bear upon a man, would show that man the dissolution of his own morals, so dead were they and carious. His mane of black hair cowled him in his evil." Yet by *Krotch's Last Stand*, Krotch is described variously as "stout," "portly," "emaciated," both a "black, scuttling beetle, low to the ground" and a "wisp torn from the wind in his ethereal height," with "dirty blonde hair" and later "reddish-tinged locks that hung like snakes to his waist." Perhaps signaling that Glaring had grown tired of the series.(*125*) See also: *Glaring, Maxwell; Krotch; Munfroe; Midnight for Munfroe.*

- L -

LACOND, JAMES. An eccentric historian whose theories of the gray caps have largely been dismissed (unfairly) by the reading public, other historians, and even by the unemployed carpenter who for years haunted the sidewalk outside Lacond's apartment near Voss Bender Memorial Square. His pamphlets have been exclusively distributed by the Ambergrisians for the Original Inhabitants Society. Among his writings is the essay "An Argument for the Gray Caps and Against the Evidence of Tonsure's Eyes."(*19, 28, 32, 38, 63, 119, 121*) See also: *Rats.*

LEOPRAN, GEORGE. A Scathadian writer and diplomat best known for his seven-page account of his journey to and from Ambergris. Also the author of the 3,000-page novel *An Eternity of Time*, which covers one day in the life of a lonely goat herd. In minute detail. The novel includes a 200-page diatribe castigating Manzikert III as an example of the abuse of power.(*58*) See also: *Scatha.*

- M -

MALID, ARCH DUKE OF. Once upon a time, the Arch Duke of Malid was a little boy who tortured insects and small animals. He kept journals of these activities that have survived down to the present day (and which are of great interest to insect collectors and taxidermists for the intense detail of their descriptions). At first the Duke's father applauded the Duke's industriousness in keeping a journal. No doubt he felt differently when he discovered himself, a little too late, on page 203: "Note to self: Above a battlement, on a wall, on a spike, the bloody head of my father."(*95*) See also: *Gray Tribes, The; Saltwater buzzard.*

MANDIBLE, RICHARD. Unfortunately, Richard's respectable reputation as a political and scientific writer has been eclipsed by his brother Roger's artwork, which was at the center of the Great Earwax Scandal, as some wags have called it. Roger, it turned out, procured earwax from the lithesome ears of his sleeping lovers and mixed it into his paint; thus the marvelous amber tint to the sunsets in his landscapes. When the source of the amber tint was discovered, Roger suffered little career damage, but staid Richard, scandalized, never fully recovered from the incident.(*47*)

MANDREL. The second eldest and more dangerous than his older brother. He tried to grab the Cappandom before his time, only to be found out and tried by his own heart-broken father. Death by hanging at age 39. See also: *Cyril; Samantha; Tiphony.*

MANZIISM. The rat-worshipping heretic religion inadvertently founded by Manzikert I near the end of his life. This cult has had little or no influence on history while at the same time inexplicably continuing to thrive, at least in Ambergris. Nothing sticks in the throats of the Truffidian priests in Ambergris more than the sight of the rat bishops, rat clerics, and just plain old rat-bastards paraded down the street during the Festival of the Freshwater Squid, a-glitter in their specially-made robes and silver crowns.(*42, 68*) See also: *Manzikert VI; Manzikert VII; Manzikert VIII; Rats.*

MANZIKERT VI. Death by bliss. In all fairness to the sixth Manzikert's moral fiber, he never really wanted to be Cappan of Ambergris. He was only too happy to retire to a monastery, especially a Manziist monastery. In those days, the only difference between a Manziist monastery and a brothel was that the latter attracted more priests.(*110*) See also: *Manziism; Manzikert VII; Manzikert VIII.*

MANZIKERT VII. Death by an extreme miscalculation while flossing. Of his actual reign, the less said the better.(*61*) See also: *Manziism; Manzikert VI; Manzikert VIII.*

MANZIKERT VIII. Death by tire tread. An expert at staging extravaganzas, Manzikert VIII had no notable political or military victories during his reign. He has the dubious distinction of being the first historical personage to be killed by a very early form of steam-powered motored vehicle (during the Festival). An entire line of motored vehicle was later named The Manzikert. See also: *Manziism; Manzikert VI; Manzikert VII.*

MANZIKERT MEMORIAL LIBRARY. Oddly enough, the ineffectual Manzikert III established the Manzikert Memorial Library. He established the library to house his ever-expanding collection of recipes and cookbooks. After his death, the Frankwrithe & Lewden publishing company temporarily housed the collection until, following a series of bizarre events and an actual assault on F&L's offices by certain security elements from Hoegbotton & Sons, Manzikert IV placed the collection under the authority of a Chief Librarian. Frankwrithe & Lewden relocated from Ambergris to Morrow soon thereafter.(*109*) See also: *Abrasis, Michael; Frankwrithe & Lewden.*

MAP, BRANDON. An unfortunate splotch.(*65*)

MARTIGAN, RED. This victim of his own curiosity would otherwise have passed out of history altogether. Instead, due to his overwhelming stupidity, Ambergris remembers him as being somehow larger-than-life. He is frequently an inhabitant of horror and ghost stories—in a sense, more substantial in memory than in the flesh.(*88*) See also: *Ambergrisians for the Original Inhabitants Society*.

MASOUF. The general who finally defeated Stretcher Jones and personally slew the great rebel leader. He is said to have wept over the body of his adversary. After so many years of battling Stretcher Jones, Masouf was distraught to have finally destroyed the only man who had proved his equal in military skill and tactics. In his journal entry that fateful day, Masouf wrote, "As I stared into that pale, bloodied face, as I cupped his head with my hands as he breathed his last, I felt as if I were staring into my own face, into an ill-fated reflection, and as the life flickered out of his eyes, so too the life briefly seemed to have left me as well." Masouf relieved himself of his own command three days later, and after an unsuccessful suicide attempt left his wife and children and spent the next 20 years as recluse in the self-imposed solitude of Zamilon. He would eventually take up Stretcher Jones' struggle and for a brief time liberated the Kalif's western-most vassals from servitude, before being defeated by a general more brilliant than even he. Masouf died when his horse, spooked by a rabbit, threw him as he fled the battlefield.(*70*) See also: *Jones, Stretcher*.

MENITES. Adherents to a Morrow-based religion that has had many fewer embarrassing incidents than the Ambergris-based Truffidianism—mainly by dint of being several centuries younger.(*68*) See also: *Morrow Religious Institute*.

MIDNIGHT FOR MUNFROE. The first volume in Maxwell Glaring's series of novels detailing the adversarial relationship between the anti-hero Munfroe and the criminally-insane Krotch. Voss Bender once considered writing an opera based on this book, but abandoned the idea after reading the complete series. Bender's purported reason? "There is too much Krotch in the world already." The book first appeared as a serial in Frankwrithe & Lewden's Dreadful Tales daily broadsheet, which may explain the staccato "voice" of the book—its inexplicably high number of cliff hangers and near-escapes. Glaring found the story's success inexplicable and, vowing never again to write a Munfroe-Krotch story, proceeded to churn out a large number of them.(*125*) See also: *Bender, Voss; Frankwrithe & Lewden; Glaring, Maxwell; Krotch; Munfroe*.

MIKAL, DRAY, PETULARCH. Dray Mikal was, as is still the custom, randomly chosen to be the Petularch by a ceremonial bull. Let loose by the Priests of the Seven-Edged Star, the ceremonial bull was allowed to roam free until it had chosen a Petularch. The choosing process consisted of any "sign" from the bull deemed sufficiently conclusive by the priests. Although the "sign" from the bull in this case has been lost on the garbage heap of unimportant facts, it is known that Mikal was a fruit-on-a-stick vendor before his Ascension. He had immigrated to Ambergris from a small city north of Morrow called Skaal. Luckily, the position of Petularch has been largely ceremonial ever since the overthrow of the Church of the Seven-Edged Star several centuries ago. See also: *Caroline of the Church of the Seven Pointed Star.*

MORROW RELIGIOUS INSTITUTE. Although Ambergris is the city of religions, Morrow is the city of religious studies. As Morrow is in all ways removed from the lustful thrust of real life, so too is it removed from its spiritual heart to the extent that it holds its faith at arm's length, the better to examine faith's anatomy. The Morrow Religious Institute is the most famously able at this dissection process. However, despite producing some great religious figures and teachers, a disturbing number of its graduates, once exposed to religion-in-the-raw, have either "gone native" or succumbed to the pleasures of this too mortal flesh. Former name: Institute of Religiosity (*132*) See also: *Menites; Signal, Cadimon.*

MUNFROE. The ever-weary anti-hero of Maxwell Glaring's Krotch and Munfroe series, Munfroe is a protean sort whose past changes from book to book. First the son of humble farmers who travels to the city to become an accountant, Munfroe later becomes the son of accountants who travels to the country to become a humble farmer. Other incarnations include parents who serve stints in the circus, the army, as doctors, and as carpenters, variously. Only one thing is for sure: Munfroe had parents.(*125*) See also: *Glaring, Maxwell, Krotch.*

- N -

NADAL, THOMAS. He who died in infamy, his fate too sad for me to relate here. Let him rest in peace as he could not in life. Faithful to his lover and faithful to his city. A curse on all of those who would defame him for his sole moment of weakness.(*82, 83, 89, 98, 101, 129*) See also: *Jones, Stretcher.*

NUNK, AUTARCH OF. Although a real historical figure, the Autarch is more commonly known to children and adults as the happy fool of Voss Bender's Nunk poems, which contain such rhymes as "The Autarch of Nunk/Was a collector of junk/Which he kept in a trunk/Beside his pet skunk" and "The Autarch of Nunk/Loved to get drunk/And, in the grip of a sudden funk,/Pass out fitfully on his bunk." Several critics complained that a less famous personage would not have been able to get such doggerel published, but the illustrations by Kinsky in the omnibus version amply make up for the simplistic verse. Recently, amongst the few possessions left by Michael Abrasis to the Manzikert Memorial Library, archivists discovered a second set of Nunk poems, decidedly more adult, as this excerpt demonstrates: "The Autarch of Nunk/Liked women with spunk/To wiggle and tickle/His enormous pink pickle." (Although some historians believe this is a gardening reference.)(*6*) See also: *Abrasis, Michael; Bender, Voss.*

NYSIMIA. A western city known for death, dust, beer, and, more recently, for ridiculous theories involving pony-riding invaders and the gray caps.(*92*)

NYSMAN, MICHAEL. A native of Nicea, Nysman was a high-ranking Truffidian priest. Although ostensibly sent to Ambergris to assuage the suffering of those who had survived The Silence, documents unearthed since his death clearly indicate that the Truffidian Church had sent him to Ambergris for other reasons entirely. Nysman's mission was two-fold: to research The Silence to determine its cause and also to develop a psychological profile of people in extreme distress and deliver a written report to the Antechamber of Nicea on ways to exploit this distress for converts. Nysman's report on psychological distress is less interesting than his report on the cause of The Silence, which includes the following sentences: "With all due respect, I do not know what good it will do us to find out the cause of this affliction. Surely the truth will be too horrible for any of us to hold within ourselves, and yet we could not loose such knowledge upon the world. The only words I can use to describe the utter despair that settles over me in this city are 'without God'. I feel entirely without God in this city." Later in the report, Nysman writes that around the time of The Silence several sheep herders saw strange lights during the night, emanating from Alfar. Nysman finds this fact to be of supreme importance, but instead of visiting Alfar, he abruptly changed his itinerary to visit Zamilon, for reasons that are lost to us. See also: *Alfar and Zamilon.*

- O -

OCCUPATION, THE. The term given to the 100 days during which the Kalif's troops occupied Ambergris. With the exception of The Silence, The Occupation was the bleakest period of Ambergrisian history. If not for the ingenuity and pluck of ordinary citizens, The Occupation would have lasted much longer. As this letter from David Ampers, the owner of a local tavern, The Ruby-Throated Cafe, to his cousin in Morrow (the infamous "fighting philosopher" Richard Peterson) demonstrates, the Kalif's troops did not have an easy time of it:

> Why, I had just said to my old friend Steen Potter (you remember Steen from your last visit—the watch salesman?) as we sat drinking at the Cafe and sharpening our knives to an unparalleled sharpness—I had just said that the city, our beloved Ambergris, had been stuck in a sort of malaise, a doldrums, the whole summer, than what should I and every other citizen of the city find nailed to our doors but a barbaric sheet of paper from the Empire of the Kalif that read thusly:

> "Noblest of the Gods, King and Master of the whole World, Son of the previous Kalif, the new Kalif, to Ambergris, his vile and insensate slave: Refusing to submit to our rule, you call yourselves lord and sovereign. You seize and distribute our treasure, you deceive our servants. You never cease to annoy us with your bands of brigands. Have I not destroyed you? I suppose I must destroy you more

utterly than you have ever been destroyed before. Beware Ambergris! Beware!"

Oh, I thought to myself, now this was promising. An ultimatum! This promised to shake us out of our rut—a real threat! And backed up too! So of course Ambergris spread her arms to the aggressor, the better to love him to death. The messenger prior to invasion was a broadsheet boy who ran past screaming, "Armies of the Kalif cross the river, crush the free armies of the Cappan!" In a stroke, Ambergris had fallen, after five years of snapping at our flanks by the Kalif—such a tease. All right, we could live with that, but did the boy have to scream it out to the world? There is such a thing as pride, my cousin, and although perhaps Steen over-reacted a little, no one complained when he took aim, let fly, and dropped the lad with a stone thrown to the head. Pride is very important to us here, although you may not understand that, not having been born in the city . . .

So the Kalif's troops invaded and we all came out to line Albumuth Boulevard for the obligatory Parade of Conquerors. It was a bright, breezy day and the swallows flew through the sky like knives. The Kalif's men formed a supposedly impenetrable wall on either side of the street, armed with spears, swords, and small cannon. It appeared they thought the local population might cause some sort of problem. Steen and I exchanged a meaningful glance. All we wanted to do was welcome the invading army to our city.

The Kalif's general, the Great One as he was called, made for an impressive sight, with his emerald turban, white ostrich plumes, silver spurs, and the eight gray oliphaunts that lurched along behind him. At least, he was impressive until someone in the crowd sent a blade flying through his throat. My, what a lot of blood he had in him—and it certainly seemed as red any anyone else's would have been in a similar situation. Alas, the assassin slipped away in the resulting turmoil.

When order had been restored, we crowded up the palace steps and watched as the mayor, the defeated Cappan at his side in chains, relinquished, in a formal ceremony, the keys to the city, and gave the sacramental sword to the new Great One (hastily recruited from among five resplendent if fiercely sweating officers). The Cappan performed these duties with a slight smirk and a conspiratorial wink to the crowd. The Cappan's personal bodyguard, too, were in a particularly mirthful mood, considering the circumstances. Indeed, one would at times during the ceremony have had difficulty determining who was slave and who was victor . . . The Great One, as he looked out on the crowd, seemed discomfited by the applause, the ready smiles, as we showed our teeth. A flicker of fear flashed across the Great One's face before tranquility once again overtook those fine, western features.

It didn't last long, of course, although I shall, in the interests of saving my hands from gripping this pen for hours and you of reading into boredom, summarize the events of the next 100 days. Inevita-

bly, the second Great One was poisoned and the third found gar-
roted in his palace, so the Kalif had no choice but to order the
mayor of our fair metropolis hanged by the neck until dead. I'm
sure he did not expect what happened at the hanging: We all
cheered as our mayor went to a better (or at least cleaner!) place.
We'd never much liked him anyway, and would probably have
done the deed ourselves in a few more months. But then, following
the execution, we rioted and killed many of the Kalif's soldiers because, after all, he was one of us, even if he had been an incompe-
tent, embezzling bastard.

From then on, it was just a matter of time. Each dawn saw another
set of foreigners' heads on spikes down by various city fountains.
Each sunset was occasion for mingled screams and pleas for mercy.
Everywhere they turned: the confluence of fate and malice in the ancient stone face of the city. When they came to my establishment,
why, I treated them like kings, using a slow-acting poison to kill several of them over a period of days. Some trickster they trusted told
them that the red flags strewn across the city were flags of defiance,
so the Kalif's men tore them up, angering the gray caps, who stirred
and clicked amongst themselves before "disappearing" the Kalif's
men in droves. The zoo keeper let the big cats free right into the bar-
racks of the Great One's personal guard. Store owners crept up to
the Kalif's cannon after dark and poured sand and glue in the muz-
zles. Priests in the Religious Quarter stoned patrols to death for vio-
lating obscure, out-of-date rules and then pleaded exemption from
punishment on grounds of conflicting faiths.

Finally, one day, they simply left, cousin, and never returned. We
boxed the bones they had left behind into the walls of abandoned
buildings. We burned their carts. We appropriated their horses. We
scrubbed the palace clean. We re-instated the Cappan. And, once
again, we cheerfully settled down to govern ourselves, ever so refreshed by this little interlude, this experiment in occupation by a
foreign empire . . . So you should come visit again soon, cousin. The
cafe is doing well and we would be glad to have you. The city is beautiful this time of year.

Fondly,
David Ampers

OLIPHAUNT. One of Tonsure's favorite mammals, these great gray creatures almost ended Stretcher Jones' rebellion at the outset. Their sudden introduction into battle, brought from the jungle plains of the far southwest, caused
such panic at the Battle of Richter that Jones was lucky to escape with his life.
Xaver Daffed found this usually gentle mammal so compelling that he devoted
two volumes of his *A History of Animals* to it. Manzikert III found oliphaunts so
succulent that toward the end of his reign he ate their flesh to the exclusion of
all else. The Kalif, upon his temporary subjugation of Ambergris, planned to
build a palace that would have represented the apogee of the oliphaunt motif in
architecture: a vast structure in the shape of an oliphaunt. The plans included
hindquarters fashioned to resemble a glen with its own running brook and a

theater in the front.(*15, 56*) See also: *Ambergris Gastronomic Association; Jones, Stretcher; and Daffed, Xaver.*

– P –

PEJORA, MIDAN. The most famous architect in Ambergris' history. He holds primary responsibility for the grandest buildings in the city, including the Cappan's Palace. Pejora could best be classified as an "idiot genius." From an early age, he erected incredible models of buildings out of wood, sand, and rock, but he could not even graduate from grade school. His parents eventually taught him as best they could at home, and many were the times neighbors would complain because Pejora had erected some new architectural monstro-city in the family's front yard.

– R –

RAMKIN. A dead man.

RATS. In sewers. In religions. In words like pirate, desperate, and narrative. Rats infest this history as surely as words and mushrooms. I smell a rat right now, in fact.(*2, 6, 7, 11, 12, 16, 18, 20, 21, 28, 38, 41, 42, 44, 49, 54, 56, 61–63, 68, 70 72, 88, 98, 102, 103, 105, 108, 120, 127, 136*) See also: *Lacond, James.*

REAL HISTORY NEWSLETTER, THE. A fringe publication that has allowed many historians in exile to have their say under the safety of pseudonyms.(*24*) See also: *Ambergrisians for the Real Inhabitants Society; Lacond, James.*

ROYAL GENEALOGIST. A position in the Kalif's Empire much shrouded in secrecy. Only the Royal Genealogist knows the true identity of the Kalif, but can publish only the vaguest facts about the royal personage. Although the theory cannot be proven, many historians, this one excluded, believe that on more than one occasion the Royal Genealogist has actually been the Kalif.(*71*) See also: *Kalif, The.*

– S –

SABON, MARY. An aggressive and sometimes brilliant historian who built her reputation on the bones of older, love-struck historians. Five-ten. One-fifteen. Red hair. Green, green eyes. An elegant dresser. Smile like fire. Foe of James Lacond. In conversation can cut with a single word. Author of several books whose titles I quite forget at the moment.(*6, 8, 26, 29, 31, 32, 38, 52, 81, 113, 116, 119, 120, 127, 129*) See also: *Lacond, James.*

SALTWATER BUZZARD. The main beneficiary of battles between Stretcher Jones and the Kalif, the Kalif and Michael Brueghel, Michael

Brueghel and Manzikert I, Manzikert I and the gray caps, the Brueghelites and the Gray Tribes, the Gray Tribes and the Arch Duke of Malid, the Arch Duke of Malid and the Kalif, the Kalif and Ambergris, Ambergris and the Haragck, the Haragck and Morrow. Scavengers, saltwater buzzards mate for life, have an average wing span of 10 feet, an average life span of 20 years, and are distinguished from other buzzards by the flashes of red and green on the tips of their otherwise black wings. See also: *Brueghel, Michael; Gray Tribes, The; Kalif, The; Jones, Stretcher; Malid, Arch Duke of.*

SAMANTHA. The smartest of the four, she eventually ruled Ambergris for 20 years. Often mistaken for her mother, she shared her parents' prudence and foresight in most things. No ill came to Ambergris under her rule. Death by bliss, in the arms of her lover, at the age of 59. See also: *Cyril; Mandrel; Tiphony.*

SAPHANT EMPIRE, THE. As empires go, this one made the Kalif's holdings look pathetic. The Saphant Empire lasted for 1,500 years and encompassed most of two continents at its zenith. Its rulers, elected by an oligarchy, demonstrated an uncanny ability to mix negotiation and ruthless military force to consolidate their successes. Under the centralized stability of Empire, an unprecedented wealth of advances in technology and the arts threatened to make the Empire a permanent institution. However, a series of inbred, weak rulers coupled with crippling attacks on shipping by Aan pirates eventually broke the Empire into five pieces. The last Emperor's chief advisor, Samuel Lewden, did his best to hold the central government together, but the five pieces became 30 autonomous regions and then splintered into even smaller kingdoms. Until finally only ghost-like cultural echoes remained of the once-great empire. For more information, read Mary Sabon's one excellent book, *The Saphant Legacy.(1)* See also: *Frankwrithe & Lewden; Sabon, Mary.*

SCATHA. A wretched place, full of novelists who think 500 words where one will suffice is a sign of sophistication. Ambassadors from Scatha have rarely liked Ambergris very much.(58)

SHARP, MAXIMILLIAN. Possibly the most talented and yet most obnoxious writer ever produced by the South. Of all the infamous tales told about him by publishers and editors, the only one backed up by actual documentation concerns his association with Frankwrithe & Lewden. Sharp published his work regularly in F&L periodicals and as stand-alone books and pamphlets. On one occasion, he apparently did not appreciate Andrew Lewden's (his editor) characterizing him at a dinner party as "somewhat arrogant" and sent Lewden the following missive (Lewden, by all accounts, read it once, smiled, threw it away, and promptly remaindered all of Sharp's books):

> **From:** Lord Sharp I, Steward of the Sacred Word & Keeper of the Torch of Life.
>
> **To:** Andrew Lewden, Lowly Knave, Steward of the Bottom Dollar & Keeper of Writers with No Alternative (currently)

Re: A Missive, To Whit, Responding to Andrew Lewden's last letter and unworthy comment of last week, in the Year 34 of our Lord Sharp. Forthsooth and with haste herewith:

Dear Lewden:

(1) My Lord Sharp thanks you for your appreciated, if rather short and wretched letter of last week and begs me to tell you (as he is himself involved in Extremely Important Matters of Writing and Editing, and has no time to deal with editors hailing from squalid and distant corners of the world) that although he appreciates the copy of your latest magazine with His exalted story "The Game of Lost and Found" printed therein, you have failed to place his name in large enough type on the cover—nor have you situated His name first and to the detriment of all other (lesser) names on said cover. Furthermore, His story was not published as the first story in the magazine, nor was it given an elaborate illustration, and, finally, the biography which accompanied the piece was not long enough, did not adequately cover Lord Sharp's career, and did not state (as is common enough custom for Lord Sharp's work, and certainly common knowledge) that Sharp is "The Premier Writer of His, or Any Other Generation."

(2) These are grave misdeeds, Mr. Lewden, and Lord Sharp, while not altogether concerned, owing to the low circulation and low pay associated with your magazine, is perplexed as to why you should seek to draw His Lordship's wrath upon you. Certainly deigning to present to you an Exalted Reprint from several years past, he has laid upon you the gravest of all duties: the proper representation not only of the Sharp Fiction but of the Sharp Image. If no illustration were available, Lord Sharp, through his many underlings, would have been glad to provide you with a glossy representation, in three-quarters profile, of His Famous Visage. This would not only have been adequate, it would have been more perfect, due to the marvelous perfections of the Sharp Visage, than any illustration (unless, of course, such mythical illustration had been of His Lordship).

(3) n any event, due to the Extreme Kindness of Lord Sharp, I am instructed by His Lordship to officially Forgive You Your Trespasses and to let you know that you may, if you ever visit Lord Sharp's estate, be allowed to kiss His hand, and even to keep a crumpled piece of paper from one of His Lordship's abortive rough drafts.

(4) Finally, as you say, Mr. Lewden, mere mortals may include appropriate return postage for a manuscript, but as your sentence implied, Lord Sharp is, like the unbroken string of Kalifs, most exceptionally Immortal, in that most enduring of ways: through the glory of the written word. Therefore, on a related topic, we ask that you immediately relinquish a tear sheet, to use a vulgar term, of the review of His Lordship's Greatest Book, *A Testament,* for His perusal. (He will not, in fact, read it, but one of His many underlings

may read it to Him; or, as is more likely, one of His underlings
gifted in the Word shall rewrite the review so that it flows like liquid
gold rather than liquid shit and thus shall not distress in any way
His noble ears; there is nothing that harms his Lordship more than
a badly-turned phrase.)

(5) In closing, I shall simply remind you, Mr. Lewden, that it will
soon again be time to pay the annual tribute to His Lordship. This
year, as you should know, it consists of three days of reading Lord
Sharp's works aloud, two days of studying them silently, and one
day of transcribing them by Your Own hand, that you may more
fully understand how Genius doth descend upon the World.

Your Obed. Ser.,

Gerold Buttox
(one of Lord Sharp's many underlings)

P.S. His Lordship would like to convey to you His appreciation for
your previous (if distant) kind words in various broadsheets which
He has, through his underlings, perused; they have, I am told to tell
you "a rough eloquence quite unlike the bastard, no doubt inspired
by my works." He so appreciates this attention that He has com-
manded me to tell you that you may skip one of the three days of
reading His works aloud.
(57)

SHRIEK, DUNCAN. An old historian, born in Stockton, who in his youth
published several famous history books, since remaindered and savaged by critics who should have known better. His father, also an historian, died of joy; or,
rather, from a heart-attack brought on by finding out he had won a major
honor from the Court of the Kalif. I was 10. I never died from my honors, but I
was once banned by the Truffidian Antechamber. Also a renowned expert on
the gray caps, although most reasonable citizens ignore even his most outland-
ish theories. Once lucky enough to meet the love of his life, but not lucky
enough to keep her, or to keep her from pillaging his ideas and discrediting
him. Still, he loves her, separated from her by the insurmountable gulf of empires, buzzards, and the successor to Aquelus/Irene.*(1–137)* See also: *Rats.*

SIRIN. A writer and editor originally born near far-fabled Zamilon. He is
primarily known for his series of fictions supposedly describing various aspects
of Ambergris history. See also: *Zamilon.*

SIGNAL, CADIMON.*(133)* A most curious man of religion who combined
elements of common crime with the utmost respect for the spiritual life. He
taught the most successful missionaries ever to graduate from the Morrow Religious Institute and spent 10 years studying with the monks of Zamilon. Famous for his fervent lectures on Living Saints and martyrs. See also: *Morrow Religious Institute; Zamilon.*

SKINDER, CAPPAN. Smoke and mirrors. Never was and never will be.(*49*)
See also: *Lacond, James.*

SPORE OF THE GRAY CAP, THE. The tavern in which much of The Early
History was written. A marvelous hide-away more fully described in *The
Hoegbotton Guide to Bars, Pubs, Taverns, Inns, Restaurants, Brothels, and Safe
Houses.(67)*

STARKIN. A dead man.

STOCKTON. Even more boring than Morrow. Might as well be populated
with monkeys or Oliphaunts than with people. Not even a religious institute to
save it from boredom. Also, the city of my birth, and the place where my father
taught me to be a historian. I guess it wasn't all that bad.(*32, 123*) See also:
Busker, Alan.

- T -

TARBUT, ARCH OF. Richard Tarbut was a very rich man who liked to have
things named after him. The Arch of Tarbut is one of those things. The Tarbuts
moved to Ambergris from Morrow, where they sold, among other items, stoves
and canaries. Tarbut named only one condition for giving money to construct
the arch: that, by means of a ladder, he and his family be allowed to hold a party
atop the arch upon its completion. This, indeed, he did, but, bothered by a mud
wasp, lost his balance, and fell to his death, attaining a condition very close to
that of Brandon Map.(*61*) See also: *Map, Brandon.*

TIPHONY. The youngest and stupidest of the four, she lived long enough to
write bad poetry, but not long enough to reread and burn it. Death by drowning, in her bathtub, at age 24. See also: *Cyril; Mandrel; Samantha.*

TRILLIAN THE GREAT BANKER. One of the greatest rulers Ambergris
has ever known. Under Trillian, Ambergris became a miniature empire, but
more importantly, a center for business and finance. Ambergrisian banks
spread across the continent and at one point accounted for 75 percent of all financial transactions in the South. Trillian, more than any ruler before him, was
able to snuff out the power of the Brueghelites through a methodical process of
depriving them of capital and resources. Strangely enough, his downfall came
at the hands of cababari pigs. A slave in love to his mistress, he bristled over a
perceived insult handed to her by a cababari breeder and signed an order that
cababari would no longer be considered fit for eating and would be banned
from the city. Just six months later, a group of Cappan Restorationists funded
by a powerful pig cartel ousted Trillian.(*70*) See also: *Cababari.*

– W –

WEATHERBY. A dead man.

– Z –

ZAMILON. A far northern place, haunted by the dizemblance of its past.(*130*)

THE TRANSFORMATION
OF MARTIN LAKE

A fresh river in a beautiful meadow
Imagined in his mind
The good Painter, who would some day paint it
—*Comanimi*

If I was strange, and strange was my art,
Such strangeness is a source of grace and strength;
And whoever adds strangeness here and there to his style,
Gives life, force and spirit to his paintings . . .
—*Engraved at Lake's request on his memorial in Trillian Square*

Few painters have risen with such speed from such obscurity as Martin Lake, and fewer still are so closely identified with a single painting, a single city. What remains obscure, even to those of us who knew him, is how and why Lake managed the extraordinary transformation from pleasing but facile collages and acrylics, to the luminous oils—both fantastical and dark, moody and playful—that would come to define both the artist and Ambergris.

Information about Lake's childhood has a husk-like quality to it, as if someone had already scooped out the meat within the shell. At the age of six he contracted a rare bone disease in his left leg that, exacerbated by a hit-and-run accident with a Manzikert motored vehicle at age 12, made it necessary for him to use a cane. We have no other information about his childhood except for a quick glimpse of his parents: Theodore and Catherine Lake. His father worked as an insect catcher outside of the town of Stockton, where the family lived in a simple rented apartment. There is some evidence, from comments Lake made to me prior to his fame, and from hints in subsequent interviews, that a tension existed between Lake and his father, created by Lake's desire to pursue art and his father's desire that the boy take up the profession of insect catcher.

Of Lake's mother there is no record, and Lake never spoke of her in any of his few interviews. The mock-historian Mary Sabon has put forth the theory that Lake's mother was a folk artist of considerable talent and also a fierce proponent of Truffidianism—that she instilled in Lake an appreciation for mysticism. Sabon believes the magnificent murals that line the walls of the Truffidian cathedral in Stockton are the anonymous work of Lake's mother. No one has yet confirmed Sabon's theory, but if true it might account for the streak of the occult, the macabre, that runs through Lake's art—stripped, of course, of the underlying religious aspect.

Lake's mother almost certainly gave him his first art lessons, and urged him to pursue lessons at the local school, under the tutelage of a Mr. Shores, who unfortunately passed away without ever being asked to recall the work of his most famous (indeed, *only* famous) student. Lake also took several anatomy classes when young; even in his most surreal paintings the figures often seem hyper-real—as if there are layers of paint unseen, beneath which exist veins, arteries, muscles, nerves, tendons. This hyper-reality creates tension by playing against Lake's assertion that the "great artist swallows up the world that surrounds him until his whole environment has been absorbed in his own self."

We may think of the Lake who arrived in Ambergris from Stockton as a contradictory creature: steeped in the technical world of anatomy and yet well-versed in the miraculous and ur-rational by his mother—a contradiction further enriched by his guilt over not following his father into the family trade. These are the elements Lake brought to Ambergris. In return, Ambergris gave Lake the freedom to be an artist while also opening his eyes to the possibilities of color.

Of the three years Lake lived in Ambergris prior to the startling change in his work, we know only that he befriended a number of artists whom he would champion, with mixed results, once he became famous. Chief among these artists was Jonathan Merrimount, a life-long friend. He also met Raffe Constance, who many believe was his life-long romantic companion. Together, Lake, Merrimount, and Constance would prove to be the most visible and influential artists of their generation. Unfortunately, neither Merrimount nor Constance has been willing to shed any illumination on the subject of Lake's life—his inspiration, his disappointments, his triumphs. Or, more importantly, how such a middle class individual could have created such sorrowful, nightmarish art.

Thus, I must attempt to fill in details from my own experience of Lake. It is with some hesitancy that I reveal Lake first showed his work at my own Gallery of Hidden Fascinations, prior to his transformation into an artist of the first rank. Although I cannot personally bear witness to that transformation, I can at least give the reader a pre-fame portrait of a very private artist who was rarely seen in public.

Lake was a tall man who appeared to be of average height because, in using his cane, he had become stooped—an aspect that always gave him the impression of listening intently to you, although in reality he was a terrible listener and never hesitated to rudely interrupt when bored by what I said to him.

His face had a severe quality to it, offset by a firm chin, a perfect set of lips, and eyes that seemed to change color but which were, at base, a fierce, arresting green. In either anger or humor, his face was a weapon—for the narrowness became even more narrow in his anger and the eyes lanced you, while in laughter his face widened and the eyes admitted you to their compelling company. Mostly, though, he remained in a mode between laughter and anger, a mood which aped that of the "tortured artist" while at the same time keeping a distance between himself and any such passion. He was shy and clever, sly and arrogant—in other words, no different from many of the other artists I handled at my gallery. —From Janice Shriek's *A Short Overview of The Art of Martin Lake and His Invitation to a Beheading*, for the *Hoegbotton Guide to Ambergris*, 5th edition.

***

One blustery spring day in the legendary metropolis of Ambergris, the artist Martin Lake received an invitation to a beheading.

It was not an auspicious day to receive such an invitation, and Lake was nursing several grudges as he made his way to the post office. First and foremost, the Reds and Greens were at war; already, a number of nasty skirmishes had spread disease-like up and down the streets, even infecting portions of Albumuth Boulevard itself.

The Reds and Greens as a phenomenon simultaneously fascinated and repulsed Lake. In short, the Greens saw the recent death of the (great) composer Voss Bender as a tragedy while the Reds thought the recent death of the (despotic) composer Voss Bender a blessing. They had taken their names from Bender's favorite and least favorite colors: the green of a youth spent in the forests of Morrow; the red flags of the indigenous mushroom dwellers who he believed had abducted his cousin.

No doubt these two political factions would vanish as quickly as they had appeared, but in the meantime Lake kept a Green flag in his right pocket and a Red flag in his left pocket, the better to express the correct patriotic fervor. (On a purely aural level, Lake sympathized with the Reds, if only because the Greens polluted the air with a thousand Bender tunes morning, noon, and night. Lake had hardly listened to Bender while the man was alive; he resented having to change his habits now the man was dead.)

Confronted by such dogma, Lake suspected his commitment to his weekly walk to the post office indicated a fatal character flaw, a fatal ar-

tistic curiosity. For he knew he would pull the wrong flag from the right
pocket before the day was done. And yet, he thought, as he limped down
Truff Avenue—even the blood-clot clusters of dog lilies, in their neat
sidewalk rows, reminding him of the conflict—how else was he to exercise his crippled left leg? Besides, no vehicle for hire would deliver him
through the disputed areas to his objective.

Lake scowled as a youth bejeweled in red buttons and waving a huge
red flag ran into the street. In the wake of the flag, Lake could see the distant edges of the post office, suffused with the extraordinary morning
light, which came down in sheets of gold.

The secondary tier of Reasons Why I Should Have Stayed At Home
concerned, much to Lake's irritation (he really was an old man at times),
the post office itself. He had no sympathy for its archaic architecture
and only moderate respect for its function; the quality of a monopolistic
private postal service being poor, most of his commissions arrived via
courier. He also found distasteful the morbid nature of the building's
history, its stacks of "corpse cases" as he called the postal boxes. These
boxes, piled atop each other down the length and breadth of the great
hall, climbed all the way to the ceiling. Surely any of the children previ-
ously shelved there had, on their ascent to heaven, found themselves
trapped by that ugly yellow ceiling and to this day were banging their
tiny ectoplasmic heads against it.

But, as the post office rounded into view—looming and guttering like
some monstrous, senile great aunt—none of these objections registered
as strongly as the recent change of name to the "Voss Bender Memorial
Post Office." A shockingly *rushed* development, as the (great, despotic)
composer and politician had died only three days before—rumors as to
cause ranging from heart attack to poison—his body sequestered secretly,
yet to be cremated and the ashes cast into the River Moth per Bender's
request. (Not to mention that a splinter faction of the Greens, in a flurry
of pamphlets and broadsheets, had advertised the resurrection of their
beloved Bender: he would reappear in the form of the first child born after midnight in one year's time. Would the child be born with arias
bursting forth from his mouth like nightingales, Lake wondered.)

The renaming alone made Lake's teeth grind together. It seemed, to
his absurdly envious eye—he *knew* how absurd he was, but could not control his feelings—that every third building of any importance had had
the composer's name rudely slapped over old assignations, with no
sense of decorum or perspective. Was it not enough that while alive
Bender had been a virtual tyrant of the arts, squashing all opera, all theater, that did not fit his outdated melodramatic sensibilities? Was it not
enough that he had come to be the de facto ruler of a city that simultaneously abhorred and embraced the cult of personality? Did he now
have to usurp the *entire* city—every last stone of it—forever and always as

his mausoleum? Apparently so. Apparently everyone soon would be permanently lost, for every avenue, alley, boulevard, dead end, and cul de sac would be renamed "Bender." "Bender" would be the name given to all new-borns; or, for variety's sake, "Voss." And a whole generation of Bender's or Voss's would trip and tangle their way through a city which from every street corner threw back their name at them like an impersonal insult.

Why—Lake warmed to his own vitriol—if another Manzikert flattened him as he crossed this very street, he would be lucky to have his own name adorn his own gravestone! No doubt, he mused sourly—but with satisfaction—as he tested the post office's front steps with his cane, his final resting place would display the legend, "Voss Bender Memorial Gravestone" with the words "(occupied by Martin Lake)" etched in tiny letters below.

Inside the post office, at the threshold of the great hall, Lake walked through the gloomy light cast by the far windows and presented himself to the attendant, a man with a face like a knife; Lake had never bothered to learn his name.

Lake held out his key. "Number 7768, please."

The attendant, legs propped against his desk, looked up from the broadsheet he was reading, scowled, and said, "I'm busy."

Lake, startled, paused for a moment. Then, showing his cane, he tossed his key onto the desk.

The attendant looked at it as if it were a dead cockroach. "That, sir, is your key, sir. Yes it is. Go to it, sir. And all good luck to you." He ruffled the broadsheet as he held it up to block out Lake.

Lake stared at the fingers holding the broadsheet and wondered if there would be a place for the man's sour features in his latest commission—if he could immortalize the unhelpfulness that was as blunt as the man's knuckles. After the long, grueling walk through hostile territory, this was really too much.

Lake peered over the broadsheet, using his cane to pull it down a little. "You *are* the attendant, aren't you? I haven't been giving you my key all these months only to now discover that you are merely a conscientious volunteer?"

The man blinked and put down his broadsheet to reveal a crooked smile.

"I *am* the attendant. That *is* your key. You *are* crippled. Sir."

"Then what is the problem?"

The man looked Lake up and down. "Your attire, sir. You are dressed somewhat . . . ambiguously."

Lake wasn't sure if the answer or the comfortable use of the word "ambiguously" surprised him more. Nonetheless, he examined his clothes.

He had thrown on a blue vest over a white shirt, blue trousers with black shoes and socks.

The attendant wore clothes the color of overripe tomatoes.

Lake burst out laughing. The attendant smirked.

"True, true," Lake managed. "I've not *declared* myself, have I? I must have a coming out party. What am I? Vegetable or mineral?"

In clipped tones, his eyes cold and empty, the attendant asked, "Red or Green: which is it, sir."

Lake stopped laughing. The buffoon was serious. This same pleasant if distant man he had seen every week for over two years had succumbed to the dark allure of Voss Bender's death. Lake stared at the attendant and saw a stranger.

Slowly, carefully, Lake said, "I am green on the outside, being as yet youthful in my chosen profession, and red on the inside, being, as is everyone, a mere mortal." He produced both flags. "I have your flag—and the flag of the other side." He dangled them in front of the attendant. "Did I dislike Voss Bender and abhor his stranglehold on the city? Yes. Did I wish him dead? No. Is this not enough? Why must I declare myself when all I wish is to toss these silly flags in the River Moth and stand aside while you and your cohorts barrel through bent on butchery? I am neutral, sir." (Lake thought this a particularly fine speech.)

"Because, sir," the attendant said, as he rose with a great show of exertion and snatched up Lake's key, "Voss Bender is not dead."

He gave Lake a stare that made the little hairs on the back of his neck rise, then walked over to the boxes while Lake smoldered like a badly-lit candle. Was the whole city going to play such games? Next time he went to the grocery store would the old lady behind the counter demand he sing a Bender aria before she would sell him a loaf of bread?

The attendant climbed one of the many ladders that leaned against the stacks like odd wooden insects. Lake hoped his journey had not been in vain—let there at least be a missive from his mother which might stave off the specter of homesickness. His father was, no doubt, still encased in the tight-lipped silence that covered him like a cicada's exoskeleton.

The attendant pulled Lake's box out, retrieved something from it, and climbed back down with an envelope.

"Here," the attendant said, glaring, and handed it to Lake, who took both it and his key with unintended gentleness, his anger losing out to bewilderment.

Bare of place and time, the maroon envelope displayed neither a return address nor his own address. More mysterious, he could find no trace of a postmark, which could only mean someone had hand-delivered it. On the back, Lake discovered a curious seal imprinted in an orange-gold wax that smelled of honey. The seal formed an owl-like mask which, when Lake turned it upside down, became transformed into a human face. The intricate pattern reminded Lake of Trillian the Great Banker's many signature casts for coins.

"Do you know how this letter got here?" Lake started to say, turning toward the desk, but the attendant had vanished, leaving only the silence and shadows of the great hall, the close air filtering the dust of one hundred years through its coppery sheen, the open door a rectangle of golden light.

From the broadsheet on the desk the name "Voss Bender," in vermilion ink, winked up at him like some infernal, recurring joke.

***

With only this feeble skeleton of a biography as our background material, we must now approach the work that has *become* Martin Lake: "Invitation to a Beheading." The piece marks the beginning of the grotesqueries, the controlled savagery of his oils—the slashes of emerald slitting open the sky, the deft, tinted green of the windows looking in, the moss green of the exterior walls: all are vintage Lake.

The subject is, of course, the Voss Bender Memorial Post Office, truly among the most imposing of Ambergris' many eccentric buildings. If we can trust the words of Bronet Raden, the noted art critic, when he writes

> The marvelous is not the same in every period of history—it partakes in some obscure way of a sort of general revelation only the fragments of which come down to us: they are the romantic ruins, the modern mannequins, or any other symbol capable of affecting the human sensibility for a period of time,

then the first of Lake's many accomplishments was to break the post office down into its fragments and recreate it from "romantic ruins" into the dream-edifice that, for 30 years, has horrified and delighted visitors to the post office.

The astute observer will note that the post office walls in Lake's painting are created with careful crosshatching brushstrokes layered over a dampened whiteness. This whiteness, upon close examination, is composed of hundreds of bones—skulls, femurs, ribs—all compressed and rendered with a pathetic delicacy that astounds the eye.

On a surface level, this imagery surely functions as a symbolic nod to the building's former usage. Conceived to house the Cappan and his family, the brooding structure that would become the Voss Bender Memorial Post Office was abandoned following the dissolution of the Cappandom and then converted into a repository for the corpses of mushroom dwellers and indigent children. After a time, it fell into disuse—as Lake effectively shows with his surfaces beneath surfaces: the white columns slowly turning gray-green, the snarling gargoyles black-ened from disrepair, the building's entire skin pocked by lichen and mold.

Lake frequently visited the post office and must have been familiar with its former function. When the old post office burned down and re-located to its present location in what was little better than an aban-doned morgue, it is rumored that the first patrons of the new service ea-gerly opened their post boxes only to find within them old and strangely delicate bones—the bones Lake has "woven" into the "fabric" of his painting.

Lake's interpretation of the building is superior in its ability to con-vey the post office's psychic or spiritual self. As the noted painter and in-structor Leonard Venturi has written:

> Take two pictures representing the same subject; one may be dismissed as illustration if it is dominated by the subject and has no other justification but the subject, the other may be called painting if the subject is completely absorbed in the style, which is its own justification, whatever the subject, and has an intrinsic value.

Lake's representation of the post office is clearly a painting in Venturi's sense, for the subject is riddled through with wormholes of style, with layers of meaning. —From Janice Shriek's *A Short Overview of The Art of Martin Lake and His Invitation to a Beheading*, for the *Hoegbotton Guide to Ambergris*, 5th edition.

***

Lake lived farthest from the docks and the River Moth, at the eastern end of Albumuth Boulevard, where it merged with the warren of middle class streets that laboriously, some thought treacherously, descended into the valley below. The neighborhood, its narrow mews crowded with cheap apartments and cafes, was filthy with writers, artists, architects, ac-tors, and performers of every kind. Two years ago it had been resplen-dently fresh and on the cutting edge of the New Art. Street parties had lasted until six in the morning, and shocking conversations about the New Art, often destined for the pages of influential journals, had perme-ated the coffee-and-mint flavored air surrounding every eatery. By now, however, the sycophants and hangers-on had caught wind of the little miracle and begun to masticate it into a safe, stable "community." Even-tually, the smell of rot—rotting ideas, rotting relationships, rotting art—would force the real artists out, to settle new frontiers. Lake hoped he would be going with them.

Lake's apartment, on the third floor of an old beehive-like tenement run by a legendary landlord known alternately as "Dame Tuff" or "Dame Truff," depending on one's religious beliefs, was a small studio cluttered with the salmon, saffron, and sapphire bluster of his art: easels made from stripped birch branches, the blank canvases upon them flap-flapping for attention; paint-splattered stools; a chair smothered in a tangle of shirts that stank of turpentine; and in the middle of all this, like a besieged island, his cot, covered with watercolor sketches curled at the edges and brushes stiff from lazy washings. The sense of a furious mess pleased him; it always looked like he had just finished attacking some new work of art. Sometimes he added to the confusion just before the arrival of visitors, not so self-deluded that he couldn't laugh at himself as he did it.

Once back in his apartment, Lake locked the door, discarded his cane, threw the shirts from his chair, and sat down to contemplate the letter. Faces cut from various magazines stared at him from across the room, waiting to be turned into collages for an as-yet-untitled autobiography in the third person written (and self-published) by a Mr. Dradin Kashmir. The collages represented a month's rent and he was late completing them. He avoided the faces as if they all wore his father's scowl.

Did the envelope contain a commission? He took it out of his pocket, weighed it in his hand. Not heavy. A single sheet of paper? The indifferent light of his apartment made the maroon envelope almost black. The seal still scintillated so beautifully in his artist's imagination that he hesitated to break it. Reluctantly—his fingers must be coerced into such an action—he broke the seal, opened the flap, and pulled out a sheet of parchment paper shot through with crimson threads. Words had been printed on the paper in a gold-orange ink, followed by the same mask symbol found on the seal. He skimmed the words several times, as if by rapid review he might discover some hidden message, some hint of closure. But the words only deepened the mystery:

Invitation To A Beheading

You Are Invited to Attend:
45 Archmont Avenue
7:30 in the evening
25th Day of This Month
Please arrive in costume

Lake stared at the message. A masquerade, but to what purpose? He suppressed an impulse to laugh and instead walked over to the balcony and opened the windows, letting in fresh air. The sudden chaos of voices from below, the rough sounds of street traffic—on foot, on horses, or in motored vehicles—gave Lake a comforting sense of community, as if he were debating the mystery of the message with the world.

From his balcony window he could see, on the right, a green-tinged slice of the valley, while straight ahead the spires and domes of the Religious Quarter burned white, gold, and silver. To the left, the solid red brick and orange marble of more apartment buildings.

Lake liked the view. It reminded him that he had survived three years in a city notorious for devouring innocents whole. Not famous, true, but not dead or defeated either. Indeed, he took a perverse pleasure from enduring and withstanding the city's countless petty cruelties, for he believed it made him stronger. One day he might rule the city, for certainly it had not ruled him.

And now this—this letter that seemed to have come from the city itself. Surely it was the work of one of his artist friends—Kinsky, Raffe, or that ruinous old scoundrel, Sonter? A practical joke, perhaps even Merrimount's doing? "Invitation To A Beheading." What could it mean? He vaguely remembered a book, a fiction, with that title, written by Sirin, wasn't it? Sirin, whose pseudonyms spread through the pages of literary journals like some mad yet strangely wonderful disease.

But perhaps it meant nothing at all and "they" intended that he waste so much time studying it that he would be late finishing his commissions.

Lake walked back to his chair and sat down. Gold ink was expensive, and the envelope, on closer inspection, was flecked with gold as well, while the paper for the invitation itself had gold threads. The paper even smelled of orange peel cologne. Lake frowned, his gaze lingering on the shimmery architecture of the Religious Quarter. The cost of such an invitation came to a sum equal to a week's commissions. Would his friends spend so much on a joke?

His frown deepened. Perhaps, merriest joke of all, the letter had been misdelivered, the sender having used the wrong address. Only, it *had* no address on it. Which made him suspect his friends again. And might the attendant, if he went back to the post office, recall who had slipped the letter through the front slot of his box? He sighed. It was hopeless; such speculations only fed the—

A pebble sailed through the open window and fell onto his lap. He started, then smiled and rose, the pebble falling to the floor. At the window, he looked down. Raffe stared up at him from the street: daring Raffe in her sarcastic red-and-green jacket.

"Good shot," he called down. He studied her face for any hint of complicity in a plot, found no mischief there, realized it meant nothing.

"We're headed for the Calf for the evening," Raffe shouted up at him. "Are you coming?"

Lake nodded. "Go on ahead. I'll be there soon."

Raffe smiled, waved, and continued on down the street.

Lake retreated into his room, put the letter back in its envelope, stuffed it all into an inner pocket, and retired to the bathroom down the hall, the better to freshen up for the night's festivities. As he washed his face and looked into the moss-tinged mirror, he considered whether he should remain mum or share the invitation. He had still not decided when he walked out onto the street and into the harsh light of late afternoon.

By the time he reached the Cafe of the Ruby-Throated Calf, Lake found that his fellow artists had, aided by large quantities of alcohol, adopted a cavalier attitude toward the War of the Reds and the Greens. As a gang of Reds ran by, dressed in their patchwork crimson robes, his friends rose together, produced their red flags and cheered as boisterously as if at some sporting event. Lake had just taken a seat, generally ignored in the hubbub, when a gang of Greens trotted by in pursuit, and once again his friends rose, green flags in hand this time, and let out a roar of approval.

Lake smiled, Raffe giving him a quick elbow to the ribs before she turned back to her conversation, and he let the smell of coffee and chocolate work its magic. His leg ached, as it did sometimes when he was under stress, but otherwise, he had no complaints. The weather had remained pleasant, neither too warm nor too cold, and a breeze ruffled the branches of the potted zindel trees with their jade leaves. The trees formed miniature forests around groups of tables, effectively blocking out rival conversations without blocking the street from view. Artists lounged in their iron latticework chairs or slouched over the black-framed round glass tables while imbibing a succession of exotic drinks and coffees. The night lanterns had just been turned on and the glow lent a cozy warmth to their own group, cocooned as they were by the foliage and the soothing murmur of conversations.

The four sitting with Lake he counted as his closest friends: Raffe, Sonter, Kinsky, and Merrimount. The rest had become as interchangeable as the bricks of Hoegbotton & Sons' many trading outposts, and about as interesting. At the moment, X, Y, and Z claimed the outer tables like petty island tyrants, their faces peering pale and glinty-eyed in at Lake's group, one ear to the inner conversation while at the same time trying to maintain an uneasy autonomy.

Merrimount, a handsome man with long, dark lashes and wide blue eyes, combined elements of painting and performance art in his work, his life itself a kind of performance art. Merrimount was Lake's on-again, off-again lover, and Lake shot him a raffish grin to let him know that, surely, they would be on-again soon? Merrimount ignored him. Last time they had seen each other, Lake had made Merri cry. "You want too much," Merri had said. "No one can give you that much love, not and still be human. Or sane." Raffe had told Lake to stay away from Merri but, painful as it was to admit, Lake knew Raffe meant *he* was bad for Merri.

Raffe, who sat next to Merrimount—a buffer between him and Lake—was a tall woman with long black hair and dark, expressive eyebrows that lent a needed intensity to her light green eyes. Raffe and Lake had become friends the day he arrived in Ambergris. She had found him on Albumuth Boulevard, watching the crowds, an overwhelmed, almost defeated, look on his face. Raffe had let him stay with her for the three months it had taken him to find his city legs. She painted huge, swirling, passionate city scapes in which the people all seemed caught in mid-step of some intricate and unbearably graceful dance. They sold well, and not just to tourists.

Lake said to Raffe, "Do you think it wise to be so . . . careless?"

"Why, whatever do you mean, Martin?" Raffe had a deep, distinctly feminine voice that he never tired of hearing.

The strong, gravely tones of Michael Kinsky, sitting on the other side of Merrimount, rumbled through Lake's answer: "He means, aren't we afraid of the donkey asses known as the Reds and the monkey butts known as the Greens."

Kinsky had a wiry frame and a sparse red beard. He made mosaics from discarded bits of stone, jewelry, and other gimcracks discovered on the city's streets. Kinsky had been well-liked by Voss Bender and Lake imagined the composer's death had dealt Kinsky's career a serious blow—although, as always, Kinsky's laconic demeanor appeared unruffled by catastrophe.

"We're not afraid of anything," Raffe said, raising her chin and putting her hands on her sides in mock bravado.

Edward Sonter, to Kinsky's right and Lake's immediate left, giggled. He had a horrible tendency to produce a high-pitched squeal of amusement, in total contrast to the sensuality of his art. Sonter made abstract pottery and sculptures, vaguely obscene in nature. His gangly frame and his face, in which the eyes floated unsteadily, could often be seen in the Religious Quarter, where his work enjoyed unusually brisk sales.

As if Sonter's giggle had been a signal, they began to talk careers, gauge the day's fortunes and misfortunes. They had tame material this time: a gallery owner—no one Lake knew—had been discovered selling wall space in return for sexual favors. Lake ordered a cup of coffee, with a chocolate chaser, and listened without enthusiasm.

Lake sensed familiar undercurrents of tension, as each artist sought to ferret out information about his or her fellows—weasels, bright-eyed and eager for the kill, that their own weasel selves might burn all the brighter. These tensions had eaten more than one conversation, leaving the table silent with barely suppressed hatred born of envy. Such a cruel and cutting silence had even eaten an artist or two. Personally, Lake enjoyed the tension because it rarely centered around him; he was by far the most obscure member of the inner circle, kept there by the strength of Raffe's patronage. Now, though, he felt a different tension, centered around the letter. It lay in a pocket against his chest like a second heart in his awareness of it.

As the shadows deepened into early dusk and the buttery light of the lanterns on their delightfully curled bronze posts held back the night, the conversation, lubricated by wine, became to Lake's ears tantalizingly anonymous, as will happen in the company of people one is comfortable with, so that Lake could never remember exactly who had said what, or who had argued for what position. Lake later wondered if anything had been said, or if they had sat there, beautifully mute, while inside his head a conversation took place between Martin and Lake.

He spent the time contemplating the pleasures of reconciliation with Merri—drank in the twinned marvels of the man's perfect mouth, the compact, sinuous body. But Lake could not forget the letter. This, and his growing ennui, led him to direct the conversation toward a more timely subject:

"I've heard it said that the Greens are disemboweling innocent folk near the docks, just off of Albumuth. If they bleed red, they are denounced as sympathizers against Voss Bender; if they bleed green, then their attackers apologize for the inconvenience and try to patch them up. Of course, if they bleed green, they're likely headed for the columbarium anyhow."

"Are you trying to disgust us?"

"It wouldn't surprise me if it *were* true—it seems in keeping with the man himself: self-proclaimed Dictator of Art, with heavy emphasis on 'Dic.' We all know he was a genius, but it's a good thing he's dead . . . unless one of you is a Green with a dagger . . . "

"Very funny."

"Certainly it is rare for a single artist to so thoroughly dominate the city's cultural life—"

"—Not to mention politics—"

("Who started the Reds and the Greens anyhow?")

"And to be discussed so thoroughly, in so many cafes—"

("It started as an argument about the worth of Bender's music, between two professors of musicology on Trotten Street. Leave it to musicians to start a war over music; now that you're caught up, listen for God's sake!")

"—Not to mention politics, you say. And isn't it a warning to us all that Art and Politics are like oil and water? To comment—"

"—'oil and water'? Now we understand why you're a painter."

"How clever."

"—as I said, to comment on it, perhaps, if forced to, but not to partici-pate?"

"But if not Bender, then some bureaucratic businessman like Trillian. Trillian, the Great Banker. Sounds like an advertisement, not a leader. Surely, Merrimount, we're damned either way. And why not let the city run itself?"

"Oh—and it's done such a good job of that so far—"

"Off topic. We're bloody well off topic—again!"

"Ah, but what you two *don't* see is that it is precisely his audience's passionate connection to his *art*—the fact that people believe the operas are the man—that has created the crisis!"

"I thought his *death* caused the crisis?"

At that moment, a group of Greens ran by. Lake, Merrimount, Kinsky, and Sonter all raised their green flags with a curious mixture of derision and drunken fervor. Raffe sat up and shouted after them, "He's dead! He's dead! He's dead!" Her face was flushed, her hair furiously tan-gled.

The last of the Greens turned at the sound of Raffe's voice, his face ghastly pale under the lamps. Lake saw that the man's hands dripped red. He forced Raffe to sit down: "Hush now, hush!" The man's gaze swept across their table, and then he was running after his comrades, soon out of sight.

"Yes, not so obvious, that's all."

"Their spies are everywhere."

"Why, I found one in my nose this morning while blowing it."

"The morning or the nose?"

Laughter, and then a voice from beyond the inner circle, muffled by the dense shrubbery, offered, "It's not certain Bender is dead. The Greens claim he is alive."

"Ah yes." The inner circle deftly appropriated the topic, slamming like a rude, massive door on the outer circle.

"Yes, he's alive."

"—or he's dead and coming back in a fortnight, just a bit rotted for the decay. Delay?"

"—no one's actually seen the body."

"—hush hush secrecy. Even his friends didn't see—"

"—and what we're witnessing is actually a *coup*."

"Coo coo."

"Shut up, you bloody pigeon."

"I'm not a pigeon—I'm a cuckoo."

"Bender hated pigeons."

"He hated cuckoos too."

"He was a cuckoo."

"Boo! Boo!"

"As if *anyone* really controls this city, anyway?"

"O fecund grand mother matron, Ambergris, bathed in the blood of versions under the gangrenous moon." Merrimount's melodramatic lilt was unmistakable, and Lake roused himself.

"Did I hear right?" Lake rubbed his ears. "Is this *poetry*? Verse? But what is this gristle: bathed in the blood of *versions*? Surely, my merry mount, you mean *virgins*. We all were one once—or had one once."

A roar of approval from the gallery.

But Merrimount countered: "No, no, my dear Lake, I *meant* versions—I protest. I meant versions: Bathed in the blood of the city's many *versions* of itself."

"A nice recovery"—Sonter again—"but I still think you're drunk."

At which point, Sonter and Merrimount fell out of the conversation, the two locked in an orbit of "version"/"virgin" that, in all likelihood, would continue until the sun and moon fell out of the sky. Lake felt a twinge of jealousy.

Kinsky offered a smug smile, stood, stretched, and said, "I'm going to the opera. Anyone with me?"

A chorus of boos, accompanied by a series of "Fuck off's!"

Kinsky, face ruddy, guffawed, threw down some coins for his bill, and stumbled off down the street which, despite the late hour, twitched and rustled with foot traffic.

"Watch out for the Reds, the Greens, and the Blues," Raffe shouted after him.

"The Blues?" Lake said, turning to Raffe.

"Yes. The Blues—you know. The sads."

"Funny. I think the Blues are more dangerous than the Greens and the Reds put together."

"Only the Browns are more deadly."

Lake laughed, stared after Kinsky. "He's not serious, is he?"

"No," Raffe said. "After all, if there is to be a massacre, it will be at the opera. You'd think the theater owners, or even the actors, would have more sense and close down for a month."

"Shouldn't we leave the city? Just the two of us—and maybe Merrimount?"

Raffe snorted. "And maybe Merrimount? And where would we go? Morrow? The Court of the Kalif? Excuse me for saying so, but I'm broke."

Lake smirked. "Then why are you drinking so much."

"Seriously. Do you mean you'd pay for a trip?"

"No—I'm just as poor as you." Lake put down the drink. "But, I would pay for some advice."

"Eat healthy foods. Do your commissions on time. Don't let Merrimount back into your life."

"No, no. Not that kind of advice. More specific."

"About what?"

He leaned forward, said softly, "Have you ever received an anonymous commission?"

"How do you mean?"

"A letter appears in your post office box. It has no return address. Your address isn't on it. It's clearly from someone wealthy. It tells you to go to a certain place at a certain time. It mentions a masquerade."

Raffe frowned, the corners of her eyes narrowing. "You're serious."

"Yes."

"I've never gotten a commission like that. You have?"

"Yes. I think. I mean, I think it's a commission."

"May I see the letter."

Lake looked at her, his best friend, and somehow he couldn't share it with her.

"I don't have it with me."

"Liar!"

As he started to protest, she took his hand and said, "No, no—it's all right. I understand. I won't take an advantage from you. But you want advice on whether you should go?"

Lake nodded, too ashamed to look at her.

"It might be your big break—a major collector who wants to remain anonymous until he's cornered the market in Lake originals. Or . . . "

She paused and a great fear settled over Lake, a fear he knew could only overwhelm him so quickly because it had been there all along.

"Or?"

"It could be a . . . special assignation."

"A *what?*"

"You don't know what I mean?"

He took a sip of his drink, set it down again, said, "I'll admit it. I've no idea what you're talking about."

"Naive, naive Martin," she said, and leaned forward to ruffle his hair.

Blushing, he drew back, said, "Just tell me, Raffe."

Raffe smiled. "Sometimes, Martin, a wealthy person will get a filthy little idea in a filthy little part of their mind—and that idea is to have personalized pornography done by an artist."

"Oh."

Quickly, she said, "But I'm probably wrong. Even if so, that kind of work pays very well. Maybe even enough to let you take time off from commissions to do your own work."

"So I should go?"

"You only become successful by taking chances . . . I've been meaning to tell you, Martin, as a friend and fellow artist—"

"What? What have you been meaning to tell me?"

Lake was acutely aware that Sonter and Merrimount had fallen silent. She took his hand in hers. "Your work is small."

"Miniatures?" Lake said incredulously.

"No. How do I say this? Small in ambition. Your art treads carefully. You need to take bigger steps. You need to paint a bigger world."

Lake looked up at the clouds, trying to disguise the hurt in his voice, the ache in his throat: *"You're saying I'm no good."*

"I'm only saying *you* don't think you're any good. Why else do you waste such a talent on facile portraits, on a thousand lesser disciplines that *require* no discipline. You, Martin, could be the Voss Bender of artists."

"And look what happened to him—he's dead."

"Martin!"

Suddenly he felt very tired, very . . . small. His father's voice rang in his head unpleasantly.

"There's something about the quality of the light in this city that I cannot capture in paint," he mumbled.

"What?"

"The quality of light is deadly."

"I don't understand. Are you angry with me?"

He managed a thin smile. "Raffe, how could I be angry with you? I need time to think about what you've said. It's not something I can just agree with. But in the meantime, I'll take your advice—I'll go."

Raffe's face brightened. "Good! Now escort me home. I need my sleep."

"Merrimount will be jealous."

"No I won't," Merrimount said, with a look that was half scowl, half grin. "You just *wish* I'd be jealous."

Raffe squeezed his arm and said, "After all, no matter what the commission is, you can always say no."

***

However, once we have explored Lake's own exploration of the post office as building and metaphor, how much closer are we to the truth? Not very close at all. If biography is too slim to help us and the post office itself too superficial, then we must turn to other sources—specifically, Lake's other paintings of note, for in the differences and similarities to "Invitation" we may uncover a kind of truth.

We can first, and most generally, discuss Lake's work in terms of architecture, in terms of his love for his adopted home. If "Invitation to a Beheading" marked Lake's emergence into maturity, it also inaugurated his fascination with Ambergris. The city is often the sole subject of Lake's art—and in almost every case the city encloses, crowds, or enmazes the people sharing the canvas. Further, the city has a palpable *presence* in Lake's work. It almost *intercedes* in the lives of its citizens.

Lake's well-known "Albumuth Boulevard" trip-tyche consists of panels that ostensibly show, at dawn, noon and dusk, the scene from a fourth story window, looking down over a block of apartment buildings beyond which lie the domes of the Religious Quarter (shiny with the transcendent quality of light that Lake first perfected in "Invitation to a Beheading"). The painting is quite massive, the predominant colors yellow, red, and green. The one human constant to the three panels is a man standing on the boulevard below, surrounded by pedestrians. At first, the architecture appears identical, but on closer inspection, the streets, the buildings, clearly change or shift in each scene, in each panel further encroaching on the man. By dusk, the buildings have grown gargoyles where once perched pigeons. The people surrounding the man have become progressively more animal-like, their heads angular, their noses snouts, their teeth fangs. The expressions on the faces of these people become progressively sadder, more melancholy and tragic, while the man, impassive, with his back to us, has no face. The buildings themselves come to resemble sad faces, so that the overall effect of the final panel is overwhelming . . . and yet, oddly, we feel sad not for the people or the buildings, but for the one immutable element of the series—the faceless man who stands with his back to the viewer.

This, then, is where Lake parts company with such symbolists as the great Darcimbaldo—Lake refuses to lose himself in his grotesque structures, or to abandon himself solely to an imagination under no causal restraints. All of his mature paintings possess a sense of overwhelming *sorrow*. This sorrow lifts his work above that of his contemporaries and provides the depth, the mystery, that so captivates the general public. —From Janice Shriek's *A Short Overview of The Art of Martin Lake and His Invitation to a Beheading*, for the *Hoegbotton Guide to Ambergris*, 5th edition.

***

Lake slept fitfully that moonless night, but when he woke the moon blossomed obscenely bright and red beyond his bed. His sheets had become, in that crimson light, violet waves of rippled fabric slick with his sweat. He smelled blood. The walls stank of it. A man stood in front of the open balcony windows, almost eclipsed by the weight of the moon at his back. Lake could not see the man's face. Lake sat up in bed.

"Merrimount? Merrimount? You've returned to me after all."

The man stood at the side of the bed. Lake stood by the balcony window. The man lay in the bed. Lake walked to the balcony. The man and Lake stood a foot apart in the middle of the room, the moon crepuscular and blood-engorged behind Lake. The moon was breathing its scarlet breath upon his back. He could not see the man's face. He was standing right in front of the man and could not see his face. The apartment, fixed in the perfect clarity of the bleeding light cried out to him in the sharpness of its detail, so that his eyes cut themselves upon such precision. Every bristle on his dried out brushes surrendered to him its slightest imperfection. Every canvas became porous with the numbling roughness of its gesso.

"You're not Merrimount," he said to the man.

The man's eyes were closed.

Lake stood facing the moon. The man stood facing Lake.

The man opened his eyes and the ferruginous light of the moon shot through them and formed two rusty spots on Lake's neck, as if the man's eyes were just holes that pierced his skull from back to front.

The moon blinked out. The light still streamed from the man's eyes. The man smiled a half-moon smile and the light trickled out from between his teeth.

The man held Lake's left hand, palm up.

The knife sliced into the middle of Lake's palm. He felt the knife tear through the skin, and into the palmar fascia muscle, and beneath that, into the tendons, vessels, and nerves. The skin peeled back until his entire hand was flayed and open. He saw the knife sever the muscle from the lower margin of the annular ligament, then felt, almost heard, the lesser muscles snap back from the bones as they were cut—six for the middle finger, three for the ring finger—the knife now grinding up against the os magnum as the man guided it into the area near Lake's wrist—slicing through extensor tendons, through the nerves, through the farthest outposts of the radial and ulnar arteries. He could see it all—the yellow of the thin fat layer, the white of bone obscured by the dull red of muscle, the gray of tendons, as surely as if his hand had been labeled and diagrammed for his own benefit. The blood came thick and heavy, draining from all of his extremities until he only had feeling in his chest. The pain was infinite, so infinite that he did not try to escape it, but tried only to escape the red gaze of the man who was butchering him while he just stood there and let him do it. The thought went through his head like a dirge, like an epitaph, *I will never paint again.*

He could not get away. He could not get away.

Lake's hand began to mutter, to mumble . . .

In response, the man sang to Lake's hand, the words incomprehensible, strange, sad.

Lake's hand began to scream—a long, drawn out scream, ever higher in pitch, the wound become a mouth into which the man continued to plunge the knife.

Lake woke up shrieking. He was drowning in sweat, his right hand clenched around his left wrist. He tried to control his breathing—he sucked in great gulps of air—but found it was impossible. Panicked, he looked toward the window. There was no moon. No one stood there. He forced his gaze down to his left hand (he had done nothing, nothing, nothing while the man cut him apart) and found it whole.

He was still shrieking.

**

In "Invitation to a Beheading," the sorrow takes the form of two figures: the insect catcher outside the building and the man highlighted in the upper window of the post office itself. (If it seems that I have kept these two figures a secret in order to make of them a revelation, it is because they *are* a revelation to the viewer—due to the mass of detail around them, they are generally the last seen, and then, in a tribute to their intensity, the *only* things seen.)

The insect catcher, his light dimmed but for a single orange spark, hurries off down the front steps, one hand held up behind him, as if to ward off the man in the window. Is this figure literally Lake's father, or does it represent some mythical insect catcher—*the* Insect Catcher? Or did Lake see his father as a mythic figure? From my conversations with Lake, the latter interpretation strikes me as most plausible.

But to what can we attribute the single clear window in the building's upper story, through which we see a man who stands in utter anguish, his head thrown back to the sky? In one hand, the man holds a letter, while the other is held palm up by a vaguely stork-like shadow that has driven a knife through it. The scene derives all of its energy from this view through the window: the greens radiate outward from the pulsing crimson spot that marks where the knife has penetrated flesh. Adding to the effect, Lake has so layered and built up his oils that a trick of perspective is created by which the figure simultaneously exists inside and outside the window.

Although the building that houses this intricate scene lends itself to fantastical interpretation, and Lake might be thought to have recreated some historical event in phantasmagorical fashion, the figure with the pierced palm is clearly a man, not a child or mushroom dweller, and the letter held in the man's right hand indicates an admission of the building's use as a post office rather than as a morgue (unless, under duress, we are forced to acknowledge the weak black humor of "dead letter office").

Further examination of the man's face reveals two disturbing elements: (1) it bears a striking resemblance to Lake's own face, and (2) under close scrutiny with a magnifying glass, there is a second, almost translucent set of features transposed over the first. This "mask," its existence disputed by some critics, mimics, like a mold made from life, the features of the first, except in two particulars: this man has teeth made of broken glass and he, unlike his counterpart, smiles with unnerving brutality. Is this the face of the faceless man from "Albumuth Boulevard?" Is this the face of Death?

Regardless of Lake's intent, all of these elements combine to create in the viewer—even the viewer who only subconsciously notes certain of the more hidden elements—a true sense of unease and dread, as well as the release of this dread through the anguished, voiceless cry of the man in the window. The man in the window provides us with the only movement in the painting, for the insect catcher, hurrying away, is already in the past, and the bones of the post office are also in the past. Only the forlorn figure in the window is still alive, caught forever in the present. Further, although foresaken by the insect catcher and pierced by a shadow that may be a manifestation of his own fear, the *light* never forsakes or betrays him. Lake's tones are, as Venturi has noted, "resonant rather than bright, and the light contained in them is not so much a physical as a psychological illumination." —From Janice Shriek's *A Short Overview of The Art of Martin Lake and His Invitation to a Beheading,* for the *Hoegbotton Guide to Ambergris,* 5th edition.

***

Lake spent the next day trying to forget his nightmare. To rid himself of its cloying atmosphere, he left his apartment—but not before receiving a stern lecture from Dame Truff on how loud noises after midnight showed no consideration for other tenants, while behind her a few neighbors, who had not come to his aid but obviously had heard his screams, gave him curious stares.

Then, punishment over, he made his way through the crowded streets to the Gallery of Hidden Fascinations, portfolio under one arm. The portfolio contained two new paintings, both of his father's hands, as he remembered them, open wide like wings as a cornucopia of insects—velvet ants, cicadas, moths, butterflies, walking sticks, praying mantises—crawled over them. It was a study he had been working on for years. His father had beautifully ruined hands, bitten and stung countless times, but as polished, as smooth, as white marble.

The gallery owner, Janice Shriek, greeted him at the door; she was a severe, hunched woman with calculating, cold blue eyes. This morning she had thrown on foppishly male trousers, and a jacket over a white shirt, the sleeves of which ended in cuffs that looked as if they had been made from doilies. Shriek rose up on tip-toe to plant a ceremonial kiss on his cheek while explaining that the short, portly gentleman currently casting his round shadow over the far end of the gallery had expressed interest in one of Lake's pieces, how fortunate that he had stopped by, and that while she continued to enflame that interest—she actually said "enflamed," much to Lake's amazement; was he to be some artistic gigolo now?—Lake should set down his portfolio and, after a decent interval, walk over and introduce himself, that was a dear—and back she scamper-lurched to the potential customer, leaving Lake rather breathless on her behalf. No one could ever say Janice Shriek lacked energy.

Lake placed his portfolio on a nearby table, the art of his countless rivals glaring down at him from the walls. The only good art (besides Lake's, of course) was a miniature entitled "Amber in the City" by Shriek's great find, Roger Mandible, who, unbeknownst to Shriek, had created his subtle amber shades from the earwax of a well-known diva who had had the misfortune to fall asleep at a cafe table where Mandible was mixing his paints. It made Lake snicker every time he saw it.

After a moment, Lake walked over to Shriek and the gentleman and engaged in the kind of obsequious small talk that nauseated him.

"Yes, I'm the artist."

"Maxwell Bibble. A pleasure to meet you."

"Likewise . . . Bibble. It is exceedingly rare to meet a true lover of art."

Bibble stank of beets. Lake could not get over it. Bibble stank of beets. He had difficulty not saying *Bibble imbibes bottled beets beautifully* . . .

"Well, you do . . . you do so well with, er, *colors*," Bibble said.

"How discerning you are. Did you hear what he said, Janice," Lake said.

Shriek nodded nervously, said, "Mr. Bibble's a businessman, but he has always wanted to be a—" *Beet?* thought Lake; but no: " . . . a critic of the arts," Shriek finished.

"Yes, marvelous colors," Bibble said, this time with more confidence.

"It is nothing. The *true artiste* can bend even the most stubborn light to his will," Lake said.

"I imagine so. I thought this piece might look good in the kitchen, next to the wife's needle point."

"'In the kitchen, next to the wife's needlepoint,'" Lake echoed blankly, and then put on a frozen smile.

"But I'm wondering if maybe it is too big . . . "

"It's smaller than it looks," Shriek offered, somewhat pathetically, Lake thought.

"Perhaps I could have it altered, cut down to size," Lake said, glaring at Shriek.

Bibble nodded, putting a hand to his chin in rapt contemplation of the possibilities.

"Or maybe I should just saw it in fourths and you can take the fourth you like best," Lake said. "Or maybe eighths would be more to your liking?"

Bibble stared blankly at him for a moment, before Shriek stepped in with, "Artists! Always joking! You know, I really don't think it will be too large. You could always buy it and if it doesn't fit, return it—not that I could refund your money, but you could pick something else."

Enough! Lake thought, and disengaged himself from the conversation. Leaving Shriek to ramble on convincingly about the cunning strength of his brushstrokes, etc.—a slick blather of nonsense that Lake despised and admired all at once. He could not complain that Shriek neglected to promote him—she was the only one who would take his work—but he hated the way she appropriated his art, speaking at times almost as if she herself had created it. A failed painter and a budding art historian, Shriek had started the gallery through the largesse of her famous brother, the historian Duncan Shriek, who had also procured for her many of her first and best clients. Lake felt that her drive to push, push, push was linked to a certain guilt at not having had to start at the bottom like everyone else.

Eventually, as Lake gave a thin-lipped smile, Bibble, still reeking of beets, announced that he couldn't possibly commit at the moment, but would come back later. Definitely, he would be back—and what a pleasure to meet the artist.

To which Lake said, and was sorry even as the words left his mouth, "It is a pleasure to *be* the artist."

A nervous laugh from Shriek. An unpleasant laugh from the almost-buyer, whose hand Lake tried his best to crush as they shook goodbye.

After Bibble had left, Shriek turned to him and said, "That was wonderful!"

"What was wonderful?"

Shriek's eyes became colder than usual. "That smug, arrogant, better-than-thou artist's demeanor. They like that, you know—it makes them feel they've bought the work of a budding genius."

"Well haven't they?" Lake said. Was she being sarcastic? He'd pretend otherwise.

Shriek patted him on the back. "Whatever it is, keep it up. Now, let's take a look at the new paintings."

Lake bit his lip to stop himself from committing career suicide, walked over to the table, and retrieved the two canvases. He spread them out with an awkward flourish.

Shriek stared at them, a quizzical look on her face.

"Well?" Lake finally said, Raffe's words from the night before buzzing in his ears. "Do you like them?"

"Hmm?" Shriek said, looking up from the paintings as if her thoughts had been far away.

Lake experienced a truth viscerally in that moment which he had only ever realized intellectually before: he was the least of Shriek's many prospects, and he was boring her.

Nonetheless, he pressed on, braced for further humiliation: "Do you like them?"

"Oh! The paintings?"

"No—the . . . " *The ear wax on your walls?* he thought. *The beets?* "Yes, the paintings."

Shriek's brows furrowed and she put a hand to her chin in unconscious mimicry of the departed Bibble. "They're very . . . interesting."

Interesting.

"They're of my father's hands," Lake said, aware that he was about to launch into a confession both unseemly and useless, as if he could help make the paintings more appealing to her by saying *this happened*, this is a person *I know*, it is *real* therefore it is *good*. But he had no choice—he plunged forward: "He is a startlingly nonverbal man, my father, as most insect catchers are, but there was one way he felt comfortable communicating with me, Janice—by coming home with his hands closed—and when he'd open them, there would be some living jewel, some rare wonder of the insect world—sparkling black, red, or green—and his eyes would sparkle too. He'd name them all for me in his soft, stumbling voice—lovingly so; how they were all so very different from one another, how although he killed them and we often ate them in hard times, how it must be with respect and out of knowledge." Lake looked at the floor. "He wanted me to be an insect catcher too, but I wouldn't. I couldn't. I had to become an artist." He remembered the way the joy had shriveled up inside his father when he realized his son would not be following in his footsteps. It had hurt Lake to see his father so alone, trapped by his reticence and his solitary profession, but he knew it hurt his father more. He missed his father; it was an ache in his chest.

"That's a lovely story, Martin. A lovely story."

"So you'll take them?"

"No. But it is a lovely story."

"But see how perfectly I've rendered the insects," Lake said, pointing to them.

"Yes, you have. But it's a slow season and I don't have the space. Maybe when your other work sells." Her tone as much as said not to press her too far.

With a great effort of will, Lake said, "I understand. I'll come visit again in a few months."

The invitation to a beheading was looking better to Lake all the time.

When Lake returned to his apartment to work on Mr. Kashmir's commission, he was decidedly out of sorts. In addition to his disappointing trip to the gallery, he had spent money on greasy sausage that now sat in his belly like an extra coil of intestines. It did not help that the image of the man from his nightmares blinked on and off in his head no matter how hard he tried to suppress it.

Nevertheless, he dutifully picked up the pages of illustrations he had torn from discarded books bought cheap at the back door of the Borges Bookstore. He set about cutting them out with his rusty paint-speckled scissors. Ideas for his commissions came to him not in flashes from his muse but as calm re-creations of past work. Lately, he knew, he had become lazy, providing literal "translations" for his commissions, while suppressing any hint of his own imagination.

Still, this did not explain why, following a period of work during which he stared at the envelope and its invitation where it lay on his easel, he looked down to find that after carefully cutting out a trio of etched dancing girls, he had just as carefully sliced off their heads and then cut star designs out of their torsos.

In disgust, Lake tossed the scissors aside and let the ruins of the dancing girls flutter to the floor like exotic confetti. Obviously, Mr. Kashmir's assignment would have to await a spark of inspiration. In the meantime, the afternoon still young, he would take Raffe's advice and work on something for himself.

Lake walked over to the crowded easel, emptied it by placing four or five canvases on the already chaotic bed, pulled his stool over, retrieved a blank canvas, and pinned it up. Slowly, he began to brushstroke oils onto the canvas. Despite three years of endless commissions, the familiar smell of fresh paint excited his senses and, even better, the light behind him was sharp, clear, so he did not have to resort to borrowing Dame Truff's lantern.

As he progressed, Lake did not know the painting's subject, or even how best to apply the oils, but he continued to create layers of paint, sensitive to the pressure of the brush against canvas. Raffe had forced the oils upon him months ago. At the time, he had given her a superior, doubtful look, since her last gift had been special paints created from a mixture of natural pigments and freshwater squid ink. Lake had used them for a week before his first paintings began to fade; soon his canvases were as blank as before. Raffe, always trying to find the good in the bad, had told him, when next they met at a cafe, that he could become famous selling "disappearing paintings." He had thrown the paint set at her. Fortunately, it missed and hit a stranger—a startled and startlingly handsome man named Merrimount.

This time, however, Raffe's idea appeared to be a good one. It had been several years since he had used oils and he had forgotten the ease of creating texture with them, how the paint built upon itself. He especially liked how he could blend colors for gradations of shadow. Assuming the current troubles were temporary—and that a drop cloth would suffice until that time—and even now giving a quick look over his shoulder, he worked on building color: emerald, jade, moss, lime, verdigris. He mixed all the shades in, until he had a luminous, shining background. Then, in dark green, he began to paint a face . . .

Only the Religious Quarter's evening call to prayer—the solemn tolling of the bell five times from the old Truffidian cathedral—roused Lake from his trance. He blinked, turned toward the window, then looked back at his canvas. In shock and horror, he let the brush fall from his hand.

The head had a brutish mouth of broken glass teeth through which it smiled cruelly, while above the ruined nose, the eyes shone like twin flames. Lake stared at the face from his nightmare.

For a long time, Lake examined his work. His first impulse, to paint over it and start fresh, gradually gave way to a second, deeper impulse: to finish it. Far better, he thought, that the face should remain in the painting than, erased, once more take up residence in his mind. A little thrill ran through him as he realized it was totally unlike anything he had done before.

"I've trapped you," he said to it, gloating.

It stared at him with its unearthly eyes and said nothing. On the canvas it might still smile, but it could not smile only at him. Now it smiled at the world.

He worked on it for a few more minutes, adding definition to the eyelids and narrowing the cheekbones, relieved, for now that he had come around to the idea that the face *belonged* in the world, that perhaps it had always been in the world, he wanted it perfect in every detail, that no trace of it should ever haunt him again.

As the shadows lengthened and deepened, falling across his canvas, he put aside his palette, cleaned his brushes with turpentine, washed them in the sink across the hall, and quickly dressed to the sounds of a busker on the street below. After he had put on his jacket, he stuck his sketchbook and two sharpened pencils into his breast pocket—in case his mysterious host should need an immediate demonstration of his skills—and, running his fingers over the ornate seal, deposited the invitation there as well.

A few moments of rummaging under his bed and he had fished out a collapsible rubber frog head he had worn to the Festival of the Freshwater Squid a year before—it would have to do for a costume. He stuffed it in a side pocket, one bulbous yellow eye staring up at him absurdly. Further rummaging uncovered his map. Every wise citizen of Ambergris carried a map of the city, for its alleys were legion and seemed to change course of their own accord.

He spent a nervous moment adjusting his tie, then locked his apartment door behind him. He took a deep breath, descended the stairs, and set off down Albumuth Boulevard as the sky melted into the orange-green hue peculiar to Ambergris and Ambergris alone.

***

We find this quality of illumination in almost all of Lake's paintings, but nowhere more strikingly than in the incendiary "The Burning House," where it is meshed to a comment on his fear of birds—the only painting with any hint of birds in it besides "Invitation to a Beheading" and "Through His Eyes" (which I will discuss shortly). "The Burning House" blends reds, yellows, and oranges much as "Invitation" blends greens, but for a different effect. The painting shows a house with its roof and front wall torn away—to expose an owl, a stork, and a raven that are burning alive, while the totality of the flames themselves form the shadow of a fire bird, done in a style similar to Lagach. Clearly, this is as close to pure fantasy as Lake ever came, a wish fulfillment work in which his fear of birds is washed away by fire. As Venturi wrote, "The charm of the picture lies in its mysteriously suggestive power—the sigh of fatality that blows over the strangely contorted figures." Here we may hold another piece of the puzzle that describes the process of Lake's transformation. If so, we do not know quite where to place it—and whether it should be placed near or far away from the puzzle piece that is "Invitation to a Beheading."

A less ambiguous link to "Invitation" can be found in the person of Voss Bender, the famous opera composer nee politician, and the tumult following his death—a death that occurred only three days before Lake began "Invitation." In later interviews, the usually taciturn Lake professed to hold Voss Bender in the highest regard, even as an inspiration (although, when I knew him, I cannot recall him ever mentioning Bender). More than one art historian, noting the repetition of Bender themes in Lake's work, has wondered if Lake obsessed over the dead composer. Perhaps, as Sabon suggests, "Invitation" represents a memorial to Voss Bender. If so, it is the first in a trilogy of such paintings, the last two, "Through His Eyes" and "Aria to the Brittle Bones of Winter," clear homages to Bender. —From Janice Shriek's *A Short Overview of The Art of Martin Lake and His Invitation to a Beheading*, for the *Hoegbotton Guide to Ambergris*, 5th edition.

***

The dusk had a mingled blood-and-orange-peel scent, and the light as it faded left behind a faint golden residue on the brass doorknobs of bank entrances, on the coppery flagpoles outside the embassies of foreign dignitaries, and on the Fountain of Trillian, with its obelisk at the top of which perched a sad rose-marble cherubim, one elbow propped atop a leering black skull. Crowds had gathered at the surrounding lantern-lit square to hear poets declaim their verse while standing on wooden crates. Nearby taverns shed music and light in equal quantities, the light breaking against the cobblestones in thick shafts, while sidewalk vendors plied passersby with all manner of refreshments, from Lake's ill-starred sausages to flagrantly sinful pastries. Few outside of Ambergris realized that the great artist Darcimbaldo had created his fruit and seafood portraits from life—stolen from the vendors, who arranged oranges, apples, figs, and melons into faces with black grapes for eyes, or layered crayfish, trout, crabs, and the lesser squid into the imperious visage of the mayor; these vendors were almost as popular as the sidewalk poets, and had taken to hanging wide-angle lanterns in front of their stalls so that passersby could appreciate their ephemeral art. Through this tightly-packed throng, occasional horse-and-carriages and motored vehicles lurched through like lighthouses for the drunk and disorderly, who would push and rock them at every opportunity.

Here, then, in the flushed faces, in the mixing of dark and light, in the swirling, shadowy facades of buildings, were a thousand scenes that lent themselves to the artist's eye, but Lake, intent on his map, saw them only as hindrances now.

And more than hindrances, for the difficulty of circumnavigating the crowds with his cane convinced Lake to flag down a for-hire motored vehicle. An old, sumptuous model, nicer than his apartment and prudently festooned with red and green flags, it had only two drawbacks: the shakes—almost certainly from watered down petrol—and a large, very dirty sheep with which he was forced to share the back seat. Man and sheep contemplated each other with equal unease while the driver smiled and shrugged apologetically (to him or the sheep?), his vehicle racing through the narrow streets. Nonetheless, Lake left the vehicle first, deposited at the edge of the requested neighborhood. The nervous driver sped off at top speed as soon as Lake had paid him. No doubt the detour to deliver Lake had made the sheep late for an appointment.

As for the neighborhood, located on the southeastern flank of the Religious Quarter, Lake had rarely seen one grimmer. The buildings, four and five stories high, had a scarcity of windows that made them appear to face away from him—inward, toward the maze of houses and apartments that contained his destination. Such stark edifices gave Lake a glimpse of the future, of the decay into which his own apartment building might fall when the New Art moved on and left behind only remnants of unkept promises. The walls were awash in fire burns, the ground level doors rotted or broken open, the balconies that hung precariously over them black with rust. In some places, Lake could see bones worked into the mortar, for there had been a time when the dead were buried in the walls of their own homes.

Lake took out his invitation, ran his hand across the maroon-gold threads. Perhaps it *was* all a practical joke. Or perhaps his host just wanted to be discreet. He wavered, hesitated, but then his conversation with Raffe came back to him, followed by the irritating image of Shriek's face as she said, "Interesting." He sighed, trembled, and began to walk between two of the buildings, uncomfortable in the shadow of their height, under the blank or cracked windows whose dust-covered panes were somehow predatory. His cane clacked against rocks, a plaintive sound in that place.

Eventually, he emerged from the alleyway onto a larger street, strewn with rubbish. A few babarusa pigs, all grunts and curved tusks, fought with anemic-looking mushroom dwellers for the offal. The light had faded to a deep blue colder in its way than the temperature. The distant calls to prayer from the Religious Quarter sounded like the cries of men drowning fifty feet underwater.

By the guttering light of a public lamp, Lake made out the name of the street—Salamander—but could not locate it on his map. For a long time, the darkness broken by irregularly-posted lamps, he walked alone, examining signs, finding none of the streets on his map. He kept himself from thinking *lost!* by trying to decide how best the surrounding shadows could be captured on canvas.

Gradually, he realized that the darkness, which at least had been broken by the lamps, had taken on a hazy quality through which he could see nothing at all. Fog, come off the River Moth. He cursed his luck. First, the stars went out, occluded by the weight of the shadows and by the dull, creeping rage of the fog. It was an angry fog, a sneering fog that ate its way through the sky, through the spaces between things, and it obscured the night. It smelled of the river: of silt and brackish water, of fish and mangroves. It rolled through Lake as if he did not exist. And because of this, the fog made Lake ethereal, for he could no longer see his arms or legs, could feel nothing but the cloying moisture of the fog as it clung to and settled over him. He was a ghost. He was free. There could be no reality to this fog-ridden world. There could be no reality to him while in it.

Lost and lost again, turning in the whiteness, not sure if he had walked forward or retraced his steps. The freedom he had felt turned to fear—fear of the unknown, fear that he might be late. So when he became aware of a dimly bobbing light ahead, he began to fast walk toward it, heedless of obstacles that might make him turn an ankle or fall on his face.

A block later, he came upon the source of the light: the tall, green-hooded, green-robed figure of an insect catcher, his great, circular slab of glass attached to a round, buoy-shaped lantern that swung below it. As with most insect catchers, who are products of famine, this one was thin, with bony but strong arms. The glass was so large that the man had to hold onto it with both gloved hands, while grasshoppers, moths, beetles, and ant queens smacked up against it, trying to get to the light.

The glass functioned like a sticky lens inserted into a circular brass frame; when filled with insects, the lens would be removed and placed in a bag. The insect catcher would then insert a new lens and repeat the process. Once home, the new catch would be carefully plucked off the lens, then boiled or baked and salted, after which the insects would hang from his belt on strings for sale the next day. Many times Lake had spent his evening tying insects into strings, using a special knot taught to him by his father.

Steeped in such memories and in the fog, his first thought was that this man *was* his father. Why couldn't it be his father? They would be ghosts together, sailing through the night.

His first words to the insect catcher were tentative, respectful of his own memories.

"Excuse me? Excuse me, sir?"

The man turned with a slow grace to peer down at this latest catch. The folds of the insect catcher's robes covered his face, but for a jutting nose like a scythe.

"Yes?" The man had a deep, sonorous voice.

"Do you know which way to Archmont Lane? My map is no help at all."

The insect catcher raised one bony finger and pointed upward.

Lake looked up. There, above the insect catcher's light, was a sign for Archmont Lane. Lake stood on Archmont Lane.

"Oh," he said. "Thank you."

But the insect catcher had already shambled on into the fog, little more than a shadow under a lantern that had already begun to fade...

From there, it was relatively easy to find 45 Archmont Lane—unlike the other entrances to left and right, it suffered few signs of disrepair and a lamp blazed above the doorway. The numerals "4" and "5" were rendered in glossy gold, the door painted maroon, the steps swept clean, the door knocker a twin to the seal on the envelope—all permeated by a sudsy smell.

Reassured by such cleanliness, Raffe's advice still whispering in his ear, Lake raised the doorknocker and lowered it—once, twice, thrice.

The door opened a crack, light flooded out, and Lake caught sight of a wild, staring eye, rimmed with crusted red. It was an animal's eye, the reflection in its black pupil his own distorted face. Lake took a quick step back.

The voice, when it came, sounded unreal, falsified: "What do you want?"

Lake held up the invitation. "I have this."

A blink of the horrible eye. "What does it say?"

"An invitation to a—"

"Quick! Put on your mask!" hissed the voice.

"My mask?"

"Your mask for the masquerade!"

"Oh! Yes. Sorry. Just a moment."

Lake pulled the rubber frog mask out of his pocket and put it over his head. It felt like slick jelly. He did not want it next to his skin. As he adjusted the mask so he could see out of the eyeholes that jutted from the frog's nostrils, the door opened, revealing a splendid foyer and the outstretched arm of the man with the false voice. The man himself stood to one side and Lake, his vision restricted to what he could see directly in front of him, had to make do with the beckoning white-gloved hand and a whispered, *"Enter now!"* He walked forward. The man slammed the door behind him and locked it.

Ahead, through glass paneled doors, Lake saw a staircase of burnished rosewood and, at the foot of the stairs, a globe of the world upon a polished mahogany table with lion paws for feet. Candles guttered in their slots, the wavery light somehow religious. On the left he glimpsed tightly stacked bookcases hemmed in by generous tables, while to the right the house opened up onto a sitting room, flanked by portraits. Black drop clothes covered the name plate and face of each portrait: a line of necks and shoulders greeted him from down the hall. The smell of soap had faded, replaced by a faint trace of rot, of mildew.

Lake turned toward the front door and the person who had opened it—a butler, he presumed—only to find himself confronted by a man with a stork head. The red-ringed eyes, the cruel beak, the dull white of the feathered face, merged with a startlingly pale neck atop a gaunt body clothed in a black-and-white suit.

"I see that you are dressed already," Lake managed, although badly shaken. "And, unfortunately, as the natural predator of the frog. Ha ha. Perhaps, though, you can now tell me why I've been summoned here, Mister . . . ?"

The joke failed miserably. The attempt to discover the man's name failed with it. The Stork stared at him as if he came from a foreign, barbaric land. The Stork said, "Your jacket and your cane."

Lake disliked relinquishing his cane, which had driven off more than one potential assailant in its day, but handed both it and his jacket to the Stork. After placing them in a closet, the Stork said, "Follow me," and led Lake past the stairs, past the library, and into a study with a decorative fireplace, several upholstered chairs, a handful of glossy black wooden tables and, adorning the walls, eight paintings by masters of the last century: hunting scenes, city scapes, still lifes—all genuine and all completely banal.

The Stork beckoned Lake to a couch farthest from the door. The couch was bounded by a magnificent, if unwieldy, rectangular box of a table that extended some six feet down the width of the room. It had decorative handles, but no drawers.

As Lake sat, making certain not to bang his gimp leg against the table, he said, "Who owns this house?" to the Stork's retreating back.

The Stork spun around, put a finger to its beak, and said, "Don't speak! Don't speak!"

Lake nodded in a gesture of apology. The master of the house obviously valued his privacy.

The Stork stared at Lake a moment longer, as if afraid he might say something more, then turned on his heel.

Leaving Lake alone in his frog mask, which had become uncomfortably hot and scratchy. It smelled of a familiar cologne—Merri must have worn it since the festival and not cleaned it out.

Claustrophobia battled with a pleasing sense of anonymity. Behind the mask he felt as if he would be capable of actions forbidden to the arrogant but staid Martin Lake. Very well, then, the new Martin Lake would undertake an examination of the room for more clues as to his host's taste—or lack thereof.

A bust of Trillian stared back at him from a far table, its white marble infiltrated by veins of some cerise stone. Also on this table lay a book entitled *The Architect of Ruins*, above which stood the stuffed and bejeweled carcass of a tortoise. Across from it, upon a dais, stood a telescope which, in quite a clever whimsy, faced a map of the world upon the wall. Atlases and other maps were strewn across the tables, but Lake had the sense that these had been placed haphazardly as the result of cold calculation. Indeed, the room conveyed an aura of artificiality, from the burgundy walls to the globe-shaped fixtures that spread a pleasant, if pinkish, light. Such a light was not conducive to reading or conversation. Despite this, the study had a rich warmth to it, both relaxing and comfortable.

Lake sat back, content. Who would have thought to find such refinement in the midst of such desolation? It appeared Raffe had been right: some wealthy patron wished to commission him, perhaps even to collect his art. He began to work out in his head an asking price that would be large enough, even if eventually knocked down by hard bargaining, to satisfy him. He could buy new canvases, replace his old, weary brushes, perhaps even convince an important gallery to carry his work.

Gradually, however, as if the opening notes of a music so subtle that the listener could not at first hear it, a tap-tap-tapping, intruded upon his pleasant daydream. It traveled around the room and into his ears with an apologetic urgency.

He sat up and tried to identify the source. It came neither from the walls nor the door. But it definitely originated from *inside* the room . . . and, although muffled, as if underground, from somewhere close to him. Such a gentle sound—not loud enough to startle him, just this cautious, moderate *tap*, this minor key *rap*.

He listened carefully—and a smile lit his face. Why, it was coming from the table in front of him! Someone or something was *inside* the table, gently rapping. What a splendid disguise for the masquerade. Lake tapped back. Whatever was inside the table tapped back twice. Lake tapped twice, answered by three taps. Lake tapped thrice.

A frenzied rapping and *smashing* erupted from the table. Lake sucked in his breath and pulled his fist back abruptly. A frisson of dread traveled up his spine. It had just occurred to him that the playful game might not be a playful game after all. The black table, on which he had laid his invitation, was not actually a table but an unadorned coffin from which someone desperately wanted to get out!

Lake rose with an "Uh!" of horror—and at that moment, the Stork returned, accompanied by two other men.

The Stork's companions were both of considerable weight and height, and from a certain weakness underlying the ponderous nature of their movements, which he remembered from his days of sketching models, Lake realized both were of advancing years. Both wore dark suits identical to that worn by the Stork, but the resemblance ended there. The larger of the two men—not fat but merely broad—wore a resplendent raven's head over his own, the glossy black feathers plucked from a real raven (there was no mistaking the distinctive sheen). The eyes shone sharp and hard and heavy. The beak, made of a silvery metal, caught the subdued light and glimmered like a distant reflection in a pool of still water.

The third man wore a mask that replicated both the doorknocker and the seal on Lake's invitation: the owl, brown-gold feathers once again genuine, the curved beak a dull gray, the human eyes peering out from the shadow of the fabricated orbits. Unfortunately, the Owl's extreme girth extended to his neck and the owl mask was a tight fit, covering his chins, but constricting the flesh around the neck into a jowly collar. This last detail made him hideous beyond belief, for it looked as if he had been denuded of feathers, revealing the plucked skin beneath.

The three stood opposite Lake across the coffin—the top of which had begun to shudder upwards as whatever was inside smashed itself against the lid.

"What . . . what is in there?" Lake asked. "Is this part of the masquerade? Is this a joke? Did Merrimount send you?"

The Owl said, "A very nice disguise," and still staring at Lake, rapped his fist so hard against the coffin lid that black paint rubbed off on his white glove. The thrashing inside the coffin subsided. "A good disguise for this masquerade. The frog, who is equally at home on land as in the water." The Owl's voice, like that of the Stork, came out distorted, as if the man had stuffed cotton or pebbles in his mouth.

"What," Lake said again, pointing a tremulous finger at the coffin, "is in there?"

The Owl laughed—a horrid coughing sound. "Our other guest will be released shortly, but first we must discuss your commission."

"My commission?" A thought flashed across his mind like heat lightning, leaving no impression behind: *Raffe was right. I am to paint their sex games for them.*

"It is an unusual commission and before I give you the details, you must resign yourself to it with all your heart. You have no choice. Now that you are here, you are our instrument."

Raffe had never suggested that he must *become* part of the pornography, and he rebelled against the notion: this was too far to take a commission, even for all the money in the world.

"Sirs," Lake said, standing, "I think there has been a misunderstanding. I am a painter and a painter only—"

"A painter," the Owl echoed, as if it were an irrelevant detail.

"—and I am going to leave now. Please forgive me. I mean no offense."

He began to sidle out from behind the coffin, but stopped when the Raven blocked his path, a long gutting knife held in one gloved hand. It shone like the twin to the Raven's beak. The sight of it paralyzed Lake. Slowly, he sidled back to the middle of the couch, the coffin between him and these predators. His hands shook. The frog mask was awash in sweat.

"What do you want?" Lake said, guarding unsuccessfully against the quaver in his voice.

The Owl rubbed his hands together and cocked his head to regard Lake with one steel-gray eye. "Simply put, your commission shall be its own reward. We shall not pay you, unless you consider allowing you to live payment. Once you have left this house, your life will be as before, except that you shall be a hero: the anonymous citizen of the city who righted a grievous wrong."

"What do you want?" Lake asked again, more terror-stricken than before.

"A murder," croaked the Raven.

"An execution," corrected the Stork.

"A beheading," specified the Owl.

"*A murder?*" Lake shouted. "A murder! Are you mad?"

The Owl ruffled its feathers, said, "Let me tell you what your response will be, and then perhaps you can move past it to your destiny all the quicker. First, you will moan. You will shriek. You will even try to escape. You will say 'No!' emphatically even after we subdue you. We will threaten you. You will weaken. Then you will say 'No' again, but this time we will be able to tell from the questioning tone of your voice that you are closer to the reality, closer to the deed. And then the cycle will repeat itself. And then, finally, whether it takes an hour or a week, you will find yourself carrying out your task, because even the most wretched dog wants to feel the sun on its face one more day.

"It would save us all some time if you just accepted the situation without all the attendant fuss."

"I will not."

"Open the coffin."

"No!"

Lake, his leg encumbering him, leapt over the coffin table. He made it as far as the bust of Trillian before the Stork and the Raven knocked him to the floor. He twisted and kicked in their grasp, but his leg was as supple as a wooden club and they were much too strong. They wrestled him back to the coffin. The Stork held him face-down on the couch, the frog mask cutting so painfully into his mouth that he could hardly draw breath. The Raven yanked his head up and held the knife to his throat. In such a position, his eyeholes skew, he could see only the interior of the mask and a portion of the maroon-gold leaf ceiling.

From somewhere above him, the Owl said, with almost sensual sloth, "Accept the commission, my dear frog, or we shall kill you and choose another citizen."

The Stork, sitting on Lake, jabbed his kidneys, then punched in the same spot—hard. Lake grunted with pain. The Raven bent Lake's left arm back behind him until it felt as if his bones would break.

He shrieked. Suddenly, they were both off of him. He flipped over on his back, adjusted his mask, and looked up—to find all three men staring down at him.

"What is your answer?" the Owl asked. "We must have your answer now."

Lake groaned and rolled over onto his side.

"Answer!"

What did a word mean? Did a single word really mean . . . anything? Could it exile whole worlds of action, of possibility?

"Yes," he said, and the word sounded like a death rattle in his throat.

"Good," said the Owl. "Now open the coffin."

They moved back so that he would have enough space. He sat up on the couch, his leg throbbing. He grappled with the locks on the side of the coffin, determined to speed up the nightmare, that it might end all the more swiftly.

Finally, the latches came free. With a grunt, he opened the lid . . . and stared down at familiar, unmistakably patrician features. The famous shock of gray hair disheveled, the sharp cheekbones bruised violet, the intelligent blue eyes bulging with fear, the fine mouth, the sensual lips, obstructed by a red cloth gag that cut into the face and left a line of blood. Blood trickled from his hairline where he had banged his head against the coffin lid. Strange symbols had been carved into his arms as if he were an offering to some cruel god.

Lake staggered backward, fell against the edge of the couch, unable to face this final, dislocating revelation—unable to comprehend that indeed the Greens were right: *Voss Bender was alive*. What game had he entered all unwitting? What nightmare?

For his part, Bender tried to get up as soon as he saw Lake, even bound as he was in coils of rope that must cruelly constrict his circulation, then thrashed about again when it became clear Lake would not help him.

The Raven stuck his head into Bender's field of vision and caw, caw, cawed like his namesake. The action sent Bender into a hysterical spasm of fear. The Raven dealt him a cracking blow across the face. Bender slumped back down into the coffin. His eyelids fluttered; the smell of urine came from the coffin. Lake couldn't look away. Lake couldn't tear his gaze away. This was Voss Bender, savior and destroyer of careers, politicians, theaters. Voss Bender, who had been dead for two days.

"Why? Why have you done this to him?" Lake said, though he had not meant to speak.

The Stork sneered, said, "He did it to *himself*. He brought everything on himself."

"He's no good," the Raven said.

"He is," the Owl added, "the very epitome of Evil."

Voss Bender moved a little. The eyes under the imperious gray eyebrows opened wide. Bender wasn't deaf or stupid—Lake had never thought him stupid—and the man followed their conversation with an intense if weary interest. Those eyes demanded that Lake save him. Lake looked away.

"The Raven here will give you his knife," the Owl said, "but do not think that just because you have a weapon you can escape." As if to prove this, the Owl produced a *gun*, one of those sleek, dangerous-looking models newly invented by the Kalif's scientists.

The Raven held out his knife.

Senses stretched and redefined, Lake glanced at Voss Bender, then at the knife. A thin line of light played over the metal and the grainy whorls of the hilt. He could read the words etched into the blade, the name of the knife's maker: *Hoegbotton & Sons*. That the knife should have a history, a pedigree, that he should know more about the knife than about the three men struck him as absurd, as horrible. As he stared at the blade, at the words engraved there, the full, terrible weight of the deed struck him. To take a life. To snuff out a life, and with it a vast network of love and admiration. To create a hole in the world. It was no small thing to take a life, no small thing at all. He saw his father smiling at him, palms opened up to reveal the shiny, sleek bodies of dead insects.

"For God's sake, don't make me kill him!"

The burst of laughter from the Owl, the Raven, the Stork, surprised him so much that he laughed with them. He shook with laughter, his jaw, his shoulders, relaxed in anticipation of the revelation that it was all a joke . . . before he understood that their laughter was throaty, fey, cruel. Slowly, his laughter turned to sobs.

The Raven's hilarity subsided before that of the Owl and the Stork. He said to Lake, "He is already dead. The whole city *knows* he's dead. You cannot kill someone who is already dead."

Voss Bender began to moan, and redoubled his efforts to break free of his bonds. The three men ignored him.

"I won't do it. I won't do it." His words sounded weak, susceptible to influence. He knew that faced with his own extinction he would do *anything* to stay alive, even if it meant corrupting, perverting, destroying, everything that made him Martin Lake. And yet his father's face still hovered in his head, and with that image everything his father had ever said about the sanctity of life.

The Owl said, with remorseless precision, "Then we will flay your face until it is only strips of flesh hanging from your head. We will lop off your fingers, your toes, as if they were carrots for the pot. You, sir, will become a bloody red riddle for some dog to solve in an alley somewhere. And Bender will still be dead."

Lake stared at the Owl and the Owl stared back, the owl mask betraying not a hint of weakness.

The eyes were cold wrinkled stones, implacable and ancient.

When the Raven offered Lake the knife, he took it. The lacquered wooden hilt had a satisfying weight to it, a smoothness that spoke of practiced ease in the arts of killing.

"A swift stroke across the throat and it will be done," the Raven said, while the Stork took a white length of cloth and tucked it over Bender's body, leaving exposed only his head and neck. How many times had he drawn his brush across a painted throat, the model before him fatally disinterested? He wished he had not taken so many anatomy classes. He found himself counting and naming the muscles in Bender's neck, cataloging arteries and veins, bones and tendons.

The Raven and the Stork withdrew to beyond the coffin. The divide between them and Lake was enormous, the knife cold and heavy in his hand. Lake could see that tiny flakes of rust had infected the center of each engraved letter of *Hoegbotton & Sons.*

He looked down at Voss Bender. Bender's eyes bulged, bloodshot, watery. The man pleaded with Lake through his gag, words Lake could only half understand. *"Don't . . . Don't . . . what have I . . . Help . . . "* Lake admired Bender's strength and yet, as he stood over his intended victim, Lake found he *enjoyed* the power he wielded over the composer. To have such *control.* This was the man he had only the other day been cursing, the man who had so changed the city that his death had polarized it, splintered it.

Voss Bender began to thrash about and, as if the movement had broken a spell, Lake's sense of triumph turned to disgust, buttressed by nausea. He let out a broken little laugh.

"I can't do it. I *won't* do it."

Lake tried to drop the knife, but the Raven's hand covered his and, turning into a fist, forced his own hand into a fist that guided the knife down into the coffin, making Lake stoop as it turned toward Bender's throat. The Stork held Bender's head straight, caressing the doomed man's temples with an odd gentleness. The Owl stood aloof, watching as an owl will the passion play beneath its perch. Lake grunted, struggling against the Raven's inexorable downward pressure. Just when it seemed he must succumb, he went limp. The knife descended at a hopeless angle, aided by Bender's mighty flinch. The blade did only half the job—laying open a flap of skin to the left of the jugular. Blood welled up truculently.

As if the stroke had been a signal, the Raven and the Stork stood back, breathing heavily. Bender made a choking gurgle; he sounded as if he might suffocate in his own blood.

Lake rocked back and forth on his knees.

The Owl said to his companions, "You lost your heads. Do you want his blood on our hands?"

Lake stared at the knife and at Voss Bender's incompetently cut throat, and back at the knife.

Blood had obscured all but the "Hoeg" in "Hoegbotton." Blood had speckled his left hand. It looked nothing like paint: it was too bright. It itched where it had begun to dry.

He closed his eyes and felt the walls of the study rush away from him until he stood at the edge of an infinite darkness. From a great distance, the Owl said, "He will die now. But slowly. Very slowly. Weaker and weaker until, having suffered considerable pain, he will succumb some days hence. And we will not lift a feather or finger to help him. We will just watch. *Your* choice remains the same—finish him and live; don't and die with him. It is a mercy killing now."

Lake looked up at the Owl. "Why me?"

"How do you know you are the first? How do you know you were chosen?"

"That is your answer?"

"That is the only answer I shall ever give you."

"What could he have done to you for you to be so merciless?"

The Owl looked to the Raven, the Raven to the Stork, and in the sudden quaver, the slight shiver, that passed between them, Lake thought he knew the answer. He had seen the same look pass between artists in the cafes along Albumuth Boulevard as they verbally dissected some new young genius.

Lake laughed bitterly. "You're afraid of him, aren't you? You're envious and you want his power, but most of all, you fear him. You're too afraid to kill him yourself."

The Owl said, "Make your choice."

"And the hilarious thing," Lake said. "The hilarious thing is, you see, that once he's dead, you'll have made him *immortal*." Was he weeping? His face was wet under the mask. Lake watched, in the silence, the blood seeping from the wound in Bender's throat. He watched Bender's hands trembling as if with palsy.

What did the genius composer see in those final moments? Lake wondered later. Did he see the knife, the arm that held it, descending, or did he see himself back in Morrow, by the river, walking through a green field and humming to himself? Did he see a lover's face contorted with passion? Did he see a moment from before the creation of the fame that had devoured him? Perhaps he saw nothing, awash in the crescendo of his most powerful symphony, still thundering across his brain in a wave of blood.

As Lake bent over Voss Bender, he saw reflected in the man's eyes the black mask of the Raven, who had stepped nearer to watch the killing.

"Back away!" Lake hissed, stabbing out with the knife. The Raven jumped back.

Lake remembered how the man in his nightmare had cut his hand apart so methodically, so completely. He remembered his father's hands opening to reveal bright treasures, Shriek's response to his painting of his father's hands. Ah, but Shriek knew nothing. Even Raffe knew nothing. None of them knew as much as he knew now.

Then, cursing and weeping, his lips pulled back in a terrible snarl, he drew the blade across the throat, pushed down with his full weight, and watched as the life drained out of the world's most famous composer. He had never seen so much blood before, but worse still there was a moment, a single instant he would carry with him forever, when Bender's eyes met his and the dullness of death crept in, extinguishing the brightness, the spark, that had once been a life.

*** .

"Through His Eyes" has an attitude toward perspective unique among Lake's works, for it is painted from the vantage point of the dead Voss Bender in an open coffin (an apocryphal event—Bender was cremated), looking up at the people who are looking down, while perspective gradually becomes meaningless, so that beyond the people looking down, we see the River Moth superimposed against the sky and mourners lining its banks. Of the people who stare down at Bender, one is Lake, one is a hooded insect catcher, and three are wearing masks—in fact, a reprisal of the owl, raven, and stork from "The Burning House." Four other figures stare as well, but they are faceless. The scenes in the background of this monstrously huge canvas exist in a world which has curved back on itself, and the details conspire to convince us that we see the sky, green fields, a city of wood, and the river banks simultaneously.

As Venturi writes, "The colors deepen the mystery: evening is about to fall and the river is growing dim; reds are intense or sullen, yellows and greens are deep-dyed; the sinister greenish sky is a cosmetic reflection of earthly death." The entirety of the painting is ringed by a thin line of red that bleeds about a quarter of an inch inward. This unique frame suggests a freshness out of keeping with the coffin, while the background scenes are thought to depict Lake's ideal of Bender's youth, when he roamed the natural world of field and river. Why did Lake choose to show Bender in a coffin? Why did he choose to use montage? Why the red line? Sabon suggests that we ignore the coffin and focus on the red line and the swirl of images, but even then can offer no coherent explanation.

Even more daring, and certainly unique, "Aria for the Brittle Bones of Winter" creates an equivalence between sounds and colors: a musical scale based on the pictorial intensity of colors in which, according to Sabon, "color is taken to speak a mute language." The "hero" rides through a crumbling graveyard to a frozen lake. The sky is dark, but the reflection of the moon, which is also a reflection of Voss Bender's face, glides across the lake's surface. The reeds which line the lake's shore are composed of musical notes, so cleverly interwoven that their identity as notes is not at first evident. Snow is falling, and the flakes are also musical notes—fading notes against the blue-black sky, almost as if Bender's aria is disintegrating even as it is being performed.

In this most ambitious of all his paintings, Lake uses subtle gradations of white, gray, and blue to mimic the progression of the aria itself—indeed, his brushstrokes, short or long, rough or smooth, duplicate the aria's movement as if we were reading a sheet of music.

All of this motion in the midst of apparent motionlessness flows in the direction of the rider, who rides against the destiny of the aria as a counterpoint, a dissenting voice. The light of the moon shines upon the face of the rider, but, again, this is the light of the *reflection* so that the rider's features are illuminated from *below*, not above. The rider, haggard and sagging in the saddle, is unmistakably Lake. (Venturi describes the rider as "a rhythmic throb of inarticulate grief.") The rider's expression is abstract, fluid, especially in relation to the starkly realistic mode of the rest of the painting. Thus, he appears ambivalent, undecided, almost unfinished—and, certainly, at the time of the painting, and in relation to Voss Bender, Lake *was* unfinished.

If "Aria for the Brittle Bones of Winter" is not as popular as even the experimental "Through His Eyes," it may be because Lake has employed too personal an iconography, the painting meaningful only to him. Whereas in "Invitation" or "Burning House," the viewer feels empowered—welcomed—to share in the personal revelation, "Aria . . . " feels like a closed system, the artist's eye looking too far inward. Even the doubling of image and name, the weak pun implicit in the painting's lake and the painter Lake, cannot help us to understand the underpinnings of such a work. As Venturi wrote, "While Lake's canvases do not generally inflict a new language upon us, when they do, we have no guide to translate for us." The controversial art critic Bibble has gone so far as to write, in reference to "Aria," "[Lake's] paintings are so many tombstones, so many little deaths—on canvases too big for the wall in their barely suppressed violence."

Be this as it may, there are linked themes, linked resonances, between "Invitation," "Through His Eyes," and "Aria . . . " These are tenuous connections, even mysterious connections, but I cannot fail to make them.

Lake appears in all three paintings—and only these three paintings. Only in the second painting, "Through His Eyes," do the insect catcher and Bender appear together. The insect catcher does appear in "Invitation" but not in "Aria . . . " (where, admittedly, he would be a bizarre and unwelcome intrusion). Bender appears in "Aria" and is implied in "Through His Eyes," but does not appear, implied or otherwise, in "Invitation." The question becomes: Does the insect catcher inhabit "Aria" unbeknownst to the casual observer—perhaps even in the frozen graveyard? And, more importantly, does the spirit of Voss Bender in some way haunt the canvas that is "Invitation to a Beheading?" —From Janice Shriek's *A Short Overview of The Art of Martin Lake and His Invitation to a Beheading*, for the *Hoegbotton Guide to Ambergris*, 5th edition.

***

Afterwards, Lake stumbled out into the night. The fog had dissipated and the stars hung like pale wounds in the sky. He flung off his frog mask, retched in the gutter, and staggered to a brackish public fountain, where he washed his hands and arms to no avail: the blood would not come off. When he looked up from his frantic efforts, he found the mushroom dwellers had abandoned their battle with the pigs to watch him with wide, knowing eyes.

"Go away!" he screamed. "Don't look at me!"

Further on, headed at first without direction, then with the vague idea of reaching his apartment, he washed his hands in public restrooms. He sanded his hands with gravel. He gnawed at them. None of it helped: the stench of blood only grew thicker. He was being destroyed by something larger than himself that was still somehow trapped inside him.

He haunted the streets, alleys, and mews through the tail end of the bureaucratic district, and down a ways into the greenery of the valley, until a snarling whippet drove him back up and into the merchant districts. The shops were closed, the lanterns and lamps turned low. The streets, in the glimmering light, seemed slick, wet, but were dry as chalk. He saw no one except for once, when a group of Reds and Greens burst past him, fighting each other as they ran, their faces contorted in a righteous anger.

"It doesn't mean *anything!*" Lake shouted after them. "He's *dead!*"

But they ignored him and soon, like some chaotic beast battling itself, moved out of sight down the street.

Over everything, as he wept and burned, Lake saw the image of Voss Bender's face as the life left it: the eyes gazing heavenward as if seeking absolution, the body taking one last full breath, the hands suddenly clutching at the ropes that bound, the legs vibrating against the coffin floor . . . and then *stillness*. Ambergris, cruel, hard city, would not let him forget the deed, for on every street corner Voss Bender's face stared at him—on posters, on markers, on signs.

Eventually, his crippled leg tense with a gnawing ache, Lake fell down on the scarlet doorstep of a bawdy house. There he slept under the indifferent canopy of the night, beneath the horrible emptiness of the stars, for an hour or two—until the Madame, brandishing curses and a broom, drove him off.

As the sun's wan light infiltrated the city, exposing Red and Green alike, Lake found himself in a place he no longer understood, the streets crowded with faces he did not want to see, for surely they all stared at him: from the sidewalk sandwich vendors in their pointy orange hats and orange-striped aprons, to the bankers with their dark tortoise-shell portfolios, their maroon suits; from the white-faced, well-fed nannies of the rich to the bravura youths encrusted in crimson make up that had outgrown them.

With this awareness of others came once again an awareness of himself. He noticed the stubble on his cheek, the grit between his teeth, the sour smell of his dirty clothes. Looking around him at the secular traffic of the city, Lake discovered a great hunger in him for the Religious Quarter, all thoughts of a return to his apartment having long since left his head.

His steps began to have purpose and speed until, arrived at his destination, he walked among the devotees, the pilgrims, the priests—stared speechless at the endless permutations of devotional grottos, spires, domes, arches of the cathedrals of the myriad faiths, as if he had never seen them before. The Reds and Greens made no trouble here, and so refugees from the fury of their convictions flooded the streets.

The Church of the Seven Pointed Star had an actual confessional box for sinners. For a long time Lake stood outside the church's modest wooden doors (above which rose an equally modest dome), torn between the need to confess, the fear of reprisal should he confess, and the conviction that he should not be forgiven. Finally, he moved on, accompanied by the horrid, gnawing sensation in his stomach that would be his burden for years. There was no one he could tell. No one. Now the Religious Quarter too confounded him, for it provided no answers, no relief. He wandered it as aimlessly as he had the city proper the night before. He thirsted, he starved, his leg tremulous with fatigue.

At last, on the Religious Quarter's outskirts, where it kissed the feet of the Bureaucratic District, Lake walked through a glade of trees and was confronted by the enormous marble head of Voss Bender. The head had been ravaged by fire and overgrown by vines, and yet the lines of the mouth, the nose, stood out more heroically than ever, the righteous eyes staring at him. Under the weight of such a gaze, Lake could walk no further. He fell against the soft grass and lay there, motionless in the shadow of the marble head.

It was not until late in the afternoon that Raffe found him there and helped him home to his apartment.

She spoke words at him, but he did not understand them. She pleaded with him. She cried and hugged him. He found her concern so tragically funny that he could not stop laughing. But he refused to tell her anything and, after she had forced food and water on him, she left him to find Merrimount.

As soon as he was alone again, Lake tore apart his half-finished commissions. Their smug fatuousness infuriated him. He spared only the paintings of his father's hands and the oil painting he had started the day before. He found himself still entranced by the greens against which the head of the man from nightmare jutted threateningly. The painting seemed to contain the soul of the city in all its wretched depravity, for of course the man with the knife was himself, the smile a grimace. He could not let the painting go, just as he could not bring himself to finish it.

***

Sometimes what the painter chooses *not* to paint can be as important as what he does paint. Sometimes an absence can leave an echo all its own. Does Bender cry out to us by his absence? Many art critics have supposed that Lake must have met Bender during his first three years in Ambergris, but no evidence for this meeting exists; certainly, if he did meet with Bender, he failed to inform any of his friends or colleagues, which seems highly unlikely. Circumstantial evidence provided by Sabon points to the stork-like shadow in "Invitation . . . ," as Bender had a well-known pathological fear of birds, but since Lake *also* had a pathological fear of birds, I cannot side with Sabon on this issue. (Sabon also finds it significant that on Lake's recent death he was cremated in similar fashion to Bender, his ashes spread over the River Moth while his friend Merrimount said the words, "To follow you, with all regret, in all humility.")

In the absence of more complete biographical information about Lake following this period, one must rely on such scanty information as exists in the history books. As is common knowledge, Bender's death was followed by a period of civil strife between the Reds and the Greens, culminating in a siege of the Voss Bender Memorial Post Office, which the Reds took by force only to be bloodily expelled by the Greens a short time later.

Could this, then, as some critics believe, be the message of "Invitation?" The screaming face of the man, the knife blade through the palm, which is wielded by Death, who has just claimed Voss Bender's life? Perhaps. But I believe in a more personal interpretation. Given what I know about Lake's relationship with his father, this personal meaning is all too clear. For in these three paintings, beginning with "Invitation," we see the repudiation of Lake by his natural father (the insect catcher) and Lake's embrace of Bender as his real, artistic father.

What, then, does "Invitation" tell us? It shows Lake's father metaphorically leaving his son. It shows his son, distraught, with a letter sent by his father—a letter which contains written confirmation of that repudiation. The "beheading" in "Invitation to a Beheading" is the dethroning of the king—his father . . . and yet, when a king is beheaded, a new king always takes his place.

Within days of this spiritual rejection, Voss Bender dies and for Lake the two events—the rejection by his father, the death of a great artist—are forever linked, and the only recourse open to him is worship of the dead artist, a path made possible through his upbringing by a mystical, religious mother. Thus, "Through His Eyes" is about the death and life of Bender, and the metaphorical death of his real father. "Aria . . . " gives Bender a resurrected face, a resurrected life, as the force, the light, behind the success of the haggard rider, who is grief-stricken because he has buried his real father in the frozen graveyard—has allowed his natural father to be eclipsed by the myth, the potency, of his new father, the moon, the reflection of himself: Bender.

In the end, these paintings are about Lake's yearning for a father he never had. Bender makes a safe father because, being dead, he can never repudiate the son who has adopted him. If the paintings discussed become increasingly more inaccessible, it is because their meaning becomes ever more personal. —From Janice Shriek's *A Short Overview of The Art of Martin Lake and His Invitation to a Beheading*, for the *Hoegbotton Guide to Ambergris*, 5th edition.

* * *

The days continued on at their normal pace, but Lake existed outside of their influence. Time could not touch him. He sat for long hours on his balcony, staring out at the clouds, at the sly swallows that cut the air like silver-blue scissors. The sun did not heat him. The breeze did not make him cold. He felt hollowed out inside, he told Raffe when she asked how he was doing. And yet, "felt" was the wrong word, because he couldn't feel anything. He was unreal. He had no soul—would never love again, never *wanted* with anyone, he was sure, and because he did not experience these emotions, he did not miss their fulfillment. They were extraneous, unimportant. Much better that he simply *be* as if he were no better, no worse, than a dead twig, a clod of dirt, a lump of coal. (Raffe: "You don't mean that, Martin! You can't mean that . . . ")

So he didn't paint. He didn't do much of anything, and he realized later that if not for the twinned love of Raffe and Merrimount, a love that he need not return, he might have died within a month. While they were helping him, he detested their help. He didn't deserve help. They must *leave him alone.* But they ignored his stares of hatred, his tantrums. Worst of all, they demanded no explanations. Raffe provided him with food and paid his rent. Merrimount shared his bed and comforted him when his nights, in stark and terrifying contrast to the dull, dead, uneventful days, were full of nightmares, detailed and hideous: the white of exposed throat, the sheen of sweat across the shadow of the chin, the lithe hairs that parted before the knife's path . . .

The week after Raffe had found him, Lake forced himself to attend Bender's funeral, Raffe and Merrimount insistent on attending with him even though he wanted to go alone.

The funeral was a splendid affair that traveled down to the docks via Albumuth Boulevard, confetti raining down all the way. The bulk of the procession formed a virtual advertisement for Hoegbotton & Sons, the import/export business that had, in recent years, grabbed the major share of Ambergris trade. Ostensibly held in honor of Bender's operas, the display centered around a springtime motif, and in addition to the twigs, stuffed birds, and oversized bumblebees attached to the participants like odd extra appendages, the music was being played by a ridiculous full orchestra pulled along on a platform drawn by draft horses.

This display was followed by the senior Hoegbotton, his eyes two shiny black tears in an immense pale face, waving from the back of a topless Manzikert and looking for all the world as if he were running for political office. Which he was: Hoegbotton, of all the city's inhabitants, stood the best chance of replacing Bender as unofficial ruler of the city . . .

In the back seat of Hoegbotton's Manzikert sat two rather reptilian-looking men, with slitted eyes and cruel, sensual mouths. Between them stood the urn with Bender's ashes: a pompous, gold-plated monstrosity. It was their number—three—and Hoegbotton's mannerisms that first roused Lake's suspicions, but suspicions they remained, for he had no *proof.* No tell-tale feathers ensnarled for a week to now slowly spin and drift down from the guilty parties to Lake's feet.

The rest of the ceremony was a blur for Lake. At the docks, community leaders including Kinsky, Hoegbotton conspicuously absent, mouthed comforting platitudes to memorialize the man, then took the urn from its platform, pried open the lid, and cast the ashes of the world's greatest composer into the blue-brown waters of the Moth.

Voss Bender was dead.

*** .

Is my interpretation correct? I would like to think so, but one of the great challenges, the great allures, of a true work of art is that it either defies analysis or provides multiple theories for its existence. Further, I cannot fully explain the presence of the three birds, nor certain aspects of "Through His Eyes" with regard to the ring of red and the montage format.

Whatever the origin of and the statement made by "Invitation to a Beheading," it marked the beginning of Lake's illustrious career. Before, he had been an obscure painter. After, he would be classed among the greatest artists of the southern cities, his popularity as a painter soon to rival that of Bender as a composer. Lake would design wildly inventive sets for Bender operas and thus be responsible for an interpretive revival of those operas. He would be commissioned, albeit disastrously, to do commemorative work for Henry Hoegbotton, de facto ruler of Ambergris after Bender's death. His illustrations for the Truffidians' famous *Journal of Samuel Tonsure* would be revered as minor miracles of the engraver's art. Exhibitions of his work would even grace the Court of Kalif himself, while nearly every year publishers would release a new book of his popular prints and drawings. In a hundred ways, he would rejuvenate Ambergris' cultural life and make it the wonder of the south. (In spite of which, he always seemed oddly annoyed, even stricken, by his success.) These facts are beyond doubt.

What, finally, was the mystery behind the letter held in the screaming man's hand, the mystery of "Invitation to a Beheading," we may never know. —From Janice Shriek's *A Short Overview of The Art of Martin Lake and His Invitation to a Beheading*, for the *Hoegbotton Guide to Ambergris*, 5th edition.

***

A year passed, during which, as Raffe and many of his other friends remarked to Lake, he appeared to be doing penance for some esoteric crime. He spent long hours in the Religious Quarter, haunting back alleys and narrow streets, searching in the dirty, antique light for those scenes, and those scenes alone which best embodied his grief and the cruelty, the dispassionate passion, of the city he had adopted as his home. He heard the whispers behind his back, the rumors that he had gone mad, that he was no longer a painter but a priest of an as yet unnamed religion, that he had participated in some unspeakable mushroom dweller ritual, but he ignored such talk; or, rather, it did not register with him.

Six months after Bender's funeral, Lake visited 45 Archmont Lane, new cane trembling in his hand. He found it a burnt out husk, the only recognizable object amidst the ruins the bust of Trillian, blackened but intact. At first he picked it up, meaning to salvage it for his apartment, but as he wandered the wreckage for some sign of what had occurred there, the idea became distasteful, and he left the head in the rubble, its laconic eyes staring up at the formless sky. Nothing remained but the faint smell of carrion and smoke, rubbing against his nostrils. It might as well have been a dream.

Later that month, Lake asked Merrimount—lovely Merrimount, precious Merrimount—to move in with him permanently. He did not know he was going to ask Merri, but as the words left his lips they felt like the right words and Merri, tears in his eyes, said yes, smiling for the first time since before Lake's ordeal. They celebrated at a cafe, Raffe giving her guarded approval, Sonter and Kinsky bringing gifts and good cheer.

Things went better for Lake after that. Although the nightmares still afflicted him, he found that Merrimount's very presence helped him to forget, or at least disremember. He went by Shriek's gallery and took all of his paintings back, burning them in a barrel behind his apartment building. He began to frequent the Ruby Throated Calf again. His father even visited in late winter, a meeting which went better than expected,

even after the guarded old man realized the nature of his son's relationship with Merrimount. He seemed genuinely touched when Lake presented him with the twin paintings of his own hands covered with insects, and with that approval Lake felt himself awakening even more.
There were cracks in the ice. A light amid the shadows.

Yet Ambergris—city of versions and virgins both—did its best to remind him of the darkness. Everywhere, new tributes to Bender sprang
up, for Bender's popularity had never been so high. It could be said with
confidence that the man might never fade from memory. Under the
vengeful eyes of Bender statues, posters, and memorial buildings, the
Reds and Greens gradually lost their focus and exhausted themselves.
Some merged with traditional political factions, but many died in a final confrontation at the Voss Bender Memorial Post Office. By spring,
Ambergris seemed much as it had before Bender's death.

It was in the spring, one chilly morning, that Lake sat down in front
of the unfinished painting of the man from his nightmare. The man
smiled with his broken teeth, as if in warning, but he wasn't fearsome
anymore. He was lonely and sad, trapped by the green paint surrounding his face.

Lake had snuck out of bed, so as not to disturb his still-sleeping lover,
but now he felt Merri's eyes upon his back. Gingerly, he picked up a
brush and a new tube of moss-green paint. The brush handle felt rough,
grainy, the paint bottle smooth and sleek. His grasp on the brush was
tentative but strong. The paint smelled good to him and he could feel
his senses awakening to its promise. The sun from the balcony embraced
him with its warmth.

"What are you doing?" Merrimount mumbled sleepily.

Lake turned, the light streaming from the window almost unbearable,
and said, with a wry, haunted grin, "I'm painting."

THE STRANGE CASE OF X

The objects that are being summoned assemble, draw near from different spots; in doing so, some of them have to overcome not only the distance of space but that of time: which named, you may wonder, is more bothersome to cope with, this one or that, the young poplar, say, that once grew in the vicinity but was cut down long ago, or the singled-out courtyard which still exists today but is situated far away from here?
—*Vladimir Nabokov, "The Leonardo"*

It was damp and unpleasant that morning, a methodical drizzle drifting down out of a dull gray sky. An ephemeral rain he might have thought, and yet the buildings, discolored and blackened in their sooty ranks, steeped in the smell of gasoline and hay mixed with dung, seemed to have been contoured and worn down by it, or at least *resigned* to it. The few passersby on the street, shivering against the cold, were subdued, anonymous, sickly; their shoes made wet *splacking* noises in the puddles. The sound, startling in the silence, depressed him and he was glad to reach his destination, glad when the glass doors closed behind him, shutting out the smell of the rain.

Inside, the ironic smell of mold and a sickly sweet sterility. He sneezed and put down his briefcase. He took off his galoshes, placed them by the door. Removed his raincoat, which looked as if the rain had worn grooves into it, and hooked it on the absurdly sinister coat rack with its seething gargoyle heads. He shook himself, stray water drops spraying in all directions, straightened his tie, and smoothed back his hair. Bemoaned the lack of coffee. Took a slip of paper from his jacket pocket. Room 54. Downstairs. Down many stairs.

He stared across the empty hall. White and gray tile. Anonymous doors. Sheets of dull lighting from above, most of it aflicker with abnormalities. And clocks—clocks created for bureaucrats so that they formed innocuous gray circles every few yards, their dull hands clucking quietly. He could only hear them because most of the staff was away for the holidays. The emptiness lent a certain ease to his task. He meant to take his time.

He picked up his briefcase and walked up the hall, shoes squeaking against the shiny tile floor; amazingly enough, the janitorial staff had recently waxed it.

He passed a trio of coat racks, all three banal in their repetition of gargoyles, and not at all in keeping with the dream of a modern facility dreamt by his superiors. Ahead, a lone security guard stood at attention in a doorway. The man, gaunt to the point of starvation, looked neither right nor left. He nodded as he passed but the guard did not even blink. Was the guard dead? He smelled of old leather and tar. Would he smell of old leather and tar if he was dead? Somehow the thought amused him.

He turned left onto another colorless, musty corridor, this time lit reluctantly by oval light bulbs in ancient fixtures that might once have been brass-colored but were now a gunky black.

As he walked, he made a note of the water dripping from the ceiling; better that the janitors fix leaks than wax floors. Before you knew it, mold would be clotting the walls and mushrooms sprouting from the most unexpected places.

He approached a length of corridor where so much mud had been tracked in by way of footprints that a detective (which, strictly speaking, he was not) would have assumed a scuffle had broken out among a large group of untidy, rather frenzied and determined, individuals. Perhaps it had; patients often did not like being labeled patients.

The mud smell thickened the air, but entwined around it, rooted within it, another smell called to him: a fragrance both fresh and unexpected. He stopped, frowned, and sniffed once, twice. He turned to his left and looked down. In the crack between the wall and the floor, amid a patch of what could only be dirt, a tiny rose blossomed, defiantly blood-red.

He bent over the flower. How rare. How lovely. He blinked, took a quick look down the corridor to his right and left. No one.

Deftly, he plucked the rose, avoiding the thorns on the stem. Straightening up, he stuck the flower through the second buttonhole of his jacket, patted his jacket back into place, and continued down the corridor.

Soon he came to a junction, with three corridors radiating out to left, right, and center. Without hesitation, he chose the left, which slanted downward. The air quickly became colder, mustier, and overlaid with the faint scent of . . . *trout*? (Were cats hoarding fish down here?) The light grew correspondingly dimmer. He had hoped to review the files on "X" before reaching Room 54, but found it an impossible task in the gloom. (Another note to the janitors? Perhaps not. They were an unruly lot, unaccustomed to reprimand, and they might make it difficult for him. No matter: the words of his colleagues still reverberated in his head: "X is trapped between the hemispheres of his own brain"; "X is a tough nut to crack"; "X will make an excellent thesis on guilt.")

No matter. And although he appreciated the position of those who believed the building should be renovated to modern standards, he *did* enjoy the walk, for it created a sense of mystery, an atmosphere conducive to exploration and discovery. He had always thought that, in a sense, he shed irrelevant parts of himself on the long walk, that he became very much *functional* in his splendid efficiency.

He turned left, then right, always descending. He had the sensation of *things flitting* through the air, just on the verge of brushing his skin. A coppery taste suffused the air, as if he were licking doorknobs or bed posts. The bulbs became irregular, three burnt out for each buttery round glow. His shoes scraped against unlikely things in the darkness that lay beneath his feet.

Finally, he reached the black spiral staircase that led to Room 54. A true baroque monstrosity, in the spirit of the gargoyle coat racks, it twisted and turned crankily, almost spitefully, into a well of darkness dispelled only by the occasional glimmer of railing as it caught the light of the single, dull bulb hanging above it. Of all the building's eccentricities, he found the staircase the most delightful. He descended slowly, savoring the feel of the wrought-iron railings, the roughness of the black paint where it had chipped and weathered to form lichen-shaped patterns. The staircase smelled of history, of ancestors, of another world.

By the time he had reached the bottom, he had shed the last of his delight, his self-interest, his selfishness, his petty irritations, his past. All that remained were curiosity, compassion, instinct, and the rose: a bit of color; a bit of misdirection.

He fumbled for the light switch, found it, and flooded the small space beneath the stairs with stale yellow. He took out his keys. Opened the door. Entered. Closed it behind him.

Inside, he blinked and shaded his eyes against the brightness of superior lighting. Smell of sour clothes. Faint musk of urine. Had "X" been marking his territory?

When his eyes adjusted, he saw a desk, a typewriter, a bed, a small provision of canned goods, and a separate room for the toilet. Windows—square, of a thick, syrupy glass—lined the walls at eyelevel, but all that lay beyond them was the blankness of dirt, of mortar, of cement.

The writer sat behind the desk, on a rickety chair. But he wasn't writing. He was staring at me.

I smiled, put down my briefcase. I took off my jacket, careful not to disturb the rose, and laid it over the arm of the nearest chair.

"Good morning," I said, still smiling.

He continued to observe me. Very well, then, I would observe him back. We circled each other with our eyes.

From the looseness of his skin, I deduced that he had once been fat, but no longer; he had attained the only thinness possible for him: a condition which suggests thinness, which *alludes to* thinness, but is only a pale facsimile at best. He had too much skin, and broad shoulders with a barrel chest. His mouth had fixed itself half-way between a laconic grin and a melancholy frown. A new beard had sprouted upon his chin (it was not unkind to him) while above a slight, almost feminine, nose, his blue eyes pierced the light from behind the golden frames of his glasses. He wore what we had given him: a nondescript pair of slacks, a white shirt, and a brown sweater over the shirt.

What did he smell of? A strangeness I could not identify. A hint of lilacs in the spring. The waft of rain-soaked air on a fishing boat, out on the river. The draft from a door opening onto a room full of old books.

Finally, he spoke: "You are here to question me. Again. I've already answered all the questions. Numerous times." A quaver in the voice. Frustration barely held in check.

"You must answer them one more time," I said. Briefcase again in hand, I walked forward until I stood in front of his desk.

He leaned back in his chair, put his hands behind his head. "What will that accomplish?"

I didn't like his ease. I did not like his comfort. I decided to break him of it.

"I'll not mislead you: I am here to decide your final disposition. Should we lock you away for five or ten years, or should we find some other solution? But do not think you can lie your way into my good graces. You have, after all, answered these questions several times. We must reach an understanding, you and I, based solely on your current state of mind. I can smell lies, you know. They may look like treacle, but they smell like poison."

I had given this speech, or a variant of it, so many times that it came all too easily to me.

"Let me not mislead you," he replied, no longer leaning back in his chair, "I am now firmly of the belief that Ambergris, and all that is associated with Ambergris, is a figment of my imagination. I no longer believe it exists."

"I see. This information does not in any way mean I will now pack up my briefcase and set you free. I must question you."

He looked as if he were about to argue with me. Instead, he said, "Then let me clear the desk. Would you like me to give you a statement first?"

"No. My questions shall provide you with the means to make a statement." I smiled as I said it, for although he need not hope too much, neither did I wish to drive him to despair.

X was not a strong man and I had to help him lift the typewriter off the desk; it was an old, clunky model and its keys made a metallic protest when we set it on the floor.

When we had sat down, I took out a pen and pad of paper. "Now, then, do you know where you are and why?"

"I am in a Chicago psychiatric ward because I have been hallucinating that a world of my creation is actually real."

"When and where were you born?"

"Belfont, Pennsylvania. In 1968."

"Where did you grow up?"

"My parents were in the Peace Corps—are you going to write all of this down again? The scribbling irritates me. It sounds like cockroaches scuttling."

"You don't like cockroaches?"

He scowled at me.

"As you like."

I pulled his file out of my briefcase. I arranged the transcripts in front of me. A few words flashed out at me: *fire . . . Trial . . . of course I loved her . . . control . . . the reality . . . It was in the room with me . . .*

"I shall simply check off on these previous interrogatories duplications of answers. I shall only write down your answers when they are new or stray from the previous truths you have been so kind as to provide us with. Now: Where did you grow up?"

"In the Fiji Islands."

"Where is that?"

"In the South Pacific."

"Ah . . . What was your family like? Any brothers or sisters?"

"Extremely dysfunctional. My parents fought a lot. One sister—Vanessa."

"Did you get along with your sister? How dysfunctional?"

"I got along with my sister better than Mom and Dad. Very dysfunctional. I'd rather not talk about that—it's all in the transcripts. Besides, it only helps explain why I write, not why I'm delusional."

In the transcripts he'd called it the "ten year divorce." Constant fighting. Verbal and some physical abuse. Nasty, but not all that unusual. It is popular to analyze a patient's childhood these days to discover that one trauma, that one unforgivable incident, which has shaped or ruined the life. But I did not care if his childhood had been a bedsore of misery, a canker of sadness. I was here to determine what he believed *now*, at this moment. I would ask him the requisite questions about that past, for such inquiries seemed to calm most patients, but let him tell or not tell. It was all the same to me.

"Any visions or hallucinations as a child?"

"No."

"None?"

"None."

"In the transcripts, you mention a hallucination you had, when you thought you saw two hummingbirds mating on the wing from a hotel room window. You were sick, and you said, rather melodramatically, `I thought if I could only hold them, suspended, with my stare, I could forever feast upon their beauty. But finally I had to call to my sister and parents, took my eyes from the window, and even as I turned back, the light had changed again, the world had changed, and I knew they were gone. There I lay, at altitude, on oxygen—'"

"—But that's not a hallucination—"

"—Please don't interrupt. I'm not finished: `on oxygen and, suddenly, at my most vulnerable, the world had revealed the very extremity of its grace. For me, the moment had been Divine, as fantastical as if those hummingbirds had flown out of my mouth, my eyes, my thoughts.' That is not a hallucination?"

"No. It's a statement on beauty. I really did see them—the hummingbirds."

"Is beauty important to you?"

"Yes. Very important."

"Do you think you entered another world when you saw those hummingbirds?"

"Only figuratively. I'm very balanced, you know, between my logical father and my illogical mother. I know what's real and what's not."

"That is not for you to determine. And what do your parents do? No one seems to have asked that question."

"My dad's an entomologist—studies bugs, not words. My mom's an artist. And an author. She's done a book on graveyard art."

"Ah!" I took out two items which had been on his person when he had been brought here: a book entitled *Dradin, In Love and Other Tales of the City* and a page of *cartoon* images. "So you are a writer. You take after your mother."

"No. Yes. Maybe."

"I guess that would explain why we gave you a typewriter: you're a writer. I'm being funny. Have the decency to laugh. Now, what have you been writing?"

"`I will not believe in hallucinations' one thousand times."

"It's my turn to be rude and not laugh." I held up *Dradin, In Love.* "You wrote this book."

"Yes. It's sold over one million copies worldwide."

"Funny. I'd never heard of it until I saw this copy."

"Lucky you. I wish *I'd* never heard of it."

"But then, I rarely read modern authors, and when I do it is always thrillers. A straight diet of thrillers. None of the poetics for me, although I do dabble in writing myself . . . I did read this one, though, when I was assigned to your case. Don't you want to hear what I thought about it?"

X snorted. "No. I get—got—over a hundred fan letters a day. After awhile, you just want to retire to a deserted island."

"Which is exactly what you have done, I suppose. Metaphorically." Only the island had turned out to be inhabited. All the worse for him.

He ignored my probing, said, "Do you think I *wanted* to write that stuff? When the book came out, all anyone wanted were more Ambergris stories. I couldn't *sell* anything *not* set in Ambergris. And then, after the initial clamor died down, I *couldn't* write anything else. It was horrible. I'd spend ten hours a day at the typewriter just making this world I'd created more and more real in this world. I felt like a sorcerer summoning up a demon."

"And this? What is this?" I held up the sheet of cartoons:

"Sample drawings from Disney—no doubt destined to become a collector's item—for the animated movie of *Dradin, In Love*. It should be coming out next month. Surely you've heard of it?"

"I don't go to the movies."

"What do you do then?"

"Question sick people about their sicknesses. It would be good to think of me as a blank slate, that I know nothing. This will make it easier for you to avoid leaving out important elements in your answers . . . I take it your books are grossly popular then?"

"Yes," he said, with obvious pride. "There are Dwarf & Missionary role-playing games, Giant Squid screen savers, a 'greatest hits' CD of Voss Bender arias sung by the Three Tenors, plastic action figures of the mushroom dwellers, even Ambergris conventions. All pretty silly."

"You made a lot of money in a relatively condensed period of time."

"I went from an income of $15,000 a year to something close to $500,000 a year, after taxes."

"And you were continually surrounded by the products of your imagination, often given physical form by other people?"

"Yes."

Razor-sharp interrogator's talons at the ready, I zeroed in, no longer anything but a series of questions in human guise, as elegant as a logarithm. I'd tear the truth right out of him, be it bright or bloody.

INTERROGATOR: When did you begin to sense something was amiss?

X: The day I was born. A bit of fetal tissue didn't form right and, presto!, a cyst, which I had to have removed from the base of my spine twenty-four years later.

I: Let me remind you that if I leave this room prematurely, *you* may never leave this room.

X: Don't threaten me. I don't respond well to threats.

I: Who does? Begin again, but please leave out the sarcasm.

X: . . . It started on a day when I was thinking out a plot line—the story for what would become "The Transformation of Martin Lake." I was walking in downtown Tallahassee, where I used to live, past some old brick buildings. The streets are all narrow and claustrophobic, and I was trying to imagine what it might be like to *live* in Ambergris. This was a year after St. Martin's Press published *Dradin, In Love*, and they wanted more stories to flesh out a second book. I was pretty deep into my own thoughts. So I turn a corner and I look up, and there, for about six seconds—too long for a mirage, too short for me to be certain—I saw, clotted with passersby—the Borges Bookstore, the Aqueduct, and, in the distance, the masts of ships at the docks: all elements from my book. I could smell the briny silt of the river and the people were so close I could have reached out and touched them. But when I started to walk forward, it all snapped back into reality. It just snapped . . .

I : So you thought it was real.

X : I could smell the street—piss and spice and horse. I could smell the savory aroma of chicken cooking in the outdoor stoves of the sidewalk vendors. I could feel the breeze off the river against my face. The light—the light was *different*.

I : How so?

X : Just different. Better. Cleaner. *Different*. I found myself saying, "I cannot capture the quality of this light in paint," and I knew I had the central problem, the central question, of my character's—Martin Lake's—life.

I : Your character, you will pardon me, does not interest me. I want to know why you started to walk forward. In at least three transcripts, you say you walked forward.

X : I don't know why.

I : How did you feel after you saw this . . . image?

X : Confused, obviously. And then horrified because I realized I must have some kind of illness—a brain tumor or something.

I stared at him and frowned until he could not meet my gaze

"You know where we are headed," I said. "You know where we are going. You may not like it, but you must face it." I gestured to the transcripts. "There are things you have not said here. I will indulge you by teasing around the edges for awhile longer, but you must prepare yourself for a more blunt approach."

X picked up my copy of *Dradin, In Love*, began to flip through it. "You know," he said, "I am so thoroughly sick of this book. I kept waiting for the inevitable backlash from the critics, the trickling off of interest from readers. I really wanted that. I didn't see how such success could come so . . . effortlessly. Imagine my distress to find this world I had grown sick of, waiting for me around the corner."

"Liar!" I shouted, rising and bending forward, so my face was inches from his face. "Liar! You walked toward that vision because it fascinated you! Because you found it irresistible. Because you saw something of the real world there! And afterwards, you weren't sorry. You weren't sorry you'd taken those steps. Those steps seemed like the only sane thing to do. You didn't even tell your wife . . . your wife"—He looked at me like I'd become a living embodiment of the coat rack gargoyles while I rummaged through the papers—"your wife Hannah that you had had a vision, that you were worried about having a brain tumor. You *told* us that already. Didn't I tell you *not* to lie to me?"

This speech, too, I had given many times, in many different forms. X looked shaken to the core by it.

X : Haven't you ever . . . Wouldn't you like to live in a place with more mystery, with more color, with more life? *Here* we know everything, we can do everything. Me, I worked for five years as a technical editor putting together city ordinances in book form. I didn't even have a window in my office. Sometimes, as I was codifying my fiftieth, my seventy-fifth, my one hundredth wastewater ordinance, I just wanted to get up, smash my computer, set my office on fire, and burn the whole rotten, horrible place down . . . The world is so small. Don't you ever want—need—more mystery in your life?

I : Not at the expense of my sanity. When did you begin to realize that, as you put it, "I had not created Ambergris, but was merely describing a place that already existed, that was real"?

X : You're a bastard, you know that?

I : It's my function. Tell me what happened next.

X : For six months, everything was normal. The second book came out and was a bigger success than the first. I was flying high. I'd almost forgotten those six seconds in Tallahassee . . . Then we took a vacation to New Orleans, my wife and me—partly to visit our friend and writer Nathan Rogers, and partly for a writer's convention. We usually go to as many bookstores as we can when we visit other cities—there are so many out-of-print books I want to get hold of, and Hannah, of course, likes to see how many of the new bookstores carry her magazine, and if they don't, get them to carry it. So I was in an old bookstore with Hannah—in the French Quarter, a real maze to get there. A real maze, which is half the fun. And once there, I was anxious to buy something, to make the effort worthwhile. But I couldn't find anything to buy, which was killing me, because sometimes I just have a compulsion to buy books. I guess it's a security blanket of sorts. But when I rummaged through the guy's discard cart—the owner was a timid old man without any eyebrows—I found a paperback of Frederick Prokosch's *The Seven Who Fled* so I bought that.

I : And it included a description of Ambergris?

X : No, but the newspaper he had wrapped it in was a weathered broadsheet published by Hoegbotton & Sons, the exporter/ importer in my novel.

I : They do travel guides, too?

X : Yes. You have a good memory . . . We didn't even notice the broadsheet until we got back to the hotel. Hannah was the one who noticed it.

I : Hannah noticed it.

X : Yeah. She thought it was a prank *I* was playing on her, that I'd put it together for her. I'll admit I've done that sort of thing before, but not this time.

I : You must have been ecstatic that she found it.

X : Wildly so. It meant I had physical proof, and an independent witness. It meant I wasn't crazy.

I : Alas, you never found that particular bookstore again.

X : More accurately, it never found us.

I : But Hannah believed you.

X : She at least knew something odd had happened.

I : You no longer possess the broadsheet, however.

X : It burned up with the house later on.

I : Yes, the much alluded to fire, which also conveniently devoured all of the other evidence. What was the other evidence?

X : Useless to discuss it—it doesn't exist anymore.

I : Discuss it briefly anyway—for my sake.

X : Okay. For example, later we visited the British Museum in London. There was an ancient, very small, almost miniature altar in a glass case in a forgotten corner of the Egyptian exhibits. Behind a sarcophagus. The piece wasn't labeled, but it certainly didn't look Egyptian. Mushroom designs were carved into it. I saw a symbol that I'd written about in a story. In short, I thought it was a mushroom dweller religious object. You remember the mushroom dwellers from *Dradin*?

I : I am familiar with them.

X : There were two tiny red flags rising from what would normally be considered incense holders. It was encrusted with gems showing a scene that could only be a mushroom dweller blood sacrifice. I took pictures. I asked an attendant what it was. He didn't know. And when we came back the next day, it was gone. Couldn't find the attendant, either. That's a pretty typical example.

I : You *wanted* to believe in Ambergris.

X : Perhaps. At the time.

I : Let us return to the question of the broadsheet. Did you believe it was real?

X : Yes.

I : What was the subject of the broadsheet?

X : Purportedly, it was put out by Hoegbotton on behalf of a group called the "Greens," denouncing the "Reds" for having somehow caused the death of the composer Voss Bender.

I : You had already written about Voss Bender in your book, correct?

X : Yes, but I'd never heard of the Greens and the Reds. That was the lucky thing—I'd put my story "The Transformation of Martin Lake" aside because I was stuck, and that broadsheet unstuck me. The Reds and Greens became an integral part of the story.

I : Nothing about the broadsheet, on first glance, struck you as familiar?

X : I'm not sure I follow you. What do you mean by "familiar?"

I : Nothing inside you, a voice perhaps, told you that you had seen it before?

X : You think I created the broadsheet and then blocked the memory of having done so? That I somehow then planted it in that bookstore?

I : No. I mean simply that sometimes one part of the brain will send a message to another part of the brain—a warning, a sign, a symbol. Sometimes there is a . . . division.

X : I don't even know how to respond to such a suggestion.

I sighed, got up from my chair, walked to the opposite end of the room, and stared back at the writer. He had his head in his hands. His breathing made his head bob slowly up and down. Was he weeping?

"Of course this process is stressful," I said, "but I must have definitive answers to reach the correct decision. I cannot spare your feelings."

"I haven't seen my wife in over a week, you know," he said in a small voice. "Isn't it against the law to deny me visitors?"

"You'll see whomever chooses to see you after we finish, no matter the outcome. *That* I can promise you."

"I want to see Hannah."

"Yes, you talk a great deal about Hannah in the transcripts. It seems to reassure you to think of her."

"If she's not real, I'm not real," he muttered. "And I know she's real."

"You loved her, didn't you?"

"I *still* love my wife."

"And yet you persisted in following your delusions?"

"Do you think I wanted it to be real?" he said, looking up at me. His eyes were red. I could smell the salt of his tears. "I thought I'd dug it all out of my imagination, and so I have, but at the time . . . I've lost the thread of what I wanted to say . . . "

Somehow, his confusion, his distress, touched me. I could tell that a part of him *was* sane, that he truly struggled with two separate versions of reality, but just as I could see this, I could also see that he would probably always remain in this limbo where, in someone else, the madness would have won out long ago . . . or the sanity.

But, unfortunately, it is the nature of the writer to question the validity of his world and yet to rely on his senses to describe it. From what other tension can great literature be born? And thus, he was trapped, condemned by his nature, those gifts and talents he had honed and perfected in pursuit of his craft. Was he a good writer? The answer meant nothing: even the worst writer sometimes sees the world in this light.

"Do you need an intermission?" I asked him. "Do you want me to come back in half an hour?"

"No," he said, suddenly stubborn and composed. "No break."

I : After the broadsheet incident, you began to see Ambergris quite often.

X : Yes. I was in New York City three weeks after New Orleans, on business—this is before we actually moved north—and I stayed at my agent's house. I took a shower one morning and as I was washing my hair, I closed my eyes. When I opened them, rain was coming down and I was naked in a dirty side alley in the Religious Quarter.

I : Of New York?

X : No—of Ambergris, of course. The rain was fresh and cold on my skin. A group of boys stared at me and giggled. The cobblestones were rough against my feet. My hair was still thick with shampoo . . . I spent five minutes huddled in that alley while the boys called to passersby beyond the alley mouth. I was an exhibit. A curiosity. They thought I was a Living Saint, you see, who had escaped from a church, and they kept asking me which church I belonged to. They threw coins and books—books!—at me as payment for my blessings while I shouted at them to go away. Finally, I ran out of the alley and hid at a public altar. I was crowded together with a thousand mendicants, many wearing only a loin cloth, who were all chanting what sounded like obscure obscenities as loudly as they could. At some point, I closed my eyes again, wondering if I could possibly be dreaming, and when I opened them, I was back in the shower.

I : Was there any evidence that you'd been "away," as it were?

X : My feet were muddy. I could swear my feet were muddy.

I : You took something with you out of Ambergris?

X : Not that I knew of at the time. Later, I realized something had come with me . . .

I : You sound as if you were terrified.

X : I *was* terrified! It was one thing to see Ambergris from afar, to glean information from book wrappings, totally different to be deposited naked into that world.

I : You found it more frightening than New York?

X : What do you mean by that?

I : A joke, I guess. Tell me more about New York. I've never been there.

X : What's to tell? It's dirty and gray and yet more alive than any city except—

I : Ambergris?

X : I didn't say that. I may have thought it, but then a city out of one's imagination would have to be more alive, wouldn't it?

I : Not necessarily. I would have liked to have heard more about New York from your unique perspective, but you seem agitated and—

X : And it's completely irrelevant.

I : No doubt. What did you do after the incident in New York?

X : I flew back to Tallahassee without finishing my business . . . what did I say? You look startled.

I : Nothing. It's nothing. Continue. You flew back without finishing your business.

X : And I told Hannah we were going on vacation *right now* for two weeks. We flew to Corfu and had a great time with my Greek publisher—no one recognized me there, see? Hannah's daughter Sarah loved the snorkeling. The water was incredible. This clear blue. You could see to the bottom.

I : What did Sarah think of Ambergris?

X : She never read the books. She was really too young, and she always made a great show of being unimpressed by my success. I can't blame her for that—she did the same thing to Hannah with her magazine.

I : Did the vacation make a difference?"

X : It seemed to. No more visions for a long time. Besides, I'd reached a decision—I wasn't going to write about Ambergris ever again.

I : Did Hannah agree with your decision?

X : Without a doubt. She saw how shaken I'd been after getting back from New York. She just wanted whatever I thought was best.

I : Did it work out?

X : Obviously not. I'm sitting here talking to you, aren't I? But at first, it did work. I really thought that Ambergris would cease to exist if I just stopped writing about it. But my sickness went deeper than that.

I : I'm afraid we have reached a point where I must probe deeper. Tell me about the fire.

X : I don't want to.

I : Then tell me about the thing in your work room first.

X : Can't it wait? For a little while?

The dripping of water had become a constant irritation for me. If it had become an irritation, then I had failed to concentrate hard enough. I had not left enough of myself outside the room. I wondered how long the session would last—more specifically, how long my patience would last. If we are to be honest, the members of my profession, then we must recognize that our judgments are based on our own endurance. How long can we go on before we simply cannot stand to hear more and leave the room? Often the subject, the patient, has nothing to do with the decision.

"I hear music down here sometimes," X said, staring at the ceiling. "It comes from above. It sounds like some infernal opera. Is there an opera house nearby, or does someone in this building play opera?"

I stared at him. This part was always difficult. How could it fail to be?

"You are avoiding the matter at hand."

"What did you think of my book?" X asked. "One writer to another," he added, not quite able to banish the condescension from his voice.

Oddly enough, *Dradin, In Love* had struck me, on a very primitive level, as evidence of an underlying sanity, for X clearly had conceptualized Dradin as a madman. No delusions there, for Dradin *was* a madman. I had even theorized that X saw Dradin as his alter ego, but dismissed the idea on the basis that it is unwise to match events in a work of fiction with events in the writer's life.

Of course, I did not think it useful to share any of these thoughts with X, so I shrugged and said, "It was fanciful in its way and yet some of its aspects were as realistic as any hardboiled thriller. I thought it moved slowly. You devote an entire chapter to Dradin's walk back to his hostel."

"No, no, no! That's foreshadowing. That's symbolism. That's showing you the beginning of the carnage, in the form of the sleeping mushroom dwellers."

"Well, perhaps it did not speak to me as forcefully as you wanted it to. But you must remember, I was reading it for clues."

"As to my mental state? Isn't that dangerous?"

"Of course. To both questions. And I must also determine whether you most identify with Dradin, or the dwarf Dvorak, or the priest Cadimon, or even the Living Saint."

"A dead end. I identify with none of them. And all of them contain a part of me."

I shrugged. "I must gather clues where I can."

"You mean if I don't give you enough information."

"Some give me information without meaning to."

"I am not sure I can give you what you want."

"Actually," I said, picking up *Dradin, In Love*, "there was a passage in here that I found quite interesting. Not from "Dradin, In Love," but from this other story, "Learning to Leave the Flesh." You make a distinction in the introduction to that tale—you call it a forerunner to the Ambergris stories, and yet in your response to the other interrogatories, you say the story was written quite recently."

"Surely you know that a writer can create a precursor tale after he has written the tales which come after, just as he can write the final tale in a series before he has finished writing the others."

The agitation had returned to X's features, almost as if he knew I was steering the conversation back toward my original objective.

"True, true," I said as I turned pages, "but there is one passage—about the dwarf, Davy Jones, that interests me most. Ah, here it is—where Jones haunts the main character. Why don't you read it for me?" I handed it to him and he took it with a certain eagerness. He had a good reading voice, neither too shrill nor too professional.

"Then he stands at the foot of my bed, staring at me. A cold blue tint dyes his flesh, as if the TV's glow has burnt him. The marble cast of his face is as perfect as the most perfect sentence I have ever written. His eyes are so sad that I cannot meet his gaze; his face holds so many years of pain, of wanting to leave the flesh. He speaks to me and although I cannot hear him, I know what he is saying. I am crying again, but softly, softly. The voices on the street are louder and the tinkling of bells so very light."

I : A very nice passage from a rather eccentric story. Whence came the dwarf? Did he walk out of your imagination or out of your life?

X : From life, at first. When I was going to college at the University of Florida, I had a classmate named David Wilson who was a dwarf. We took statistics together. He tutored me past the rough bits. He was poor but couldn't get enough financial aid and his overall grades weren't good enough for scholarships, so he rented himself out for dwarf-tossing contests at local bars. He had a talent for math, but here he was renting himself out to bars, and sometimes to the county fair when it came by. One day, he stopped coming to class and the next week I learned from a rather lurid article in the local paper that he had drunk himself to death.

I : Did he visit *you* at the foot of your bed?

X : You will remember I had resolved not to write about Ambergris ever again, but at first I resolved not to write at all. So I didn't. For five months I quit writing. It was hell. I had to turn a part of myself off. It was like a relentless itching in my brain. I had to unlearn taking notes on little pieces of paper. I had to unlearn making observations. Or, rather, I had to ignore these urges. And I was thinking about David Wilson because I had always wanted to write about him and couldn't. I guess I figured that if I thought about a story I couldn't write, I'd scratch the itch in a harmless way . . . And it was then that the dwarf—or what I thought was the dwarf—began to haunt me. He'd stand at the foot of the bed and . . . well, you read the story. To stop him from haunting me, I relented and sat down to write what became "Learning to Leave the Flesh."

I : But he was already Dvorak.

X : No. Dvorak was just a dwarf. He had nothing of David Wilson in him. David Wilson was a kind and gentle soul.

I : The story mentions Albumuth Boulevard.

X : Yes, it does. I had not only broken my vow not to write, but Ambergris had, in somewhat distorted form, crept back into my work.

I : Did you see the dwarf again?

X : One last time. When he became the manta ray. That was when I realized that I had brought something back from Ambergris with me. It scared the shit out of me.

I : The manta ray is mentioned in the transcripts, but never described. What is a manta ray?

X : You've never heard of a manta ray?

I : Perhaps under another name. What is it, please?

X : A big, black, saltwater . . . fish, I guess, but wide, with flaps like huge, graceful wings. Sleek. Smooth. Like a very large skate or flounder.

I : Ah! A flounder! You'll forgive my ignorance.

X : Clearly you devote too much time to your job.

I : You may be right, but to return to our topic: you were given this *fish* by the apparition of the dwarf. It is important that we get the symbolism correct.

X : No. The "fish" was the dwarf all along, leading me astray. The dwarf *became* the manta ray.

I : How did this happen?

X : I wish I could say Hannah saw it too, but she had fallen asleep. It was a cold night and I was wide awake, every muscle in my body tense. Suddenly, as before, Wilson stood at the foot of my bed. He just watched me for a long time, a smile upon his face . . . and then, as I watched him, he became like a pen-and-ink drawing of himself—only lines, with the rest of him translucent. And then this drawing began to fill up with cloudy black ink—like from a squid; do you know what a squid is?

I : Yes.

X : And when he was completely black with ink, the blackness oozed out from his body, until his body was eclipsed by the creature that looked exactly like a manta ray. It had tiny red eyes and it swam through the air. It terrified me. It horrified me. For the creature *was* Ambergris, come to reclaim me. The blackness of it was diffused by flashes of light through which I could see scenes of the city, of Ambergris, tattooed into its flesh—and they were *moving*. I hid under the covers, and when I looked again, in the morning, it was gone.

I : Did you tell your wife?

X : No! I should have, but I didn't. I felt as if I were going mad. I couldn't sleep. I could hardly eat.

I : This is when you lost all the weight?

X : Yes.

I : What, specifically, did you think this black creature was? Surely not "Ambergris," as you say?

X : I thought I'd brought it back with me from Ambergris—that it was a physical manifestation of my psychosis.

I : You thought it was a part of you. I know you were terrified by it, but did you ever, for a moment, consider that it might have been benevolent?

X : No!

I : I see. It has been my experience—and my experience is substantial—that some men learn to master their madness, so that even if all
manner of horrific hallucinations surround them, they do not react.
They live in a world where they cannot trust their senses, and yet no one
would guess this from their outward composure.

X : I am not one of those men. It terrified me to my soul.

I : And yet such men find such hallucinations a blessing, for they
give warning of a skewed reality. How much worse to slip—to just *slip*, as
if slouching in your chair, as if blinking—into madness with no immediate sign that you had done so. So I call your visitation a helper, not a destroyer.

X : You may call it what you will. I did not think to call it anything.

I : What did you do to reestablish your equilibrium after this incident?

X : I began to write again. I spent eight to ten hours in my work room,
scribbling away. Now I felt my only salvation *was* to write—and I wrote
children's stories. "Sarah and the Land of Sighs" was the first one, and it
went well. My agent liked it. It sold. Eventually, it won an honorable
mention for the Caldecott. So I wrote more stories, except that at some
point—and I still can't recall when exactly—the manta ray reappeared.

I : What was your reaction?

X : Fear. Pure, unadulterated fear.

I : Tell me what happened.

X : I will not discuss what happened. But I have written about it—a
story fragment you could call it.

X reached under the desk and handed me a thin sheaf of papers. I
took them with barely disguised reluctance.

"Fiction lies."

X snorted. "So do people."

"I will read with reservations."

"Yes, and if you'll excuse me . . . " He trotted off to use the bathroom.

Leaving me with the manuscript. The title was "The Strange Case of
X."

I began to read.

> The man sat in the room and wrote on a legal sheet. The
> room was small, with insufficient light, but the man had
> good pens so he did not care. The man was a writer. This is
> why he wrote. Because he was a writer. He sat alone in the
> room which had no windows and he wrote a story. Some-
> times he listened to music while he wrote because music in-
> spired him to write. The story he wrote was called "Sarah and
> the Land of Sighs" and it was his attempt to befriend the
> daughter of his wife, who was not his own daughter. His chil-

dren were his stories, and they were not always particularly well-behaved. "Sarah and the Land of Sighs" was not particularly well-behaved. It had nothing at all to do with the world of Ambergris, which was the world he wrote about for adults (all writers have separate worlds they write about, even those writers who think they do not have separate worlds they write about). And yet, when he had finished writing for the day and reread what he had written, he found that bits and pieces of Ambergris were in his story. He did not know how they had gotten into his story but because he was a writer and therefore a god—a tiny god, a tiny, insignificant god, but a god nonetheless—he took his pen and he slew the bits and pieces of Ambergris he found in his children's story. By this time, it was dusk. He knew it was dusk because he could feel the dusk inside of him, choking his lungs, moving across that part of him which housed his imagination. He coughed up a little darkness, but thought nothing of it. There is a little darkness in every writer. And so he sat down to dinner with his wife and her daughter and they asked him how the writing had gone that day and he said, "Rotten! Horrible! I am not a writer. I am a baker. A carpenter. A truck driver. I am not a writer." And they laughed because they knew he was a writer, and writers lie. And when he coughed up a little more darkness, they ignored it because they knew that there is a little more darkness in a writer than in other souls.

All night the writer coughed up bits of darkness—shiny darkness, rough darkness, slick darkness, dull darkness—so that by dawn all of the darkness had left him. He awoke refreshed. He smiled. He yawned. He ate breakfast and brushed his teeth. He kissed his wife and his wife's daughter as they left for work and for school. He had forgotten the darkness. Only when he entered his work room did he remember the darkness, and how much of it had left him. For his darkness had taken shape and taken wing, and had flown up to a corner of the wall where it met the ceiling and flattened itself against the stone, the tips of its wings fluttering slightly. The writer considered the creature for a moment before he sat down to write. It was dark. It was beautiful. It looked like a sleek, black manta ray with cat-like amber-red eyes. It looked like a stealth bomber given flesh. It looked like the most elegant, the wisest creature in the world. And it had come out of him, out of his darkness. The writer had been fearful, but now he decided to be flattered, to be glad, that he had helped to create such a gorgeous apparition. Besides, he no longer coughed. His lungs were free of darkness. He was a writer. He would write. And so he did—all day.

Weeks passed. He finished "Sarah and the Land of Sighs" and
moved on to other stories. The writer kept the lights ever
dimmer so that when his wife entered his work room she
would not see the vast shadow which clung to the part of the
wall where it met the ceiling. But she never saw it, no matter
how bright the room was, so the writer stopped dimming the
room. It did not matter. She could not see the gorgeous darkness. It glowed black, pulsed black, while he wrote below it.
And although the creature had done him no harm, and he
found it fascinating, the writer began to end his evenings
early and take the work he had done for the day out into the
living room. There he would reread it. He was a writer.
Writers write. But writers also edit. And it was as he sat there
one day, lips pursed, eyebrows knit, absorbed in the birth of
his latest creation, that he noticed a very disturbing fact.
Some of the lines were not his own. That one, for instance.
The writer distinctly remembered writing, "Silly Sarah didn't
question the weeping turtle, but, trusting its wise old eyes,
followed it cheerfully into the unknown city." But what the
writer read on the page was, "Silly Sarah didn't question the
mushroom dweller, and when she had turned her back on it,
it snatched her up cheerfully and took her back into Ambergris." There were others—a facet of character, a stray description, a place name or two. The story had been taken over by
Ambergris. The story had been usurped by the city. How
could this have happened? Writers work hard, sometimes too
hard. Perhaps he had been working too hard. That must be it.
The writer thought only fleetingly of the beautiful, sleek
manta ray. All writers had a little darkness. And even though
this darkness had become externalized, it was still a little
darkness, and now it did not clot his lungs so. The writer
thought of the calming silence of the creature, unmoving but
for the slight rippling of its massive wings. The writer
frowned as he sat in his chair and corrected the story. Could a
thing his wife could not see impact upon the world? On him?

The next day, as the writer wrote, he felt the weight of the
dark creature on his shoulder, but when he looked up, it still
hugged the wall where it met the ceiling. He returned to his
work, but found himself overcome by thoughts of Ambergris. Surely, these thoughts said, he had abandoned Ambergris for too long. Surely, it was time to come home to the city.
His pen, almost against his will, began to write of the city: the
tendrils of vines against the sides of buildings in the burnt
out bureaucratic district; the sad, lonely faces on the statues
in Trillian Square; the rough lapping of water at the docks.
The pen was a black pen. Writers write with black pens. He
dropped the pen, picked up the blue pens he used for editing,

but the best he could do when he tried to run a line through
what he had written was to correct his poor spelling. Writers
may write, writers may edit, but writers are lousy spellers. He
looked up again at the manta ray. He looked up at the little
darkness and he said, "You are dark, and all writers have a little darkness inside them, but not all writers have a little darkness outside them. What are you? Who are you?" But the
darkness did not answer. The darkness could only write. And
edit. As if it too were a writer.

Within a short time, the writer wrote only about Ambergris.
He described every detail of its glistening spires as the morning light hit them. He described the inner workings of the
Truffidian religion that so dominated the city's spiritual life.
He described houses and orphans, furniture and social customs. He wrote stories and he wrote essays. He wrote stories
which were disguised as essays. A part of him delighted in the
speed with which the pen sped effortlessly, like a talented figure skater, across the ice of his pages. A part of him pomp-
ously scorned the children's stories he had worked on before
his transformation. A part of him was so frightened that it
could not articulate its fear. A part of him screamed and gib-
bered and raged against the darkness. It seemed that Ambergris was intent on becoming real in the world that the writer
knew as real, that it meant to seduce him, to trick him into
believing it existed without him. But a writer writes, even
when he doesn't want to write, and so he wrote, but not without pain. Not without fear. For days he ate nothing and fed
the creature on the wall everything, hoping it would reveal
more of Ambergris to him. His wife began to worry, but he
impatiently told her everything was fine, was fine, was fine.
He began to carry a notebook everywhere and write notes at
embarrassing times during social events. Soon, he stopped attending social events. Soon, he slept in his work room, with
the bright darkness above him as a night light. Being a writer
is addictive. Being a writer is an addiction. All those words,
all those words. The act of writing is addictive. But the writer
didn't feel like a writer anymore. He felt like a drug addict.
He felt like a drug addict in constant need of a fix. Could he
be fixed? His fingers and his wrist were constantly sore and
arthritic from over-use. His mind was a soaring, wheeling
roller coaster of exhilaration and fear. When the creature
held back information or he was forced away from his desk
by his wife, or even the need to perform bodily functions, he
had the shakes, the sweats. He vomited. He was sick with Ambergris. It was a virus within him, attacking his red and white
blood cells. It was a cancer, eating away at corpuscles. It was a
great, black darkness in the corner of his mind. He was drunk

on another world. And the thing on the wall, always growing larger, stared down at him and rippled its wings and mewled for more food, which was, of course, pieces of the writer's soul. His whole life had become a quest for Ambergris, to make Ambergris more real. He would find notes on the city that he did not remember writing scattered around the house, even the manuscripts of librettos by Bender, stories by Sirin. His wife thought he had written them, but he knew better. He knew that the creature on the wall had written them, and then left them, like bread crumbs, for him to follow, to the gingerbread house, to the witch, to death.

Finally, one wan autumn day, when the leaves outside the house had turned golden brown and distributed themselves across the lawn, the writer knew he must destroy the creature or be destroyed by it. He was sad that he must destroy it, for he knew that he was destroying a part of himself. It had come out of him. He had created it. But he was writer. All writers write. All writers edit. All writers, surely must, on occasion, destroy their creations before their creations turn stale and destroy them. The writer had no love for the creature any more, only hatred, but he did love his wife and his wife's daughter, and he thought that such love was the greatest justification he could ever have for his actions. And so he entered his work room and attacked the darkness. His wife heard terrible sounds coming from the work room—a man crying, a man screaming, a man pounding on the walls; and was that the smell of fire?—but before she could come to his rescue, he stumbled out of the room, his features stricken with fear and failure. She asked what was wrong and held him tight. "All writers write," he whispered. "All writers edit," he muttered. "All writers have a little darkness in them," he sobbed. "All writers must sometimes destroy their creations," he shouted. But only one writer has a darkness that cannot be destroyed, he thought to himself as he clutched his wife to him and kissed her and sought comfort in her, for she was the most precious thing in his life and he was afraid—afraid of loss, afraid of the darkness, and, most of all, afraid of himself.

***

After I had finished reading, I turned to the writer and I said gently, "This is an interesting allegory in its way, although the ending seems a little . . . bleak? And a most valuable document as well. I can see how people would like your writing."

The writer again sat behind the desk. "It's not an allegory. It's my life." He seemed defeated, as if he had reread the tale over my shoulder.

"Don't you think it is time to discuss the fire?" I asked him. "Isn't this all leading to the fire?"

He turned his head to one side, as if he were a horse resisting a bit. "Maybe. Maybe it is. When can I see my wife?"

"Not until we're done," I said. Who knew when he would see his wife? It has been my experience that I must lie, or half-lie, in order to preserve a certain equilibrium in the patient. I do not enjoy it. I do not relish it. But I do it.

"You have to understand," X said, "that I don't fully understand what happened. I can only guess."

"I will gladly accept your best guess."

But, despite my control, a grim smile played across my lips. I could smell his desperation: it smelled like yellow grass, like stale biscuits, like sour milk.

X : Gradually, the manta ray grew in size until it covered more than ten feet of the wall. As it grew, it began to change the room. Not visual changes, at first, but I began to smell the jungle, and then auto exhaust, and then to hear noises as of a bustling but far away city. Gradually, the manta ray fit itself into its corner and shaped itself to the wall like a second skin. It also began to smell—not a pleasant smell: like fruit rotting, I guess.

I : And this continued until . . . ?

X : Until one day I woke up early from a terrible nightmare: I was being stabbed in the palm by a man with no face, and I didn't even try to pull away while he was doing it . . . I walked into my work room and there was an intense light coming from the corner where the creature had been—just a creature-shaped hole through which Ambergris peeked through. It was the Religious Quarter—endless calls to prayer and lots of icons and pilgrims.

I : How did you feel?

X : Anger. I wanted to tear Ambergris apart stone-by-stone. I wanted to lead a great army and batter down its gates and kill its people and raze the city. Anger would be too weak a word.

I : And do you believe this was the manta ray's purpose when it gave you the gift of returning to Ambergris?

X : "Gift?" It was not a gift, unless you consider madness a gift.

I : Forgive me. I did not mean to upset you. Do you believe the curse visited upon you by the manta ray was given so you could destroy Ambergris?

X : No. I was always, deep down, at cross purposes with the creature. It destroyed my life.

I : What did you do when confronted by the sight of Ambergris? Or what do you think you did?

X : I climbed up the wall and over into the other world.

I : And this, according to the transcripts, is where your memory grows uncertain. Would it still be accurate to say your memory is "hazy?"

X : Yes.

I : Then I will redirect my questioning and come back to that later. Tell me about Janice Shriek.

X : I've already—never mind. She was a fan of my work, and Hannah and I both liked her, so we had let her stay with us—she was on sabbatical. She painted, but made her living as an art historian. Her brother Duncan was a famous historian—had made his fortune writing about the Byzantine Empire. Duncan was in Istanbul doing research at the time, or he would have come to see us too. He didn't get to see his sister much.

I : And you wrote them into your stories?

X : Yes, I'd given them both "parts" in stories of mine, and they'd been delighted. Janice even helped me to smooth out the art history portions of "The Transformation of Martin Lake."

I : Did you feel any animosity toward Janice Shriek or her brother?

X : No. Why would I?

I : Describe Janice Shriek for me.

X : She was a small woman, not as small as, for example, the actress Linda Hunt, but getting there. She was a bit stooped. A comfortable weight. About fifty-four years old. Her forehead had many, many worry wrinkles. She liked to wear women's business suits and she smoked these horrible cigars she got from Syria. She had a presence about her, and a wit. She was a polyglot, too.

I : You said in an earlier interrogation that "sometimes I had the feeling she existed in two places at once, and I wondered if one of those worlds wasn't Ambergris." What did you mean?

X : I wondered if I hadn't so much written her into Ambergris as she'd already had a life in Ambergris. What it came down to was this: Were my stories verbatim truths about the city, including its inhabitants, or were only the settings true, and the characters out of my head?

I : I ask you again: Did you feel any animosity toward Janice Shriek?

X : No!

I : You did not resent her teasing you about the reality of Ambergris?

X : Yes, but that's no motive for . . .

I : You did not feel envy that, if she indeed existed in both worlds, she seemed so self-possessed, so in control. You wanted that kind of control, didn't you?

X : Envy is not animosity. And, again, not a motive for . . . for what you are suggesting.

I : Had you any empirical evidence—such as it might be—that she existed in both worlds?

X : She hinted at it through jokes—you're right about that. She'd read all of my books, of course, and she would make references to Ambergris as if it were real. She said to me once that the reason she'd wanted to meet me was because I'd written about the real world. And once she gave me a peculiar birthday gift.

I : Which was?

X : *The Hoegbotton Travel Guide to Ambergris.* She said it was real. That she'd just ducked into the Borges Bookstore in Ambergris and bought it, and here it was. I got quite pissed off, but she wouldn't say it was a lie. Hannah said the woman was a fanatic. That of course she had created it, and that I'd better either take it as a compliment or start asking lawyers about copyright infringement.

I : Why did you doubt your wife?

X : The guidebook was so *complete*, so perfect. So detailed. How could it be a fake?

I : Surely a polyglot art historian like Janice Shriek could create such a work?

X : I don't know. Maybe. Anyway, that's where I got the idea about her.

I : Let us return to your foray into Ambergris. The manta ray had become an opening to that world. I know your memory is confused, but what do you recall finding there?

X : I was walking down Albumuth Boulevard. It was very chilly. The street was crowded with pedestrians and motor vehicles. I wasn't nude this time, of course, for which I was very appreciative, and I just . . . I just lost myself in the crowds. I didn't think. I didn't analyze. I just walked. I walked down to the docks to see the ships. Took in a parade near Trillian Square. Then I explored the food markets and, after awhile, I went into the Bureaucratic District.

I : Where exactly did it happen?

X : I don't . . . I can't . . .

I : I'll spare you the recall. It's all down here in the transcripts anyway. You say you saw a woman crossing the street. A vehicle bore down on her at a great speed, and you say you pushed her out of harm's way. Would that be accurate?

X : Yes.

I : What did the woman look like?

X : I only saw her from behind. She was shortish. Older than middle aged. Kind of shuffled as she walked. I *think* she was carrying a briefcase or portfolio or something . . .

I : What color was the vehicle?

X : Red.

I : And after you pushed the woman, what happened?

X : The van passed between me and the woman, and I was back in the real world. I felt a great heat on my face, searing my eyebrows. I had collapsed outside of my writing room, which I had set on fire. Soon the whole house would be on fire. Hannah had already taken Sarah outside and now she trying to drag me away from it when I "woke up." She was screaming in my ear, "Why did you do it? Why did you do it?"

I : And what had you done?

X : I had pushed Janice Shriek into the flames of the fire I had set.

I : You had murdered her.

X : I had pushed her into the fire.

We faced each other across the desk in that small, barren room and I could see from his expression that he still did not understand the crux of the matter, that he did not understand what had truly happened to Janice Shriek. How much would I tell him? Very little. For his sake. Merciless, I continued with my questioning, aware that he now saw me as the darkness, as his betrayer.

I : How happy do you feel having saved the life of the woman in Ambergris in relation to the sadness you feel for having killed Janice Shriek?

X : It's not that simple.

I : But it is that simple. Do you feel guilt, remorse, for having murdered Janice Shriek?

X : Of course!

I : Did you feel responsible for your actions?

X : No, not at first.

I : But now?

X : Yes.

I : Did you feel responsible for saving the woman in Ambergris?

X : No. How could I? Ambergris isn't *real*.

I : And yet, you say in these transcripts that in the trial that resulted from Shriek's death, you claimed Ambergris was real! Which is it? Is Ambergris real or isn't it?

X : That was then.

I : You seem inordinately proud that, as you say, the first jury came back hung. That it took two juries to convict. Indecently proud, I'd say.

X : That's just a writer's pride at the beautiful trickery of my fabrication.

I : "That's just a writer's pride at the beautiful trickery of my fabrication." Listen to yourself. Your pride is ghastly. A human being had been murdered. You were on trial for that murder. Or did you think that Janice Shriek led a more real existence in Ambergris? That you had, in essence, killed only an echo of her true self?

X : No! I didn't think Ambergris was more real. *Nothing* was real to me at that point. The arrogance, the pride, was a wall—a way for me to cope. A way for me not to think.

I : How did you get certain members of the jury to believe in Ambergris?

X : It wasn't easy. It wasn't even easy to get my attorney to pursue the case in the rather insane way I suggested. He went along with it because he believed the jury would find me crazy and remand me to the psychiatric care I'm sure he thought I needed. There seemed no question that I would be convicted—my own wife was a witness.

I : But you convinced some of the jurors.

X : Perhaps. Maybe they just didn't like the prosecuting attorney. It helped that nearly everyone had read the books or heard about them. And, yes, it proves my imagination is magnificent. The world was so complete, so fully-realized, that I'm sure it became as real to the jurors as that squalid, musty backroom they did all their deliberations in.

I : So you convinced them by the totality of your vision. And by your sincerity—that *you* believed Ambergris was real.

X : Don't *do* that. As I told you before we began, I don't believe in Ambergris anymore.

I : Can you describe the jurors at the first trial for me?

X : What?

I : I said, describe the jurors. What did they look like? Use your famous imagination if you need to.

X : They were jurors. A group of my peers. They looked like . . . people.

I : So you cannot remember their faces.

X : No, not really.

I : If you made them believe in Ambergris so strongly that they would not convict you, why can't you believe in it?

X : Because it doesn't exist! It doesn't exist, Alice! I made it up. Or, more properly, *it* made *me* up. It does not exist.

X was breathing heavily. He had brought his left fist down hard on the desk.

"Let us sum up, for there are two crucial points that have been uncovered by this interrogation. At least two. The first concerns the manta ray. The second concerns the jury. I am going to ask you again: *Did you never think that the manta ray might be a positive influence, a saving impulse?*

"Never."

"I see it as a manifestation of your sanity—perhaps a manifestation of your subconscious, come to lead you into the light."

"It led me into the darkness. It led me into never never land."

"Second, there was no trial, except in your head as you ran from the scene of the crime. Your jurors who believed in Ambergris—they represented the part of you that still clung to the idea that Ambergris was real. No matter how you fought them, they—faceless, anonymous—continued to tell you Ambergris was real!"

"Now you are trying to trick me," X said. He was trembling. His right hand had closed around his left wrist in a vice-like grip.

"Do you remember how you got here?" I asked.

"No. Probably through the front door, don't you think?"

"Don't you find it odd that you don't remember?"

"In comparison to what?" He laughed bitterly.

I stared at him. I said nothing. I think it was my silence, in which I hoped for some last minute redemption, that forced him to the conclusion my decision would not be favorable.

"I don't believe in Ambergris. How many times do I have to say it?" He was sweating now. He was shaking.

When I did not reply, he said, "Are there any more questions?"

I shook my head. I put the transcripts back in my briefcase and locked it. I pushed the chair back and got up.

"Then I am free to go. My wife is probably waiting in—"

"No," I said, putting on my jacket. "You are not free to go."

He rose quickly, again pounded his fist against the desk. "But I've told you, I've told you—I don't believe in my fantasy! I'm rational! I'm logical! *I'm over it!*"

"But you see," I said, with as much kindness as I could muster as I opened the door, "that's precisely the problem. This *is* Ambergris. You are *in* Ambergris."

The expression on X's face was quite indescribable.

As he locked the door behind him and ascended the staircase, he realized that it was all a horrible shame. Clearly, the writer had lost contact with reality, no matter how desperately that reality had struggled to get his attention. And that poor woman, Janice Shriek, that X had pushed into the path of a motored vehicle (he hadn't quite had it in him to tell X just how faulty his memory was)—she was proof enough of his illness. In the end, the fantasy had been too strong. And what a fantasy it was! A place where people flew and "made movies." Disney, tee-vee, New York City, New Orleans, Chicago. It was all very convincing and, within limits, it made sense—to X. But as he well knew, writers were a shifty lot—not to be trusted—and there were far too many lunatics on the streets already. How would X have coped with freedom anyhow? With his twin fantasy of literary success and a happy marriage revealed as a lie? (And there were X's last words as the door had closed: "All writers write. All writers edit. All writers have a little darkness in them.")

They had found no record of him in the city upon his arrest, so he had probably come from abroad—from the southern islands, perhaps—carrying his pathetic book, no doubt self-published by "Cosmos Books," a vanity operation by the sound of it. He knew those sounds himself from his modest dabbling in the written arts. In fact, he reflected, the only real benefit of the session, between the previous transcripts and the conversation itself, had been to his fiction; he now had some very interesting elements with which to compose a fantasy of his own. Why, he could already see that the report on this session would be a kind of fiction itself, as he had long since concluded that no delusion could ever truly be understood. He might even tell the story in first *and* third person, to both personalize and distance the events.

When he reached the place where he had plucked the rose, he took it from his buttonhole and stuck its stem back in the crack. He regretted having picked it. But even if he had not, it would have been doomed to a short, brutish life in the darkness.

Out on the street the rain had stopped, although the moist rain smell lingered, and the noontime calls to prayer from the Religious Quarter echoed through the narrow streets. He could almost taste the wonderful savoriness of the hot sausage sold by the sidewalk vendors. After lunch, he would take in some entertainment. The Manzikert Opera Theater had decided to do a Voss Bender revival this season, and with any luck he could still catch the matinee and be home to the wife before dinner. With this thought uppermost in his mind, he stepped out onto the street and was soon lost to view amongst the lunchtime crowds.

ABOUT THE AUTHOR

Jeff VanderMeer's work has appeared in eight languages in 15 countries, including in such magazines and anthologies as *Asimov's SF Magazine, Amazing Stories, Weird Tales, Interzone, The Silver Web, Ikarie B (Czech Republic), The Third Alternative, Nebula Awards 30, Best New Horror 7, The Year's Best Fantastical Fiction, Infinity Plus: The Anthology, Dark Terrors,* and *Dark Fantasy 2000.* Honors include winning the 2000 World Fantasy Award for Best Novella, the 1994 Rhysling Award, Fear Magazine's Best Short Story Award, and a $5,000 Florida Individual Artist Fellowship. VanderMeer has also been a finalist for the Theodore Sturgeon Award.

VanderMeer's nonfiction has appeared in *Novel & Short Story Writer's Markets, SF Eye, Tangent, Zene, The St. James Guide to Gothic, Ghost, and Horror Writers, Fantasy & Science Fiction, The New York Review of SF, Magill's Guide to SF & Fantasy Literature,* and publications from Gale Research. Books include *The Book of Lost Places* (Dark Regions Press), *Dradin, In Love* (Buzzcity Press), and *Dradin, In Love & Other Stories* (Oxy Publishing, Greece). His latest book is *The Exchange,* a collaboration with artist Eric Schaller. VanderMeer is 32 years old.